WHILE YOU WERE GONE

Sybil Baker

C&R Press
Conscious & Responsible

Cover art: Other Side by Eugenia Loli
Interior design by C&R Press
Exterior design by C&R Press and Victoria Dinning

Library of Congress Cataloging-in-Publication Data

ISBN: 978-1-936196-65-4
LCCN: 2016952190

C&R Press
Conscious & Responsible
www.crpress.org
Winston-Salem, North Carolina

For special discounted bulk purchases, please contact:
C&R Press sales@crpress.org
Contact lharms@crpress.org to book events, readings and author signings.

In memory of
Calvin Baker, Silvia Tartarini,
William Gay, Cathy Holton, Lee
Johnson

and Lizette Potgieter: the one who
disappeared

JEREMY'S CAR I
1995

Because it's not too far to the Walnut Street Bridge, Shannon's cousin and prom date Jeremy insists on driving with the top down. Even though it's chilly for early May, Shannon doesn't stop him, nor does the girl sitting behind her in Jeremy's Mustang convertible.

Julie, her name is. David's date. Of course Shannon knows. Julie's one of the popular girls, pretty in a way that is not extraordinary, because who in high school wants to be extraordinary? Julie's beauty, the thick shell of hair she'll cut after she marries ten years from now, the long gangly legs that will eventually thicken and soften, the pale dewy face that will also succumb to early wrinkles, is at its peak, but Julie, Shannon thinks, at least has this. Shannon is not a beauty nor will she ever be one, especially on this night, with the red chicken pox spots and scabs dotting her body as if she were some crazed pointillist painting. She'll not be even almost-pretty the way her older sister Claire is, her features uniformly bland and nonconfrontational, nor will she be striking, the way her younger sister Paige will be someday, though for now she just looks strange with her broad face and wide cheekbones. Shannon knows she will have to rely on other things, boring things like perseverance and commitment and ambition to get ahead, to maybe find love. But for now, there is no love, no success; there is just getting through one of these final, awful moments that is high school so she can start life over as the new, improved Shannon when she begins college in the fall.

She'd not even wanted to go to the senior prom, but Jeremy had talked her into it, said he'd make all of her friends jealous, and besides he'd always wanted to go to a public school dance. Like being in a John Hughes movie, he said. He was darkly handsome, from one of the old Chattanooga families, and attended the city's most prestigious boys' school. A veritable Prince Charming, except for the being gay part, which most people didn't know about. She believed him when he told her he was doing this for her out of kindness and not pity, as her cousin and best friend for as far back as she can remember. He's her cousin on her mother's side, the side with inheritances and trust funds. The side that started forgetting her and her sisters after Jeremy's father had died thirteen years ago and their mother, his sister, had followed three years later. Now Shannon's father works a nice white-collar job as an engineer, and she is graduating from a magnet public school and going to college, but this is not enough for Shannon, who envies Jeremy's world, envies what she might have had.

Because he means well, she's agreed to let him take her to the prom, but then she'd contracted chicken pox and even though she would no longer be contagious, she refused to go. Her face was puffy, her skin mottled and angry looking. She would not endure the humiliation. But Jeremy would not have it and showed up one afternoon with a dress that she would have never bought for herself, even if she could have afforded it, even if her mother had been alive to choose one with her. He was stereotypically gay in that sense, with a flair for fashion she didn't have or care about. The dress was a sleek violet Thai silk, and there was nothing public school about it. She tried the dress on for him, her face and arms covered in red bumps, her skin tender as a bruised plum.

"You've lost a few pounds," Jeremy had said.

"The chicken pox diet." The dress had a mandarin collar and capped sleeves, covering much of her pocked and swollen skin. "This is not me."

"It is now," Jeremy said. "I'll pick you up at seven."

He'd arrived in his new convertible, the first time Shannon had seen it, a slightly early graduation present (a thank-God-he-graduated-and-made-it-into-college present, he said), as darkly handsome as he always was, but more so in the suit, Brooks Brothers, for although he had an eye for women's fashion, his own sartorial choices tended toward his family's traditional Southern prep. Her corsage was an orchid, an expensive but scentless variety that would look diminished instead of elegant next to the other girls' outsized corsages smelling of honey and violets. He took her to a fancy restaurant overlooking the river, where they ate flesh from exotic animals and shared a bottle of wine, even though they were both underage, a feat only Jeremy could get away with. Her face, barely camouflaged under layers of thick foundation, flamed like a recently struck match. Shannon, who felt like a red popsicle on a purple stick, reminded herself this too would pass.

She self-righteously suffered through the humiliation of the prom with a modicum of grace, for she knew that soon she'd be away from all this, at college, becoming a journalist, never looking back. And Jeremy, well, was Jeremy. Charming and smart and good-looking, from the right family, from the right school. Except for the gay thing, he was an ideal Southern boy. He was doing what he thought was a favor for Shannon, who had on more than one occasion suffered through his own school's dances because he didn't want to bring a date who might want more from him. Suffered his friends' dates' appraisals that found her lacking, the slight head shakes, eyes wide with surprise: you're with him? Suffered the questions in the bathroom as she tried to revive her wilted corsage in a spotted sink. *Why is he taking you? Why won't he take a real girl out? What's he hiding?* And now here she was suffering again, where she was sure the girls were just like the ones at Jeremy's dances, thinking the same things. Why would he think her classmates would envy her, when they knew that he was, after all, her cousin and she was the pity date?

But now, as Jeremy idles the car in front of the bridge, ignoring the blasts of cars passing around them, she catches him looking in the rearview mirror. David, with his sun-streaked shaggy hair touching his collarbone, sinewed skinniness, doe-like eyes, tie-and coat-less, barefoot, smoking endlessly into the night: Jeremy's type. She punches Jeremy hard in the arm, angry more at herself than him for being so slow on the uptake. The real reason he wanted to go to her prom is now smoking in his car. He smiles more than grimaces, winks as he rubs where she punched him.

"You can't stop here in the middle of the road," Julie says. "You'll get a DUI."

"I'm idling," Jeremy says. "Because I want y'all to appreciate our lovely pedestrian bridge, saved from dissipation and destruction, thanks to the efforts of Chattanooga's citizens. Our pride and joy. 'Course y'all know this bridge is not just famous, but notorious."

"The lynching of Ed Johnson," David says. "I read Shannon's piece about it in our paper."

"You and Dad were the only ones," Shannon says. But she smiles. Her face cracks from what's left of her caked-on makeup.

"I don't remember any lynching," Julie says.

Jeremy gestures for one of David's cigarettes, and he passes his lit one to the front seat. "It was in 1906."

"Oh. Doesn't really count then."

"Well, it kind of does," Shannon says. "Ed Johnson's lynching resulted in the only Supreme Court criminal trial in history. Not that his was the only lynching on the bridge."

"Blah blah school blah," Julie says. "So that's why the river smells so foul."

"That and all the chemicals dumped in it. Remember, we were once the most polluted city in America."

"But not anymore. Why dwell on the past?" Julie reaches into David's jacket pocket and pulls out a flask. She unscrews the top, takes a swig, and then passes it to David. "Let's have some fun."

"You know who the ringleader of that mob that lynched poor old Ed Johnson was?" Jeremy asks. "My great-great-great-grandfather on my mother's side. That's who. A black man falsely accused of raping a white woman, and they shot him and hung him."

"You related to this guy too, Shannon?" Julie says.

In the rearview mirror, Shannon watches Julie scoot closer to David. Shannon's convinced: Julie thinks she's winning now, that she's putting Shannon in her place by reminding everyone that Jeremy's her cousin. She actually believes, Shannon thinks, that she'll have sex with David later. She wants to tell her to give up now, but she knows Julie won't listen. "It's the South. We're all related one way or another, aren't we?" Shannon says.

Jeremy laughs, and a few seconds later, David joins in.

A siren wails, coming closer.

"Let's go," Julie says.

"Not yet."

Shannon closes her eyes, flutters her hands over her face. Her skin feels hot and bare, tender, the makeup smeared and sweated off. She hears Jeremy's door open, the shift in his seat. She reaches out to touch his thigh, to stop him, even though it's futile, even though he's gone. She hears Julie's voice, anxious, terrified. Shannon could tell her not to worry, that the emergency brake is on, they are safe for now, but doesn't. She opens her eyes, watches Jeremy at the rails of the bridge, climbing them. It's a pale darkness, one grainy from the diffused light of late sunset. The mornings are dark here almost year-round, but those nights in summer, it's like the sun will never set.

He's on the rails now, screaming like a god or condemned man; it's hard to tell. Below, the water sparkles; above, the sky absorbs the light. He's done this before, drunk and sober, and she's always there to pull him back, talk him down from jumping. Just as she's held him, wracked and sobbing, smoothed his curly hair, her steady voice convincing him that even in the most painful moments of being Jeremy Hamilton, it is still worthwhile being alive.

But this show is not for her. David gets out of the car, jogs down the middle of the bridge. She watches him gesture to Jeremy. He takes a small camera from his jacket pocket. Jeremy laughs, poses for David, arm and leg stretched toward sky and water. She knows Jeremy is smiling for David, who holds his hand out, helps Jeremy down.

"He's crazy," Julie says.

"Maybe."

"We got a room at the Read House," Julie says. "They say it's haunted."

"Well, a woman's head was severed there. And Civil War soldiers were murdered. And there were the suicides. Just because that stuff happened doesn't mean it's haunted more than anyplace else."

"I don't want to think about it," Julie says. She leans toward Shannon, cupping her hands over her mouth as if they are in a crowded room. "Momma thinks I'm spending the night at Abbie's house."

Shannon pantomimes locking her mouth, tossing the key out the window.

The boys are back in the car, breathless, slightly sweaty from the excitement. Jeremy releases the brake and shifts the car into gear.

"One more place, then I'll let you two get back to the night of your lives."

David snorts as Jeremy turns and drives up Third Street, toward the worn-down neighborhoods at the foot of Missionary Ridge. With each block, the houses become tinier and neater, as if darkened curtains and well-kept gardens strain to maintain order against the neighborhood's slide into ruin. The air, heavy with wild honeysuckles and uncollected trash, rushes past them.

"Can you put the top up?" Julie whispers. "I'm scared." She leans into David.

"We're all right," Jeremy says slowly. "For now." A smile creeps up his face.

He parks the car in a gravel space overlooking an overgrown cemetery. "This is where we buried the black people, 'cause we didn't want them next to us even in death." By now the darkness has seeped into the sky, the ground, the air around them. Jeremy and Shannon get out of the car, and David opens his door. Julie whimpers and then steps out, last. They walk past the worn grave markers, many still unidentified, through the ghosts they can all feel, up and down faded paths to the gravesite of Ed Johnson. Jeremy sits next to the headstone and pats the ground for the others to join him. The moon is half full, the stars dimmed by the city lights. Shannon can feel Julie's shoulders shaking. David drapes an arm around her, and her body stills. The flask of whisky is ceremoniously passed around. Shannon takes the smallest of sips. Jeremy whispers the words on the gravestone, but loud enough that they all can hear.

"God Bless You All. I Am An Innocent Man." Jeremy's voice breaks at the end. He touches the top of the grave. "On behalf of my country, my family, I'm sorry, Ed."

The thing is, even though she's seen him do this before, this routine, this ploy, Shannon knows he's not exactly faking either. Jeremy rises and disappears into the woods.

"Is he coming back?" Julie asks.

"He'll be okay." Shannon waits for David to stand. Finally he does.

"I better go check on him. Y'all go on back to the car," he says. Then he too disappears into the dark.

Back in the car, the two are silent for a long time. Finally Julie speaks. "I don't know why Jeremy's so upset about something he didn't do."

"You ever read Faulkner?" Shannon says.

"Why?"

Shannon closes her eyes. Nothing lasts forever, she reminds herself, and then the other voice, her little girl voice, adds: except death.

"I just want him to take us to our hotel," Julie finally says.

"He will."

"He seems a little crazy."

"Just emotional."

"David's going to Virginia Tech. ROTC."

"So I heard."

"Real marriage material." Julie snaps open her clutch, removes a compact, dusts her face even though it's too dark for anyone to see her. Shannon thinks of her own mother, and the other dead people lying in the ground around them. "What about Jeremy?" Julie says. "He's going to Sewanee, right? You're not hooking up with him?"

"Jeremy? God, no."

"I mean y'all are cousins and all, but," she giggles, "it is the South. Ha ha."

"Not going to happen. Ever."

"It's the first time for me and David. That's why I want to get out of here. He's so hot."

"Mmhm." Right now, she guesses, David and Jeremy are making out, fumbling under shirts, tugging pants down. Perhaps a blowjob—or two—is in the equation. "Jeremy's not my type."

"Who is your type?"

"My type is John Reed."

"He go to school around here?"

"He died in 1920 of typhus."

"Oh." Julie plucks the pins out of her hair one by one, leaving them on the seat beside her. "That's creepy." Hair clumps shoot wildly in all kinds of directions. She runs her hands over the sections, finger combs through the hairspray. "That's pretty brave for you to go to prom with your face like that. I could never do that."

"Don't worry," Shannon says. "It's not contagious." Just a while longer. Soon Jeremy will be back and she can go home and she will graduate and leave the Julies of Chattanooga behind. She lays the back of her hand on her forehead, bumpy like a rough road of gravel. She imagines herself witnessing revolutions and writing about them, accepting the Pulitzer Prize.

Then she hears their voices, low and conspiratorial, approaching. Even though her eyes are still closed, Shannon knows Jeremy's shirt is untucked, the tails of white fabric almost glowing under his suit coat.

"The good thing is," she can hear Jeremy say as he gets into the car, "I'll never be as bad as my great-great-great-grandfather, no matter what my mother says."

Shannon opens her eyes, watches David slide into the back and Julie wrap her arms around him. "Everything okay?"

"Dandy," David says. "You two want to stop by our room for a drink?"

"No, thanks." Shannon hates that she's taken Julie's side on this one. If she had the energy, if she cared enough, she and Jeremy would go with them to the hotel room, and Julie would never get what she wants.

"David," Julie says, dragging his name out. "I have to pee."

"Can't it wait?" David sinks a bit in the seat.

"I've been holding it for-ev-er." She opens the door, swings her legs out. "Just walk with me down the hill. I'm not walking by myself. I might get raped or knifed or something."

"Go on, Davey," Jeremy says, waving his hand. "We won't leave you."

After the two disappear, Jeremy reclines his seat, massages his forehead. "So, I got some news."

"You moving to New York?"

"Not without you." This is their plan. Right after college. He takes a breath. "The big news is I told Mother I'm gay."

Shannon sits up, turns so she faces him. Since her mother died ten years ago, Shannon has avoided talking about the things that hurt. She touches his shoulder, thin and bony even under the suit coat. "When?"

"Last week. After I got the car, of course." His hands trace the steering wheel, in smooth, even circles. "You know what she said?"

Shannon is afraid to fill in the blank. None of the answers are good ones.

"That I was adopted."

"She's lying."

He turns to her, scrunches his face. "Did you know about it?"

Shannon shakes her head. "You know I didn't."

"She said I must have inherited being gay from my biological parents, so it's not her fault. I told her I'd rather have the gay gene than the lynch mob KKK gene."

"Hah," Shannon says. "Sure that went over well."

"She said she can just as easily leave her money to some charity."

"She'll get over it."

But they both know she won't. Shannon wants to say more, to comfort him properly, but her throat feels clotted. Closed. She reaches for him and he folds into her as he's done before. Ever since she can remember she's been terrified of losing Jeremy, to love or despair or both. "I'm sorry," she says.

"Break it up, you two."

Jeremy pulls away. She's glad he hasn't been crying; at least he's spared that. And she's grateful now for David, barefoot and rumpled, his hand momentarily on Jeremy's shoulder as he climbs in.

After everyone's in the car, the wheels crunch out of the parking spot and they're back on Third Street again. At the stoplight on Third and Market, Julie taps Jeremy's shoulder. "Shannon says you're not her type."

"Don't worry, Jules. Me and Shannon are still kissing cousins." Jeremy pulls Shannon close to him so suddenly she doesn't resist and kisses her hard on the mouth, a flick of tongue even.

"Oh my God, she's diseased."

Jeremy laughs, but it sounds more like a bark than a human laugh.

Shannon turns around and sticks her balloon-face over the seat. "It's not contagious." She rakes her nails over the fading pox bumps. She's been good about not scratching, not leaving scars, but this is worth it. She rubs her hand on Julie's exposed thigh.

"You freak."

"You know what, Julie? Me and you, we're going to remember this day for the rest of our lives. For you, it's because you went to the prom with big man David here and, if he can get it up for you, you get to fuck him. It's going to be the best day of your life—after this it's a boring husband or two and screaming children and a dead-end job and bad haircuts for you." Shannon turns and faces the front as the light turns green. "But for me, this is the last day of life sucking. It only gets better from here."

"You wish, loser bitch."

"Shannon's right," Jeremy says, pulling up in front of the hotel. "In the words of Ol' Blue Eyes himself, the best is yet to come." The car idles. He reaches his hand back to David, pats his knee.

"Go on. I won't miss you."

After David and Julie disappear into the lobby of the hotel downtown, Jeremy leans back in his seat and closes his eyes. "You got a present for your dad's birthday?"

Shannon hits the dashboard with her hand. "Shit, I forgot."

"The party's not till dinner, right? We've still got time. I'll pick you up for lunch and we can go shopping then."

Shannon reaches over and squeezes his hand. "I swear I didn't know you were adopted," she says.

"I know." He opens his eyes, pulls the top up so that it blocks the night stars, shifts into gear. "God, will I ever love anyone as much as him?"

Soon, Shannon thinks, soon she'll be happy. She can feel it. "If we only knew, Jeremy. If we only knew."

1999

Why do I feel so happy today! I feel as if I had sails flying in the wind, and the sky over me was bright blue and full of white birds.
Three Sisters, Act I

How sharper than a serpent's tooth it is
To have a thankless child!
King Lear, Act I, Scene 4

SHANNON

Years later, this is how Shannon would remember it: she and Ben kissed for the first time, lightly, with promise, in the corner of the basement, and then the lights went out. It was just after midnight. They'd been listening to Paige's band playing songs of love and loss they'd had yet to experience to a small crowd of semi-adoring fans. But then Shannon took their teacups and gestured for Ben, the camera bag strap slung over his shoulder, to follow her to another corner of the basement, empty, almost alone. She was wearing Ben's blazer with the fraying pocket, a blazer his mother had had tailored for him in Seoul. She'd pretended to be cold just so she could wear him for a while.

They'd been working up to that kiss, all day, all year, and now that they could pretend they were alone, they reached for each other. No tongue, lips only slightly parted. She kept her eyes closed even after he pulled away. When she opened her eyes, it was dark and suddenly quiet.

"Jo-ah," Ben said. They were the first Korean words he'd said to her, and for a moment she thought she was kissing another man. "It means 'I like this.' It means this is good."

"Jo-ah," she said, her voice tight. The word sounded strange in her mouth. She thought: I want more. She thought: the world has stopped.

Then Paige yelled something and the partiers lit up like stars with cigarette embers and half-burned candles and flicked-on lighters in a semicircle around Paige and her band. (Was it fair to call it Paige's band? Paige was her sister and Paige was the singer, so yes.) Paige started singing something—Bessie Smith, Shannon guessed—without the mic and Becky backed her up with a soft, steady beat on the drums. The party collectively quieted to hear her scratched-record voice. No one seemed to care too much that the electricity had gone out. They were used to it. Old houses and amps didn't mix.

"Someone will eventually make it to the circuit box," Shannon said.

"Eventually." Ben slipped his hand into the frayed blazer pocket with Shannon's, then leaned forward and kissed her again.

Could they have sex here, because wasn't that where this kiss was leading? They slithered to the floor, their teacups beside them. They huddled like the last survivors of a storm, their only sustenance some alcoholic concoction, ruby punch in china teacups set beside folded knees. "I feel like we're back in the darkroom."

They'd been there just that afternoon, in the darkroom at their campus an hour away in Rome, Georgia. As Ben had affixed glistening photos with a clothespin to a taut, fraying rope, they decided which photos would go best with her story, her last for the school paper. Then she'd driven them to Chattanooga for Paige's CD release party and her father's birthday party the next day. It was to be a lunch thing her sister Claire had organized as she'd always done, even though she was eight months pregnant and engrossed with her job—career, Claire would be quick to correct her—in accounts management.

"What if it's not a tripped circuit?" Shannon said. "What if it's something else?"

"Like a nuclear attack?"

"Or a tornado? Or Y2K?"

"Eight months early?"

"Why not?" Shannon said. "What would you do? Theoretically?"

"Stay here in this basement and wait for the world to end."

"But really? What if it happens like they say? What will you do?" She wished she could take the question back. Why speak of the real world?

Ben shrugged. "Well, I'll be in Seoul, of course, working for my father. But we'd probably go to my grandmother's house on Jeju Island. She practically lives off the land there anyway. What about you?"

"I guess go to Dad's. With Claire and Jim and the baby. And Paige. And Jeremy hates his mother, so he'd probably come, too."

They were quiet. At least Ben had not mentioned her, the loyal fiancée back in Seoul, the one who wrote him letters every week in a language Shannon couldn't read. She hoped the lights would never turn back on. For as long as it was dark, she could pretend the world had ended, she could pretend they'd never leave the basement. She would not graduate from college and she would not begin her job at the newspaper in Knoxville writing obituaries. Ben would not return to South Korea to work at his father's tire company, and most importantly, Ben would not marry the girl in Seoul, the one who had waited for him during Ben's mandatory military service and time at the tiny liberal arts college in Georgia, the one he promised he would come back for. Jeremy would not pick them up tomorrow at eleven-thirty in the morning and drive her and Paige and Ben to her childhood home for her father's fifty-fifth birthday party, with its unwanted presents and unnecessary women.

She uncurled from Ben's shoulder. "I don't have a present for Daddy."

"You're figuring this out now?" She could feel his disapproval. He would never not have a present ready for his parents, for his fiancée, for her.

"I meant to. But then the article just kind of took over." Interviews with her classmates, the last class of the millennium. The word for the class of 1999, her interviews suggested, was "surplus." A surplus of opportunity, of friends, of money, of possibility. The cold war was over. The US had a balanced budget. The Internet would allow everything.

"I'm a terrible daughter." She would get up in the morning and go to the nearest open store and get him something silly and stupid.

"You are."

"Gas station's open. Maybe I should go now." She gently tugged the ragged sleeve of Ben's T-shirt, the one he always wore in the darkroom, the one that read, "One by One the Penguins Steal My Sanity," the threads of its fabric weakened from wear and washings. His shirt smelled like chemicals, which she would forever find nostalgic because the smell was Ben and not-Ben. On days when he wasn't in the darkroom, he smelled almost like nothing, no cologne, no male sweat, only something ineffable, a smell that she associated with a rare spice or fern plant or conifer that she could not name.

She stood, trying to pull Ben up with her. Paige in her black jeans and combat boots, her cropped hair like a helmet, turned to Shannon, who was not even a shadow in that dark corner with Ben, and waved. She waved back, although she wasn't sure Paige could see her. The air was thick and vaporous with cigarette and pot smoke. Her legs crumbled just as Ben grabbed her hand and pulled her back down to him.

"We're stuck here, remember?" he said. "We'll worry about your dad's present in the morning."

We. She loved the sound of it. We. Yes. She closed her eyes, settled back into his arm, rested her head on his chest. "I guess I don't have to get him a present if we never leave the basement."

"You know what I'll miss most?" he said.

"What?" *Me. You'll miss me.*

"IHOP."

They went there after deadlines, often in the middle of the night, when the restaurant was empty except for truckers coming off the highway. Shannon usually ordered eggs sunny side up, biscuits, and grits. Ben had waffles drenched in butter and strawberry syrup and a side of scrambled eggs. Breakfasts in America, he said, were the best, with their bottomless coffee and generous portions. He complained that he was gaining weight, getting soft around the middle, but Shannon could not tell; he seemed the same, slim, elegant. One night at IHOP she'd told him she knew the newspaper staff thought she was too serious with her story assignments, that she should lighten up and assign more fun topics. "They think I want to go back to the sixties, that I was born in the wrong era, that I long for those fights and protests just for a good news story. That I can't enjoy the world as it is now. But that's not it."

Ben had studied the soggy bite of waffle on his fork. "You want to be Louise Bryant," he'd said.

She'd looked at her plate, the grits congealing under a film of butter. She'd almost stopped being surprised when Ben seemed to read her mind. She'd watched the movie *Reds* when she was in high school and that was when it had started. Diane Keaton as the feminist Marxist reporter married to Warren Beatty's John Reed. "Yes," she half-whispered. "Louise Bryant. She's the one." Then she smiled. "When did it start for you?"

Ben wiped his mouth and hands with a crumpled napkin. From one of the side pockets of his camera bag he removed a glossy square of paper. The picture was from a magazine, excised neatly with scissors or a razor. He smoothed the photo on the table. It was of a starving African girl and a vulture hovering nearby.

"This won the Pulitzer," he said. "Do you know the story behind it?"

"The photographer, I forget his name."

"Carter. Kevin Carter."

"He was criticized for not helping the girl," Shannon said. "And then he committed suicide."

"We were living in South Africa for Dad's business when that happened. Carter was part of a group of photographers known as the Bang Bang Club. But this photograph, it's not the entire story. The girl was crawling to a food station, and some say the vulture was interested in the food out of the frame, not the girl. Later, some people said the girl was not a girl at all, but a boy, who died many years later from another disease. They criticized Carter for not help-ing the girl, but if he had, then there would have been no photo, no attention to starvation in Sudan. He had to wait twenty minutes for the light and the composition to align because that's what it comes down to. After he took the photo, he carried the girl to the food station and wept."

Shannon traced the edges of the photo. "This is why you always tell me there is so much left out of the frame."

"He didn't know that six days after he won the Pulitzer, his friend would be killed on an assignment that Carter thought he should have been on, that he felt guilt over his friend's death, felt despair at all the violence he'd witnessed, the pain in the world. He didn't know that after winning he would drive to his old childhood neighborhood, run a garden hose from his truck's exhaust into the cab, and kill himself."

Shannon remembered looking at the photo on the Formica, somewhat bleached under the fluorescent's glare. She'd felt nothing but sadness. "Why do you want to be someone like that?"

"Because he took that photo."

"Maybe he shouldn't have."

Ben smiled. "You want to change the world."

Ben had told her more than once at their IHOP debriefings that only a white American girl born into a certain era (post–Second World War) from a certain class (her father was an engineer) and from a certain family (respectable yet not complete) could wholeheartedly believe she could make a difference.

She blinked, as if startled. "Of course I want to change the world," she said. "What else is there?"

"What if that's why Carter killed himself? Trying to change a world that won't. Or can't."

And now, here they were in this basement, not giving up on themselves, on their future without each other. Despite their mutual attraction, they'd not gotten together until this moment for all the responsible reasons: her boyfriend, his loyal fiancée, the future geographic and cultural impossibilities. Besides, Shannon had to remind herself, even if they had gotten together for real, if the obstacles evaporated, how long would they have lasted, really? A summer? A year?

And maybe because deep down they'd known they wouldn't last, now that the semester was just about over, now that they were away from their tiny campus and the dorms they lived in, here, without too much judgment or regret, they were going to at least have this. They would have their kiss, and later, not here, not in this noisy, dank basement but somewhere else, they would have sex, once, maybe a few times if they could. Then they'd say goodbye and go on to live the lives they were meant to live.

"I guess I won't miss IHOP because I can go whenever I want, but I will miss going there with you." She rested her hand on his stomach, counted the seconds between its rise and fall. She could move her hands a few inches lower, pull the edges of his T-shirt, rub the fabric of his jeans. She pushed herself up, reached for the teacup of spiked punch, rinsed her mouth. Not here. Not here. "I have to get a present for Daddy."

Ben raked his hand through his hair, shook his head as if to awaken. "Wait. For the electricity to come back on." He held his arms out to her, so open in that moment she suddenly wanted to weep. She took his cup of punch and handed it to him before settling back into their corner. She rubbed the sleeve of his shirt, allowed her fingers to touch the damp chill of his slim bicep, compact but sturdy. This was it. Soon it would all change, and after this nothing would change again. But not sex, not here in the basement on this sticky floor, in this acrid air, with the band still playing. It would remind her too much of the awkwardness and bruises of that time on the Outer Banks when she and her old boyfriend Kurt had had sex in the sand along the edge of an abandoned shore. Both of them were drunk and horny; they'd been together three months and still could not get enough of each other, their bathing suits barely damp, like handcuffs around their ankles. For once he'd wanted to be on top; he was drunk and was taking longer. The sand ground into her, abrading her skin, and she'd wondered when the sex would end. The next day she was still trying to rinse the sand out of all her skin's cracks and folds, little tiny grains everywhere, her skin a pink corrugated landscape of minor pain, and of course she'd started her period, and the blood and bits of sand mixed together on her skin and washcloth. Kurt, hung over, apologetic, rubbed aloe vera on her broken, tender skin, waiting until the fourth day, when her period was almost over, to approach her again for sex, this time on the cool smoothness of the sheets in their hotel room, her on top please, her skin a sheet of goose bumps blooming from her abrasions. This time while they were having sex she saw it: Kurt was selfish, and that was when she knew they would not last.

But Ben, he was not selfish, and this could be their first and possibly last chance, here in the corner. She imagined her body against the wall, jeans bunched below her knees, not enough time for her to come. She knew so much about him, but so little about his body beyond his corded arms, his angular yet soft face. He was a beautiful man, but he did not realize it. But if not now, when? There was only a week left in the semester. And if not here, where? They lived in dorms with roommates where squishes and gasps and grunts leaked through the walls.

Once she and Kurt had started fooling around in one of the administration buildings. It was late at night and the building was unlocked. They'd walked around the empty halls in a renovated old house, feeling haunted, abandoned. On the stairs to the second floor Kurt had pulled her to him and then they were kissing and their clothes came off as if of their own accord. That's how she felt when the security guard's flashlight was on them, she in her bra and panties, Kurt his boxers, pink striped, she remembered, like a candy cane, and she covered her breasts even though her bra was on and she dressed before giving the guard her ID, pleading silently that she would not see her name in the school's police report, which would result in her being a headline for the paper she edited. But the next day there was no report. The security guard had done nothing but warn them to not trespass in school buildings at night.

That was how she thought of her time with Kurt, seeking, searching for places to have sex, as if their love, or whatever it was called, could survive anywhere. And then, five months ago, as soon as she'd arrived back in Chattanooga for Christmas break, he'd emailed her, telling her he didn't feel "that way" anymore. It was not the breakup that rankled but the email, the petty indignity of it, and because of it she'd impulsively sworn off boys and sex for at least a year. As if to mock her earnestness, she'd had a one-night stand the last day of that very break—her first! her only!—with a high school friend, a long-simmering attraction that didn't feel like a one-nighter because of its inevitability. They'd done it in his room when his parents were out, the sex unspectacular, as if the act of just doing it, after all this time, had been enough. She remembered that as soon as they were finished, he'd wiped his limp penis with a Kleenex.

But with Ben she knew it would be different. If she turned her head up, they'd be kissing again, slowly, deeply, and then, maybe, everyone would disappear and the electricity would never turn on again. He'd unbutton her shirt, hike her tank top underneath it above her shoulders, so that she was naked from the waist up. Then she'd remove his T-shirt, which she'd keep forever, toss it on top of hers. Their mouths would explore ridges, skin, spaces, the hollow of clavicles, elbow creases; lightly trace nipples, earlobes. Only after they were acquainted with each other's bodies—certainly it would take a lifetime in this basement to learn everything—would they unbutton their jeans, shuck them off their socked feet, and then sink to the floor, a collapsing tower. He'd slip a finger inside her and taste her and then she'd wrap her legs around him, rubbing herself while he moved inside her, their bodies slick, suctioned together, and that was how their first time would be.

Then what? Well, she might become pregnant, because when she and Kurt broke up she went off the pill, and Ben did not keep condoms in his wallet as far as she knew. Would she tell him? Perhaps she would not, instead choosing to raise the child, fatherless, until one day the boy—it would be a boy—was old enough, and she would take him to South Korea to research an article about the DMZ, for she'd be an award-winning journalist by then, and there the three of them would meet at some restaurant in Seoul, and Ben would recognize the boy as his. He'd be divorced by then, childless except for their son. He'd agree to shoot the photos for her article, and they would travel the world, spinning stories of hope and loss through their words and pictures.

Or maybe she would tell him she was pregnant just as he was packing in his dorm room to return to South Korea. She'd sit on his bed and watch him fold his shirts, carefully, neatly, the way those who have spent their lives packing and unpacking might do, and then once she told him, he'd remove the shirts one by one until the suitcase was dark and empty. They'd marry and live in Tennessee, but he'd miss Korea and his family too much, wonder how he'd dodged his fate, his destiny, and he'd resent her for it and their child too, a boy named Dodson, her father's middle name. Or more likely, she wouldn't get pregnant. After that reckless first time in the basement with the lights out, whenever they could, they'd sneak away and have sex, protected, until it was time for him to leave. She'd wait for him to change his mind, to stay with her, but he wouldn't. He wouldn't even write her or send emails. He'd marry the long-suffering fiancée and she'd never see him again. But he'd secretly follow her career, and then one day, during her acceptance speech for the Pulitzer, she'd mention an old friend and his love for a Pulitzer Prize–winning photograph, and he'd regret the life he didn't choose.

Or maybe he'd realize that he loved her, that they were *meant to be,* that they *could not live without each other.* He'd ask her to move with him to Korea, to marry him, to build a life there. Could she do it? She felt the place to be cold and bleak, much more alien than exotic, although she knew nothing about it except what Ben had told her, which wasn't much. She didn't tell him, but Asia in its foreignness scared her in a way Europe did not. When she thought of Asia, she thought of Vietnam. She thought of herself standing out, as Ben did here, but he seemed to take it in stride or not notice it in a way she feared she could not.

Besides, in a few years, after she got a little more journalism experience, she was moving to New York with Jeremy, just as they'd always planned. After she got her foothold, she'd ask Ben to move to New York with her. They'd visit his parents once a year, as a compromise for him staying with her. His father could run his own company. Ben would be a photographer, as she believed he was born to be.

"I've got it," she said. "You could take photos of my dad's party. We'll develop them and put the best ones in an album."

"And we didn't even have to leave this room."

"That would be nice. Never leaving this room."

Shannon waited. She felt him moving closer. She tilted her head up toward him and prepared her mouth for the kiss she knew was coming, the one that would lead to one of those possibilities she'd just imagined. And then the lights came back on and the band was amped up and Paige stepped to the mike and resumed her singing of love and loss. Just like before. Just like now.

PAIGE

The band stopped playing just as the light was shifting from gray to pink because Paige's voice, scraped and strained from singing and cigarettes, had finally given out. A few hours later when the sun was thin and yellow, Paige arrived upstairs and stretched out on her bed beside a girl whose name she did not know. By the time she closed her eyes, the room was already warming to the mid-morning sun slanting through half-closed blinds. Her head felt as if it had been wrapped in damp cotton. Outside, a car horn sounded three times, impatient.

She was sure it was Jeremy summoning her and Shannon, who was downstairs, somewhere, with Ben. They were late for their father's birthday party.

The girl beside her was spread-legged, belly down, in a wine-stained tank top and boy shorts. Her eyes were smeared with black eyeliner, and a purple shock of hair shot upward, so that she resembled a crazed skunk-raccoon hybrid. Paige pushed herself up and gently slid the girl's leg off hers. She reached for the teacup on the scarred dresser and took a swig of the blood-red spiked punch she was certain had stained her teeth a vampire red. A vine of leaves spread like tentacles on the side of the cup. Where were the flowers? Before she'd moved out of her father's house last summer, she'd found her mother's old china set, forgotten in dusty boxes in the basement. The boxes had Paige's name magic-markered on them in her own childish handwriting, claiming a relic no one else wanted. She'd brought the set when she moved into the overlarge house in Fort Wood near the University of Tennessee's Chattanooga campus, intent on using the pieces in all kinds of inappropriately ruinous social situations.

Paige lit a cigarette from the almost-empty pack that had been dropped on the mottled wood floor. She padded to the window and peeled away the gauze curtain. Outside, a convertible Mustang, top down, was idling. Moody trance music traveled, muffled, into the house. Jeremy, handsomely rumpled in a black T-shirt, sunglasses wrapped around his face, reclined in the driver's seat, smoking a cigarette, most likely hungover. They'd all be, except Claire, who was about to have a baby, but even if she weren't, she'd never be hung over, ever.

The window was stuck. She'd tried to open it last month, after the first warm days seemed to hold, and it wouldn't open then either. Paige tapped the window and willed Jeremy to look up. She held up ten fingers in front of the window, her thumb and forefinger looped around her teacup, cigarette in her mouth. His hand shaped the okay sign and then returned to the steering wheel, drumming to the beat. She guessed he'd not slept at all yet, boys and drugs keeping him up. But for as long as she could remember, he'd never missed one of their dad's birthday parties, even after Jeremy's father and their mother had died. Jeremy's mother had long quit going to anything that involved "that side of the family," as she referred to them. But Jeremy, loyal to all of them, still came. He was a good Southern boy that way.

Paige set her teacup on the dresser and drifted to her open closet. A white dress, her only dress, rested on a hanger, a thrift-shop eighties throwback, an era she was almost too young to remember. It had a bodice and puffy sleeves and a slightly flared skirt. When her mother had died when she was six, Paige had wanted to wear her white tea-party dress with its red sash to the funeral, but they did not allow her. Now, she shucked her tank top and slid the dress off the hanger. In front of the smudged mirror above the dresser she slipped the dress on and dabbed her wrists with Joy perfume, her mother's bottle (she believed it was magic and would never be empty), the only perfume they both ever wore.

Her mother had allowed Paige to dot her own wrists with the perfume while they sat at the kitchen table for their tea parties. When Paige wore it she smelled like her mother then, like jasmine and roses all stirred together. At their tea parties for two (How many were there? One? Five? Ten? She could not remember) Paige, encased in a poofy white dress, would sit primly in the chair across from her mother, who was already dying. The white dress had been one of the few she owned that was not a hand-me-down from Claire to Shannon to her, something already stretched and worn for their bodies, out of fashion, dated. This white dress was one she'd wanted before she could dream it, white with a red sash wrapped around her waist, like a bow on a present. She was adamant about the red even though her mother and Shannon wanted blue and Claire and her father wanted pink. Pink! Even now she hated pink, refused to have sex with anyone who dyed their hair, even a strand of it, pink. She did not allow pink T-shirts, pink lettering, pink panties, bras, or lipstick to touch her skin. Pink was for weak little girls. Pink was the color of cancer. She hated those pink ribbons people felt so good about wearing, as if a scrap of silk would make it disappear, as if wearing a pin or a bow was the same as having it or watching someone die from it.

They were at the fabric store to choose the material for the sash of her dress, she and her mother, staring at spools of ribbon, more colors than her box of crayons. Any color, her mother urged. Any. And still she'd chosen the rich color of blood from the scrape on her knee when she'd fallen down in the driveway the week before, not the muddied red her mother sometimes coughed into a bunched napkin or the waxy red of Shannon's play lipstick. It was not even the fake red of the spiked punch she was drinking now, not the color of potions and crystals and powders that were her mother's medicine. This sash was the living red of all that could hurt and bleed, of all that was alive. After Paige had selected the ribbon, they'd chosen the white material, a calico with holes to let the air in. And her mother had made it, the last thing she sewed before her fingers would no longer work for her, before she gave up and sank into her bed watching soap operas with Claire.

For their tea parties, Paige wore that dress with the puffed sleeves and red sash and they sipped Kool-Aid (or was it tea with milk and sugar?) and ate fancy cookies from a box that tasted better than homemade because each was identically circle-shaped. They both wore white gloves with tiny pearl clasps, holding their pinkies out while they sipped from the teacups. Her mother told her how the teacups, made in England, had been used at her great-great-grandmother's plantation in Georgia, when regular entertaining was expected. *The South has lost so much of its hospitality.* She had a soft lulling accent, one that hinted at her upbringing and education. *It's all gone now. The good and the bad.* And then she'd sniff and sip her milky tea, her cookie untouched. *The good and the bad,* Paige would echo, trying to sound like a grownup. She wore the white dress whenever she could, slept in it when her mother became too sick to make her take it off. After the tea parties ended, Paige wore that dress when her mother lay in the antique bed in the yellow spare room that smelled of old kitty litter and unwashed clothes. *Can you sing for me, Paige, honey, you know that Bessie song Tammy would sing? Once I lived the life of a millionaire, spending money, I didn't care.* This was how Paige learned Bessie Smith songs, which she would sing to her mother those last days because the doctor told them the hearing was the last to go, and later she sang one at her mother's funeral, where everyone thought motherless Paige was the saddest thing in the world.

That's what it was about the morning-after parties, Paige thought now, setting the perfume bottle back on the dresser, it's like the morning my mother died. That morning, she'd awakened early when the house was heavy with sleep and she thought she would find her mother's perfume and put some on both of them to bring the jasmine and the roses back into the house. She walked past the open doors of her sisters—Shannon strangling her stuffed bear, Claire in her room of pop star posters Paige would never like, past her father's bedroom, the door closed, but she heard him rumbling inside like the trains at the bottom of the ridge they lived on. Past all of them and down the stairs to the room her mother lay in, the door closed and dark.

Now, outside her bedroom and down the stairs was the hangover of last night's party, one that had not ended for her until now. Bodies were strewn about, frozen figures fleeing Pompeii, grotesque appendages in some cultish dance. The spiked punch ringed her dead mother's china cups, raided when the plastic cups had run out. Last night had resembled some kind of unholy tea party, both males and females adorned in floral thrift-shop dresses and scuffed Doc Martens, drinking from those china cups, joints and cigarettes necessary props of affectation. Paige smoked and wandered among the passed-out partiers, careful not to ash the worn wood floor, smooth beneath her bare unpainted feet. The floor was cool, as if it were clinging to the last of winter, fighting against the inevitable thaw. She carried the china cup of spiked punch with her, stopping only to occasionally tap her cigarette on a stray saucer. She opened the door in the hallway off the kitchen and descended another level into the cool dark of the basement.

The basement in their house had not been ideal for their CD release party, as the midnight outage showed, but playing at a bar was not yet an option. While Johnny (the bass player) and Brian (the lead guitarist) were twenty-one, Becky (the drummer) and Paige would not be legal for a few more months. Paige wondered how the music scene in the States even managed to exist. How could there be so many great bands when music lovers couldn't even go to the bars to hear them? Concerts in arenas didn't count, Paige thought, picking her way through the minefield of bodies, trying to find her sister, because anyone could go to those and they were not where great music started. In fact, Paige thought, most significant bands began at parties like these, in basements and living rooms, making music in spite of backward laws designed to kill America's creative spirit. Twenty-one! What if the Beatles had been subjected to that rule, or the Rolling Stones, or Big Star, or even the Replacements? What would music be like today if bars back then had only allowed people over twenty-one? What would music be like in the next decade, and the decade after that, when it would be decided and disseminated by people old enough to be out of college? She was not optimistic.

But soon, Paige thought, searching for Shannon, it wouldn't matter, at least for them. Last night before the party, the band had gathered in Brian's room to share a ceremonial joint, their pre-performance ritual. They discussed the set list, haggled over the order of a few songs. They agreed again that the CD cover, a black-and-white photo of them peeking out from trees in the leafless woods, represented their aesthetic. As soon as Becky turned twenty-one they were going on the road, playing wherever someone would let them. They talked of getting out of the South, out of Tennessee, away from the manufactured country glitz of Nashville, of the twangs and simplistic hokey stories that did not speak to them, away from racism and backwardness and small-hearted religion. None of them had ever been to Seattle, but in their minds, the place and the music was everything Chattanooga was not. If—if the tour this summer left them intact—then in the fall they would not return and instead would keep playing across the country until they arrived in Seattle. There they'd start over, opening for tiny acts in tiny bars, but that was okay, because that was where they would make it happen.

Paige had wanted to leave after high school, take her guitar and board a bus to New York, but as the youngest child she couldn't abide the loneliness and disappointment her father would feel, at least not yet. So she'd stayed at home and enrolled at the University of Tennessee at Chattanooga, her major undeclared, taking poetry classes, theater, music appreciation, none of which inspired her. At night in her bedroom she sang into a tape recorder songs she'd written in classes when she should have been taking notes. She'd met Becky at one of Brian's sprawling parties, where the people her age who counted congregated as regularly as church goers. Becky's band had been set up in the corner, a three-piece punk affair, but the only good one was Becky, who played her drums standing up. Becky with her wild, almost red hair and curves not quite hidden under a shapeless dress. After the first set Paige had brought her a beer and they sat on the floor and smoked cigarettes beside the drums and that was how it began. They stayed until the final edges of the party had burned away with the rising sun. Paige helped Becky pack her drum kit in her car and rode home with her, scooted in close, her thigh pressed against Becky's. In Becky's room they collapsed on her bare mattress, their desire fast and sudden, afterward falling asleep in each other's arms. Paige awoke first, midmorning, and wandered around the house, just as she had this morning, amid the clutter and debris, lives abandoned for a few hours of sleep. This moment now, the morning after the CD party, the morning of her father's birthday, reminded her of those other mornings, and for a moment she forgot what year it was, what she was doing here. She forgot that she was not condemned to walk houses like this for the rest of her life, alone, abandoned, afraid to open doors.

That first morning she'd stayed with Becky, Paige had wandered the house and then returned to her and waited for her to awake. When Becky did, her breath like mud, her curls like flattened cotton, Paige suggested having a band together, and that the band should live in this house. That was how she started it. Before then it had just been her and her guitar and her tape recorder, her voice jagged with frustrated desire because she was not yet living the life she should be. That was last summer. At first Becky didn't want Johnny and Brian in the band—she didn't like musician guys, their energy and ego, the silly girls they would attract to the shows—but Paige convinced her. "It's a new era," she said. "We don't have to do things that way anymore." She'd spent the last few years with anyone her age who had stayed in Chattanooga who was remotely cool, going to the same parties where her friends played in a conveyer belt of bands, changing slots and positions as needed. She knew who was good, who was serious, and who was just in it for fun or show. Johnny had gone to school with Jeremy, her cousin, and he and Brian had played in a sometimes-band for a while. Becky liked the Velvet Underground, Yo La Tengo, Sleater-Kinney; Paige, Liz Phair, Ani DiFranco, Michelle Shocked, PJ Harvey, Neko Case; Johnny and Brian, Wilco, Radiohead, Beck, the Smashing Pumpkins. They were united in their worship of Big Star, the most influential pop band from Tennessee that no one knew about. They practiced in the basement of their rented ancient house, trying their music out at parties, playing more covers than they would have liked but knowing that was the way to grow an audience. They leaked more and more original songs into their sets, until they had a dozen or so they could feel good about. And then Johnny knew someone in Atlanta with a tiny studio who liked their sound and now they had a CD.

Paige was not surprised to find Becky in the basement, sleeping beside her drum kit, one hand still clutching a drumstick. She lightly smoothed Becky's hair, half-curly and rust-colored. A line from one of the Bessie Smith songs she'd sung for her mother came to her: *My heart is sad and I'm all alone.* Back then she'd performed those songs because they made her mother happy; now she understood her mother enjoyed Paige's performances because they reminded her of the Old South and Tammy, and for a long time Paige recalled her singing them with embarrassment and shame. She had only grown to love Bessie again a few years ago, thanks to her father.

When the song finally left her, she turned back up the basement stairs, without waking Becky, to resume her search for Shannon. She was in the living room, curled up with Ben on a faded Turkish rug, Ben's arm, threaded through the strap of his camera bag, resting on Shannon's chest.

Paige hovered over Shannon, whose arm was around Ben's neck, almost strangling him the way she used to squeeze her bear so close to her at night. Typical Shannon, hooking up with the guy she loved a few weeks before he would leave her forever. She toed her sister's hip, rocked her to life. "Rise and shine, lovebirds."

Ben shot up. He pulled his camera bag to him before he picked up his jacket, which had been spread on the floor, resembling the shadow of a dead man, a body evaporated into the night. Vaporized. Shannon followed, more slowly, as if she were resisting reentering the waking world. "I dreamed we were in the basement, never leaving," she said, blinking her eyes. "How disappointing to wake up here." She was wearing an oversized T-shirt that said something about penguins. Ben put the jacket over a plain white T-shirt that looked suspiciously clean.

"Is that mine?"

"He'll give it back."

"Whatever. Jeremy's outside," Paige said.

Ben reached for his camera and took a few shots of Paige, cigarette pursed between stained lips. "You know, in Korea, white is the color of mourning."

"What's the color for afternoon?" Paige said.

"He means funerals," Shannon said, lacing her hand in Ben's.

"Blue. Afternoons are blue," Paige murmured. After her mother's funeral, Paige could not find the white tea dress. When she asked, her father and her sisters pretended not to know. What dress, they'd said. You don't have a dress like that. She did, though, the white dress with the red sash her mother had made her. She remembered it, so it must be true. She would not let them deny her that.

Paige dropped her cigarette butt in a teacup on the coffee table scattered with the night's debris. The horn wailed a final impatient call. "All right, guys. Daddy's waiting. Time to serve some cake."

JEREMY'S CAR II

Outside the Fort Wood house, Jeremy reclines on the driver's side, his eyes closed against the pale April sun until he hears them open the doors and settle in. Paige claims the front, and Ben and Shannon take the tiny back seats of the convertible.

"Thanks for keeping me waiting, ladies." He shifts into gear and guns down the street.

"You missed a party," Paige says.

"I was detained." Jeremy looks in the rearview mirror. "Is this the Asian photographer you're always going on about?"

"His name is Ben and he's from Korea." Shannon snuggles under Ben's arm, burrows in his jacket, the chilly air blasting past them.

"Is that right? My ex is from Korea. Except that Koreans don't have gay people. That's what my ex told me after we'd been together for about three months, right before he went back and married some girl from Daegu. Famous for its apples and pretty girls, right?"

"That's right," Ben says.

Shannon knees Jeremy's seat from the back, and he howls in mock pain.

In the front, Paige punches the car lighter in for the unlit cigarette clenched between her lips. She ejects the CD of Jeremy's trance music and slots in her band's debut, which is mostly jangly guitar, muscular drums, and a thrumming bass. Paige's voice, full of twenty-something longing, sounds like cut glass.

"What do you think?" Paige says, as Jeremy speeds onto Brainerd.

"Derivative Alanis Morissette," Jeremy says.

"Fuck you. More like PJ Harvey meets Liz Phair."

"Oh, you mean rich white girls complaining because boys—excuse me, girls—don't love them," Jeremy says.

"We're not rich; you are." Paige settles into the seat, spreads the skirt of her white dress as if it were a napkin. "Where were you, anyway?"

"I drove in last night because Mother wanted to have dinner. I set up in the guest cottage and thought I'd have a little look-see at Alan's before the party."

"Alan's is a bar, not a person," Shannon says to Ben.

"Well, guess who I ran into? A certain somebody from senior prom."

"David?"

"Let's say we stopped by the cottage before heading to the party, to, you know, reconnect."

As they talk, Jeremy winds the convertible up Missionary Ridge along South Crest, a narrow road that takes them above the city. The farther they climb, the larger the houses become.

"Isn't he in the Army?"

"Graduated ROTC. Starts officer training camp in a month and then he gets to go to Germany to drive tanks. Not a bad gig."

"Except for that whole Don't Ask, Don't Tell thing."

"Well, nobody's asking and I'm not telling," Jeremy says.

"Except you just did," Paige says.

"Y'all don't count." Jeremy sighs. "He was the love of my life once upon a time. Anyway, I doubt I'll see him again."

"Fight?"

"Mother has the key to the cottage and made a surprise early morning visit. He ran out the door before I could say goodbye."

"Should have come to the party instead," Paige says.

"She threatened in her predictably tiresome way to cut my inheritance." They pass ruined battlefields from the Civil War, marked by crumbling stones and rusted cannons. The battles fought on Missionary Ridge were numerous and minor, and now residents drive by them without noticing or remarking upon them. Only Ben notes the open patches, the scarred grass. With his free hand he takes a few photos as they blur past the relics.

They stop at a house, not one of the largest but a stately stone building, which boasts views of the city and mountains from the front and back yards.

"You grew up here?" Ben waits for Shannon to lift her head from his shoulder so he can take pictures.

"Crazy, I know."

The four of them stretch, catlike, as if waking from a long sleep, and slowly climb out of the car. It's almost noon, and the sun shines with prisms and spangles of light on the city below them, rendering it deceptively, misleadingly benign. Shannon and Ben hold hands, fingers intertwined. Jeremy and Paige fall in behind them, she in her white dress, he in his black T-shirt and jeans, like some deranged bride and groom stumbling their way to the altar. The four pause at the door, smoothing hair, patting pockets, prying eyelids open for squirts of Shannon's eye drops.

"It's not true what they say about Asians and small dicks, right, Shannon?" Jeremy says. "At least not with mine. Sung was his name. Sung was hung. Ha ha. I bet he's fucking another married guy behind pretty apple girl's back."

"Stop it," Shannon says.

"Don't listen to him, Ben. Jeremy's being an asshole because he's jealous, that's all. It's probably worse here in Chattanooga than in Korea," Paige says. "I'm so tired of the back-ass South."

"Me too," Jeremy says.

"I'm tired of country music. I'm tired of poor-old-me songs," Paige says. "I hate the South."

"I don't hate it he thought, panting in the cold air, the iron New England dark: I don't. I don't! I don't hate it! I don't hate it!" Ben says.

"Faulkner's so tiresome," Jeremy says.

"Why are you being such a pill?" Shannon says. It was something her mother would have said, years ago.

"He was the love of my life," Jeremy says in a voice so low they can barely hear him. He reaches for the doorknob.

"Who?" Shannon says.

"Both."

Without knocking, they enter the girls' childhood home.

CLAIRE

Claire rubbed the slope of her belly just as the baby kicked. She was eight months pregnant, but she felt as if the baby—a girl—already wanted out. She'd just returned from the bathroom, and she wondered if she could ice the cake before she had to go again. She was in her father's kitchen, avocado walls and laminate countertops unchanged since her childhood, waiting for the cake to cool so she could ice it. She turned on the mixer, spun the frosting until it peaked, and tested the cake with the pad of her index finger. Still warm. Her sisters, as usual, were late.

Jim was on the deck with her father, keeping him company with the small group of women who'd arrived with the usual casseroles and fried chicken and Jell-O molds. She'd taken the morning off for her father's birthday, but she had to be back in the office after lunch for a planning session. She had a month to delegate, plan, and delay projects and deadlines before her maternity leave started. She knew the higher-ups did not expect her to come back. When they stopped her in the hall, asking over and over when the baby was due, they'd tell her she'd be a good mother, just like her poor sweet Lila, who had devoted herself to her daughters until the Good Lord decided heaven needed her early. Claire hated the insinuation, the assumption that she'd stay at home because she could, because that's what mothers did. But her mother's death had shown her that nothing could be counted on. She would be back and she would continue to work her way up in the company. She would make it to vice president. She would show them all.

About four months before her mother died, before she was in the hospital as much as she was out of it, Claire had crawled in bed with her to watch soap operas, as they'd started doing in the afternoons. They'd converted the office on the first floor to a bedroom for Lila and bought her a cane and a wheelchair, which she refused to use. Her father brought a new TV home, one with a large, forgiving screen. Her mother had never watched TV much before, except to spend time with the family, and when she did, she was always mending or knitting or cleaning something. Claire remembered her mother polishing silver while they watched TV, the stained cloth tattered with use, saying, "Mother never polished the silver. That was Miss Eva's job." Her mother often mentioned Miss Eva, the housekeeper who'd lived in a cottage on their property, and her daughter Tammy. Miss Eva not only cooked dinner but also cleaned the house and had practically raised their mother and her brother Thad, who had died in his thirties as well. Claire had once asked her mother, "Well, if Miss Eva did everything, what did your mother do?"

"Mother didn't 'do,'" her mother had answered, wide-eyed. "She simply was."

In those last months of afternoons her mother was dying, Paige and Shannon would entertain their mother with their singing and stories and then retreat to Paige's room to play with the crochet dollhouse Momma Hamilton had made for Claire before she died, which they inhabited with Fisher-Price people because Barbies were too big. Her sisters were four and six years younger, and a vast chasm separated twelve-year-old Claire from their world of dolls and miniature houses. Claire, who, anticipating her first period, had read and reread the sections on Maxi Pads in *Are You There God? It's Me, Margaret* since she had no one to talk to about it. Who nursed her mother while trying to protect her sisters from the worst of her dying. Who worried their father was too quiet and stoic, almost secretive. Who felt it was up to her to keep their family from falling apart.

While her sisters played with their dolls, Claire would join her mother in bed and they would watch the soaps for a few hours before Claire's father came home and replaced her in the bed so that she could make dinner and do her homework. That time with her mother in bed, watching soaps, Claire remembered secretly, fondly. They were not time wasters, she and her mother. In regular circumstances, they would not sit in bed and watch the pretend-lives of others. Even now, those days in bed with her mother were the only times she remembered actually resting. Her whole life she'd been busy, taking care of her mother, ushering her into death, and then raising her sisters, protecting her father against opportunistic women, doing well enough to get a full honors scholarship, and then doing well enough to be accepted into the University of Tennessee at Knoxville's MBA program. Next were the life steps, which she'd followed with ruthless planning and dedication: marriage, career, house, family. Now, about to give birth to her first child (there would be two, she and Jim had decided), she saw that she would never rest again, for resting meant death.

One night during her fourth month of pregnancy Claire had tried to roll onto her side but could not, and instead she lay on her back and thought of that day when her mother, concave, the inverse of Claire now, rested on her stomach for a few seconds, shifted to her side, and then settled on her back. Claire's cheek was pressed into the sheets that, no matter how often they were laundered, smelled sweaty and damp. Her mother's tears were dried before they'd touched her cheek, small stubborn things, the last of the liquid left in her mother's body. She asked, "What is it, Momma?" and her mother croaked, "I can't sleep on my side anymore. Never will again. From now on, I'll be on my back, facing that blank ceiling. The only thing keeping me from heaven." Claire shifted to her back to survey the ceiling, colored golden now from the late afternoon sun, which cast a sallow glow in the room that held them.

"That's not the ceiling; it's the sky," Claire told her mother. "We're on a raft drifting in the sea. Where do you want to go?" She saw a trace of her mother's smile, upturned slightly, as if in pain. "I'd like to go to Africa." She patted Claire's hand. "It would be a nice long ride in a boat, drifting. And then when I got to Africa—Kenya, actually—I'd meet my sister Tammy for tea."

Claire listened to her mother's breathing, synchronized, shallow. She didn't know if her mother was hallucinating. "You don't have a sister."

She sighed, turned back to the ceiling. "When I went off to college, Tammy went to Kenya. She didn't even leave an address for me to write her. I wonder if she wears those colorful clothes I see in *National Geographic*. Maybe she's got her own help there."

"You said she was your sister," Claire said. "What do you mean?"

Her mother closed her eyes. "I wonder what kind of tea she'd serve. Probably Earl Grey, with British scones and cream. We'd have lots to talk about." Outside, clouds obscured the sun and the room dimmed. Her mother's breathing was as light as a feather's falling.

Sometimes, Claire would wonder if anyone had ever tried to contact Tammy after her mother had died. Someone should have, she thought; they should have at least done that. But who was there to do it? Her mother's side of the family had been sickly, frail, a withering vine, all dead. Her uncle Thad had died three years before their mother, before he was thirty-five, his heart weakened by childhood scarlet fever. Her grandfather and grandmother died of sorrow and waste after that. Only Susan—Thad's wife and Jeremy's mother, not a blood relative—survived. There was no one who would even go to the trouble of trying to find Tammy.

The baby—Aimee, they'd already named her—kicked again, and Claire felt something else, a deep burrowing pain that claimed her breath for a second. She pressed the cake layers, which were now cool enough to frost. With a frosting knife, she spread chocolate frosting on the bottom layer, then carefully positioned the second layer on top.

Maybe now with the Internet she could track Tammy down and ask her about her mother, what she'd been like as a girl. She wondered if Tammy really was in Kenya, or if that had been one of her mother's hallucinations, frequent toward the end. Maybe Tammy was not far away at all—but if Claire did find her, what would she ask her? What was she prepared to know? What had her mother meant: *sister.* Why had her mother burdened her with what could not be known? She would not do such a thing to Aimee, use her as a confessional for her own dark secrets, as if she would ever have any. She would not use her daughter as a priest on her deathbed.

The door burst open and her sisters spilled inside, followed by Jeremy and a man she'd never seen, Asian, wiry, a camera aloft in his hand. Paige was wearing that awful white dress and Shannon, in an oversized, ratty T-shirt that said something about penguins, looked like she'd been wearing the same clothes for a week. Jeremy was slick and shaven, dressed in black, and she could smell his heavy cologne and cigarettes from here.

"I know, I know," Paige said. The white dress looked as if it had come from an ancient fairy tale. On her feet were her scuffed purple Doc Martens, the only shoes she'd seen Paige wear for the past year. She'd inched up behind Claire, wrapped her arms around Claire's full belly, and the faintest smell of her mother's perfume brushed her neck. "They kept wanting us to play. I couldn't say no, could I?"

"You reek," Claire said. She looked up at the other three congregating in the kitchen. "All of you. And you didn't even dress up for Dad." They smelled like cigarettes and rotting cheese dipped in sweet perfume. Paige loosened her hold. "I hope you remembered presents."

"Of course." Jeremy slid the patio door open and disappeared outside with Paige. Her father's voice rose, booming. She was sure they were slapping backs. He'd always loved Jeremy, all these years, despite everything. Paige was talking, her voice high and fast, no breaths in between. A range of women's voices from high-pitched to Southern-honey smooth to cigarette-throaty trilled into the kitchen. Their father had never remarried, but now that the girls were out of the house, single women in Chattanooga had renewed hope.

Shannon was beside her, a butter knife magically in her hand, helping spread the icing. "This is Ben," she said. "Mind if he takes a few photos?"

"I'm sweaty and fat," Claire said, wiping a smear of frosting off her cheek.

"It's for Daddy." Shannon called Paige from the porch. Ben took several shots of the three of them huddled, exhausted, their smiles hurting from effort. Claire was in the middle, flanked by Paige and Shannon, all three standing preposterously over the bowl of icing, giving the impression that they were dedicated homemakers. She blew a stray hair away from her face. The camera clicked successively.

Claire felt her father behind them then, his arms circling their shoulders, folding them into himself, tucking them between his ribs, as if there were space for them there. She imagined how the photo would turn out. Claire, bloated and sweaty; Shannon, swallowed in a nonsensical T-shirt; Paige, Snow White after the apocalypse. Their father, a youthful fifty-five, with full bristly hair spiked with gray, his plaid shirt still creased from the pins and cardboard packaging it had been released from that morning. He still wore the same aftershave from when they were children. He had tried to change it once, after their mother had died, but the girls had begged him to go back. They didn't recognize him without it—deep woods and dark spices and something like tobacco. Their mother had worn only Joy, and it had not eluded Claire that Paige wore the same perfume, probably from her mother's bottle, which made her smell like a woman who volunteered at the Junior League.

The photo taken, their father released them. "I want to talk to you girls for a minute, in my office."

"We're frosting," Shannon said.

"The cake isn't going anywhere."

Ben left for the porch, and the three daughters followed their father to his office, a spare room that had once been their mother's room when she was sick and dying.

His study was cluttered, shelves stacked with useless artifacts from that past that he seemed unable or unwilling to dispose of:

dated children's books, unremarkable drawings, thin tapes of country music now on CD, an old oak desk from surplus at work decorated with Post-its of passwords and usernames. He'd just discovered the Internet a few years ago, when Claire signed him up for dial-up and a Hotmail account. Every now and then he'd sent her a few emails, sporadic bursts of stream-of-consciousness memories from when he'd grown up. He opened a deep, dark drawer at the bottom of the desk and retrieved a thick spiral notebook. He flipped the cover open and showed them the pages of recorded payments, records of bills due and paid, monthly investment statements, insurance forms, copies of checks cashed.

"In case something happens." He thumbed the pages. Paige put her hand on top of his to stop him rifling.

"Nothing's going to happen to you, Daddy."

He grabbed her hand and slid it away from the book. "You smell like your mother," he said, his voice soft. He allowed the space of a pause to say what he did not need to say: your mother died when she was thirty-four. "I'm going to be a grandfather soon. It's time." He let go of Paige's hand and closed the book. "I've updated my will. Claire's the executor. She's the oldest and she's the only one I can count on staying in Chattanooga."

The good daughter, thought Claire. The one who stays put, who does everything at the right time. She'd never envied her sisters and their dreams before, but in that moment she did. That they did not have the burden of the bureaucracy of their parents' deaths. Her mother had done the same before she died. She and Claire were lying in bed watching *General Hospital* and during one of the dying-person-in-a-hospital scenes, her mother had said, "I'm counting on you to take care of your sisters and father." And Claire had promised her mother that of course she would. And she had. That promise had shaped the rest of her life.

"Everyone okay with that?"

"Sure, Daddy," Shannon said.

"But we don't have to worry about that for a long time," Paige said.

"Of course not," he said. "The other thing is I've added a Living Will. No end-of-life measures. And it's not explicit, but especially if I get cancer and it's terminal, no chemo, no radiation. When it's my time, that's that."

"Stop it, Daddy," Paige said.

"And cremated. I want to be cremated."

"No, Daddy. I'm doing whatever it takes to keep you alive—chemo, radiation, whatever. I won't give up on you."

"That's why Claire's in charge."

Claire said nothing.

Of course she'd follow his wishes. She was thinking about his ashes already. Did he want them scattered somewhere or did he want to be buried next to their mother? She'd ask him later, when the other two were gone. She didn't like surprises. Her hot, swollen feet pushed out of her shoes, like lava spilling over, trying to escape.

"I'm not helping you die," Paige said.

"I'm not dying."

"Not if I have anything to do with it." She turned, her dress twirling, Doc Martens stomping out of the room.

"She'll come around," he said. "Besides, she'll be gone soon anyway, gallivanting around the country with that band of hers. I'll talk to her." The phone rang. He reached for the phone on the desk. "Y'all go on. I'll take this call here."

As they walked away their father answered the phone with a bright, intimate hello.

"Probably one of his lady friends," Shannon said, entering the kitchen. "Finish frosting the cake?"

Claire was a champion froster; she knew how to swirl the frost in even circles, how to write names in a uniform cursive, having done it for Shannon and Paige's birthdays for so many years. She knew how to arrange candles so that they'd blow out easily. She didn't know if Shannon knew any of this. And while she was frosting the cake, she would ask Shannon about Ben, who he was to her. He seemed tall to her for an Asian. His hair flopped forward in a way that surprised her. She wanted to warn Shannon about falling for the wrong person, as their own mother had warned her, and she'd known Jim was the right person because her mother would have approved of him.

"Don't worry," Shannon said. "I'm not going to marry him."

"I didn't say anything," Claire said.

"He's moving back to Korea after graduation. He has a fiancée."

"I'm sure it's for the best. There are enough obstacles in the world without making more."

Shannon was talking again, arguing, but Claire had stopped listening. Aimee was thrashing again, and she desperately had to pee. Again. She wasn't sure if she could handle another month of this.

She left Shannon to finish the cake, went to the bathroom and sat on the commode, kicked off her flats, wondering if she could just fall asleep for a few minutes. The room was quiet and cool and full of memories, good and not-so-good. Trying on makeup in the mirror, applying different layers and levels of eye shadow, watching her face transform into something no longer plain, then washing it off, her secret. Walking her mother to that bathroom, rinsing a damp cloth in the sink to wipe her mouth after she vomited. Sponging the vomit and blood off the dusty rose wallpaper, still on the wall. Getting her period just a few months after her mother died. She'd found some old pads of her mother's, and she felt guilty using them, peeling the adhesive and affixing the pad to her underwear. Appropriating her mother's stolen life. She felt shame and did not say anything, but the next day her father gave her a bag full of tampons and pads for all types of flows. He'd gone to the drug store and just bought a little of everything. He'd of course spotted the pads wrapped in toilet paper in the trashcan. He was a good man that way, her father, quiet and unassuming. She'd never heard him complain, and that was why she worried about him. She worried that he was thinking too early about death and the management of it. She did not want to think of those things, did not want to be the one to administer it, not when a baby was about to be born.

Claire flushed the commode, washed her hands, and waddled out to the deck. Jim scrambled to find her a seat next to him. His solicitude alternately pleased and annoyed her. She lowered herself into the deck chair, her breath full and wheezy. Jim patted her hand and briefly palmed her belly. "Everything okay," he mouthed. She squeezed his hand. She'd not told him about the false labor contractions, for fear he'd want her to go to the doctor again. The sun was like a laser beyond the deck, and she wanted to sit under the sun, even though her skin was damp and clammy. Paige had claimed the seat next to their father, who was surrounded by a half dozen single women Claire had vaguely known most of her life. They were coiffed and groomed, dressed smartly in their pressed stain-guard cotton slacks, trim knee-length skirts, and color-coordinated short-sleeved blouses and capris. From a distance, the kaleidoscope of plums, blacks, tans, reds, and oranges resembled exotic animals showing off their spots and plumage. Since their mother's death, the women had floated in and out of their lives, with casseroles and fried chicken and red velvet cakes and female advice and appraisals of their house that Claire took as personal judgment. She worked hard to prove their father had not needed them then. But now she was married, with a position in accounts at Chattasys, expecting her first baby, and she thought, *Have at it, Daddy*.

Beyond them lay a long falling hill that ended with a thick forest of trees framed by gentle dark mountains. The view and the house were the last of their mother's legacy, bought with a generous financial gift when their parents had first married. The rest of their life had been comfortably middle class, their house the only nod toward a past that was grander, might have offered more. After their mother died, their father had wanted to sell the house and move to the bottom of Missionary Ridge, where people "like them" lived, but his daughters would not let him give up that last connection to their mother.

One of the women, who resembled a fire hydrant with her sturdy, compact body and shock of red hair, placed a tall, pointy hat coated with balloons and sparkles on their father's head; her hands lingered on the elastic band she had tucked under his taut chin. Jeremy was huddled next to Jim, talking in low tones. Ben, almost invisible, was taking pictures. Shannon called Paige, who pushed herself from the chair and disappeared into the kitchen.

Claire cleared her throat and tried to sit a bit straighter. She breathed in with the contraction, hoping no one would notice. "Thanks for coming, everyone." She raised her hand like a choir director, and started the group in a double-time version of "Happy Birthday." Shannon and Paige pranced through the patio door, each holding the cake platter, keeping the cake aloft. A few steps from their father, the toe of Paige's Doc Martens caught in the crack of one of the deck's slats. She pitched forward, taking the cake with her. The ladies gasped as Shannon caught the cake while Paige fell on the deck. Some of the ladies began to rush toward her, but Paige pushed herself up and threw her hands in the air, her fingers shaped in the victory sign. Claire raised her hands again and waved her invisible baton, and the three sisters sang the last line, "Happy Birthday to you." Shannon and Paige finished the song with a can-can. The ladies laughed and applauded, for what else could they do?

"The first time we did that, Paige was nine and fell by accident. It made such a good stunt, we've done it every year since." Shannon stood behind their father, who was patting her hand that rested on his shoulder.

"Never dropped a cake," Paige added and then pecked her father on the cheek. She scooted a chair nearer the table.

The crowd counted to three, and the girls helped their father blow out the candles on the first try. "I guess that means I'll get my wish," he said, winking at the ladies.

"What's that, Daddy?" said Claire.

"That my three daughters find love, prosperity, and happiness without bankrupting me on the way."

"Good luck with that," Jim said. The ladies laughed, a little too easily, a little too loudly, Claire thought. She didn't like to see them simper over and pander to him. It wasn't that she was against him meeting someone or even marrying again, or that no one would match up to their mother. In fact, she knew her mother had been difficult in some ways, moody and put upon, even before she got sick. She was never sure why her parents had even married, why her mother didn't marry a man from the same world she'd grown up in. Another question she'd not had answered, another question she should ask. She wasn't sure why her mind was on these things lately, except that it must be because of Aimee, and what she felt she already owed her. Truth and time.

She'd hardly noticed Ben until she saw the lens zooming toward her face. He'd quietly been threading among the few guests, documenting the day with more photos than they'd ever need to look at. She'd save them and show them to Aimee one day. Your first birthday party, before you were even born.

Claire glanced at her watch. It would not occur to anyone that she actually had somewhere to be soon. Yes, it was a Saturday, but some people still had to work. Her sisters still lived in that floating, timeless world of college students. The women either seemed to have jobs that did not require them to be at the office at specific times or were wealthy enough, from divorce or widowhood, that they did not need one. Even Jim, who worked hard at his business as a kitchen and bath remodeling contractor, could make his own hours as long as he got the work done. But Claire was trying to get as much done as possible before her maternity leave, and that meant late nights and Saturdays until then. There was always more work. She wondered how much longer she had to stay before she could make her exit.

"Daddy, open your presents," she said. "I've got to get going."

"You work too hard," her father said. "It's not good for the baby."

The women agreed with or chastised her father, depending where they were on the feminist continuum. Claire noticed that some of the women were still put-together and attractive—late forty-something women with degrees and important jobs. Her father was not bad looking, he'd raised three daughters, he had a job, and he was a single widower. A catch. Her father was a catch.

The presents were shirts he would never wear, Paige's band's CD he would listen to out of obligation but not pleasure, monogrammed towels from her and Jim, which he pretended to appreciate, the promise of framed photos that Ben took. It wasn't fair. Those towels of his were all worn and ratty. Hers was the most useful and appealing of the gifts, and the most expensive, but it never mattered. The other two sisters were always outshining her with their dances and music and surprises.

She felt another contraction, but this one was deeper, from her back, bearing down. She gasped involuntarily, but everyone was laughing about something their father had said, and even Jim hadn't noticed. She exhaled slowly. Not now. Not yet. She had not packed her bag for the hospital or finished setting up the baby's room. Her baby shower was next weekend, and she had not bought anything because she was waiting to see what she'd need. They had a crib, but it lay unassembled, still in its box, a project Jim had promised to finish during the baby shower. If she had the baby now, her work projects would be left in chaos. Her bosses, the old Southern men, would tell her: "I told you so."

She stood and excused herself to the bathroom. She had a few minutes before Jim came looking for her, demanding she go to the doctor. This was her first real contraction. If another didn't come in a few minutes, then she still had time to get to work and at least clean up her desk. She'd have to sneak out before they missed her.

She made it to the front door before she felt something wet between her legs, a spurt of liquid, and at first she thought she'd peed in her pants. Another suit to dry-clean. Her face was clammy with a cold sweat. She felt the wet spot spread, warm and comforting in some ways, because she could not hold it back. Her mother, wet stains on the bed, after they laughed at the overly dramatic dialogue in a soap opera. "Another loss," her mother had said. "I never wanted to be like a baby." If only she could get to her car, if only she could clear her desk.

She lay down on the sofa in the living room and closed her eyes. "Are you okay?"

It was the Asian guy, Ben, squatting next to her, camera resting in a V around his neck, pointed down. She shook her head as a second contraction came, deep and buried. She was embarrassed that she'd wet her pants, a little girl thing, an old lady thing, a dying person thing. She took in long gulps of air and then pushed them out as she'd practiced after the one Lamaze class she'd gone to before she'd become too busy. She took the throw from the sofa and spread it over the half-circle stain spreading on her pants. "My water broke."

"I'll get your husband."

Claire grabbed his arm to stop him. "Don't say anything until they've finished their cake," she said. "It's a very good cake. Bring me a slice. Please."

Just a few more minutes. A few. She pushed herself up and waddled to the door. She wasn't sure what she'd do if she made it to her car; she couldn't really go in and work now, but something gripped her stronger than her contractions, something that told her: run.

She turned the doorknob. She closed her eyes and breathed in and out. When she opened her eyes, Jim's arm was on her, pulling her away from the door. Shannon was on the phone in the kitchen. The women bustled on the deck. She turned and faced her father, who had grabbed her other arm, as if she were suddenly an invalid.

"Where were you going?" Jim said.

"Nowhere," Claire said. "Happy birthday, Daddy. Your granddaughter is on her way."

SHANNON

At 1:30 in the morning on April 28, 1999, Aimee Lila Patrick was born. The baby was tiny and sweet and beautiful, of course, and Claire let Ben take some photos of Aimee cradled in her arms. And then, almost as exhausted as Claire, Shannon and Ben left the hospital, drove back to their campus in Georgia, and went directly to the IHOP. She did not need to say out loud what they'd both thought—that in a public place they would talk instead of falling into each other again, clothes shedding, limbs attaching, lips doing everything but talking, making it even harder to say goodbye.

They chatted about how Shannon felt too young to already be an aunt. They discussed the school newspaper, whose last issue on the class of 1999 was now out, stacked in kiosks around campus, and the small prizes they hoped it might win. They spoke with ankles touching. She was still wearing Ben's penguin T-shirt and she'd already decided she would never give it back. They finished their meal and he dropped her off at her dorm and then she walked over to his room around lunchtime and they ordered pizza and watched videos of Elvis movies, which Ben adored without irony or reservation. When Shannon, who found them corny, not even worthy of her generation's brand of irony, asked him why he liked them, he'd respond simply, "He's the King," an answer that broached neither derision nor questioning. He made barley green tea for her, which she'd never had before. The tea was not green at all, but more the color of used dishwater, and she couldn't drink it without honey, while Ben slurped his unadorned from cups without handles. They watched Elvis croon and thrust, their own knees touching once again. Shannon's hand trembled ever so slightly as she raised her cup to her lips, parched with desire. At the commercial break Ben took her to him and kissed her, first lightly, like friends almost, and then with urgent pressure, like the time in the basement, which was without time or end. They still had not talked about what needed talking about. He pulled away and studied her.

"What are you thinking?" he said softly.

"Nothing," she said. She felt like a bug under a light, with nowhere to escape. She was used to hiding herself from the world.

"I'm thinking about Ji Young," he said. The fiancée, finally named.

"Good." But she didn't mean it.

"It's complicated. Very Korean. She's waited for a long time." He touched Shannon's hair, smoothed it back. "It's not the same as with you."

"How?"

"With you it's easy. But it's easy because you don't really know me."

"I do." She was offended.

"What do you know of Korea? Of my family? Of what is required of me? Ji Young understands."

"Not fair. You never told me."

"You never asked." He said it gently.

Shannon closed her eyes, felt his hand on her hair, tried to memorize its weight and warmth, so that she could remember it always. "We can't do this anymore," she said finally, her voice breaking. "If we did, I don't think I could recover." She knew she was being dramatic, but that was how she felt then.

Slowly, Ben let his hand move down her hair to her neck. With his thumb he traced her collarbone to her shoulder. "You'll be surprised what you can recover from." He let his hand drop and he edged slightly away from her. He did not touch her again, but her skin remembered where he'd laid his fingers on her as if she'd been branded.

And then, that night, as if she were in a bad movie, she ran into her ex-boyfriend Kurt in one of the few bars in town, got drunk, and went home with him. She thought it might be easier this way, letting Ben go, pretending there was someone else. But it wasn't.

She saw Ben one last time, a few weeks later at graduation, after the overlong ceremony had taxed her lipstick, her lower back, her exuberance. She'd rushed out of the building into the sunshine so bright and strong it seemed to have erased any shadows that should have been cast. He'd found her with her father and Paige, waved to her from across the lawn. Ben was wearing a suit, and in that alone he seemed like a different person already, not the guy in his T-shirt smelling like chemicals, but a suited-up salary man, all business, no art, stiff and starched. Not the sinewy, fluid Ben Lee, almost invisible behind his camera, but the serious Ha Bin Lee, his real name. He'd half jogged to her, as if he were on important business or had an urgent message to deliver from another world. When he came up to them, he bowed ever so slightly to her father. It was as if he'd already returned to his country and re-adopted the customs of his family and land. She'd already lost him. He told her that his family wanted to meet her, the editor of the award-winning paper he'd worked on, and she reminded him that they had not won an award yet. (But they would; a few months later Shannon received a first-place plaque confirming they'd won the General Excellence Award in the Georgia College Press Association Better Newspaper Contest, which she displayed for years until she moved back to Chattanooga and threw it away.) A few weeks ago, they'd gone to IHOP with the other editors, and amid plates of steaming grits and biscuits and pancakes and oily sausages and overcooked scrambled eggs, they'd agreed that the paper would never be as good again as it was that year. Ben took photographs of the group scooping and forking and spooning in what had become a collective feeding frenzy.

Now, at graduation, he presented her with a print of the photo sealed in a manila envelope. She showed the photo of them, all steamy and slick from grease, to her father and Paige. Then Ben handed her a small photo album. She flipped to the first page, closed the album, and then handed it to her father.

"Happy belated, Daddy."

Her father and Paige said they would look at the photos while they waited for her in the car. They would drive back to Chattanooga and to Claire and Jim's house up on Signal Mountain, where they would celebrate Shannon's graduation. Claire was still at home with Aimee, ministering to the newborn's demands, Jim ministering to hers.

Shannon walked across the field of clipped grass that scratched her ankles. Ben's black leather shoes trampled over the grass without care or concern, toward other claims more urgent. This is it, she thought, this is your chance to tell him whatever it is you want to tell him, and yet he walked so briskly she could barely keep up with him. He was not lingering; he was no longer waiting for her to speak. Not that she even knew what to say.

At the edge of the field, near the university commons, his family stood straight in a row, with a degree or two more pomp and formality than the others around them, like the featured guests at a party where they knew no one. There were his father and mother, dressed better than anyone else on campus, he in a charcoal suit and red and blue silk tie, she in a gold-thread brocade jacket and skirt, like something Jackie Kennedy may have worn. His sister Min Ju was dressed slightly more casually, in a short shift and ballet flats. She was studying at Brown, had already been accepted into Wharton's MBA program for the fall. Even though he was two years older, Ben and his sister were graduating at the same time; his mandatory military service had delayed university for two years. Ben had told Shannon that his sister should have been the one to succeed his father in running the company, but his father, even in 1999, was certain Korean customers could not accept the two strikes against her—being the younger and female sibling.

There was another girl with them who, Shannon knew immediately, was Ji Young, Ben's fiancée. She wore a cashmere sweater buttoned to her throat, even in the early May warmth, and a knee-length light wool skirt, with black kitten heels as narrow as her ankles. A strand of pearls adorned her throat, and her hair was straight and lustrous, with a rulered side part. She was reed-like, elbows and hipbones and shoulder blades sharp under the simple yet expensive fabrics, an Asian embodiment of a fifties Radcliffe girl. The only makeup she seemed to wear was a meticulous black line rimming her eyelids, and the feathered strokes on her carefully plucked and arched brows. She carried what Shannon's mother would have called a pocketbook, a hard rectangular purse with a shiny gold clasp whose handle rested in the crook of her arm. Her eyes stretched open past their normal size, as if she were being forced to see something she'd rather not. She looked petrified, like an animal trapped in a dark and angry corner. The girl's oversized eyes were on Ben, as if as long as she could see him she would stay alive. Shannon thought she understood why Ben could not abandon Ji Young, why they all depended on him the way she did. In that moment, Shannon wanted to put her arm around Ji Young's fragile shoulders and shield her from the world that would be too harsh and sharp on her. Seeing all of them lined up like that, she saw what Ben meant. She hardly thought of him as a man from another country, whose native language was not English. As a man from another culture and history she was ignorant of. Yes, she thought, let them marry, let them have their family, their future. There could be nothing else.

Ben introduced her to his family, and Ji Young edged closer to Ben, bowing slightly to Shannon. "Nice to meet you," she said in accented English, her voice high and vulnerable. She held her purse out to Ben and he took it, without confusion or question. She extended her hand to Shannon and took hers in a surprisingly strong grip. Her mouth quivered slightly, upturned as if she were suppressing a smile or a mirthless laugh. It was the slightest condescension of the victor, along with a swift rake of her eyes as she took Shannon in and found her wanting: her fuzzy, poorly parted hair and her body, soft, undisciplined, her thick-soled shoes that advertised comfort over fashion, her smear of red lipstick, garish against Ji Young's pastel palette. She knows, Shannon thought, she knows, and now that she's met me and found me lacking, she's no longer worried. She'd seen the same swift assessment in high school from the private school girls when she'd been Jeremy's date at school dances. An unworthy adversary. She'd misjudged Ji Young's vulnerability. Shannon flicked her eyes at Ben, thinking surely he knows she's stronger than she appears, for Ben sees everything, surely he must see the duplicity of Ji Young. But Ben was not looking at her or Ji Young; instead he was gazing far off, as if he'd spotted an exotic bird and was following its path until it disappeared on the horizon. He himself looked, if not exotic, then out of place, diminished even, with Ji Young's pocketbook dangling from his hand in his stiff, overly fitted suit. Saying hello to his family was the most horrible way for them to say goodbye, Shannon thought. Or perhaps it was better, or easier at least for her to turn away without saying how much she loved him, without begging him to stay. She would not have to pretend there was anything left for them.

She chatted briefly with his family while Ben watched the distance. His father spoke fluent, accented English, while his sister's English, like Ben's, without accent or flaw, was just a bit more careful and considered than a native speaker's. The family thanked her for her work with Ben, that it must have been her that enabled him to do such good work as a photographer, that she gave him a chance to enjoy himself in a worthwhile hobby before beginning the real work with the company. She told them that it was the opposite, that it was Ben's photographs that enabled her to write the articles she had, and she doubted she would ever be as good without him. When she said that she saw him visor his eyes and squint, as if the sun had suddenly become too terrible and harsh to stare into.

And then she heard her name and saw Kurt waving at her as he approached them. He ran up, out of breath, telling Shannon he was sorry she couldn't make the thing with his parents, but that he'd see her tomorrow. Quick introductions and handshakes, and then Kurt disappearing back down the hill toward the parking lot. Ben looked stricken. She felt slightly satisfied. You have a fiancée and you are moving to Seoul. What did you expect?

When it was time to leave them, she wished them all the best, and then she took Ben's hand and shook it. Quickly he pulled her to him in a tight hug, one that stole her breath, as their bodies aligned smoothly for one last time. Then he released her.

"Good luck, Shannon," he said, this time looking at her. This was it. No emails or expensive overseas phone calls. She turned to Ji Young, returned her slight, upturned smile, and walked away from the fantasy of what might have been.

TIME PASSES

It seems to me that everything on this earth must gradually change, and it is changing already in front of our eyes.
Three Sisters, Act II

Winter's not gone yet if the wild geese fly that way.
King Lear, Act II, Scene 4

SHANNON

Shannon had her first encounter with obituary writers when she was eight. She'd been trapped in the kitchen after her mother's funeral when the phone rang. The house seemed crowded with well-meaning Southern ladies depositing casseroles and fried chicken and their empty-handed men in seersucker suits, sneaking cigarettes in the backyard. Paige, two years younger than Shannon, was in her room playing with dolls. Shannon answered the phone because it seemed no one heard the incessant rings over the women fussing over their father. Claire, twelve years old, but world-weary from nursing their mother through cancer, remission, recurrence, and now death, sat beside their father, her hand protectively on his knee to deflect the women's ministrations. Shannon had been told to let the answering machine pick up, but the ringing would not stop. It was like some kind of shrill nagging, and she decided she'd have to answer it just to stop the sound. Then she thought that somehow the phone was ringing for her, that it was possibly her mother calling from heaven, even though she knew that was not how you talked to people from heaven, that you prayed and they might answer you at night in your dreams, but she'd convinced herself that if she didn't answer she'd never talk to her mother again, that her mother would think they hadn't loved her because in those final days Shannon had refused to see her, this woman sick-smelling and undernourished, a skeleton with skin, this imposter she'd refused to touch or witness, but that didn't mean she didn't love her mother, no, far from it. So she'd picked up the phone because it was ringing for her and answered in a whisper, "Mommy?"

"This is Linda Thompson from the *Chattanooga Times*. Can I speak to your father? I have a few questions to ask him."

Shannon pressed the hot plastic of the circular dial against her ear and said nothing. Later in high school when she'd studied James Joyce's "Araby" for English class, Shannon read that story's somewhat overwrought final alliterative phrase, "and my eyes burned with anguish and anger," and remembered that moment in the kitchen, the phone's receiver too large, heat smothering her ear, the curve of the handle reaching past her throat. A rotary phone, almost antiquated even then, in 1985. She had thought her mother, or God even, had called her, had defied death to speak to her, to explain the how and the why, to say that her mother's love for Shannon surpassed death and sickness and the richness of heaven, but that was not it at all, it was just a newspaper lady who wanted to speak to her father. A woman whose twang stretched out her syllables in that Tennessee way, now calling her "honey" and "sweetie," a voice muffled and cajoling, relentless, hypnotizing her so that she was nodding into the phone but not speaking. Then Claire was gently prying the receiver from Shannon's sweaty grip and speaking to the lady in that self-same smooth Southern tone, telling her that she should be ashamed upsetting her little sister, and she didn't care if her mother was important to the community or not, they'd have to find their information somewhere else. Then Claire, her face ashen, had unplugged the phone and with the pads of her thumbs smeared Shannon's tears along the apples of her cheeks.

And now Shannon's first job out of college was obituaries. It would be her job to follow the dead and the dying, to call grieving families, prodding them for facts and dates, because that person would be considered important enough to warrant such intrusions. That would be her job and she would have to do it well so she could move to something bigger and better that made her student loan and her ambitions worth it.

Shannon found a tiny apartment near the university in Knox-ville—a basement efficiency with a built-in desk for her books and computer. Its most charming feature was a Murphy bed, which fit into the wall during the day. She loved coming home at night and playing whatever CD she was into at the time (U2, Hootie and the Blowfish, No Doubt, Paige's band) over and over and dancing naked in the center of the room for no one. She loved pulling the bed down before sleep, the mattress tumbling out of the wall, sheets bunched together, messed like morning hair. She felt happy and alone in those early days. When she came home from work and only had her room and the hidden bed and the ten CDs to play over and over, she felt some kind of settling in, a reconfiguring of what she was to become.

She and Kurt, who'd started law school a few hours away, were still together, long distance, seeing each other every other weekend, but they both knew their reunion was just a bridge to other people. They would not last much longer. And, even though she tried not to think of Ben too much, a small part of her hoped he would re-appear. He'd call her father one night, confessing that the marriage had fallen through and he was coming back to the States. He could live with her in Knoxville, do some freelance photography. But she tried to indulge those fantasies as little as possible. The truth was he was marrying someone else and working for his father's company in Korea, and it was not productive for her to pretend otherwise.

On Shannon's first day of work she met Dennis, who had done the obituaries before her and, with her hiring, had been pro-moted to the police beat. He'd been at the paper for not quite two years, a graduate of the University of Tennessee at Knoxville and, like Shannon, editor of the college paper. The summer before his senior year he'd gotten an internship at the Knoxville paper, and when a position opened that next summer they brought him on. That first day Dennis presented her with a document detailing what her new job entailed. It was a Venn diagram of outcomes, anticipat-ing any scenarios that might befall her on the obituary beat. Dennis confessed he'd worked on the project off the clock in his room in a group house he shared with three former frat guys. Her success at the job seemed guaranteed in that volume of detailed notes, but the minutiae and digressions, full of caveats and conditions, overwhelmed any useful information she might have gleaned, like an expensive gift she could not use. Later, she wondered if the document had really been for her or if it had been for him, a reflection of his own strange vanity, his own desire to control outcomes.

She did not think that at the time, though. Instead, she saw Dennis's document and his patient, persistent mentoring as the most exquisite kind of care and attention. He was affably attractive, with sandy brown hair, thick, almost poofy. He inhabited the prep school look of Jeremy and his private school friends, living in button-down oxfords and chinos and scuffed worn loafers from L. L. Bean. He had two pairs—when one became too worn he mailed it in for refurbishing, and a few weeks later he received a like-new pair for the price of postage. Lifetime guarantee. She took his commitment to wearing the same pair of shoes as a sign of his ability to commit long term and to be content with what he had.

He was a solid if slightly unimaginative worker, which made him well-suited to ascend the paper's chain of command. She liked that about him, too, that he was consistent and reliable, that they could talk about work and reporting and would understand the rhythm of each other's lives. She also liked that there was none of the confusing seduction there had been with Ben, when work felt like sex, all foreplay and fucking. She liked that she could pat his arm or grab his hand and not have her mind so disturbed. She thought this way was better for the long term. With Dennis she felt protected, not exposed. Dennis liked her for the reasons she wanted people to like her, he liked her for the self she projected, the aspirational reporter, and had no desire to probe the dark spaces where she so easily hid. He was not curious, as Ben was, about what might be beyond or beneath her projected self, or that she even had one. And it seemed that those emotions became so small and hidden they did not disrupt her sleep or the rhythms of her life at all, and for a while she believed they'd all but disappeared.

At the end of that summer after graduation, Shannon and Kurt mutually parted ways. After a few months of careful, slow work-to-getherness, she and Dennis kissed one drunken evening at a Moroccan restaurant. A B-plus kiss, Shannon decided after he pulled away, the plus for potential and possibility. And then, a month after that, he told her seriously, with gravity, that he loved her, a word he did not use often or without apprehension. Then they had sex for the first time on her Murphy bed, and that too was good enough, with promises of even better things to come. It was what she'd hoped for.

Years later, even after it all fell apart, Shannon knew it would be unfair to Dennis to say that he was merely a long-term diversion from Ben. Love, the falling in and out of it, was more complicated than that. The problem with Ben, she'd decided, was they'd never have a chance to see what might have been, and so because of that, he and their relationship could always be wonderful. She remembered the way he looked at her, underneath her, like she was a photograph made of tissues he was carefully peeling off. She remembered his hand palmed against her ribs, his kisses as just about perfect, gentle wet secrets probing mouth, skin, bone.

But in the beginning, Shannon was not unhappy with Dennis. After six months together, she and Dennis no longer hid their relationship from their coworkers, and when Shannon's apartment lease was up that next summer, they found a two-bedroom apartment and moved in together, settling into a domestic serenity with ease. Their surface compatibility enabled her to ignore those small, dense moments when she'd hear Ben's voice, soft but urgent: what are you feeling? How afraid she was of that question, how hard it was to answer, for what he was really asking her was, where are your feelings, especially the ones you believe you should not have, especially the ones you are certain will keep the world from loving you?

In the afternoons at work, after she'd made the last phone call to someone whose spouse or parent had died, written up the last tiny article about the so-called important person, and sent her pieces to her editor, she would look up from her computer and around the room. The veteran employees, the ones who'd started with typewriters, the ones close to retirement, they were looking up like her, their eyes dead, faces slack, bodies soft and heavy with accumulation of years in the newsroom. They'd sit ever so still at their desks and stare at the blank wall in front of them, a screen for their failed visions, the color of their life draining, seeping over time into the stained carpets, spotted ceilings, flickering fluorescent lights. Under deadline, briefly juiced, they performed tasks they had for days and years automatically, the rush of the deadline now an old and tired drug they administered out of habit rather than thrill. From her own almost-mid-twenties perch, Shannon felt nothing but dread and horror toward these deadened office workers, these people whose obituaries she could have easily written as if they were already dead.

It seemed the world was conspiring against her, she who was born twenty years too late to be the kind of reporter she'd dreamed of. She who had planned her trajectory so carefully, first Knoxville, then a larger paper—perhaps Atlanta, or even DC, and eventually New York. But the Internet and its new world of blogs and free content had not been part of her plan. As newspapers cut staff or folded, with circulations in free fall, ads diminishing, paid positions disappearing, and more people publishing their articles for free on the Internet, she saw that the career she'd chosen was quickly becoming an anachronism. Like becoming a silent-screen actress just as talkies were invented, or deciding to get into radio plays just as TV was born. Her dream was dependent on a fixed place and time, on a way of being and living in the world that was quickly becoming outmoded. Reading the paper at breakfast with a cup of coffee to learn of the news was becoming quaint and nostalgic, like a black-and-white advertisement for a fifties TV show. But unable or unwilling to change course, she fought for the odd available assignments, saved her clips, and readied to move up. In the meantime, she wrote about the dead and the small pieces of their lives, people who, if remembered at all, would soon be forgotten.

Then the Twin Towers collapsed, with one of Dennis's cousins inside, and Shannon reconsidered what she'd wanted. Was it worth giving up the life she had for the dangerous unknown? If she'd followed her ambitions unimpeded, she might have been at the Twin Towers that very day. She wondered what was so wrong with the life she and Dennis were to have, a life of relative ease and comfort with jobs they didn't hate, a house in a city near her father, and, possibly, a family? She took 9/11 as an omen, a sign that New York was not for her, that she need not miss what had not been. Jeremy was still living there in Brooklyn. She'd called him as soon as she heard the news, and he answered her, high on something but safe. He'd seen the smoke, he said, had smelled it, and all he could think of was David, the guy he'd had a crush on in high school, an officer stationed in Germany, whose life was about to change in unforeseeable ways. New York was vulnerable, Knoxville was protected—who would want to fly a plane into a building in Knoxville? There was something to be said, she thought, for being off the radar, hidden, unwatched, for her life to move on without threat or danger. She decided that instead of dwelling on what she'd wanted, she should be thankful for what she had, for a man who loved her and whom she loved, for the promise of their life together—mundane and extraordinary at the same time.

Shannon told herself she'd not given up on her dream, that she'd merely faced up to the incontrovertible realities of the market and adjusted her goals. She no longer had the stomach to fight for the ever-diminishing piece of the pie. Now she just hoped to make it out of obituaries and into a news beat where she might have some hope of making a difference, or at least having a job in what she wanted to do. She would focus on being a bigger fish in a small pond, of writing articles that might Mean Something or Enlighten Her Readers. That would be enough.

She and Dennis married on a cold day in December 2001 in a church ceremony with fifty of their friends and family. Paige had flown in from Seattle, their band still together, not famous but on the rise, with the possibility of being the opening act for a band Shannon had not heard of but, according to Paige, was huge. They were on the road more days than not and, more importantly, did not have day jobs. Paige played a song she'd written at the wedding, something about cotton and sheets and dreams, the sentimentality undermined by her raspy rumbling voice. The rest were there too, her father, Jeremy, Claire, Jim, Aimee, with her Buddha belly and wispy curls tendrilling past her ears, and baby Desmond, just a few months old.

Because flying was now more trouble than it was worth so soon after 9/11, Shannon and Dennis honeymooned in a cabin on a mountain in Gatlinburg for a week, drinking large glasses of wine, soaking naked in the hot tub with the snow falling around them. Every few days they'd drive thirty minutes into town to buy provisions of whatever was available for simple meals—spaghetti and vodka sauce, steaks and fresh-cooked spinach, cheese plates with olives and prosciutto. A few nights Dennis cooked elegant meals from his favorite cookbook *Secret Ingredients*; in his usual forward-thinking way, he'd selected the recipes and necessary ingredients before leaving home—fresh cinnamon or lime or cumin or honey. He made game hens with roast garlic and candied anise, shoulder of lamb with port, jalapeno, and Stilton. He'd selected the wines for the week as well, chosen carefully from the wine collection he was starting to curate. He documented each wine he tasted in a small spiral notebook with notes on flavors and stars from one to five. Beside each bottle of wine he bought and catalogued, he had a card noting when it could be opened. 2005, 2007, 2010. She loved that he was already planning their drinks and meals far into the future, anticipating them, counting on them. She wondered what they'd be doing in those future years, how old their children might be, what kind of jobs they might be working at the paper, or if they might branch out into some other kind of work—PR, nonprofits, technical writing. The vision of them growing older, possibly raising a family, the future measured and predicted by wines and birthdays and sports seasons, was something that comforted her more often than not.

With that in mind, her life as a married woman was not an unhappy one. They drove to work separately, as she had to go in earlier for the obituaries, but they had lunch together once or twice a week, sometimes with colleagues, sometimes not. In the evenings, they'd watch a movie Shannon had picked up at Blockbuster on the way home or she'd read a book or a magazine while Dennis retreated to the spare bedroom to play games on his computer. They spent some of their weekends on household hobbies and projects, painting rooms, rearranging furniture, shopping. When it was warm enough, Shannon started a small garden, something her mother had done until she no longer could. Shannon remembered her mother waking the family up in the night to throw tarps on her seedlings if there was a threat of a late frost. It seemed to Shannon she'd tended and fussed over the fate of her garden more than her own daughters. Was that good or bad? Shannon thought about this as she worked their tiny garden in the backyard of the starter home she and Dennis had bought, urging seedlings and plantings to grow into shapes and colors both intimate and profound. She and Dennis met friends on the weekends for dinner parties and on Sundays for brunch. With decreasing frequency they would gather at house parties, with some guests descending to the basement to get high and play music from nineties bands already bathed in nostalgia while others stayed upstairs with glasses of wines they were learning the names of, nibbling cheeses and discussing home décor. Dennis shared his wine notebooks with the upstairs group. One night, as another bottle of wine was opened, Shannon remarked that she could no longer hear the thump of music from downstairs, and that was the moment they realized everyone was now upstairs, listening to jazz on a CD player, swirling wine in long-stemmed glasses to release its bouquet. They were adults.

The only problem was now it was 2002 and Shannon was still in obituary hell, with no sign of purgatory. It was the longest anyone had stayed on the obituary beat at the paper without promise of promotion, as people usually moved into a new position after a year or two at most. But in this age, any vacated positions were eliminated instead of filled, leaving Shannon in her position indefinitely. The daily incremental dealing with death on such a small unspectacular scale was getting to her. So many people dying, forgotten, or remembered, but for what? What was the point?

Still, she felt that she could not complain, for at least she had a job, at least she was safe, at least she was loved. And then one morning about six months after they'd married, Dennis stopped talking to her for a week. This kind husband who had cooked complicated dinners and cleaned the bathrooms, who made tender and respectful love, always making sure she orgasmed, who brought home special bottles of wine for dinner, almost, if she thought too much about it, as if he were following a detailed and secret list of All Things Good Husbands Should Do, this kind husband was giving her the silent treatment. Now the man who had never raised his voice had silenced it in a cold, cutting way and she didn't know why. For the next week he kept his code of silence, and she felt her life had become a strange silent movie. Shannon would say something and he would not answer, as if he were deaf and she were mute, as if she were imagining her speech to him, that she was the one who had the problem, not him. He still fulfilled his domestic obligations—cooking dinner (she did the washing up), making the bed, putting the commode seat back down, and one night, making love, although it was not making love, it was like having dutiful sex with a silent ghost.

A week after the silent treatment began, she woke up one morning and Dennis was talking to her again, as if his week of silence had only been some terrible dream she was now awakening from. She did not ask Dennis what had happened, what had she done to bring upon his silence and rebuke. They never spoke of it. They pretended the silence had never occurred. Their lives returned to the way they had been, except now there was the silence about the silence. Shannon wondered if his silence would return. And then, three months later, it did. For three days. Then four months later, another week. When she finally asked him why he wasn't talking to her, he didn't answer her. It was as if she'd never spoken.

For the next few years, life became increasingly heavy for Shannon. In the mornings she felt as if there were someone or something lying on her, a weight that was hard to push off. Still, she made herself get out of bed, shower, drive to work. She performed her job as required, writing up her tiny paragraphs chronicling the recently dead. But the air was so thick it was hard for her to walk or type. Everyone's voices were low and heavy, like growling animals crouched under trees. She protected herself by acting normally, creating a safe space for her to nurse the heaviness without intervention. She suspected her problems were psychological and that she should see a therapist, but she did not know what she would say, what her complaint was against the world. She'd never been depressed before, didn't know its shape or tenor. She thought Jeremy might be able to tell her, but he was erratic with email. Occasionally she'd receive a drunken phone message dispatched from a stranger's home, from bars, from a noisy late-night street. He'd leave rambling messages about a *Bonanza* episode he was watching or that he'd caught a re-run of *Little Big Man* or binged on a *Three Stooges* marathon. He'd call her to tell her how beautiful life was, that he missed those days in high school, and his tormented love for David, who he'd heard through the grapevine had been deployed to Iraq. She wondered if he really missed it—a time when he could not come out and she had been one of the few people he could talk to about it. The days he'd fall into sullen depression, hide in his bed, only allowing Shannon in to see him. She'd hold him and tell him to wait for college, where they could be who they were meant to be. She promised him that after college they could move to New York together away from Chattanooga, with its petty small-minded ambitions. In New York they could find the fullest, truest expression of themselves. That was when her dream of living in New York had started for her, not the real place, but the imagined one she invented for herself and Jeremy, a place where she bustled down windblown streets, reporter's pad in hand, meeting Jeremy and his boyfriend for drinks in Chelsea. And now that she was having her own problems leaving her bed, she wanted to ask Jeremy to explain the heavy air phenomenon, what it meant, how to thin it out. But for that she'd have to see him, and to see him meant she'd have to go to New York, a place that now terrified her. She was afraid to see it as it was and as it might have been.

Dennis had taken on a long-term investigative piece on a top secret subject that required him to spend more nights away from home, and on those nights when she was alone Shannon would cut out the longer obituaries from the paper she'd written and put them in a shoebox. Sometimes she'd read her mother's obituary and the ones she'd written, trying to remember which family member she'd talked to for each one. She remembered what it felt like when she was eight, picking up the phone and expecting her mother on the other end, calling from heaven. How each time she wrote an obituary, she felt she was dying a little. Perhaps, she thought, this is what I need a therapist for. To help me survive these little deaths.

Instead of seeing a therapist, she conjured Ben's voice asking her about these people in the obituaries. She would make up stories for each person, recite them in her head before sleep, committing them to memory. The next day she would speak the stories out loud, so that she could then release them. But they stayed with her, until she was crowded with the voices of the dead. To still her mind, she wrote them out in longhand in her cheap composition books, the published obituary taped to each page, each life reimagined so it might have meant something. She wrote of the former right-wing state senator who built a shelter in his yard to give all the stray animals comfort and food in the winter. She wrote of a philanthropist getting drunk one night and burning hundred-dollar bills one by one in his fireplace, just to watch them disappear. She wrote of the pastor's wife who dreamed each night of the secret child she'd given up for adoption. She believed that the notebooks would bring about her own redemption if only someone knew how to read them.

One evening, Dennis was upstairs on the computer as he often was, and Shannon was downstairs staring into the refrigerator, wondering why it was so empty. She did not hear him come down the stairs, quietly, stealthily. When she shut the door, she saw him sitting at the table with his hands on her black-and-white notebook creased to a page of her frantic writing.

"Something's wrong with you," Dennis said.

"They're just stories."

"It's a violation." He ran his hands down the text as if he were reading Braille. "I don't think we should try having children until you've fixed it."

They had not mentioned children since they'd married, although she'd assumed they'd have them when the timing was right. It was the spring of 2004. Shannon had turned twenty-seven a month ago. She was a year older than her mother had been when she'd given birth to Shannon. Too young, Shannon had always thought. Everything about her mother had been too young: marriage, babies, illness, dying, all of it. Forever too young.

She wanted the notebook back, but she was afraid making a grab for it might alarm him. She had a vision of him burning her notebooks in a bonfire, her missives to the other world. He had not understood, and that itself was a little death. Unbidden, it came to her: Ben would understand. He would have read the notebooks and have understood what she was trying to say. But how did she know, really? What did she know of Ben? Ben was just a receptacle for what was missing in her own life, just like her dream of moving to New York had been in high school.

"You need to be medicated." Dennis closed the cover of the notebook, a finality.

"I'll make an appointment tomorrow." She laid her hand on top of his covering the notebook. "I'll need this back. To show the therapist."

"You need to stop this," he said. "I'd hate to see you lose your job." He slid his hand out from under hers, allowing her to take the notebook, which she allowed to remain on the kitchen table, a reminder of their agreement.

She found a therapist, a woman, her only requirement, and made an appointment a few days after her encounter with Dennis.

She brought her notebooks (luckily Dennis had only found one, the most recent; the others were folded in the unused comforter on the top shelf of the linen closet) and showed them to the therapist, to prove her craziness, to obtain a prescription for something to make her feel light again, to dissipate the fog.

The therapist, a pleasantly bland woman who looked reassuringly like a therapist one might see in a movie with her chiseled bob, squarish glasses, and dark suit from a store like Banana Republic or Ann Taylor, flipped through the pages without comment before returning the notebooks back to Shannon.

"Sometimes depression is telling you something about your life. Why don't we listen to what this is telling you and wait on any medication."

"My husband thought it might help."

"That's kind that he's so concerned." The therapist's face was unreadable. "How's your marriage?"

"Dennis? Wonderful. He's kind and considerate. That's not the problem. The problem is me. It's all me." Shannon thought of Dennis's silences, but they seemed so far away and strange she wondered if they had happened at all.

Each session Shannon brought in the obituaries she'd rewritten that week. They were secret missives, ones she was careful to hide from Dennis because they were proof she wasn't making progress, and he would want her to go to another therapist of his choosing, one that would prescribe pills for her instead of reading her notebooks. One revised obituary was about a man who'd died in a motorcycle crash, a man who before his death had not spoken to anyone for a year. Another was of an older woman who wandered her neighborhood, tending people's neglected gardens, planting random, surprising plants among the withering vines. Another was of a father who'd married the wrong woman and had the wrong children and lived in the wrong town but didn't realize it until he was dying and saw a vision of the life he should have lived.

On her fourth appointment Shannon brought in an obituary not based on any of the real obituaries. This was of a man who was loved by those on the outside, but at home could be cruel and withholding. He wouldn't talk for weeks and called his wife incompetent and sick. He would disappear for hours, with the vaguest of excuses. He believed that all their problems were her fault and that if she were drugged, he could control her even better.

Only when the therapist read that one did Shannon bow her head and weep, ashamed at what her life had become. The next morning the heavy weight on her was a bit lighter, the fog less dense, and she knew she would not need any medication.

For her fifth appointment with the therapist, Shannon brought her latest obituary—the one of herself. She and the therapist had agreed that by writing her own death she could begin a new life, with or without Dennis. In her obituary she was found dead, in a small house in the woods, a house with a window that looked out onto endless trees. She did not know what she was doing in the house, only that she was alone and content, and she was not doing anything she was doing now.

When she arrived at the therapist's office with her obituary, the receptionist said her appointment had been cancelled—she'd left messages on her work and home phones; did she not get them? Shannon had not. The therapist had food poisoning; she was terribly sorry but also unable to get out of bed. She would be available next week.

Back in her car, Shannon did not start the engine, but stared out the window, her hands clenched on the steering wheel. The car radio was tuned to the soothing background of an NPR broadcast, the correspondent's voice distant yet kind, like the therapist's. She had not realized how dependent she'd become on the therapist, how, in the end, she had no one else to talk to, and it was her own fault. There was Claire, of course, but she wasn't sure how sympathetic she'd be to Shannon's invisible plight—Claire with her daughter and son and marriage and her high-stakes job, checking in on their father, rushed and harried, without time to focus on anyone or anything. Paige was more often than not somewhere unreachable, rumbling across America in a van, playing angst-filled songs of women-denied. Her sisters were achieving their dreams, while Shannon was not. Would they even understand? She thought of their friends in Knoxville, all couples, most of them Dennis's friends, which made sense since he'd grown up here and had brought her into his world. She'd appreciated it at first, how easy it was, an instant group of friends without effort. But that meant their friends' allegiances and loyalties would ultimately be with him. There was Jeremy, of course, but he was only around late at night, when Dennis was home and she was supposed to be sleeping. She'd always assumed she could talk to Dennis if she really needed to, even with those periods of silence, but that night when he'd found her notebook she could not explain to him what she herself was not ready to face: I don't want this.

She thought she should try again. Dennis was her husband. They should talk. He spent the evenings of her therapy sessions at Half Barrel on the strip with his old college friends, his night out with the guys. She started her car. She would go there and see him and try to explain why she no longer wanted to write obituaries even if it meant quitting the newspaper, and in return he'd tell her about his silences, his mean withholding. Maybe they were the same thing, maybe they no longer wanted what they thought they did, and now, they could work on that, make something new together.

But when she walked into the bar she did not see him or his friends. The tables were populated with unknown faces, of people their age or older, people who seemed to have settled into their future better than she had. She could not find any of his friends, all of them clean-shaven, Oxford-shirt-wearing versions of him. She drove home and waited. She checked the answering machine for a message from him. There was one from her therapist about having to cancel the appointment, which she deleted. The other was from Jeremy, from this morning, his voice slurred and syrupy telling her how much he missed her.

Dennis was usually only a bit later coming home than she was on her therapy nights, but this time he arrived more than an hour past the time her appointment would have ended. She was in the living room drinking a glass of wine, pretending to read a magazine about fashions she did not wear, when he came home. She heard the ice machine rumble, then water from the fridge tap filling his glass. He entered the living room and bent to kiss her cheek. He sat in the easy chair and flipped on the TV.

"Sorry I'm late," he said. "Craig got drunk, and I had to take him home."

"From the Half Barrel?"

"Sure. Where else?"

There was a roaring in her ears then, the same feeling she had when he held her notebook and told her she needed to fix her problem. She observed him from a place that was not hers, a place high on the ceiling in the corner of the room. He looked tiny from that vantage point, his hair slightly mussed, the hints of a bald spot in the center of his scalp, the blades of his hunched back sticking out like the wings of a nervous insect.

"How was therapy?"

"Fine." Shannon had never known Dennis to lie. As a journalist, he claimed to hate liars of all stripes. That was one of the things she'd loved about him, his straightforward unambiguous integrity. He'd told her more than once there were no situations or extenuating circumstances for even a white lie. Now she found herself in a situation in which she was sure hers was justified. "I feel much better about things."

"That's great," he said. "I hope she's changed her mind about the pills. You'll think about asking her for some?"

Shannon nodded, afraid to say anything more.

She lay awake that night, unable to sleep, trying to make sense of this Dennis she had not known—the silent Dennis, and now, the lying Dennis. What had she done to drive him to those extremes? Why had he changed? Even worse, what if he had not changed at all?

The next morning she told him she had an upset stomach and would come to work later if she felt better. He brought a steaming cup of broth to her bedside as well as the paper and some hot tea. He told her he would call later to check in on her. The kind, solicitous Dennis she had married. She wondered if she was wrong to doubt him. She should have told him the truth, that she'd stopped by Half Barrel and he wasn't there. Perhaps there were reasonable explanations for things, still. Perhaps. As soon as he drove away, she went to his computer and logged in to his email.

They had each other's passwords in case something happened since, as Dennis was always quick to say, they had nothing to hide. And because they didn't, Shannon had never looked at his emails, although she had asked Dennis to check hers on occasion, at night when he was at the computer, to save her the bother. She was on the computer so much at work that she tried to avoid it at home, and she'd always been thankful that Dennis had done that chore for her.

She felt like she'd been transported to some thriller movie, where each second passed and the bomb was ticking and the killer would be returning at any moment. What if Dennis had forgotten something or returned to check on her? What would she say if he found her looking at his email? He might not talk to her for years.

There were only a few emails in his inbox, innocent missives about work and short notes from family and friends, all names and topics she recognized. Maybe Dennis was right. Maybe she really did need medication, something to bring her back to her own problems, her acceptance of the world the way it was, to begin the disassembling of her misplaced sorrow. Maybe he'd been in the bar after all, on another floor or in the restroom, or she'd somehow missed him in the crowd, or they'd arrived late. Maybe she was the problem after all.

Then she saw them. Folders with women's names not even hidden in subfolders or given secret names. Sharon. Lisa. Kristina. She clicked on one, and there tumbled a skein of emails, his and hers. Conversations starting with a flirtation then escalating to open declarations of desire and ending with entreaties to meet.

She clicked on each folder, scanning the subjects and content, one woman after another, affair after affair, each in a different stage of consummation. Beginnings, middles, ends, most of them engendered from his unapologetic and somewhat oppressive pursuit. She saw another folder titled "Photos." In that was one subfolder titled "Travel." In that were photos of the women he had emailed to himself, images scanned or uploaded with the digital camera she'd bought him for his birthday last year. The photos were bland, postcard-like, a clichéd photo shoot: a woman with long black hair sitting in the grass, another lean-legged in tight jeans resting against a tree, a third pixie-like straddling a bicycle. Dennis was in a few of the photos—in each one he held hands with a different woman, their dark hair the only physical connection Shannon discerned. She recognized the riverboat, the Star of Knoxville, with its wide outdoor deck and slick plastic chairs, because he had held her hand there on one of their first dates.

Before she felt or thought anything, Shannon pulled open the desk drawer and grabbed a blank CD. She copied each of the emails and photos, her heart thumping, her chest expanding, her skin a sheen of sweat. Even though Dennis would not be home for hours, she was afraid the files would disappear if she didn't copy them right then. She wanted to make sure the files and the photos were not a projection of her own hallucinations, that his silences, his nonappearance at the bar were real. She wanted to examine them in detail later, when she had time to understand them, parse their meaning, decipher their code. By the time she'd exited his email and burned the CD, only fifteen minutes had passed. She sat at the computer, her body still thrumming, electric. She rasped shallow breaths, the only sound in the house besides the refrigerator's low hum. She taped the CD under the bottom of her nightstand, poured the broth and tea down the sink, rinsed the dishes and put them in the dishwasher, showered, and dressed for work.

She arrived at work after the dead had been sorted, Dennis dutifully returning briefly to his former post. He put a solicitous hand on her shoulder, asked her if she felt okay, that she still looked pale. She told him it was just bad cramps and that she was fine now. She felt serene as she worked through her tasks, for once thankful that she could do so much of her job by rote. At lunchtime, Dennis stopped by with some takeout chicken noodle soup. One of their coworkers sighed: the doting husband. He inquired again about her condition. She said she felt better, although her appetite had not returned, which was true. She could not imagine when she would be hungry again.

Their interaction was like the thousands before. A security camera would not have detected any difference, except that now she knew there was a current of another world for both of them humming beneath. Dennis's actions, so apparently sincere and smooth, belied something duplicitous that had probably been going on even before their marriage. And now she, with the evidence, was also duplicitous, unable or unwilling to confront him and so also continuing the façade.

For the next six days when she was with him, she acted as normally as she could. She met him for lunch, waited up for him in the evenings when he was supposedly working late, lightly gossiped about friends or coworkers. He acted as if he didn't notice any change in her. At night she pretended to watch TV, her stomach and intestines a Gordian knot she would one day have to cut. When her husband was home at night she listened to him clack away on his computer, now knowing he was writing women, creating folders, curating photos.

Whenever her husband was not around, she opened her laptop and scrutinized the CD with his emails to the others, the photos of them ridiculously posed, and each time she did this, she felt as if she were willingly sticking her finger in a live socket. She'd open her notebook and write obituaries for the women in the emails. They had sad, tragic deaths from drug addiction and sexually transmitted diseases. She'd hide her obituary notebook in an old backpack in the spare closet, buried under empty suitcases, hidden among the boxes of old college newspapers, artifacts from a time she could no longer bear to reflect on.

She congratulated herself at how well she played his game. The trick, she realized, was floating. She'd learned to float above the both of them, to watch the world from some corner of the ceiling. To embody a space of silence, so penetrating and protective she did not share it with anyone. When he wanted to have sex one night, she acquiesced. She ran her hand over the tiny hairs on the back of his thigh, thinking *This may be the last time I ever have sex with him, this may be the last time I kiss him, the last time he slides his hand down my stomach, the last time I rest my head on his slightly salty back.*

And that was how she got through her week until her next therapy appointment, in which she planned to tell the therapist all she knew. The night before the appointment, while she was pretending to watch TV, Dennis came down the stairs holding her black-and-white notebook she'd so carefully hidden in the spare closet.

"What's this?"

She looked up from the TV show, *Seinfeld*, a show about nothing, in which, as usual, things were going horribly, hilariously awry.

"I know," Shannon said, her voice accusing. Her insides felt like a boa constrictor tightening, circling up from her heart to her throat so that she feared she'd never speak again.

"You know what?" he said, his voice smooth, calm.

"About your girlfriends," she said, her voice a rasp. Is that what they were?

"How do you know they're my girlfriends?"

"I've read the emails."

"They're my pretend girlfriends," he said. "For the article I've been working on. Undercover work."

She almost snorted. The photos, which he did not know she knew about, said otherwise. But perhaps they too were part of being undercover. She drew the blanket she had draped around herself closer.

Dennis sat down beside her on the couch, tossed the notebook on the table. "I thought you said therapy was helping you.

But you're becoming delusional and dangerous. These obituaries of my sources, it's pathological." Dennis put his arm around her, drew her to him. "You need a break from work. No one has been writing obituaries as long as you have. We can live on my salary for a while."

His voice was heavy and slow. Her eardrums roared. She did not think to ask him how he had found the notebook, so carefully hidden. "Will you finally ask your therapist for some meds?" he asked. "Will you tell her about your delusions?"

"Yes," she whispered.

He squatted in front of her so that he was looking up to her. "Don't tell anyone about my story or my informants," he said. "If you do, I'll have to kill you." His voice was so far away she wondered if she'd heard him correctly, if she'd not registered his tone, which, he would tell her if she said anything, was joking. If she'd heard him at all. Because she felt so heavy, like she could barely walk, she let Dennis lead her to bed.

She'd planned to tell her therapist everything, what she saw, or thought she saw, and what Dennis had told her. The therapist would help her, prescribe something to lift the weight and fog, to make sense of what Dennis had said. Then at work the next morning, she'd gone in to see the editor about taking time off, but instead asked him about Dennis's special assignment.

"Don't you know?" he said.

"He doesn't want me to worry," she said.

"That's silly. It's just garbage."

"Sorry?"

"He's doing an exposé on the sanitation workers. They disappear for hours on their route. Apparently they're gathering at some empty warehouse, gambling and drinking, on duty, while the garbage piles up, stinking and rotting the city. He's working as a garbage—excuse me—sanitation worker. Couldn't you smell it on his clothes?"

Shannon shook her head. "He must shower at the gym," she murmured.

"Ah, well. Don't say anything." The editor grinned at her. "Don't look so terrible. At least it's nothing dangerous. Maybe he's worried they'll quit picking up your trash or something. You know Dennis—he likes his secrets."

She did not drive to her appointment that evening, but went home as soon as Dennis left for his alleged weekly night with the guys. She packed as much as she could in the dusty suitcases and backpack where Dennis had found her notebook. She made another copy of the CD of the emails and photos. At least he had not found that. She moved quickly, in case, for some reason, he came back early. Was his threat to kill her imagined, a joke, a hallucination? She felt afraid of him, that if she didn't slip away secretly, he might keep her from leaving.

She took her computer, her notebooks, the stacks of her college newspapers. She left a note for him, scrawled in shaky, hasty handwriting.

Shannon Nash Thornton and Dennis Thornton. Born December 15, 2001. Died July 21, 2004. Shannon Nash met Dennis Thornton on her first day of work in May 1999 at the newspaper in Knoxville when she started working as the obituary writer. She was attracted to his helpfulness and his easygoing demeanor. They moved in together in 2000. They were married in December 2001. Their marriage was pleasant and uneventful, until one day Dennis, for reasons unclear to Shannon, stopped talking to her for a week. Feeling depressed about her job, she started rewriting the obituaries, offering more context to people's lives. Dennis thought she should see a therapist and she did. One evening when her therapy session was canceled she discovered Dennis had been lying to her and was having multiple affairs. When he threatened to kill her, she knew she had to leave and file for divorce. He tried to convince her she was delusional, but his boss confirmed her suspicions. Dennis Thornton was unavailable for comment.

And then she left.

For the next three years she lived in a house in the woods with a window that looked onto endless trees. She was one of three reporters who wrote articles for a newspaper so small in a town so tiny she couldn't find it on a map.

PAIGE

The first few years in Seattle were great, traveling in a van from gig to gig, all that time on the road. Then two years after they'd settled in Seattle, two years of touring, of sharing toothbrushes and pajamas and occasionally bras (Becky was a cup size larger), of reading each other's thoughts, speaking through music and language and drums and voice, there came someone else. The someone else was a woman in her thirties, married with two children. She frequented the coffee shop around the corner from the townhome the band lived in, one of the few places Paige inhabited without Becky, who found the place too pretentious, too Seattle. Of the band members, Becky had taken to Seattle the least; she'd never really planned on or wanted to leave Tennessee, but she'd fallen in love with Paige and would have followed her anywhere, at least for a while. Paige, however, was loving Seattle, and she'd spend mornings at the coffee shop, jotting lyrics in her journal, never to be used, and humming parts of songs, never to be played. One afternoon in the café, the woman sat next to her. She was a Seattle native, never with an umbrella, always dressed in thin seductive layers, like a present waiting to be unwrapped. After the woman had a few sips of her coffee, she'd peel off her fleece, sweaters, scarves to reveal a lean body in worn jeans and a tight T-shirt. Only later, after they'd had sex, did Paige learn that Christine was thirty-four, a married stay-at-home mother of two young children tucked away in day care. She belonged to a demographic of smart ambitious mothers who had traded their promising careers for the job of raising children, whose husbands worked crazy hours at Microsoft or Amazon or other high-tech companies most people had not heard of that enabled them to make enough money so that all of it—the home, the nanny, the yoga classes, the good bottles of wine, the vacations abroad, the new SUV—was possible. It was a world Paige glimpsed through windows and on streets, couples dining at chic intimate restaurants where meals cost more than her rent. These couples came sometimes to hear her band at festivals, but never at the late-night smoky bars in Seattle. The women had careful blonde hair, each strand a different hue, like stripes on a pale, exotic animal. Their roots never showed. They did not have tattoos or nose rings. They wore fitted jackets in buttery leather with complicated zippers. They were rich enough to all look similarly beautiful. They went to yoga. They were in a book club. They drank one generous glass of wine with dinner. They ate a lot of salmon. They played hands-on educational games with their children. They filled their calendars with lessons and play dates. Christine was one of those women, and she was not unhappy with her marriage or her children or her life. Her husband was a wonderful, enlightened man who worked too hard, but when he came home he always greeted her and the children with cheerful hugs and kisses. There was nothing to complain about, and she would not change her place with anyone, she said.

"So why am I doing this?" Christine said to the ceiling. They were naked in her bed, Paige lying beside her waiting for the answer to the question she had not asked. "Most men lead lives of quiet desperation and go to their grave with the song still in them."

"Thoreau," Paige said. She'd loved that quotation in high school.

"It's a misquotation, actually. He never said anything about graves and songs, but I like it anyway."

"I will not die with my song still in me," Paige said. "And I'm neither quiet nor desperate."

Christine was silent for a moment. "You'll get older."

The sex was the best Paige had ever had. Because of what Christine dared to do. She liked to wear billowy skirts with no underwear and garters holding up sheer black stockings with a black seam running up. She liked to go down on Paige, who would have to scoot her jeans down so that they dangled off one knee, on the kitchen counter, in the laundry room, in the guest bathroom, and once, when he was away on business, on the desk of her husband's office downtown. Whenever Christine wore a skirt to the coffee shop, Paige knew they would have sex somewhere, someway. Some days she came in wearing fur-lined boots and stiff jeans and she would not unwrap herself, and those days Paige knew that nothing would happen. Afterward if they were in her house, Christine, an art history major, would pull out books of paintings and talk her through them. Paige learned of Picasso and his Blue period, of Pollock and Miro, and Christine's favorite, Clyfford Still.

"We'll take a trip to San Francisco sometime; that's where most of his paintings are. And Paris, you've never been to Paris, have you?"

Paige shook her head dumbly. She felt innocent, uneducated, so unworldly, when at shows she felt the opposite. There the people looked to her as someone who knew and felt everything.

But the people at her shows loved her when she was on stage. Christine loved the other parts of her. That Paige loved Bessie Smith. That Paige was from Chattanooga—Bessie's hometown. That Paige as a child had sung some of Bessie's songs for her mother and then had rediscovered her in high school. Christine would ask her to sing Bessie's songs, and Paige would, sometimes still in bed, sometimes after, dressed, ready to go. She sang for Christine and this time, instead of when she sang for her mother, she knew why Bessie, with her deep-throated longing, was so loved.

She did not think of it as cheating on Becky, even though she knew she should. She guessed it was because Christine acted as if their affair was organically right, that Paige fit into her world without effort or blame. A few times Paige even babysat for Christine, and even then, she did not feel that she was doing them or their family harm. In many ways Christine made her a better person. Paige didn't smoke or do drugs around her. She learned about art and classical music, which Christine would play on the piano in the living room. Paige was even nicer to Becky, a better lover, more accommodating, and while they were on tour, she and Becky were still as tight as ever. She did not wonder how things would end or if she would be caught. She simply lived in the moment, each day folding into the next, hoping that things would never change.

And then one day Becky insisted on going with Paige to the coffee shop. It was another misty-rainy day, had been for as long as they could remember. Becky, fighting depression, had decided to stop spending the days looking out the window, searching for a sliver of light. That morning Becky was out of her sweatpants, dressed, her deep copper hair combed and fluffy, her porcelain face scrubbed clean, vulnerable.

"Anything is better than here, even a new-age coffee shop," she said, following Paige down the stairs of the house.

Christine was wearing a gray wool skirt, her sheer stockings peeking out of her Frye boots. She'd looked up with a sly smile when Paige walked in. They were planning on going to the museum for some artistic foreplay before sex in the museum's bathroom stall, Paige's jacket on the toilet seat, her pants bunched on one leg, Christine between her legs. Paige smiled at her just as Becky grabbed her hand and briefly squeezed it. Christine's smile did not disappear, and Paige thought she heard a small laugh.

They sat next to Christine, who was sitting at a tiny table, and Paige introduced Becky as the drummer of her band and her girlfriend. She usually did not introduce Becky as her girlfriend as they tried to keep their relationship private for themselves and for the band, but in her attempt to hide everything, she thought it best to pretend she had nothing to hide.

"Do you want to go to the museum with us today? We'd love to have you come along." Christine unfolded her legs from under the table, stretched them so that her skirt rode up slightly, exposing the thin black line of her stockings.

"Why not?" Becky said. "Let's make it a threesome."

When they were back home, Becky poured a glass of Jack Daniels on the rocks, the bottle a permanent fixture on their kitchen table. Down the hall, the boys were playing around, electric guitar and bass, working on bars to some new songs. Band practice was in an hour. She sat at the table and silently sipped the whisky. Paige cracked a window and lit a cigarette. She took a smudged glass from the sink and rinsed it in the tap water. She poured some Jack into her own glass and went back to the window.

"That is the person you're willing to break the band—us—up for?" Becky finally said. "Her?"

Paige quickly smoked her cigarette and lit another. Her glass was empty and she refilled it.

"I don't want to break up the band," she finally said, her voice low. "Or us."

"It's too late for that." Becky was an old-fashioned Tennessee girl at heart, Paige knew, who would not abide cheating or an open relationship.

"What's wrong with Christine?"

"Besides that you're fucking her? Just that she's a walking West Coast rich bitch cliché, and there's nothing beneath that but more of the same." Becky stood up from the table and went to the sink. She lowered her head so that hair curtained her face. "You're just a play-thing for her. Some kind of diversion from her boring life."

"She's taught me about art and music. Plus she's really into Bessie."

"Why? Because it's cool to like her now? Does she ever ask you about your music? How you write a song? Or does she ask you to sing Bessie, like some kind of Sambo entertaining the whiteys?"

"It's not like that."

The boys were laughing. Paige could picture them in their flannel shirts and soft beards, poking each other in the ribs over some joke they'd never share with them. And then the house was quiet, and she could not even hear the boys' whispers. Becky sipped her drink and stared. "I didn't even give a fuck about Seattle."

The boys were laughing again, edging down the hall, zooming into the kitchen.

"Hey, y'all are here. Want to start practice early?"

"Y'all can do whatever you want," Becky said. "I don't give a fuck anymore." She stepped outside into the forever dark and raining sky.

The first few months were the hardest. The band did not break up—the boys begged Becky to come back, for they couldn't imagine anyone else but her playing the drums. They went on tour, but now the sleeping arrangements were more complicated. It had been boys in one room, girls in the other, and if one of the boys brought a girl to the hotel or room they were crashing in, the other would pretend he was asleep, not really there. They took turns. Now, Becky would not share a room with Paige, and so they switched up. Paige, in some kind of perverse and belated loyalty to Becky and Christine, remained celibate on tour, but a month in, she saw Becky one night after the show, leaning into some earnest girl, and Paige knew that Becky would take that girl with her back to her room. Her stomach lurched because she missed Becky's warmth, missed their early days together back in Chattanooga on the futon. She knew that her significance would diminish with each girl Becky slept with, and one day Becky would meet someone she loved even more than she'd loved Paige.

In honor of her loss, she got the band to play a Bessie Smith song for each show. Her own singing became sadder, heavier. She emailed Christine safe things about paintings or music, never anything that suggested they were more than friends. She tried to go to the art museums if she was in a town that had one, listened to CDs of classical music Christine had loaned her. Would it have surprised anyone that Beethoven was Paige's favorite? When she was in town, she and Christine would meet when they could, and Paige would talk about art and Beethoven, but now that she was learning something, Christine seemed bored with Paige's ideas.

On one of the tours, the last shows were cancelled and Paige got back to Seattle a few days early. She didn't email Christine; instead she went to the coffee shop hoping to surprise her. Christine was there with her husband and the two children Paige had watched and cared for. For the first time in that café she thought of her own sister, Claire, and her children, Aimee, four now, and Desmond, almost two. What if Jim were having an affair with someone? Would she be okay with that? She would not. The Husband's (she'd never cared to learn his name) attention was focused on Christine, listening intently to whatever she was saying, his arm encircling the oldest child, the youngest caught between his legs. He was keeping them all close, as if he feared some unknown and sudden danger might befall them. Christine was talking animatedly, her fingers feathering the air while she spoke about, Paige imagined, Miro or Still or Rothko.

She should have stopped seeing Christine then, but she did not. Whenever she went to Christine's house she felt like she was going to Europe—the coffee was darker, the chocolate more bitter, the cheese more pungent. Her education was not yet complete, and she could not stop thinking about Christine's body and the skirt and stockings, things out of some novel she had not yet read. Sometimes Christine would ask her to read out loud a passage from Anaïs Nin or the Marquis de Sade or the all-female sections from *The Story of O*. Christine began to ask Paige for digital photos of her naked outdoors, in streets and parks, and Paige happily obliged. When Paige asked Christine for photos, she gave her blurry Polaroids of sections of naked limbs that could belong to anyone. Once they met at a party pretending to be strangers, Christine's husband with her, Paige with a friend, and at one point someone introduced them, and she officially met the Husband for the first time. Later, at Christine's signal, they met in the master bathroom of the house and had fast, furious sex. At Christine's urging Paige got a tattoo on the blade of her back, a red and black block, representing one of Miro's paintings. Clyfford Still, they'd agreed, would have been impossible to tattoo.

Paige began to wonder about the other young women in Christine's life—the babysitters, the afternoon nanny. Christine denied there were others, but Paige could not be sure. Each night grew darker earlier, and the skies were permanently gray. When they weren't on tour, the band played around town a few nights a week, allowing them to earn enough to pay rent, keep them out of menial jobs. Paige's own voice, tattered, raw with her desire for Christine, for things she did not yet know about herself, this voice connected with the crowds, which kept getting larger. The band went on tour again, this time more extensively, opening for an act that had opened for the Smashing Pumpkins. They were climbing the rung, ever so slowly. Becky would still not share a room with Paige but no longer ignored her. Occasionally Paige would hook up with someone who waited for her after the show, told her how much her singing meant to her. She liked girls with long hair, girls with no makeup, girls with hidden tattoos. She liked girls who brought drugs—that was the band's rule, you could use but not buy. In her hotel room, with or without the other band members, they'd do lines of coke and talk fast to catch up to their racing thoughts, or take mushrooms and talk about little things like boxes within boxes and what might be inside them. Sometimes they'd take pills that took away all the bad feelings and they'd talk about nothing at all.

And this continued until it did not. After Paige came home from one of the longer tours, Christine had disappeared. She did not arrive at the coffee shop. Her emails bounced back; her cell phone was no longer in service. Paige went to Christine's house, but when she rang the bell a different woman, also blonde with a supple leather jacket, answered, and two children older than Christine's came running up behind her. "Can I help you?" the woman asked, and Paige said, "Where's Christine?" and the woman said, "Christine who?" It was as if Christine had never existed.

Paige mourned her for a week. She stayed in her room, crying from loss, from abandonment, from someone not just leaving her but disappearing like a ghost. She had no one to talk to about it, not

Becky, her former best friend, not her sisters, not her father because she was crying over her affair with a married mother. She stayed in her room and the floor filled with tissues, like large balls of snow, like crumpled clouds. Then the day came when the band had to go back on tour. When she stood, the world spun, and she could not remember the last time she'd eaten. Cigarettes smoldered in ashtrays; ashes stuck to her skin.

This was how she got over them: at the gig that night she met a girl named Raine who braided her long chestnut hair into two pigtails and did not shave her legs. That infatuation lasted four months until Casey came along. After that was Brandy. Then others whose names she didn't bother to remember. Not only women, sometimes men. There was one with long hair and blue eyes, his face narrow and angular, but his body as if it were without joints, just liquid. She loved his hairless chest, the way he took forever to kiss her body. They'd get high and have sex that seemed to not begin or end anyplace, they'd just pick a spot and see where it took them. There was the black woman going to the University of Washington, almost six feet, who didn't drink or smoke, and so Paige could only see her when she was clean, which was one day a week, and the woman would read *Vogue* and Paige would look at art photos and they'd watch videos and listen to bands on the radio, for she'd never even heard of Paige's band. They didn't have much to talk about, but Paige liked their pseudo-domesticated relationship that revolved around consuming rented movies and magazines of no significance. It must have been like her parents' marriage, she thought, or like all those couples she saw not talking to each other in restaurants and cafés. Then she met someone else, another girl who wanted to know what Paige thought about everything, a girl who knew all her band's music, who wanted to write her own. Who always had something to say.

CLAIRE

Y ears passed. Her life unfolded just as she'd planned. If anyone had asked her, if she'd asked herself, she would have said she
was happy. And meant it.

She was happy the day she'd met Jim, sophomore year, in a
keg line at his fraternity party. He stood in front of her, talking to no
one, his blue button-down shirt and khakis nerdy and serious at the
same time. When he reached the keg, he turned and offered to pour
her beer first. She'd not known he'd even noticed her. Her friends
were already in another room flirting with other guys. She took the
beer, which she was not going to drink, and thanked him, and then
he followed her to the room where her friends were, and he told her
she reminded him of his mother, in a good, not weird way. It was her
curly hair and the pearl necklace. His mother had died just this past
summer from breast cancer and he missed her, but not the illness.
She was the first person he'd seen who reminded him of her. What
was her name?

She told him her name and that her mother had died, too, six
years ago.

The one thing they would always have. That evening they also
found out they'd both been raised Presbyterian, their favorite movie
was *ET*, and they both loved U2. His southern accent was stronger
than hers, a bit more country, but she didn't mind that because it
sounded like he was meant to stay with her, that he wouldn't go

away. They didn't even kiss that night, but Claire knew, later in her dorm room, smothering her giggles with her hands so as not to wake her roommates, that Jim was the man she would marry. All that had followed—graduation, marriage, graduate school, careers, Aimee, Dez—unfolded more or less as she'd always imagined it would, and this made her happy, too. Jim was easy to talk to because they agreed on almost everything, so that even from the beginning they didn't have to talk a lot, but it wasn't awkward. It was more like they already knew what the other was thinking.

They'd had a large disagreement only once, when Claire broke her promise that she'd stay home with their children until they were in school. Even while she nursed Aimee and held the most beautiful being she'd ever seen, even while she kissed Aimee's tender powdery skin and changed her diapers, Claire also missed being at work. She missed her office with its contained and defined projects, she missed the one photo of her and Jim, a wedding photo in a silver frame positioned next to her computer. She missed the office drama and the sudden deadlines. She missed surprising her superiors with her productivity. Besides, taking care of Aimee full time was too much like before, growing up and taking care of her mother, her sisters, her father. At night in the short hours that Aimee slept, Claire, exhausted, used up, counted the days until she could return to work.

But she did not tell Jim that, because that would make her a bad mother. Instead she asked Jim, what if something happened to him, how could she support the kids if she gave up her career? "I don't want to be morbid," she told him, "but we know things can happen to parents." He grudgingly caved.

First there were nannies, then day care, and finally, when Dez started kindergarten, babysitters. She loved her kids, their exuberance, their shelteredness, how they didn't have to worry about depressed, dying moms or take care of younger siblings. She loved the challenge of her job most days, and Jim loved his well enough. They bought Claire's dream house, a five-bedroom house on an acre on Signal Mountain. Large and new, comforting in its sameness to the other houses in the neighborhood, filled with people like them, professionals with families. She wanted their lives to be normal, boring even, so that her kids would not feel different, so that life would be so smooth they could base their decisions—who they wanted to be, what they wanted to study, where they wanted to go—on nothing but their own reasonable desires. They would not be children with a dead mother, they would not live in a house that was old and musty in a neighborhood without kids their age. They would go to the private schools her father had thought too snobby, so they would not be looked down upon. They would not worry about her or Jim, but would instead focus on the possibilities of their own lives. Their house was clean and bright and new, with big airy rooms painted in soothing colors like pewter and sand and mist. No wallpaper. No puke green. They'd barely been able to afford it, but she and Jim both had good jobs and they planned on living there forever. They'd sit on the deck at night and watch the children play in the backyard and they'd have neighbors with families like theirs over.

That was how, for a while at least, the years would pass.

SHANNON

Dear Ben,

Long time no talk to. ~~After some half-hearted Internet stalking, I finally found your email address.~~

I found your email address while doing research for an article on ~~Korean tire companies,~~ Korean actresses. Imagine my surprise to see that Ji Young is a famous ~~B-list~~ actress for a ~~shitty~~ nighttime soap opera! I ran across an article in English about you and her, just a mention, how you were some kind of celebrity couple and that you had a daughter. Congratulations!! I had no idea that your father's company was so big. No wonder ~~you abandoned me~~ you had to go back to Korea. Anyway, life is going well for me, ~~aside from a divorce and the journalism industry tanking.~~ I decided that writing for a large newspaper was not my thing, so for the last few years I've been managing editor for a paper in small-town Tennessee. The editor, ~~a closeted depressive homosexual,~~ is great to work with and throws a lot of parties ~~for the other closeted men in town.~~ I have a few ~~desperate housewives~~ friends here, but I can feel the call for the next step. I'm moving back to Chattanooga in the interim. Right now I'm thinking of either joining Jeremy in New York (~~fat chance~~) or moving to Atlanta or Raleigh and focusing on writing long-form articles for magazines ~~(or selling out, getting a job in PR or tech writing).~~ Anyway, I just wanted to say hello and glad you are doing well. ~~Love, yours, sincerely,~~ best ~~wishes,~~ Shannon

[Dear Ben,

I just wanted to thank you for being such a good friend to me. I've had some tough times since college—marriage, divorce, downward career trajectory, working for a nothing paper in the middle of nowhere. It's not as bad as it sounds, though. There's something good about living by yourself in a house by the woods in a town small enough to know you but also leave you alone. I mean that. I've enjoyed a lot of what I never thought I'd enjoy. Whenever things got really bad, I'd just imagine you asking me what I really felt, and then I'd answer, and somehow I'd feel better. Other times, I'd look at some of your photos I still had, and remember what you said about so much of the story being out of the frame. I know the newspapers say you and Ji Young are famous, rich, and happy and that you have a beautiful daughter, but is that it, really? What's outside the frame? I miss those conversations. But either way, I wish you a happy life. Love, Shannon.] DELETED

Dear Ben,

Just found your email address and thought I'd write and say hi. I'm still in Tennessee, heading back to Chattanooga for a while to spend some time with my family before moving to a bigger city. Drop me a line when you have a chance. Your friend, Shannon.

She emailed the last version to his work address on the company's website. For a few weeks she waited to hear back from him, but she never did. Then she quit her job and moved back to Chattanooga, a city, suddenly—it seemed—bustling with coffee shops and music festivals and outdoor events. It was home, but it was also somewhere new.

2009

I would like to confess, my dearest sisters. My heart is breaking. I will confess to you, and then to nobody else, never, never ... I will tell you this minute. (*Quietly.*) This is my secret, but you all know it already ... I can't keep quiet any longer ...
>   *Three Sisters*, Act III

And thou, all-shaking thunder,
Smite flat the thick rotundity o' the world!
Crack nature's moulds, all germens spill at once,
That make ingrateful man!
>   *King Lear*, Act III, Scene 2

SHANNON

Wet and dripping like a stray dog, Shannon opened the door to her North Shore house and announced to Jeremy she was home. Outside it was warm and raining. She'd just run from her car without an umbrella, her arms balancing a stack of the latest issue of *Jail Break,* now smeared and soggy, with her overstuffed black leather tote, which had left a semi-permanent red indentation in her right shoulder. She'd bought the tote a year ago hoping to represent the professional yet quirky female cops and lawyers on TV shows whose sleek leather totes were always crammed with important and surprising bits that helped them out of jams. Her own tote was also full of useful things like tampons and ibuprofen and hand cream, but they weren't surprising or that important, and she could never find the right item when she needed it. The spare tampon had settled somewhere on the bottom, its delicate wrapper torn by the spikes of her miniature hairbrush, also nesting at the bottom, and more than once she'd pulled the frayed tampon out, expecting a pen. Just a few hours ago her period had started in the bathroom at McDonald's, and when she'd triumphantly extracted the tampon, it was flattened and unusable. She'd had to use a wad of toilet paper instead, just like in high school, as if the past ten years—college, marriage, divorce, career reconfigured—had only been some alternate world she'd dreamed of in her darkest moments. Now here she was, fingers smeared with newsprint, hoping she had some tampons left in the bathroom.

Jeremy was in the kitchen spearing fat olives on toothpicks. On the counter was a bottle of gin, three martini glasses, and a martini shaker. As soon as she closed the door, he scurried from the kitchen and smacked his gin-flavored lips on hers. He relieved her of her tote, groaning dramatically under its weight, and then grabbed the stack of papers, which he chucked on the coffee table.

"Well, look what the cat dragged in," he said. "Martini?"

"Just one. We can't be late for Dad's. You got a present, right?" Jeremy had offered to pick something up when she realized last night she'd forgot to buy something. Her father's sixty-fifth birthday was tonight, and instead of going out as they'd done the last few years, he'd said he wanted to celebrate at home.

"Of course." Jeremy scanned the front page of *Jail Break*, covered with photos of the recently arrested. He tossed it back on the coffee table. "Anyone we know?"

"Not this week." As distribution manager for *Jail Break*, a below-the-bottom-of-the-food-chain rag that published the information of the recently arrested, Shannon fed Jeremy's hunger for seedy local gossip. A few weeks ago, a prominent Chattanooga attorney from Lookout Mountain had crashed into a mailbox while driving home from one of the members-only clubs. It was his third DUI. His photo had been on the front page of *JB*, sandwiched between two gap-toothed girls arrested for solicitation and running a meth lab. Jeremy's mother had babysat that attorney when she was in high school. He was incorrigible even back then, she'd said, always pulling up her skirt when she walked past him, and once she caught him pouring vodka into his ginger ale. He was ten. This week's edition of the paper was more typical, populated with the usual suspects: drug dealers, habitual drunk drivers, prostitutes, meth and pill addicts. The people in the photos always looked rough, surprised, tired, not quite believing that this was where life had led them.

"Bathroom free?"

"David's just showered. It's all yours."

She grabbed her tote, hurried to the bathroom, still pleasantly fogged and steamy, and threw open the door under the sink. "What did you get," she yelled through the bathroom door.

"It's a surprise."

Small victories: a half-full box of tampons remained smooshed in the back. She tugged her underwear down, disposed of the bunched-up toilet paper, and slipped off her soggy but reliable Scandinavian-brand shoes. From the bottom of her tote bag, she dug out the frayed tampon, which she tossed into the trash, and her cell phone. The text from Anna, the former features editor of her college paper, was still there, unread. They'd reconnected last year on Facebook, and Shannon had taken a few weekend trips to Atlanta to see her. Unlike her friends in Chattanooga who all seemed to be smug marrieds with children, Anna, who worked as a feature writer for the city magazine, was single. Whenever Shannon visited her, they'd go out for dinner at restaurants too cosmopolitan for Chattanooga with some of Anna's friends or to someone's house for a dinner party. She'd met several interesting men and even made out with one in the bathroom at one of the dinner parties. Earlier that day, Anna had emailed Shannon, letting her know their copyeditor had suddenly quit and they were desperate for a replacement. The pay wasn't great, the work tedious, but was she interested? Yes, she was, and she attached her résumé. Shannon had seen the text message earlier but had refused to read it. Now she opened it. *Interview tomorrow at 3*. She put a new tampon in her tote and flushed the toilet.

Time for a drink.

Shannon joined Jeremy on their tiny front porch, where they listened to the rain patter on the roof. Jeremy was in love, again. He'd bumped into David, his high school crush, a few months ago at Alan Gold's. David, who had just left the Army, had been visiting his parents, deciding what his next step was. Only a few days after they reunited at Alan's, David moved in.

David, smelling of citrus, his blond hair thinning and almost brown, a lighter version of Jeremy's, appeared. He took his martini and kissed Jeremy on the cheek before sitting next to him.

"Any news from the front?" Shannon said. It was their joke. As an officer, David had been in charge of building a school and an orphanage. He knew people who knew people who had been killed or maimed, but he'd experienced none of it personally.

"Salim wrote." David's Iraqi Kurdish interpreter friend. "He's worried about his son."

"Ali?" David had shown them pictures on his computer. In one, even though he was almost too big, Salim's son was sitting on David's lap, his arm around David's neck as if David were a life preserver, his long gangly legs touching the ground.

"I told him if they can make it through the next few years, they might be able to come here as refugees," David said. "Once the Americans leave, things will get worse."

"I hope it works out," Shannon said. That's how their conversations usually ended. She hadn't been there. She didn't know, and these days, so far removed from her dreams of being a journalist covering those very things, she didn't even know how to begin to know.

Shannon stood, but Jeremy patted the chair next to him.

"Maybe this should wait." David drained his martini.

"What?"

Jeremy took David's hand.

"You're leaving me for San Francisco?"

"We want to have a baby," Jeremy said.

"Well, I want to have a baby, too, someday. Maybe." Shannon said. "So what?"

Jeremy laughed. "We want to have a baby now."

"Isn't it a bit soon?" She looked at them, holding hands. She thought of that time at prom, with Jeremy on the rails of the Walnut Street Bridge, waiting for David to save him. "I mean, you two have just got together."

"Define *soon*. I've loved him since high school."

"Okay," she said. "Isn't it kind of hard to adopt here if you're gay?"

"That's why we're going the biological route."

"And?"

"We want you to be the mother," Jeremy said. "I'll provide the sperm. That way the kid can inherit whatever Mother leaves me."

She laughed, brittle, horse-like. "Funny."

"Come on. We'd be great parents. Admit it."

"We're cousins."

"I'm adopted, remember?" He put his free hand on hers. "It would be fun. The three of us. We'll all raise her. A family."

She stood, decided to ignore them. "What did you get Dad?"

"An espresso machine."

"A fancy one," David added.

"Dad's not an espresso kind of guy." She went inside, grabbed her tote, and headed to the bathroom. She sat on the commode and plunged her hand to the bottom of the bag, feeling around the scattered contents until she found her wallet.

She didn't look at it that often any more, but she knew it was there, folded, tucked in one of the credit card pockets. A copy of the obituary of her marriage she'd taped to the kitchen counter when she'd left Dennis five years ago. Back when she thought she and Dennis would have a family. When she still thought she'd write articles one day that mattered. About stuff like Iraq, trying to figure out why her government was still there. Now she had a chance, for not quite those dreams, but for something good. She heard banging on the door.

"You'll live with us. Like *Three's Company*."

"Except it's two guys. Who really are gay."

"My life will not be a bad reality show." Shannon opened the door. "This," she said, catching Jeremy, David, and the house in one sweep of her hand, "is temporary. I got plans. And they don't include you or this place."

"So that means no?"

"Bottoms up, boys. We're going to be late. I hope that espresso machine's wrapped."

Her father was snoring softly on the couch, a book cleaved open, glasses slid forward so they rested on the flared nostrils of his large red nose, a position he assumed when he was pretending to be awake. His plaid shirt was pressed and a blue tie crested his stomach. Shannon sat on the armrest next to her father and picked up the book he was reading, a vintage edition of Shakespeare's plays. *King Lear*. He mumbled something that sounded like "Where's all the candy?" and then pushed his glasses back on his nose as he blinked himself awake. He turned his hands so that his palms rested on his lap. He studied them for a moment, as if he were unsure what to do now that his book had been taken away from him. Then the cloudy confused look disappeared, and he smiled.

"Shakespeare, Daddy?" she said.

"Isn't that what people do in retirement?"

Shannon laughed because she thought he was joking, but he seemed to be looking at her for some kind of reassurance. "Whatever you want," she said, hugging him. When they pulled away, Shannon studied her father's face. His skin was an ever-growing constellation of sunspots and dark moles, and his eyes seemed puffier than the last time she'd seen him a few weeks ago. At least he still smelled like Old Spice.

Jeremy stood in front of her father, his hand extended. Her father stuck his hand out and Jeremy pulled him up, embracing him.

"Glad you came," her father said.

"Uncle Ed, this is David," Jeremy said.

"Pleased to meet you." He shook David's hand.

"Why are you so formal, Daddy?"

"I don't know." Her father looked toward the deck, which was populated by people in party hats. "I just came in for a few minutes rest. I guess we should rejoin the party."

They watched him slide the patio door open to the deck.

"He okay?" Jeremy said.

"Maybe he's sick," Shannon said. "Maybe Claire knows. Why don't you go sit with him and I'll talk to her."

Claire had quietly materialized in the kitchen with a stack of plates she was easing into the sink. Outside Jim was walking around the crowded table refilling drinks. From the deck, Aimee, ten, and Desmond, eight, yelled Shannon's name as they ran into her outstretched arms and chatted excitedly about the party outside.

"Dez put a party hat on Papa Nash. He looks silly," Aimee said. She was wearing a pale blue dress and a matching blue ribbon clipped onto her cropped blond hair. "He's got a lot of presents too!" She hugged the kids close to her. "Is Papa Nash ready for his cake?"

"I know I am," Dez said. And then, as quickly as they'd appeared they were back on the deck, throwing themselves on Jeremy, showing off in front of David how much Jeremy was theirs. In the kitchen Shannon admired the coconut cake, where Claire had drawn their father in a Hawaiian shirt reclining in a lounge chair. "Happy Birthday & Happy Retirement" was written in an even, attractive script.

"That's Jeremy's new BF?" Claire said. "He looks very respectable."

"I suppose he is. Used to be an officer. Went to my high school." Shannon took the spoon from the frosting bowl and licked it. "They want me to have a baby with them."

"You're joking, right?" Claire met her eyes, but then Shannon laughed and Claire did, too.

"Sure." She had thought about telling Claire about her interview, but she wasn't ready for her sister's unsolicited advice about making a good impression, for more of her judgment. "Does Dad seem a bit off?"

"He said he thinks he might have the flu or something. That he just feels tired."

"I'm going to make a doctor's appointment," Shannon said.

"It's probably nothing, just the changes with retirement and everything. Let him rest a bit, and I bet he'll be fine. I know that's what I could use. Sleep."

They'd turned to the window looking out the deck. Desmond and Aimee were on the table dancing and singing Miley Cyrus's "Party in the USA."

"They've been practicing that song for weeks," Claire said. "It's driving Jim crazy."

"She reminds me of Paige. She had that pixie cut when she was five or six."

Claire fingered her own chin-length bob. "That's right. She begged Mom to chop it all off, then cried the second she did it." David and Jeremy were sitting next to their father, their shoulders almost touching, both cheering Dez and Aimee on.

Claire swirled her finger on the side of the cake and then slid her finger into her mouth. "I wonder why Mom didn't try to protect us?"

"From what?"

"Sickness. Dying."

"Maybe she did protect us from some things."

"But not like Sethe protected Beloved."

"Who?"

"In the novel."

"Since when did you start reading novels?"

"Since, I don't know. A few months."

"Expanding your horizons. I approve," Shannon said. "Time for cake."

Dez and Aimee climbed down from the table as Claire and Shannon brought out the cake glowing with candles. Replaying the old routine, Claire pretended to drop the cake, and the kids joined them in the birthday can-can. They were outgoing, charming children who craved attention and approval from adults in a way Shannon did not remember she and her sisters needing. After their mother had died, whenever their father had people over, which was not often, she and Paige would hide in one of their bedrooms and play with their dolls until their father called them out to say hello, after which they were allowed to disappear again. Claire would be in her own bedroom, as Shannon remembered it, studying. But Dez and Aimee soaked up praise and attention from the adults. After they'd finished singing, they flanked their grandfather, ready to help him blow out the candles. A pile of presents, most of them shirts, Shannon suspected, were stacked in front of him. In the past ten years, as the divorced or widowed women demographic increased, their father had become even more popular with the ladies. Shannon recognized some of the women from birthday parties stretching back more than a decade.

The crowd counted to three, and their father looked up at Claire, as if unsure what to do. "Blow out the candles, Papa Nash," Dez screamed.

"Is that what you think I should do?" he said, looking at Claire for approval. He puffed at the candles, and Dez joined in at the last minute. Shannon locked eyes with Claire, who shrugged her shoulders. Jim popped open champagne and poured some into plastic flutes while their father cut the cake. The late April afternoon had been humid from the rain, which had ended, but now that evening was upon them, the air was beginning to cool. Sipping the warming champagne and eating their squares of chocolate cake, the ladies joked that it was a shame to cut up such a handsome face, but at least everyone got a piece of him. Their father methodically ate his cake, as if he were alone. Later, Paige called and sang "Happy Birthday" in a throaty, ragged voice.

Shannon tried to remember the last time she'd been alone with him, just the two of them, and she couldn't. Usually she saw him Sunday afternoons for lunch with the family after he'd gone to church, or at the kids' soccer games. Now, she watched him in the corner, the same but not, somewhat confused by the attention. Last year, after dinner at a restaurant and a few glasses of wine, he'd put on some Bessie Smith and had danced with Claire, her, and then Aimee on the deck.

This year as the party drew to a close, he remained slumped in his chair, dutifully thanking the guests as they left one by one. Jeremy and David had already said goodbye and were waiting in the car for her, but Shannon lingered until she had a moment to talk with him alone. He'd returned to the spot on the sofa where she'd found him. This time he was reading the collected plays of Chekhov. His hand ran over the first page of *Three Sisters*.

"Did you have a good birthday?"

"Did I?" He seemed to be genuinely asking.

"You didn't seem very talkative."

"I was listening."

"Okay."

The house was empty. She rarely thought about how lonely her father might be in this house by himself. She'd assumed he was happy living alone, secretly thought that the reason he never remarried was because he'd not enjoyed marriage the first time. Shannon remembered her mother as being moody, and her mood each morning predicted the day for the rest of the family. Some mornings, they'd wake up to pancakes decorated with a smiley face of berries. Other times her mother would not get out of bed until they'd left for school; on those mornings her father laid out bowls and boxes of cereal, tops already open, wax bags unsealed, a carton of milk, and tiny glasses of sour-tasting orange juice. If their mother had lived, she'd probably be medicated, her emotions smoothed out, flatlined—there would be neither smiley pancakes nor neglected boxes of cereal, just a certain sameness of the emotionally stable, as her father had always been. Even when their mother had died, his grief had been subdued or at least submerged, probably because he did not have time to grieve or a place to allow the grieving.

Shannon heard Jeremy honk the horn. How many times had he done that, sounded the horn with the car running? Waiting for her or someone, always ready to go.

"Where's Paige?" Her father closed the Chekhov.

"In Seattle. Remember, she called earlier?"

"What about Maria? Where's she?"

"Maria? Who's Maria?"

"Nobody you know." He sounded sullen.

"Hey, Dad, I'm going to come over Saturday and set up the espresso machine and spend the night here. We'll just hang out, do whatever you want, maybe barbeque at Memos? We'll go to church together Sunday morning."

"Suits me." He closed his eyes. She was almost afraid to leave him then, as if she was abandoning him in his hour of need. But she had to get up early for work, and he was already sleeping, as if he had been waiting for this moment for her to go. She had planned to tell him about her interview, but decided to wait until Saturday after she knew about the job. By then he should be feeling better.

Saturday evening they went to Memos on Martin Luther King and ate pulled pork sandwiches at a tiny booth with checked plastic tablecloths. Her father was quiet, but he ate his food while Shannon talked. When he asked her why Claire wasn't with them, she offered that Claire was spending time with her kids, although Shannon was just guessing. Claire had been hard to reach lately, her calls dumped to voicemail, emails often unanswered. He chewed methodically, allowing bits of pork to fall onto the plate. He was usually a fastidious eater. He was staring at her shirt—Ben's old penguin T-shirt from long ago, still one of her favorites.

"Dad, we have a doctor's appointment next week, just a checkup."

"There's nothing wrong. I'm just tired."

"I know, but I'll feel better if we go in." Shannon stirred the baked beans on her plate. "I got a new job at a magazine. In Atlanta."

"That's nice."

"I'll be starting at the bottom, and I'm taking a pay cut. But it's got lots of potential." She took his hand. Her father looked up at her, his face blank. "What do you think, Daddy, about me moving to Atlanta?" A month ago her father would have been happy for her, glad to see her moving on.

"Suits me."

She told herself not to get too worried. Not until they went to the doctor on Monday.

"One by one the penguins steal my sanity," he said, reading the words on her T-shirt out loud, like a first grader just learning to read. He stood. "I have to go the Aquarium. To see the penguins. They're waiting for me."

"Tuesday, Dad. Not until Tuesday."

Back at his house, they watched a show on the History Channel, the only TV her father seemed to watch besides the Weather Channel and college football. When the show, something about World War II and submarines, was over, Shannon saw that her father had already fallen asleep, his eyes closed and his mouth open. She helped him to bed and then went to her old bedroom and settled in for the night. The room had not changed since she'd moved out to go to college almost fifteen years ago. Her twin bed was covered with the same pale blue comforter—she'd not gone for the small floral prints that Claire favored or the bold stripes in primary colors that Paige liked. She'd not wanted anything too feminine or distracting.

Her room still housed the dusty biographies of journalists and investigative pieces on scandals uncovered. Her senior year of high school she'd been obsessed with *All the President's Men*. She'd dreamed of having her own secret source like Deep Throat one day, someone who would help her uncover a scandal that upon its publishing would make the world a better place. Something like discovering a network of forced prostitution or illegal immigrants made to work for free or cancer-causing chemicals dumped illegally in streams. The source would be shadowy and unknown, and Shannon would be threatened with jail if she did not reveal it, but she would not yield. Or she was Louise Bryant, restlessly reporting on the hopes of people wanting a better, different world, sharing life with a man as committed as she. She no longer dreamed of that kind of life. She wanted love, and, yes, a child, but with a proper husband, and a job that she enjoyed. Those desires were not compatible with reporting on wars and scandals and facing threats and jail sentences. The idea of going to places like Iraq or Afghanistan to report on the ongoing wars now frightened her. She'd spent the last few years in Chattanooga recovering from her life not turning out the way she'd thought it would. But now she was okay with that because her life might turn out another way, a way she'd not imagined, that might even be better. The interview had been breezy and friendly. She'd been offered the job that evening after she'd returned, with promises of potential promotion. She imagined herself at the vacant office cubicle, her mug and photos of Jeremy and Aimee and Dez. It would almost be like college again, except this time without Ben. She was ready.

It was still dark out when Shannon was awakened by a noise in the hall, the creak of floorboard as someone descended the stairs. She found her father in the kitchen, fumbling with the new espresso machine.

"Dad?"

"It's time to make coffee, isn't it?"

"It's still a little early," she said. The stove's digital clock read 3:41. She led him back to bed, and then she went to her father's office and turned on the computer. She typed in his symptoms in the search engine and waited for the results. With relief she landed upon the possible cause: sleep apnea. Her father had always been a snorer, and his absent-mindedness and nocturnal wandering could be explained by that diagnosis. She would tell the doctor her theory.

Then she logged onto Facebook. Her ex-husband Dennis's friend request stared at her from the top of the page, as it had for the past year. She wasn't sure what he wanted: friendship? To apologize? To blame her for everything? So far, she'd neither accepted nor denied his request. She enjoyed keeping him in purgatory while she decided what to do. After looking at a few feeds and liking a few posts, she typed in Ben's name, as she did every few months. Of course he wasn't on Facebook. He would not be a Facebook person. She'd written him that one email at his work address, a few years ago before she moved back to Chattanooga, but never heard from him.

Ben. Even now she nursed her memory of him so that it was private and meaningful and secret. She missed Ben the way she missed being married—as beautiful shiny things that had little relationship to how they were in the real world. When she missed being married, a couple, she did not think of Dennis and his withholding, just as she did not dwell on what Ben was probably like now, a rich Korean businessman married to Ji Young, a beautiful TV star, with children, as removed from her life as anyone could be.

Imaginary Ben was the person she confessed everything to, a compassionate God or shrink or priest, someone who listened without condemnation. Real Ben could never live up to him.

Still she felt the need to boast a bit after her unanswered email to him confessing temporary defeat. She wanted him to know that soon she would be living in a real city with a real job in journalism. Sure, that email might also go unanswered, but at least he'd know she wasn't down yet. She supposed he'd be easier to find online if she could spell his name in Korean. But she couldn't. Then as she sometimes did, although she hadn't done it in about six months, she Googled his Korean name in English: Ha Bin Lee.

He was mentioned in an article from a few weeks ago in the English-language Korean newspaper about a spate of celebrity suicides, including that of his wife Ji Young Kim. She'd differentiated herself from the other models and actors who'd hung themselves by jumping off the roof of their apartment building in Gangnam. Ha Bin Lee, son of the owner of Leesung Tire and vice president of management, had taken an undetermined leave of absence. He was reportedly at a family residence on Jeju Island with their daughter.

His grandmother's house. Where he'd go if the world were to end.

She started an email to him but couldn't get past writing his name. She didn't know if she should call him Ben or Ha Bin. She didn't know where to send the email or what to say other than that she was sorry. Suddenly writing to him felt like calling someone for the obituaries she used to write—like an unwanted, unnecessary intrusion. Her own tiny news was now of no importance. She turned her computer off and went to sleep.

In the morning, Shannon took two bowls from the cabinet and poured bran cereal into them, sliced a banana, half into each bowl, soaked the flakes with low-fat milk from the carton, and sat at the kitchen table. She ground beans in the espresso maker and made her father an espresso as well as putting on a pot of coffee. If her father were still sleeping, a possibility with the sleep apnea, she would not wake him for church.

He was sitting on the bed, fully dressed, checkbook open in his hand. "How much do you think I should give for church?"

"How about twenty dollars?"

"That sounds about right." He wrote the check out in that amount, slowly composing the letters as if he were writing in a foreign language. Shannon gave him the cup of espresso, which he sipped slowly. "This is good."

"Do you remember my friend Ben, from college? He came to your birthday once."

"Should I?"

"Probably not. I just found out his wife killed herself."

"That's terrible." He set the espresso cup down on his nightstand. "Lila died of cancer."

"She did." Shannon gripped his hands, pulled him off the bed. "Dad, we have to hurry and eat breakfast. Otherwise we'll be late."

"The service will go on without me."

That was certainly not their father, a man who was never late for anything. She remembered when she was fourteen and she and her sisters had been late getting ready for church. Her father had waited for them in the driveway, the engine whirring, as the girls tumbled in. He'd been silent during the drive, pulling into the church driveway just as the service was beginning. He'd made them sit in the car and listen to an evangelical church service instead on the radio. Shannon had been especially annoyed because she'd wanted to get the attention of a boy her age who would be at the service. What was his name? Two initials—she tried to remember now—JD or TK or BD? Her father had been waiting in the car for them with the engine running because she'd taken extra time to layer her earth-colored eye shadow so that her eyes might look bigger, and she couldn't decide between the dangly green feather earrings and blue sparkly ones, and kept changing her part from middle to side. Claire and Paige had been late too, for their own reasons, and instead of eyeing the two-initial boy in church, Shannon had sat in the car with her sisters and silent father, pretending to listen to a station that promised everyone would go to hell unless they repented now. When the service was over, their father started the car and drove them home and didn't talk to them the rest of the day. Like Dennis, she now thought. Now he was dawdling over his cereal, with no concern about being late.

Back in her bedroom, Shannon made a call to Claire, but as had been the case lately, it went straight to voicemail. She tried the home phone and Jim answered. "You have to come to church today."

"I don't think we're going to make it," Jim said, his voice weary. She heard Dez in the background whining about something.

"Can you put Claire on?"

"She's trying to sleep in."

"Daddy's sick. Wake her up."

Claire sounded far away, as if she were on the other side of the world, but Shannon made her promise she'd come to the service, even if she was late. "It's probably just sleep apnea," Shannon said, "but I need you to see him and tell me what you think." The unspoken: because you know best about parents being sick.

Shannon finally had to take the bowl of cereal away and usher her father to the car. She'd been thinking of Ben, widowed, on that island with his daughter, dealing with loss. They arrived a few minutes late, sneaking into the back pew. Claire arrived alone during the opening hymn, sliding in next to Shannon. Her father stood and sat with the congregation. He repeated the liturgy. He put his envelope with his check for twenty dollars in the collection plate. During the service, Shannon wrote a note on the back of the visitor registration card. *Ben's wife killed herself.* Claire scribbled back: *Who's Ben?*

As they walked out of the service, Claire whispered in Shannon's ear. "He seems okay. Better than me."

Claire did not look well, puffy and wan at the same time, her eyes bruise-colored, her hands flaky and dry. The price she had to pay for Having It All.

"Just wait until you talk to him," Shannon said.

"And who's Ben?"

"That guy from college, the photographer from Korea that you disapproved of?"

"I didn't disapprove of him. I don't even remember him. You're still in touch?"

"I kind of Internet-stalked him."

"Figures."

"Do you think I should email him?"

"No. Leave well enough alone."

Shannon walked ahead to her father as he approached the car. "Do you want to go out for lunch, Dad?"

"Oh, I don't know. Claire, what do you think?" He was opening the door and getting into the front passenger seat. Claire held the door open, leaned in so he could hear her.

"I think that sounds great," Claire said. "How about City Café?"

Their father did not like the newer brunch places that populated Chattanooga. Wally's was his favorite for breakfast, but it was closed on Sundays.

"Suits me," he said.

As soon as they were seated in the restaurant, Claire ordered coffee for all three while their father scrutinized the menu. He read each item on the menu out loud as if he were discovering new food from an unknown country. He finally ordered a bowl of the soup of the day, his usual lunch meal.

"What did you think about the sermon, Dad?"

"It was pretty good," he said. "Didn't you think so?"

"It was a bit Old Testament for me," Claire said. She sprinkled artificial sweetener in her coffee. "You know James Baldwin said something about the most segregated time in America being Sunday morning, and that pretty much sums up our Christian hypocrisy. It's getting old." She sipped her coffee and then reached for another packet.

"If you say so," their father said.

Shannon caught Claire's eye. "You've changed your tune."

Claire shrugged and drank her coffee.

They ate their lunch, changing the topic to Dez and Aimee, their usual fallback conversation. Dez was no longer interested in dinosaurs and had moved on to action heroes. Aimee had decided she wanted to be an actress. While they chatted, their father crushed Saltines in his soup until it was thick and mushy, paste-like on his spoon. He seemed not to be listening, instead focused on crumbling cracker after cracker into his soup.

"Dad?" Claire said. He looked up. "When we get home, can you help me find that photo album from your fifty-fifth birthday? I wanted to show it to Aimee and Dez."

He stirred his soup. "Suits me."

When they got home, their father started up the stairs. Claire reminded him about the album. He said he was going to get it.

They waited in the living room for him to come back down.

"Something's wrong," Claire said.

"I told you."

"Do you want me to go with you to the doctor's tomorrow?"

"There's nothing you can do. I'll call you after. Will you bother to answer?"

"Of course." Claire closed her eyes.

Shannon thought Claire might fall asleep on the sofa. "Let me see what's taking him so long." Upstairs Shannon found him staring into the computer screen, playing a game of Hearts. "Dad, what about the photo album?"

"I'm supposed to play Hearts now, aren't I?"

"No. You were supposed to get your birthday photo album."

"Oh," he said, not turning to her. "I didn't think it was important."

The phone rang. Her father looked at the phone beside his bed.

"Daddy, who is Maria?"

He smiled. "My wife."

"Is that her calling?"

"I don't know." They let the phone ring until the answering machine turned on. The person hung up, not leaving a message.

"Daddy, you don't have a wife."

"If you say so. I'm going to lie down for a while, if that's okay."

"Sure, Daddy. We can look for the photo album later."

Downstairs Claire was crashed on the sofa. Shannon wanted to go home, to see Jeremy and David and drink martinis on their porch. She would even endure listening to their harebrained baby scheme. Then she would tell them she was moving to Atlanta and starting a new job in a week, and watch their jaws drop because for once she'd surprised them. She wanted to do all this, but instead she went into the kitchen and rinsed the cereal bowls, quietly, because she wanted to let them sleep just a little longer, and that was when she found the stack of unopened bills in the silverware drawer.

The next day Shannon picked up her father and took him to the doctor, the same one he'd had for thirty years. Her father did not want her to come in the doctor's office with him, so Shannon waited in the reception area. When her father came out, the doctor called Shannon in.

"His vitals are normal. He says everything is okay except that he's rundown. He probably just needs more rest."

"He's resting plenty in the day. And he's getting up in the middle of the night to make coffee. He's starting to hallucinate. He thinks he's married to a woman named Maria." She dug into her purse and pulled out a stack of bills. "I found these in the kitchen, unopened."

The doctor shook his head. "It could be nothing. Could be stress."

"Maybe it's sleep apnea."

The doctor scrunched his nose. "I suppose you found that diagnosis on the Internet." He sighed. "We'll send him over for an MRI, just for peace of mind."

They went directly to the hospital for an MRI. While they waited for the results, Shannon wondered what the other people in the waiting room, some obviously sick, others not, were waiting to hear. Many were overweight, with oxygen tanks and wheelchairs; others were sunken, with caps futilely trying to hide their post-chemo pates. Others, like her and her father, did not seem sick. The possibilities for bad news overwhelmed her—broken bones, diabetes, bad blood, tumors, closed-up hearts. She thought of Ji Young jumping off her apartment building, of the other celebrities hanging themselves. She briefly wondered about their obituaries, relieved that it was not her job to write them. She patted her father's leg.

"I don't know why I had to get this test. I'm just tired, that's all," he said.

"That's not just tired, Daddy. You don't do what you say you will; you don't care about being late. And what about your bills?" She showed him the stack of envelopes with angry lettering stamped on the envelope.

"People worry about unnecessary things," he said.

"And what about Maria, your wife?"

"I don't know what you're talking about." He looked around the room, as if he'd forgotten where they were or why. "Where's Paige?"

"In Seattle." Paige. Shannon had not contacted her just in case their father was okay. Even when Paige wasn't on tour, conversations were rare and rushed. She slept during the day, so that early morning calls when Shannon was up for work at *Jail Break* and Paige was winding down after a show, both slow-brained for different reasons, worked the best. "We'll call her tomorrow morning if you want." Meaning, another night with her father, another night away from packing up her things for Atlanta.

"Suits me."

Shannon was still holding the bills. She'd have to talk to her father tomorrow, get everything up-to-date, set up his bills to be paid automatically, even though her father had resisted anything to do with online banking. He didn't trust them, not even ATMs. She shuffled through the envelopes. Most were minor things, the newspaper, his dial-up Internet service, the water bill. There was one envelope that had been opened, not a bill but a birthday card, Shannon guessed. On the front was a beach with two empty deck chairs and "Happy Birthday" spelled out in seashells. Inside was blank, except for the note, written in elegant script. "Happy Birthday My Darling. Enjoy the day with your girls. All my love, M."

For a second, Shannon thought "M" stood for Mom, but of course her mother had been dead for almost twenty-five years, and then she remembered the mysterious Maria. So she was real. She showed him the card. He snatched it from her.

"Daddy, who is this Maria?"

"My friend."

"Just a friend. Or your wife? Can I meet her?"

"I suppose so. She's not a prostitute anymore."

"I don't understand."

"She has to wake up early. She doesn't want you to know about the yellow sponges."

"Daddy. Please tell me. What do you mean?"

But he didn't answer.

A few weeks ago, as she was adding the latest issue of *Jail Break* to her informal filing system in her bedroom, Shannon had lingered on a front-page photo of a woman looking much older than she probably was, with lanky hair the color of mud, stained teeth, and sallow skin. She'd been arrested for a DUI. Her face was streaked; her eyes were downcast as if she could not look directly into the camera. There was something strangely familiar about this woman who appeared ashamed of and surprised at her life. She'd stacked the issue on top of the others in the corner of her closet, a pile of sad tales of pedophiles and public drunkards, of pill poppers and meth cookers, of itinerants who wandered the streets arguing with the voices in their heads. It was a dark and terrible world. She wondered if any of them could recover from that moment when the police photo was taken. And then just as she was about to close the closet door, Shannon looked at the photo of the familiar woman again. It was the stringy piece of hair falling over the woman's forehead, her sad attempt to hide from the world. Shannon reread the woman's name, and then she remembered. David's date Julie from senior prom. Shannon remembered feeling jealous and superior at the same time that night, certain that her own life would be so much better than Julie's. But here she was back in Chattanooga publishing mug shots of people who made mistakes and fell into addiction and might forever pay for it. Here she was about to move to Atlanta and start over just when her father was very, very sick. Life was still unfair.

What are you thinking?

I'm thinking that life changes quickly. That people disappear when you least expect them to. That if I have to choose either job or family, I choose family.

She took her cell phone out of her tote bag. She pulled up Jeremy's number and texted him: *Let's have a baby.*

And then their names were called. Shannon helped her father up and they followed the doctor down the corridor to an office door, still out of sight.

CLAIRE

When Claire first shook Joseph's hand, dry and calloused, she thought: he is not black and I am not white. She had not thought about the color of her own skin before, but now she saw hers was not white but a light yellow, like a slice of cake from a mix. His was also yellow but darker, more of a warm copper, and yet she and other people called him black. His aunt Alma was lighter than Joseph, the dark moles on her arms and neck like black stars against a sky stained from a setting sun. In light, white is the presence of all colors. In pigment, white is the absence of color. There was no white or black, just variations and shades, degrees and tones. She wondered why this was a revelation to her, something that she was sure was not a revelation to him, and she felt ashamed.

She thought: this man could understand me. She let go of his hand and the current she'd felt flow from him to her was severed, and she thought, don't be silly. In his deep and careful voice as crisp as the suit he wore, he told her he was looking forward to working for her, and she thought again, this man understands because he knows the importance of concealment, of hiding yourself, of infiltrating the enemy to get ahead when no one wants you to.

That's how Claire remembered her first paid job in her field, an internship for an insurance company in Nashville—the time she'd learn to infiltrate the enemy. She'd learned much about office politics by reading the faxes she'd sent and retrieved, delivering folders and coffee to upper management, sitting silent and invisible in manager's meetings, taking notes like a secretary. An infiltrator. Here at Chattasys, which was much larger than the company she'd interned for, she'd applied the lessons she'd learned. Each step up the ladder had to be carefully planned, and to succeed she felt she'd whittled herself down to a caricature of who she wanted to be. She'd wrung all personality out of her, and now she was a dry dishrag. By the time Joseph arrived, she wasn't even sure who she was outside her roles as manager, mother, wife, and daughter, roles she inhabited except when she was sleeping. One more promotion and she'd be a vice president, and then she promised herself she could become more of herself again. But until then, she tried to follow her father's advice when she'd gone off to college: keep your eyes open and your mouth shut.

And that was what Joseph did from that first day in January. Joseph was quiet and contained, displaying an austere discipline that intrigued her. Compared to him, her coworkers looked careless, sloppy. Unlike the rest of them, including her, who trailed in bleary-eyed, clutching their travel mugs and Starbucks tumblers, uncurling paper bags of donuts or bagels with containers of cream cheese to share, he arrived every morning clear-eyed and alert, his eyes as bright as polished teeth. Unlike her aging colleagues who strained the buttons of their suits and wore shirts inevitably stained and rumpled by the end of the day, Joseph's button-downs remained spotless, creased along the arms and vertical down to his pants and tie. He wore two suits, blue and charcoal, rotating them every other day, but they always smelled as if they'd just been released from the dry cleaner bag. His scalp was close shaved so that he was almost bald, and from his broad shoulders and trim waist, she guessed the callouses she'd felt on his hands were from lifting weights in the gym, not from manual labor. He did not drink the coffee brewed in smudged pots in the kitchens of each floor, nor did he drink sweet tea or sodas or join the other younger employees for lunch downtown. Instead, he disappeared every day at noon with his backpack, and returned promptly at five to one, never mentioning where he'd been.

Joseph had been hired by her boss Henry Grimsley, VP of Finance. That Joseph was executive secretary Alma Washington's great-nephew, and that Henry had barely escaped a sexual harassment claim Alma had defended him on, was not a coincidence. It also helped that Joseph was a conservative's American Dream, earning his economics degree from UTC and already studying for the GMAT, with plans to pursue an MBA. Joseph was an example of how Chattasys was part of the new Chattanooga, offering opportunities to people from all walks of life, Henry said, an example of Chattasys Reaching Out to the Community. Of course it was no coincidence that Henry assigned Joseph to work with Claire, leaving the nine other white upper-class prep school hires (that's why she so desperately wanted Aimee and Dez to go to one of those private schools— how much easier life would be for them!) to work for the other similarly educated white male managers.

Despite the circumstances of Joseph's hiring, from the beginning he understood the importance and function of his job the way the other entry-level employees who had worked for her had not, performing all tasks, no matter how mundane, with grace and ease. He never complained or felt compelled to confess the details of his personal life like the teary female employees who, because they believed they were in a post-feminist world, could not understand sexism when it happened and had no mechanisms to identify or cope with its presence. Confused, tottering in their heels and tight skirts, consumed with being sexy in a way Claire and her friends had not been, these young women would weep on Claire's desk, complaining that a certain remark or slight was *not fair.* (Claire's undergrad uniform had been preppy unisex, a holdover from the eighties with her chinos, loafers, and V-neck sweaters; Shannon had been more utilitarian, living in jeans and T-shirts hiding under baggy sweaters, while Paige had, not surprisingly, adopted the thrift-shop punk grunge look with ripped stockings, Doc Martens, and smudged black eyeliner. Now, Claire was glad she and her sisters had escaped this world of thong underwear and belly rings and cleavage: reveal,

reveal, reveal. Bodies without secrets.) There were also the females who wept on her shoulder after yet another guy they'd slept with had moved on, despairing they would *never* get a proper boyfriend, *ever*, which left Claire feeling nothing but relief that she had found Jim and their relationship had progressed in predictable yet reassuring ways. And the guys, they seemed entitled and emasculated at once, boys, she thought, not men at all, even though they were in their mid-twenties, drifting from one girl to another, for the last thing they seemed to be looking for was something that might limit them. Because of this attitude, Claire theorized, the young males didn't try as hard at work as the females. The males seemed to expect Claire and the other females to clean up their messes, physical and metaphorical. They were forever leaving a trail of something behind them: tissues, cracker crumbs, broken pens, crumbled paper balls circling waste paper baskets. They did not seem to mind when the females took the initiative on projects.

Claire could not see how this new generation represented progress, enlightenment, or happiness. They seemed incapable of living their own lives with purpose and dignity, without whining, of inhabiting the stoicism she'd embraced after her mother died. They seemed unable to comprehend how hard this new world of a shrinking economy, environmental doom, global competition, and an aging populace would be on them. They seemed unprepared for what they would have to soon shoulder as the world crumpled around them. When she voiced these complaints to Jim, he would tell her she was judging them unfairly, too harshly. That she was overworked and frustrated and had little sympathy for others she felt were not trying as hard as she was. "You don't know their lives," he said. Sometimes she resented his empathy for others.

The only life Claire wanted to know more about was Joseph's. She knew he lived with his aunt Alma in the Martin Luther King neighborhood, and that they came and left work together, but that was it. Did he have a girlfriend? What did he do on the weekends while she was at home watching a movie with her kids that she pretended to be interested in while Jim napped in his easy chair? At lunch one day she followed Joseph to the Riverwalk a few blocks from their office. She'd walked past him sitting on a bench, reading a library book, as still and calm as always, wearing only his suit jacket even though it was a frosty February day. She was relieved that he did not look up from his book as she walked by, because she felt suddenly like a stalker, embarrassed that she'd trailed an employee on his lunch break. She should have let it drop, then. Person eats bag lunch and reads a book during lunch— mystery solved! But when he came into her office that afternoon to drop off some files, before he could turn to go, she asked him what book he was reading, a question that seemed to surprise her more than him.

He told her he was rereading *Invisible Man*.

"I think I saw the movie," Claire said. "Sci-fi, right?"

He stared at his fingers spread and still on her desk, his nails neat and trimmed. "Different book. You should read it."

"Oh, that's okay. I'm so busy with my kids and all, I hardly ever read whole books anymore." She realized how dumb she sounded. "Except for book club. We read a book a month."

"What are you reading now?"

"*The Help*?" The truth was, she was a member of her neighborhood book club in name only and had not been to a meeting in months. She vaguely remembered an email last month announcing the title, and Claire remembered thinking, that's what I could use. Help.

"What do you think about that one?"

She recalled some controversy about the book now, that it might be condescending to African Americans, but she couldn't remember why. "I haven't started it. So busy." She swept her hands over the stack on her desk. "But your book. I was hoping you'd tell me what it's about."

He looked at her hard then, as if he were trying to decide how much patience to have with an ignorant child. "It's about a man who is invisible."

"Literally or metaphorically?" There, that was smart. She was trying to smile, trying to pretend the conversation was light, funny, that it was nothing more than that.

"Do you see him?" Joseph said, not smiling back.

"I don't know," she whispered, feeling she was confessing to something she'd not even known she'd done.

Claire had not read much African American literature. In college she'd not been interested in gender- or race-based courses. Why not just take a literature class? She'd not believed in special attention or treatment for herself or others. She wasn't interested in spending a semester reading books about people who hated her, a white Southern woman, a descendent of a rich white Southern and, yes, slave-owning family. Of course slavery was wrong and bad, but that was the past. She hadn't done those things. That's what she thought then because she hadn't been ready for anything else. But these days, as Claire stretched tighter and tighter, determined to be a good mother to her children but also to prove to the people at work that she was worthy of being at the top, she kept thinking of Tammy, the woman who had grown up with her mother. Tammy, who may or may not have been her mother's half-sister. Invisible.

That night she ordered *Invisible Man* online. For reasons she didn't want to examine too closely, she knew she would feel self-conscious if she'd been seen buying the book at the bookstore downtown. She'd planned to give it to Joseph if she couldn't finish it, but when she started reading the following week, she was drawn in from the opening paragraph in which the narrator declares he is invisible because people don't want to see him.

"Invisible to everyone," Claire murmured. That was the first night she stayed up late, after Jim had gone to sleep, furtively reading the pages with a flashlight until two in the morning when she finally put the book in her dresser drawer and fell into fitful sleep.

She kept the book with her highlights and turned-down corners but bought a new one for Joseph, a hardback that she kept in the drawer of her office, waiting until a good time to give it to him.

But why not just give it to him, she thought: why did she feel there needed to be a time, in secret, to give him a book? Hadn't Henry given her a book when she'd started at Chattasys, some how-to travesty advising women on using their traditional charms to do well in corporate America? She'd been dumb enough to take that book seriously, following its rules to the letter until she felt like some kind of cross-dresser, inhabiting a gender at once alien and appealing. Following the book's advice, she ritualistically applied earth-toned makeup each morning, attired herself in suits from Brooks Brothers and Talbots, stuffed her feet into two-inch pumps, bought packages of sheer hose with reinforced toes by the dozens, wore tiny pearl or diamond-stud earrings. She made cookies and brought them to work. She kept track of office birthdays and made sure everyone signed the card. She organized the Secret Santa and collected money each year for bonuses for the people who emptied their trashcans and vacuumed their carpets. She laughed off sexist comments from the men, pretended not to hear the racist ones, since they didn't apply to her. She attracted flies with honey instead of vinegar. She became a paragon of the stereotype of the Woman Executive, and when she became pregnant, the men in the office said "finally" and waited for her to implode. And now, she was still here, still wearing Brooks Brothers suits and sheer hose and two-inch pumps, still applying makeup in front of a steamy mirror every morning, so that she was no longer an impersonator inhabiting a corporate woman's body. She'd become the thing and, without prompting, without manuals or how-to guides, applied her makeup and wore her suits as a defensive armor she could not imagine being without.

But this was not the same case as with Joseph. If she gave him the book, it would mean something else than Henry's presenting her with *Honey & Flies* twelve years ago. She wasn't sure what that "something else" was, other than she knew it had to be secret because it would appear inappropriate. She kept the book in her drawer for a week, furtively opening and closing it, gazing upon the title, closing the drawer again, the book invisible as well, she noted, to everyone except her.

One evening, Joseph, as he always did before he left for the day, came in to her office to ask her if she needed anything else. She felt sweaty, rumpled. Her lipstick was faded and smeared. A tiny run in her hose had started to inch up her heel, and she'd stopped it with clear nail polish, which stuck to her skin. She could smell a slight odor from under her arms, rising from her crotch, while Joseph looked as fresh as he had that morning, as if he'd just stepped out of the shower. He too was following some corporate success how-to manual, written or unwritten, something that should have a name like *Negotiating the Southern White Man's Business World, or How to Keep the Crackers Happy*. So far she had not seen him take one misstep.

She told him she had something for him, a book, which was what she gave each person when they started working for her (why did she feel compelled to lie?), and she remembered he'd been reading the library book, and so here was a book for him. She opened her drawer and took the book out, extending her hand over the desk, but he did not take it. The top half of the cover was a block of dark brown; the bottom half contained the name of the book and author in black and brown lettering against a white background. She laid it on the desk, and waited. Finally he tentatively reached out for it, opened the cover, and flipped the pages. She'd not written anything in them, although she'd agonized about that, wondering if inscribing something would make the gift more or less appropriate, but she saw that he seemed relieved that the pages were not inscribed. He closed the cover and left the book on her desk.

"Thank you, but I can't accept this," he said.

"It's just a book," she said. But it was not just a book; it was a book that she'd read surreptitiously with a flashlight, like a girl at camp reading a soft porn secret, a book that had awakened in her something she did not even know had been sleeping.

"I appreciate the gesture," he said, not unkindly. "But I can get my own books."

Then she was crying, the first time in twelve years she'd ever cried in the office, although she'd had plenty of reasons in the past, much worse and embarrassing situations than the one she was in now, and he offered her a handkerchief from his pocket, ironed and folded as if he'd tucked it in his breast pocket every morning in anticipation of this very moment. She dabbed her eyes like a heroine in a silent movie, staining the cloth with her smudged mascara, but she refused to wipe her runny nose—not on that handkerchief; she couldn't bear it. Instead she sniffed and said, her voice damp and throaty, "Can we at least talk about the book? I loved it."

He waited to answer. She watched him think. "Okay."

She told him she had not thought about how it might feel to be a black person in America, in the South, until she read that novel, and even though her life was nothing like the narrator's she felt invisible, like him. She told him that her husband had been unemployed since the recession and she was worried that they might have to sell their house if he didn't find work soon. Joseph told her he'd started reading it the summer after junior high school.

"I was getting into some bad stuff, and so they sent me to live with Aunt Alma. She made me read a book a week. That saved me."

"I know it's not right, the world," she said. "But until I read that book, I didn't know, really, that something's not right with me. I want to be bigger than this." She didn't tell him about Tammy, the invisible family member, who to Claire represented everything she would not know about her family's past. "Can we read more books together and talk about them? Would that be okay?"

"I don't think it's a good idea," he said.

"But this is like a book club. It's not work. Anyone can belong."

He looked at her in a way that no one else had, and it made her uncomfortable. As if he already knew things about her that she did not know herself. "We only discuss the books. No more personal questions," he said.

"Okay." But she was disappointed.

"Next book is *Beloved.*"

And so began their weekly Friday lunches on one of the picnic tables by the river no matter the weather, where they discussed books. From his backpack he'd take out a large salad with shredded chicken and carefully eat it, without dressing, while Claire munched on a peanut butter and jelly sandwich or whatever kind of lunch Jim had hastily assembled that morning for her and the kids. (She told him she was trying to economize, and she didn't care what he made, as long as she had something to bring to work every Friday.) The first day of their lunch she'd sat down, removed the sandwich from its Ziploc bag, and asked him to explain *Beloved*.

"That's not how it works," he told her. "You can ask questions and I'll ask questions. The questions are more important than the answers."

Three Fridays into their lunch meetings, she cried again, this time because Sethe killed her daughter to save her from slavery in *Beloved*. "Poor Sethe," she said. "Poor, poor Sethe." He let her cry, and, as he'd made her promise, he didn't ask her why she was crying, and so she didn't tell him.

She cried because she worried about Aimee and what the world held for her, and she worried whether she had the strength to do what might be needed when she was called upon to do it. She cried because her own mother had not taken Claire with her when she died. She cried because she could not cry anywhere else, for Jim would feel that it was about him and his unemployment, and she could never, never, never cry at work (except that one time, that night with Joseph) or in front of her children. She cried knowing that Joseph would not mock her or belittle her or think she was using feminine wiles or all the other reasons she didn't cry in front of men the way her mother had cried in front of her father. She'd not cried in front of her father after her mother died or in front of her sisters because her mother had made her promise to be the strong one, the one to carry on the household. Stoic. There was no outward grieving for her, only a buried bitter loss. Now, for the first time (ever, was it really ever?) she could cry and Joseph would know it for what it was, would let her be, not needing an explanation from her, never telling her it would all be okay when it might not. She was grateful for their surprising, secret friendship.

After reading each night, Claire would wait for her brain to shut down, thinking of the words and the world she'd just inhabited, forming her questions she'd ask Joseph at the end of the week. She never felt he judged her or embarrassed her, although he could have. He told her the first book Alma had made him read: *Makes Me Wanna Holler.* After that, he said, there was no turning back. That's what she thought as well—no turning back. But from what?

During this time, she saw her father only a few times. On Palm Sunday she rode with him to church. Her own family was going later, but he'd wanted to go to the morning service because it wouldn't be as crowded. The air was cold, a last-minute winter day, and she turned the heat on in the car. On the way to church Claire complained about her father's driving, that he wasn't staying within the lines, but he brushed her off. She was still thinking of *Beloved,* and she was distracted, thinking of her own children, wondering what she would or could sacrifice for them, what she could bring herself to do, what would be the right thing to do, and if she did do the right thing if she would be forever haunted, like Sethe.

On Easter her father came by for brunch after church with his sometime-church companion. In the past decade he'd accumulated an array of female companions: his work-function companion; his Aquarium volunteer companion; his plant-nursery-shopping companion, none of them serious as far as Claire could tell and so she'd not bothered to remember their names. Aimee was demanding her father's full attention as usual, with her pirouettes and ballet positions, and Dez, more because he adored his sister and did whatever she did, spun and yelled in echo. Shannon, late as usual, had promised to bring dessert. Jim was with them in the living room while Claire was in the kitchen slicing the baguette, checking on the quiche, whipping up the dressing. Her mind was on the Baldwin story she and Joseph were to discuss later in the week, "Going to Meet the Man." She wanted to ask him about Jesse and his witnessing of the lynching of a black man as a child. Of Jesse and, therefore, the reader witnessing this event, and the horror she felt, the shame.

A week ago, on her father's birthday, Claire had taken some dishes into the kitchen, but before she opened the sliding door to return to the porch she saw her reflection in the glass, and it was like her ghost-self was already out there with them. She backed away from the glass and slid out through the front door, car keys suddenly in her hand. She drove recklessly down the mountain, the back seats empty, cracker crumbs and dolls and cars littering the floor, the mirror adjusted for Jim, who had driven the family over, XM radio tuned to one of those coffeehouse rock stations, a singer who was named after some kind of gem like Diamond or Sapphire or Ruby, the kind of music Paige hated, was forever resisting comparisons to. "I'm not like them," Paige would say, "fake singers, with fake emotions." Why hadn't she called? Certainly it wasn't too much to remember their father's birthday. He always forgave Paige for those things. For her careless forgetting. Claire was careening down Missionary Ridge, braking fast at the corners, taking the curves too quickly. She would tell them she'd gone out for—what? Ice cream? Whipped cream? Toilet paper? She took Paige's latest CD from the glove compartment and with one hand opened the case and slid the CD in the player so she could hear her sister's voice as she drove down the mountain, a voice raspy and indignant and full of pain Claire had never before understood until now, and down the mountain she went, until she was in Joseph's aunt's neighborhood, and she drove by their house like a deranged criminal on a drive-by. He was on a ladder painting the window trim as white as his T-shirt, but the sun had almost set, so that Joseph and the landscape around him looked like an old sepia photo from a time before she was born. Even there on the ladder, with his back to her, he stood straight and sharp, and she, sitting in the crumbs and debris of her own life, wondered how he did it. The windows were up tight so all she could hear was Paige's singing, all cigarettes and desire, and then she drove back up the mountain, without ice cream or toilet paper or whipped cream. She parked the car and walked in the house then to the deck, where Paige was singing "Happy Birthday" on Shannon's cell phone, flipped open on the table. No one had even noticed she'd been gone.

And now, a week after her father's birthday, Claire was not thinking of her father's doctor's appointment that day or of his strange distant behavior on his birthday that had motivated Shannon to take him to the doctor. She was thinking again of the ending of Baldwin's story. The white cop was having sex and the cock crowed, a biblical echo. The sounds of dogs barking and gravel on the road. A promise or a warning? She'd told Joseph that the story depressed her. It seemed that nothing would change. But Joseph said, "Haven't you changed?" She was thinking that the books, more than Joseph, had opened her life up and that after he left for his MBA in August she would be fine. She would spearhead some kind of Friday office book club where, for once, they could talk about things that did not concern the petty lives and machinations of the office system. She was thinking those things even as she sat in the family room with the kids and pretended to watch them play some Xbox game while Jim rinsed and stacked dishes in the dishwasher, when Shannon called from the hospital.

The doctor's appointment had led to an MRI scan, which had detected a large enough mass snaking up to his brain to warrant immediate admission into the hospital to begin treatment to reduce the swelling and await a biopsy.

Claire put the phone down and looked at Jim in the kitchen, bent over the dishwasher like an old man. *He did not deserve this.* He did not deserve her exasperation and exhaustion. He did not deserve to now have to deal with her dying father. She wanted to wait to tell him, to allow him a few more minutes to load the dishwasher, a task he enjoyed doing. He claimed the process of finding places for all the dishes brought a brief but meditative calm. After the cycle finished, he enjoyed returning each hot and steamy dish or cup or piece of silverware to its home. She would wait until the dirty dishes were loaded and then cleaned and returned to their rightful places.

Then she would tell him that her father had cancer, that it was all beginning again.

But before then, while the dishes were being washed and Jim returned to the living room and the kids and TV, she would excuse herself and call Joseph. She had his cell number in case of a work emergency, but she had never called him before. She'd unconsciously memorized the numbers, and she punched them without thinking. She called him from the guest bathroom, so no one could hear her, not that they would notice she was gone.

She had planned on leaving a voicemail, but Joseph answered after a few rings, his voice smooth and distant. "My father is dying. His brain is exploding," she said, her voice a flat contrast to her hidden hysteria.

There was a long silence, but Claire had become used to Joseph's silences now and was in fact comfortable with them, enjoyed them, expected them, knew not to rush him, to wait them out.

"Do you want to talk about it?" he finally offered.

"Can we? Now? At our bench?" It was the first time she'd used the plural possessive and the word escaped her lips naturally, without thought. She wished she'd not said it as soon as the word came out. The bench was innocent in that way, a humble meeting place in a public space, where they'd set aside their personal lives to discuss books and, therefore, the world. But that evening "the bench" became "our bench." She had broken her promise not to discuss anything personal with Joseph, and he had allowed her to break it.

She told her family she had to go pick up something from work, and they waved her away, not even registering that she was leaving. These days it could be an hour or more before someone noticed her absence, from work, from home. Her children were getting older; they needed her less. And Jim—he would wake up sometimes while she was reading, his eyes open but not seeing her, a wide-eyed dream, pat her leg the same way he patted their dog, and then fall back asleep.

Now, it was early evening, and pedestrians and people on bikes and dog walkers could see them sitting across from each other, still not touching, never touching, and as the darkness fell and the street lamps flickered on one by one, she told him she didn't know if she could do it, help them all through her father's death. She was, after all, of the three sisters, the expert on dying parents. She'd been the one to take care of her sisters and ease the pain with her mother and read stories and feed her spoonfuls of soup. She'd been the one to wash her mother's face and count her pills and sit with her during the chemo treatments when her father had to return to work. And so now that even though it wasn't official (but she knew, she knew—that's what made her the dying parent expert) that her father had cancer and was dying, what she felt more than sadness or fear or grief was a thud, a tiredness already in her bones: here we go again. Shannon and Paige didn't know what was coming, what would be required of them. And there were her own children, Aimee and Dez, not much older than Shannon and Paige had been when their mother had died. There was Jim's despair of never really working again. ("We're on the downward spiral," he'd tell her at night after reading articles of doom on the Internet. "The economy will never be the same, and neither will my career. I might as well get a job at Lowe's and accept the new normal," he'd say to her, to no one, the last words she'd hear before he fell asleep.) There was her career and her imminent promotion, which they all needed more than ever. The house, the embodiment of everything she'd wanted, was a cavernous maw, threatening to devour them. And now her father was dying.

Joseph sat across from her at the picnic table under the lamplight, not moving, his eyes directly on her, listening without comment or question. No one had listened to her before, not in this way, not even Jim because they were so similar they never needed to explain themselves. Because she and Jim assumed they understood each other, Claire realized, she and Jim had reached an impasse where they didn't talk about anything, and now she was not sure how to change that. But that evening she talked and talked, unburdening herself of things she'd not even known she'd been burdened with. She didn't cry and her voice remained even. She'd learned from her mother's death. Distance without drama. There were ways to get through this. In her mind at least, as she confessed everything to Joseph first instead of Jim, that evening was when her affair with Joseph began. Other people, readers of novels, perhaps Joseph himself, would say otherwise. They would say it began months later, in a cabin room lit by candles.

The next morning, she stopped by the hospital on her way to work. Her father, tucked and sleeping in the hospital bed, looked normal, and for a moment Claire wondered if she'd jumped to conclusions too quickly. She sat in one of the chairs in the room, which had improved since her mother had been hooked up and shrinking there. Her mother's hospital room, the last one, before she came home to die, had smelled of some kind of industrial-strength cleaner that singed her nostrils but could not ameliorate that smell of someone's body being eaten away from the inside out. In her mother's room, the walls had been painted a sickly pus yellow instead of a pale healing blue as they were now. The color Claire had wanted the kitchen to be. She remembered the plastic on the chair she'd sat on when she visited her mother had been peeling off and cut into the bottoms of her thighs. One time she'd found unclaimed balls of tissue under her mother's bed, tissue flecked with someone else's blood. Now the rooms were cleaner and smelled somewhat better, the chemicals more subtle, the agent of death not so menacing. The chair she sat on was functional and comfortable. Shannon had gone to get them some coffee. Her father's eyes were closed, his head lolled to one side, and his hand loosely curled the remote-control switch for the turned-off TV.

"Daddy," Claire whispered. There was a curtain or a fog that separated her from him, and that separation would keep her from feeling pain. He opened his eyes.

"It's good to see you," he said.

"You too." She leaned over to kiss his forehead, which was uneven, almost pumped up, inflated. She'd never noticed that before. Had that always been there, that strange, slightly bulging forehead, or was this the cancer, menacingly visible under that stretch of skin? Shannon returned with lattes from the hospital's Starbucks. So different from the tiny cups of watered-down coffee thick with creamer and sweetener she'd brought for her mother so long ago.

"Where's Paige?" He brought the remote control close to his face and turned the TV on.

"She's on her way," Shannon said. "She's going to come and stay with you a while. Isn't that great?"

"Suits me." He seemed to not be listening anymore and instead was focused on the TV, changing the channels listlessly and relentlessly, as if he were sure he would find a show he liked, if only he didn't give up.

"Paige is coming back?" Claire said.

"She left Seattle yesterday. She's driving cross-country. She says she can stay with Dad for as long as we need her." Shannon tipped her coffee back. Her eyes were a watery brown, her hair haphazardly pulled back, loose, scattered ends falling out. "You don't have to do all the work this time, Claire."

Claire squeezed her eyes shut. You don't know, she wanted to say, what it's like. But they would find that all out soon enough.

A few days later, the three sisters were together when the doctor told them what they'd suspected: their father had a malignant tumor that was eating away at his frontal lobe and would kill him in a few months, unless they began chemo and radiation to extend his life, for how long, no one knew. Claire and Shannon were certain their father would not want any treatment. On his birthday ten years ago, he'd told them as much. He'd said he didn't want to go through what Lila had, and Claire understood why, even if Paige at the time had not. So when they told him that he had terminal cancer, they were surprised when he told them he wanted treatment.

"Just get it out of me," he said.

"Sure, Daddy," Paige said. She gave her sisters a look, the one that said, *See, I told you.* Claire wondered if he'd changed his mind about chemo and radiation because the cancer, eating away at the decision-making part of his frontal lobe, had changed it for him. But there was nothing they could do about that. And so his chemo and radiation treatments were scheduled, with Paige taking him to most of the appointments and caring for him at home.

Over the next few months, Claire decided there was only one way to cope with all that was required of her: to sleep less. She was now getting by on four or five hours each evening, supplemented with carefully timed micro-naps. She vaguely recalled a time she'd slept eight or nine hours each night before Aimee was born, but she now wondered if that was a hallucination or just a fantasy of a life she'd dreamed she had. Jim had taken the news about her father better than she thought he would, reassuring her that he would keep the home front moving smoothly, making sure the kids were fed and transported and did their homework. Paige had moved back home, inhabiting her old room in the finished basement. When asked about her band, she vaguely replied that they were on hiatus. With Paige driving their father to appointments during the day and Shannon taking the late afternoon shifts, Claire only needed to stop by in the evenings or during his chemo treatments when she could clear a space in her calendar. After work, Claire would go home first and spend time with her children. They'd tell her about her day and read to her from a *Harry Potter* book before she tucked them into bed and then went to see her father. When they were at Papa Nash's on the weekend, Aimee and Dez wanted to nurse him, take him his pills, fetch his cane. They took to wearing eye patches like the one he now wore over his swollen left eye, so that the three of them looked like an outcast band of pirates. Other times they were impatient, wondering why he wouldn't talk with them or why he didn't care about what they were doing in school or ballet or soccer. Claire wanted to protect Aimee and Dez from watching their grandfather die, but she could not. Instead she allowed them to sleep with her and Jim some nights, to watch TV during the week, to spend the nights at friends' houses more often than they usually did.

At work she garnered the predictable sympathy for an illness in the family. She was asked in concerned voices about her father, was told to make sure she did what she had to do to make sure he was okay, as long—it went unsaid but was understood—as she kept up with her work. Some of the other women in the firm consoled her with frozen casseroles and baskets of cucumbers, tomatoes, and okra from their gardens, which she would pass on to Jim, who would spring to the Internet and search for ways to reinvent cucumber salad and fried okra. Claire knew the women meant well, but she took the women's gifts as warnings not to slack off at work and let them down, because Claire's father's dying would be *one more thing*, one more chance for her to fail, for the men to say, *I told you so, women can't have it all, you can't take it all on.*

Claire was taking on more than anyone knew. Joseph was on her mind more than her dying father, her clingy yet aloof children, or her unemployed, depressed husband. Whenever she thought of a phrase or scene from one of the books they'd read and how it applied to her life, she filed it in her mind to tell Joseph. When she remembered her mother in those last days making Claire promise to take care of the family and now saw the unfairness of that request, she waited to talk about it with Joseph. Whenever he would allow it, she would meet with him at the picnic table by the river and unburden herself. She knew that what she was doing was dangerous. Even though the relationship was still platonic, each meeting in which, she emphasized, she needed to talk to him *as a friend* was an unarticulated attempt on her side to escalate their relationship, to what she was not sure, except that she wanted more, even though it would be ruinous.

And yet. She couldn't imagine not having Joseph in her life, for he was the only person who made things bearable. When she was with him those days and nights at the picnic table all her worries and anxieties fell away, like dead leaves from a tree. There was only

Joseph, the one person who made her feel un-invisible, and therefore alive.

It was Doris Lessing's "To Room 19" that gave her the idea. Joseph suggested she read the story when she'd confessed that she fantasized about leaving everything and everyone. That when she imagined herself happy and serene, she was alone, in a cabin, sitting by a window with a view of dense, dark woods. He loaned her his copy of a short story anthology, with that story marked by a paper clip. That night, pushed out of her bed by the sprawling kids and Jim and the dog, all webbed and intertwined so that she could not see where one began and the other ended, hot and breathy like puppies curled and wet-nosed, dreaming of balls and endless hills and collapsing stars, that night downstairs on the chocolate leather sofa, she read of Susan Rawling's desire to disappear. Claire felt the story was written for her. She would not disappear completely, of course, she would not commit suicide as Susan had done, she would not abandon her children, but she would get a room, and she would call it her own.

A few months after her father's diagnosis, she found a cabin to rent just outside of the city, a musty place on a side dirt road, but it had what she wanted—a tiny window looking out into the endless woods. While the cabin was not expensive, she was still using money that could have gone to something to keep the family organism thriving: bills and lessons and clothes and upgrades and repairs that even a new house seemed to constantly demand. She signed a three-month lease, telling herself that she just needed a bit of time alone. To combat the dinginess of the cabin, with its stained, faded carpet and naked fluorescent bulb, she'd furnished the place with bright plastic furniture from Target, so unlike the heavy wood furniture in their own house, inherited and passed down from both sides of the family, pieces bought in antique shops and estate sales. This cabin with its tiny living room, kitchen, and bedroom held nothing that could remind her of the world outside the one she was trying to create.

She supposed she could have told Jim about the cabin and he would have understood. He was a good man, and the more she pulled away from him the more she knew that he'd been nothing but the things he'd promised her he'd be. It was not his fault the recession had happened. But she didn't tell Jim about the cabin. And she didn't tell him about Joseph. She couldn't explain exactly why, except that she felt those two secrets were the only things she had that were hers, the very things that allowed her to do the rest.

That first week Claire rented the cabin she spent three nights there. Those nights she would work late, stop at home, and spend time with her children before they went to sleep. Then she'd hug Jim goodbye and tell him she was staying at her father's that night, drive to the cabin, and read *A Lesson Before Dying*, underlining the passages she wanted to discuss later. She fantasized about moving permanently into the cabin, of reading and watching the trees outside the window by her twin bed. In that cabin, her love for her children was so pure and painful she felt as if their names were being seared all over her body with a branding iron forged in gold. She wanted always to feel that way about them, instead of the watered-down, distracted love that she took for granted when she was with them. She missed Jim, too, his thick hair side-parted in the same style as in college, showing off his perfectly shaped ears, and his cappuccinos with their heart-shaped froth he made for her each morning. She missed him, but she missed him the way one might miss a dying planet or a setting sun. Could loving someone else make you love others more? She would lie awake missing the people she could not bear to be with in the new-smelling bed until two in the morning, and then she'd drive to her childhood home and fall asleep in the bedroom she'd grown up in.

It took her a few weeks to admit to herself that her two secrets—the cabin and Joseph—were really one. She imagined her fingers tracing the inside of his arms, her tongue tipped in the small of his back. She imagined washing his feet and then placing each toe in her mouth. She imagined staying in the bed in the cabin with him for years. She could not imagine them leaving it. She imagined feeling pleasure and pain, instead of dreaming of it.

After the first week, she told Joseph about the cabin and gave him the address. She told him that even if he never came, he should know that she was there, waiting for him.

Another week passed. She waited for Joseph to come to her.

He did, finally, one night when Claire had stopped counting them. It was dark out, she'd lit some candles by the bed, and she'd arranged herself so that she could look up from her reading and look out the window, imagining the animals—deer, raccoons, and coyotes—living in the woods outside her door, foraging for food, taking care of their young, living without thought or effort. She wanted to empty her mind and live like them. She was staring into the darkness outside when she heard the door open, heard his quiet, gentle steps. He closed the door and locked it. She knew her face was illuminated by the glow of the candle beside her on the ocean blue plastic nightstand. She wondered if she looked as peaceful as she felt.

He sat beside her on the bed, their sides barely touching. He took the book from her hands and placed it beside the candle.

"So what's the lesson before dying?" he said.

"That to die, one must live," she whispered. He said nothing and they sat in the dark and the silence except for the flickering candles for more minutes than she could count.

"You just want to know what it's like to have sex with a black man."

"And you just want to be the agent of a white woman's ruin."

"You don't need me to ruin yourself."

She picked her cell phone up from the dresser and powered it off. It was already late. "I'll make sure you are transferred so I'm not your boss."

"No. That would look bad for me. Besides, I don't want to work for those guys."

"Okay, then."

That sat like that for a while, silent, beside each other, not touching.

"Okay," Joseph finally said. His T-shirt, smelling of detergent, glowed from the candlelight. He stood to face her, sitting on the edge of the bed. "Take off your clothes. Slowly."

She unbuttoned her blouse and then unfastened her skirt, which she'd still not changed out of, watching his eyes on her. She'd already removed her pantyhose and shoes before he'd arrived. Before, she would have felt self-conscious about being naked, but her body was quick and lean from the Adderall she'd been taking lately, quivering like the deer outside the cabin. The buttons felt wet, clumsy between her fingers. When she was down to her bra and panties, he told her to stop. He backed away so that he was against the wall, standing. She stood and walked to him and noticed for the first time that he was only a few inches taller, much shorter than Jim, who was six feet. She'd always thought him taller. She stepped closer to embrace him but he grabbed her wrists and pinned her hands to her sides.

"Undress me," he said. She untucked his T-shirt and slid it over his head. She felt the heat from his chest and reached to touch the spare, curly, dark hairs but he grabbed her wrists again and pulled them down. Only when her arms had relaxed did he let her go. She unfastened his belt and slid it out of its loops. She felt she was performing an act of devotion rather than servitude. He still had not touched her. She reached for the button on his chinos. He placed his hand on hers to stop her.

"Give me the belt," he said. She took the belt, coiled it, and handed it to him. She thought of the stories they'd read together, and because of that she trusted him. "Turn around," he said. Her skin was chilled and damp. She had never fainted before, but she feared her legs might give way and she'd crumple like a woman from another century. He grabbed her wrists and his chest pressed against hers and his erection pushed onto her belly and she trusted him, even when he pulled her wrists behind her back and looped the belt around them, even as tears leaked from her eyes as she felt the leather tighten, but no pain, there was no pain, even when her legs finally did give, she trusted him in a way she'd never trusted anyone ever, except maybe her mother, before. Maybe. He caught her as she collapsed and carried her to the bed where he proceeded to ravish, yes that was the word, ravish, even though it was a silly word, it sounded like radish, a vegetable, a tuber, she'd always hated them, and who said ravish, except those romance novels her mother read once she'd gotten sick because she couldn't concentrate on anything else, abandoning her Jane Austen and Dickens to dusty shelves in the house, probably still untouched. Who uses ravish, thought Claire, what does it mean, she didn't know except that he was doing it, exploring, tasting, kissing, everything but her lips, he still had not kissed her on the lips, and she could not touch him except where he allowed his skin, warm and moist, to touch her. She gave up watching him and closed her eyes and instead smelled his sweat, pungent and alluring. She didn't know time, or she knew it but thought the concept archaic, simple, too primitive, a simplistic notion of how the world worked. What was time anyway when her body was being licked and kissed and petted to wakefulness while somewhere her mother was dying in her sleep, the romance novels long neglected, and somewhere else her father's death was delayed, something to happen another day that would never come?

That first night with Joseph in the cabin, she did not know how much time had passed, only that at some point her hands were released from the belt. She opened her eyes and there was Joseph naked, lying beside her, watching her attentively, as he always did. She wrapped her arms around him and they kissed for the first time, eyes open. In that moment she promised herself that no matter what else happened, whatever ruin she was to bring on her and him and her family, she would never again look away.

PAIGE

One early morning after returning from a lackluster tour, Paige was drinking in her room when Becky came in and told her the band had taken a vote. Paige was fired. Like she was in a corporation or something. Becky told her she needed to "commit" to her sobriety. Paige snorted, like a pig. Bessie Smith had been a sometime-drunk, a lover of men and women, a profligate spender until the day she died, Paige thought, but first and foremost she was a singer. "And you are not Bessie Smith," Becky had added, as if she were reading Paige's mind. "I guess I'm not," Paige had said and she hid in her room while the newly reformed band launched a Kickstarter fund to record their new CD.

Paige might have stayed in the room until the world ended, but then Shannon called with the news their father was dying. She'd arrived in Seattle in a rundown van filled with music and her best friends. Along the way they'd slept in dark hotels that smelled of stale smoke, piling into beds like siblings, wearing each other's T-shirts and boxers, sharing spoons and packs of cigarettes, reveling in the communal life. Now she departed in a beat-up pickup truck, alone.

That first night back in Chattanooga, Paige slept in her old twin bed in the basement, where she'd lived from eleventh grade until she'd moved in with Becky. She lay on the faded blue-striped sheets and tried not to think about her dying father or her former band. Instead she thought about her first sexual experience in this very bed on these very sheets with her best friend Veronica—whom Paige had always called V.—years before Becky and the others who followed. She and V. were in the ninth grade, and she'd kissed some boys at parties, but their lips had felt like disconnected pieces of rubber, wet, with too much spit and intention. For the past six months, she'd been in love with V. and her braces, her broad shoulders, her wild untamed brick-powder hair. V. was sleeping over, that was not unusual, but this time Paige could not sleep because the underside of V.'s arm, soft and pale, was tempting Paige to press her finger into the accommodating flesh, as tempting as poking a finger into a malleable marshmallow. She carefully prodded V.'s skin, tiptoed to her breastbone, barely hidden under V.'s tank top. She wondered if V.'s breasts, plumper than her own, felt like hers. V. rolled away, so that her back was to Paige. Paige shifted to her side and pressed her chest against V.'s back, allowing her hand to rest on the flat of V.'s stomach. She spent the remaining dark hours of the night inching her fingers up rib by rib, resting briefly between the space of each one, her own breath held in, waiting for V. to push her hands away, but she did not. She either slept or pretended to sleep. Paige finally reached V.'s breasts, her nipples hard and goose-bumped, and she caressed them ever so gently, afraid to pull V. out of her dreams. The next morning V. said nothing and Paige said nothing. Then a boy V. had a crush on asked her out and she started seeing more of him and less of Paige, and that was that for Paige and Veronica. Now Paige wondered how many times she'd tried to recreate that night of anticipation and wonder with V., each rib a piano key waiting to be played, each ridge a chasm she was not sure she'd successfully cross, until she finally cupped V.'s breasts, which protected her beating heart.

That first morning, Paige stripped the blue sheets and threw them away. She unpacked her mother's old china set, the one that went back to before the Civil War, and rinsed the dust off the plates and cups. The bottle of Joy perfume that she'd left behind when she moved to Seattle was still on top of her dresser. She dabbed some perfume on her wrists and went upstairs.

When the direct light hurt her father's swollen eye, she took one of her many sleep masks she'd collected and made an eye patch so her father could keep his one good eye open longer. He looked like a crazed pirate, with his balding, swollen head and ominous patch, impressing Dez so much that Paige made an eye patch for him too, which he wore around the house while brandishing his grandfather's wooden cane as a sword.

When the TV became too loud and hard for her father to follow, Paige checked out books on tape at the library, long historical novels that he enjoyed falling asleep to, the words no longer connecting but creating some kind of pleasant background buzz for whatever was floating in his mind. Sometimes he would say a word out loud, as if he were surprised he could still pronounce it but was unsure of its meaning: criminal, fire, truck, magnet.

When it was time for her father's pain pill, which he called Big Red, Dez, when he was around, would deliver the medication with a flourish, his eye patch mirroring his grandfather's. A few times the family would play Goldfish, her father pairing up with Paige because he couldn't see the cards properly or remember the rules, and then he'd get disinterested or tired and make his way back to the recliner, where he'd rest his eyes. She knew he was waiting until the pain was pulsing before he asked for the pill. She wished he'd ask sooner so that he would not have to feel the pressure put on his brain by those cancer-eating cells, growing so fast she swore that her father's forehead pushed outward a bit more each day.

She remembered her father saying on his fifty-fifth birthday that if he were ever diagnosed with cancer he wanted none of it, not the chemo or the radiation or people wheeling him around, counting his pills. She'd not wanted to think about it then, about him not being around. Now all Paige could think was, Why had her sisters allowed it? Why hadn't they noticed he was getting sick? It wasn't fair, she knew, she the absent one. She had not been the best daughter, calling only when she remembered or was reminded, which wasn't often enough, or stopping by hungover for lunch whenever the band was touring in the area. But now she would be the good daughter. She would be the one to help him to death, the way she had not been able to with her mother. She hoped, selfishly, that he would love her the most for those things. She hoped that she would be the last person he saw before he died.

She would be the one to do the things he needed: change diapers, wheel him around the garden, spoon him small bits of oatmeal, stick bendable straws in cans of Ensure. He had not wanted this, and yet it had happened anyway. This year was supposed to be the beginning of his so-called twilight years, instead of the ending to his life. In his emails and on the phone, he'd tell Paige about his retirement plans: traveling, gardening, walks by the river, more volunteering at the Aquarium, and enrolling in all kinds of appreciation courses at UTC—music, art, great books, wine, he'd appreciate it all right, he said; he'd savor it all. Not that he hadn't appreciated life before—he'd appreciated his girls and Lila, even if she drained him, he appreciated that he'd escaped Vietnam and all its attendant horrors, he appreciated that desegregation happened before his girls were born, and he appreciated feminism even if some people took it too far, because he also appreciated opening car doors for women and fetching their drinks. Even if some of the mystery and allure of the fairer sex was gone, he said he was happy what the new era and its ways brought for his daughters. The world would be hard for them but not in the ways it had been for women from his time, the way it had been for Lila. He appreciated that Aimee and Dez were entirely new creatures, with their Xboxes and computers and gadgets, creatures who still loved to sit on his lap, who drew pictures for him with crayons of infinite colors that could never be crammed back into their crumpled box.

When her father slept, Paige wandered the rooms; memories, random, unimportant, would rise like bubbles, wet and round. Here in the living room was the closet where she had once banished herself. She'd hidden there, curled like a shrimp under the vacuum cleaner, just to see how long it would take for her father and sisters to discover she was missing. She wanted to hear wailing, keening. She wanted to see her own funeral. She wanted to know who would sing for her. Paige had just turned eight, and, as her father would later remind her, she'd informed him at her birthday party that she did not appreciate getting older, because each passing year brought her closer to death. Her own mother had been dead for two years. She folded herself in the closet where she remained egg-shaped and still when they called her name, their voices rising in pitch and earnestness. She wondered how long they would mourn her, how long she could stay in this closet while the world continued. She hoped they would miss her the way she missed her mother, or at least the idea of her. Through the space between the door and floor of the closet she watched the lights turn on, imagined the world outside darkening. Her stomach rumbled, and she cursed it, afraid they would hear it. She had to pee, and she feared that was what would break her, for she wasn't sure if she could suffer the humiliation of peeing in the closet. She heard her father make calls, and then, when they still could not find her, they decided to canvas the neighborhood and the forest at the edge of the sloping hill of their house, taking the dog with them. When the house was dark and quiet, Paige opened the door slowly, allowing the artificial light in. She made it to the bathroom just in time, her underwear tugged down to her knees. In the kitchen she fixed herself a bowl of cereal, and after she slurped the last of the sugared milk, she rinsed the bowl and slotted it in the dishwasher. She sat on the sofa and turned on the TV to something she was allowed to watch. When her family returned, they hugged her so fiercely they forgot to be angry. She told them she'd crawled in the closet and fallen asleep and had awakened to them all gone. Their arms wrapped around her, forgiving her this one time, and although she said she was too big, she sat on her father's lap and breathed in the warm flannel of his shirt. That was the day she almost forgot she didn't have a mother. That was the day when she thought it might not be so bad to live a while longer.

When their father felt well enough, they would all meet at the Episcopal church. They'd been raised Presbyterian but changed denomination when the church's anti-homosexuality stance ran up against her father's loyalty to her and Jeremy. It was a small thing to do for their father, going to church, even though Paige was an atheist. The church seemed to soothe her dying father, who would sit in the back pew and listen, although Paige was never sure if the words made sense to him or if they were just sounds that floated and combined in his head, which was desperate to make meaning.

After church, they'd all go to the house, and Claire and Shannon would make lunch, while Paige played with the kids or sat near the kitchen and watched her sisters do the work. They were still that way at gatherings, huddling in the kitchen, slicing vegetables, making sauces, baking cookies, providing more food than anyone could eat. It was as if they were still trying to avoid the sting of judgment from well-meaning women who had worried about them growing up without a mother. She knew Claire had tried to fill that space, but Paige's wildness and Shannon's ambition were met with sad shakes of heads: *if only they'd had a momma.* Claire was given the most sympathy, *the poor girl, trying to be a momma to her sisters, when she needs one herself.* The women from church had always wondered why their father never remarried. He said he already had three wonderful women in his life and that was enough, but Paige wondered if there had been other reasons.

One Friday early in August, all three sisters and their father met with the doctor for the post-chemo prognosis. The doctor had been frank, saying it was time to call in hospice, that the focus from here on out would be on their father's comfort. He told them their father had a year left, at the most. The girls had thanked the doctor for telling them what they already knew, while their father, in his wheelchair, a patch over his lid, said nothing. Paige was not even sure if he'd understood what the doctor had told them. That Sunday, though, right after church, their father informed the family he wanted an official meeting to discuss the future, something he'd not done since he'd been sick.

A little before noon the family gathered on the deck. Below them Aimee and Dez were jumping through the sprinkler that arced water over the lawn. Tea was poured into clear glasses stuffed with ice. Shannon sat with a notebook and pen—she had been the recorder of her father's illness from the beginning, as if her journalism training had been preparing her for this very event. They sat around the table, the sisters and Jim, their father's wheelchair parked at the table's edge. He sipped the slightest bit of sweet tea through a straw.

"There's a cancer center in Houston," Jim said. "They could maybe do something."

"The doctor says it's too late for that," their father said. "You heard him."

"I think the doctor is right," Paige said. Ten years ago she would have sided with Jim. But seeing her father now, she didn't want to put him through any more. She wanted him to go as painlessly as possible.

"Papa Nash," Aimee cried. "Look at me!"

Their father did not turn to watch his grandchildren. The sun hurt his eyes and it was hard for him to see anyway. He continued. "I'd like to be cremated. Throw my ashes over the Walnut Street Bridge."

Shannon turned the page in her notebook and continued writing.

"Whatever you want, Daddy," Paige said.

"I don't want a fancy service or anything too serious. None of that."

They were silent, not looking at him. Dez screamed, "Not fair" and whimpered. Jim stood to watch the children.

"I don't want the usual trite speeches—he was a good man, a good father. Keep it light, maybe some funny stories. Paige, I got a George Jones song I want you to sing."

He closed his eyes and sang in a low, toneless voice, "He stopped loving her today…"

"Daddy, I can't sing country."

"You sang for Lila."

The guilt put on the living, Paige thought. She had not expected him to be that way.

"Whatever you want, Daddy."

"I want this settled now, before I forget again."

And so it was settled. Cremated. A bag of ashes scattered over the Tennessee River. The rest in an urn next to their mother at Forest Hills Cemetery. George Jones. Funny stories. Nothing maudlin or sentimental.

Then he said, "So I'll be dead within a year."

But the rest knew, from how the doctor had talked, the way he looked and acted, that death would come much sooner.

The kids came running up the deck stairs, trailing water to the table.

"Papa Nash," Dez said as he reached for his mom's iced tea, "my eye patch got all wet. Aimee made me walk the plank." He threw his arms, pearled with water, around Claire. After church, Paige had found Claire weeping in a corner of the kitchen. "They need him. He's the only one left." Paige had said nothing, because she could not say what she thought: at least they have both parents.

"Mommy, I'm hungry. When can we eat?"

Claire stood. "Now, honey, we can eat now."

The next Sunday, the girls were in the house again, and they watched with optimism as their father slowly ate a dinner of fried chicken, mashed potatoes, biscuits and gravy, and green beans. The doctor had told them about this, the brief period after chemo, when he'd start feeling better again before he entered his final decline.

"I'm tired of being cooped up in this house," he said. "I'm ready to get on the road." The fried chicken crumbles had fallen around him and on his lap. A dab of mashed potatoes clung to his chin. Before, he had been a meticulous eater, wiping his mouth after each swallow, but now he didn't seem to notice or care about the mess he made.

"Just tell us where you want to go, Daddy," Claire said.

"The Mountain Opry," he said. "Let's hope it's a good show."

That was how on a Friday in August, they converged in the parking lot of the Mountain Opry, just past Signal Mountain in Walden.

Claire was meeting them from work, and Shannon and Jeremy picked up Paige and their father in the convertible. Their father sat in front, and they drove with the top down, the late evening sun still bright in the sky.

The Mountain Opry was held in an old auditorium, with three separate sections of rows of foldout chairs. The stage was elevated, and behind the stage were more rows of foldout chairs. Some of the audience sat in these chairs, so that they merely needed to stand if they wanted to start clogging on stage.

When they arrived, they sat in the back of the auditorium, just as they did in church, except here their father was not the only person in a wheelchair, not the only person dying in the room. He'd taken the girls a few times when they were young, but to them it was a boring, uncool way to spend a Friday night, with hicks and backward country people, the old-timey music just a reminder of a South that was quickly, thankfully, falling away. Paige was struck by how the place seemed to house only the very young and the very old. The old people looked the same as the old people she remembered when she was young. There were women with bouffant hair so white it shone blue, men in worn flannel shirts buttoned over bulging bellies or so thin and creaking she thought they might blow away. The children, too, seemed of another era. These children were not static creatures glowing from the light of their electronic devices; these children were dancing behind the musicians or clapping their hands in their seats. Jim returned with Cokes and popcorn and hotdogs, and they settled in their seats as the house band began playing.

The house band was as Paige remembered, an earnest if uneven group in overalls and faded jeans, singing many of the crowd favorites like "Fox on the Run" and "Rocky Top." When that song began, Paige's memory of being a child singing the song on stage flashed before her, the lights blinding her while she sang, the heat warming her face, her hands slick and salty from the buttery popcorn she'd been eating. Maybe she had only been in one of the rows behind the stage, singing in her chair there, to herself, maybe she had only pretended she was on stage singing to the audience. No matter, she thought, it's my memory and no one can take that from me. But they'd taken away her father's memories, at least the recent ones, so who was to say that hers were safe as well? She supposed she could write a song about the lights and the popcorn and the singing, but surely that would be forgotten one day, too. Anyway, she thought, what was wrong with losing our memories, just as we lose ourselves when we die? If we didn't, the world would be choking in memories, leaving no room for new ones.

While the house band played, a man, his big bones shrinking under baggy overalls, lumbered to the stage. Occasionally he removed his cap and wiped his bald pate with a red kerchief. Before, Paige would not have thought much of it, but now she was certain that the man's baldness was from chemo. When he began singing his voice was so deep she felt the room shake just a bit. His voice was the deepest bass she'd ever heard live, a tired rumble, the voice of a wounded giant.

She couldn't tell if her father was enjoying the music or not. He stared at the stage with his good eye. Dez sat beside him, wearing his own patch, holding his grandpa's cane. Aimee was slowly creeping up to the stage where other girls clogged behind the band. Paige wondered if her father even heard them or if he were somewhere else in the past or future. Claire, distracted as usual these days, kept checking her phone, while Jim anxiously watched Aimee as she made her way forward. Shannon and Jeremy were whispering and poking each other with their own secret signals, probably making fun of the people here, Paige thought, and she was surprisingly angry that they were doing so.

After the house band finished, a few more groups played, old timers who had driven hours to play in front of an appreciative audience. Most of them had been playing for years every Friday night, and Paige began falling into the music, which alternated between Americana, bluegrass, and gospel. Once she allowed the music to seep in, she felt it in the same way she'd felt Bessie Smith. Connected to something larger than herself. And then a man so comfortable in his wrinkled visage it was as if he'd been born old came up to the stage with a guitar. He was thin and drawn, and a pack of smokes bulged from his flannel shirt pocket. He sat on a stool but did not engage in the patter and repartee that the other players had. Instead he just introduced himself, saying, "I'm Billy Wilson," and he began playing songs that Paige did not recognize, songs, from the way he played and sang them, she was sure were his.

During those years with the band, Paige had heard so much great music, met so many talented musicians and singers who plugged away without much recognition, that she'd felt simultaneously uplifted by the music and depressed by the industry. Many nights she'd been transported and carried away, pulled in by the energy of the music and the crowd. She'd shaken her head with respect and admiration when a song went a different way than she'd thought it would, took her and the crowd to an unexpected but inevitable place. And yet, until now, she'd never quite known what it must have felt like to hear Bessie Smith or Janis Joplin or Billie Holiday or any of her other idols live. That was how she felt when Billy Wilson played his guitar and sang one song after another. He was singing to outlast this moment, to outlast them all. It was the lyrics, simple, direct yet complicated, and the melody, catchy but not show-offy, surprising in where the words and music took her, and then his voice, so bare and open, unguarded, that Paige's body hurt with the pain of it. Suddenly, someone shook her shoulder. She'd been listening with eyes closed, and she'd lost track of time. She opened her eyes and saw everyone standing except her father.

"We're going," Shannon said.

She blinked her eyes at them, at their father, eyes closed in his chair. "Now?" She shook herself as if waking from a dream. She couldn't imagine leaving.

"Daddy's tired."

"Daddy's listening to the music."

"Look at him," Shannon said. "He's worn out."

Paige thought about staying, trying to hitch a ride home with someone here, but she didn't know these people and didn't think they'd give someone who looked like her a ride. They were in a small mountain town, many miles from their home. "Can't we stay until Billy finishes? It's like leaving a Beatles concert an hour early."

"Look at him," Shannon said again. Her father was breathing through his mouth, which was slightly open, the breaths of someone who was far away from the place his body was resting, although Paige was convinced he still heard the music. She slowly stood and exited the row with the rest of them, but before she left the building, she turned to wave at the man on stage, and just at that moment, he looked up, and, she was sure of it, nodded at her before she left the room.

On the way home their father slept and complained. The journey was taking too long. His head hurt. The roads were bumpy. They weren't sure if he'd remembered the trip or even cared. When they got him home they put him to bed and he fell into a deep sleep before they'd turned off the light. No one said it, but they knew that, except for doctor's appointments, that would be his last trip out of the house.

By September their father's energy seemed to flow from living to dying, and the small things he'd once again enjoyed post-chemo, the birds fluttering around the feeder, the twang of country in his headphones, a bitter espresso made at home, wine, white and chilled in a shot glass, dwindled until he only seemed to enjoy sleeping and the first hour after he'd taken his pain pill. He was still chicken-leg skinny, but the drugs and cortisone treatments had made his face and belly swell so that he resembled some kind of famine-ravaged refugee with his sunken chest and distended belly. "I'm getting fat," he'd lament, unintentionally comic, like a starved model who could not accurately see her own reflection. Hospice came weekly to weigh him, check his blood pressure, refill his medication. Each day he seemed to care less about the world around him, retreating more into his disordered mind. Paige would tell him about a new song she was writing (she'd started writing again after her visit to the Opry, but she feared the songs were sappy and melodramatic) and he'd nod or absently say it was good. He stopped having opinions; instead everything suited him fine. He sometimes engaged with those who visited, the few far-flung relatives he had not seen in years, couples they'd known from church, the same ones who had appeared when their mother died, but had Paige seen them in between that time? She thought not. They were good at that, appearing in a crisis, then disappearing. But her father had probably turned down many invitations to play bridge or go to dinner or attend some church event over the years as well. Yes, Paige thought, it was not fair for her to blame them for something her family had chosen not to be a part of. By September he started needing stronger and more frequent pain pills. His forehead seemed to throb with the tumor, an alien creature pushing inward and outward, a deformed mass begging to escape.

One Sunday night, about a month before he died, the three sisters sat in the living room, retreating into their worlds, when their father spoke from the La-Z-Boy he reclined in.

"Where is the green and red cable?" he asked.

"What are you talking about?"

"You know, in the hospice brochure," he said. The girls looked at each other. Claire shook her head. Shannon disappeared to find the brochure, already thumbed through and well read.

"What do you mean, Daddy?"

"The red cable and the green cable. So I can end it. Hospice says so."

"There's nothing in the brochure about that."

"I've had a good life, but I'm ready to go."

"Maybe God isn't ready to let you go," Claire said.

Paige mouthed to Claire, "Really?"

"We love you, Daddy," Shannon said, her hand in her father's.

"I love you too, but I'm ready to go. Call Dr. K." Then he pushed his hands together like he was holding two cables. "I should have done it when I could have."

"I bet your head hurts, Daddy, doesn't it?" Paige lightly touched his swollen brow. "Time for a Big Red." They still called his pills Big Red, although they were now something much stronger. Paige went to the kitchen, opened the bottle, and came back with two pills.

"How many are you giving him?" Shannon said.

"Enough so he's not hurting," Paige said.

"Those things are addictive," Claire said.

Paige looked at her. "So?"

Claire bit her lip.

Paige gently opened her father's mouth and placed the pills on his tongue. She lifted the cup to his lips and told him to swallow. And he did. Soon he was asleep.

The next morning, as Paige fed him his morning pain pills, he held out his empty hand and said, "Where's the green pill?"

"What green pill?"

"The one I can end it with."

"There isn't one, Daddy."

He sighed. "Even if there was one, I wonder if I'd take it." Paige wondered then if, despite his insistence he was ready to die, he really meant it.

One morning Paige found him on the floor. He'd rolled off the bed, possibly trying to get up in the night. She tried to pull him up by herself and couldn't, so she called Shannon, who was on her distribution route. She stopped by and together they pulled him up and gave him his pills and his Ensure and moved him onto the deck so he could see the yard and the mountains and the city below it.

"I was fine until the doctors got a hold of me," he said.

"That's not true," Paige said.

"I woke up in the hospital and the doctors said my blood pressure was too low and I was going to die. I was fine until then."

"Don't you remember getting the MRI?"

He did not. He did not remember much of his illness; he only remembered waking up in the hospital half-starved to death, dying, wanting to go home.

"Do you remember," Paige ventured. She wanted a cigarette, coffee, her body heavy with sleep, her own headache forming at the front of her head. But she knew there would not be many more times like this, when he could—would—talk. "The other night, Dad, you said you wanted to kill yourself with the red and the green cables from hospice. Do you remember?"

"No," he said. "But it sounds like a good idea."

"You asked us to help you."

"Why didn't you?"

"We could end up in jail. Do you want that?"

"No," he said, sighing. "I feel okay now." He closed his eyes. "Maybe tomorrow we can see the penguins."

"Sure."

She moved her chair far from him, so she could smoke without bothering him and lit her first cigarette of the day. She thought he was asleep, but then he said, "Did Maria stop by?"

"Who's Maria?"

He didn't answer. After a minute she heard him wheezing in his sleep.

When the pills no longer worked, fentanyl patches were prescribed, to be changed once every two days. She tried to remember what the going rate for those was in Seattle on the black market, but she couldn't. She had done them once or twice, but like most of the drugs she'd used, they'd always been given to her. Band rules. When she couldn't wake her father up to change the patch, she let him sleep until he was awake, and then she'd roll him over, remove the old patch and carefully apply the new one. Because his sleeping delayed the patch application, she accrued a few extra patches over the weeks, which she kept in her bedside drawer in the basement.

Those last weeks he was alive he was usually too tired to talk, but she tried sometimes. She wanted something from him, his wisdom to her, some advice for how to live. But the only thing he would tell her was, "Keep your eyes open and your mouth shut." She didn't know what to do with that. It seemed almost everyone else in the world was all too happy to give her advice, especially Claire. She did not like Paige's tattoos or smoking or her bisexuality. One evening when she'd stopped by after work, Claire told her, "I don't care if you're a lesbian; I just wish you'd choose a side. I don't even know who to set up you up with."

"You don't have to set me up with anyone," Paige said. "I don't think I'm cut out for relationships," she added. And then Claire told her she was being emotionally immature, that she was a product of her generation's narcissism.

"Or our disillusionment," Paige said. "We were promised everything and have nothing. You, you have it all."

"Are you kidding? We're barely holding on to our house. You have no idea." Claire began weeping into her hands. Next to her, their father slept on a cot hospice had provided. He rarely left it. Paige draped her hand over her sister's curved back. She could not remember comforting her before.

"I know it's not easy, with Jim being out of work. But look, you have such great kids and a great husband. How much better does it get?"

And with that Claire only wept harder. Finally she stopped, wiped her eyes. "I appreciate you taking care of Daddy, really. But what are you going to do after he's gone?"

Paige did not know the answer to the question, except that she was not returning to Seattle. It had been good for a long time, but now the city was just a Rorschach of her own tragedies, personal and public. On Facebook she learned the band had signed with a new label under a new name: the Caves. On YouTube she saw their first video, Becca (formally Becky) now the lead singer, her voice as smooth as Karen Carpenter's, the handsome new drummer, the band scruffily attractive with their over-the-top angst. The Caves' sound had broader appeal. Paige's voice was deep and raw, which connected better live than on CD. But now after years of tours and the lifestyle that went with it, she felt used, worn. She no longer cared about communicating to the so-called audience because she had nothing more to say to them. When she watched the views of the Caves' single on YouTube increase by the thousands each day, she knew they were better without her, that she was what had been holding the rest of them back.

Now that her father was in the hospice cot in the living room, Paige would sleep on the couch, and sometimes she could not catch him when he started to roll over and fall as he'd done in the bedroom. He'd forget that he could not walk, that he wore Depends and he did not need to go to the bathroom. Visitors usually arrived with a casserole or a prayer quilt. They reassured him and Paige that they were putting him on their prayer list and had asked the pastor to do the same. He pretended to remember them most of the time. Other times, toward the end, he did not care, could not care, it seemed, about anyone who visited. They would come and sit and chat with Paige, and their father would ignore them, doze off or flip through TV stations he never watched. But once they saw him and his body, with its swollen look of death consuming him from the inside out, they did not return. After he'd checked out and the visitors had left, Paige would get on the computer and follow the Caves' rapid ascendancy, from record deal to the hastily assembled tour opening for an arena-sized band.

She and her father would sit on the porch, the hot sun baking her skin, something she had not felt in years. She didn't realize how cold she'd been living in Seattle's wet, chilly air and weak, diluted light. Those evenings she would position his eye patch over his shut and swollen eye and then affix the fentanyl patch on the base of his back. She eased her father into his wheelchair, made sure he had on fresh Depends under his faded gray sweatpants with their elasticized cuffs hiding his shriveled legs. They listened to records, softly so as not to hurt his head, until he'd fallen asleep. She positioned the stereo console as close to the deck as possible, so that she need only move a few feet to change the record. The music helped her forget the new world, to remember that she and her father and her mother had not invented pain and suffering, that the world wallowed in it.

She tried to remind herself that she had brought herself here, that in some ways she was born to help her father die, that it was a privilege she would not forsake. She smoked cigarettes and wore Joy perfume and drank sweet tea from a teacup and listened to George Jones until she drifted to sleep.

Some evenings Claire or Shannon would come over to watch their father to give Paige a night off. She usually drove to JJs to hear whatever band was rolling into town. Sometimes she'd recognize the bands, people she'd seen in Seattle or played with in the same show or festival circuit or she'd recognize people in old bands with new names, sometimes with a new sound, sometimes the same one. She never spoke to these musicians she half knew. Instead she hid in the corners of the bar or sat outside in the shabby patio lit by Christmas lights and glowing cigarette cherries. She remembered when she was in high school, those last days when the bar had been the Chameleon, and she wished back then she'd been born ten years earlier. She would have been one of those people who saw the famous bands when they were first starting out. She would have seen Nirvana or the Meat Puppets or Hole or any of the others before they became big. The Chameleon had been Chattanooga's first really integrated bar, with jazz and poetry readings and a jar you put your money into to pay for your beer, and out back you could smoke weed and be left alone. To hear her friends' brothers and sisters talk about it, the Chameleon was just about the coolest place south of New York, run by the coolest black dudes in town, both six-three, handsome, and charming: George, with a gravelly cigarette voice so deep it was made for radio, and Paul, his chilled-out doppelgänger, his skin a shade darker, his demeanor a shade less intense. She'd see George sometimes around town, but she was too intimidated to speak to him, the coolest guy she'd ever seen, with his dreadlocks and green eyes like hers—she fantasized that they might be related, that her great-great-great-grandfather, the plantation owner on her mother's side, was also George's great-great-great-grandfather. But except for their eyes, there was nothing that connected them. And then, just before she'd turned twenty-one, the Chameleon had shut down. Paul had skipped town, and then George followed, leaving the club to run itself, which it could not. So Paige never got to see if the bar lived up to the stories she heard; she never got to introduce herself to George as his cousin, never got to sing there. Back then she'd once asked Claire why she'd never gone to the Chameleon, and Claire had said that places like that didn't interest her, that they were full of drugs and trouble and were on the bad side of town. That was typical for Claire even then, no curiosity, no daring. Was it because she'd had to take care of so much so soon?

Paige felt a bone-deep exhaustion from taking care of their father, even with help, and she was not twelve and did not have two sisters or school to worry about. To Paige, Claire had always been the older sister who did the boring, safe things. But now Paige wondered if Claire had not been right after all. She had a career, a family, a home. Paige had none of those and didn't know if she ever would. She didn't even have a college degree, and she couldn't see what the future held for her. While Paige would most likely struggle her entire life, Claire would soon be able to relax and to live out her older years in comfort, surrounded by people who loved her. And sometimes when Paige babysat Aimee and Desmond, she could see the appeal, how fulfilling it would be to have children to love and live for, someone else to focus your life on instead of yourself.

No, she would never have been like Claire, even if their mother had lived. Paige would have outgrown the tea parties and they would have fought. Her mother would not have accepted Paige's sexuality the way her father eventually had. Her mother would not have approved of her moving to Seattle to sing in a loud, angry band. She would have forced her to go to the girls prep school, a place Paige would have hated. Her mother would not have approved of most of what Paige had done. Had her life so far just been one long rebellion against her dead mother? Did her mother have that kind of reach, still? Why was she trying to piss off her mother, even in death? As far as their mother-daughter relationship went, her mother had died at the perfect time, before things would inevitably sour between them, before they disappointed each other in a dozen different ways. And that's why Paige was angry, still.

She remembered so little of that time, suspected that most of her memories of her mother were not hers at all, but her sisters'. They were the ones who told the stories of Paige playing with her dolls in her bedroom while the others mourned elsewhere. How she'd talk to them in a language no one else knew. How she loved church and singing in the choir, how she worried about people who didn't go to church because they had not been saved. How those last few months her mother was alive, she'd go to church with other families. In that sense, she understood how her father must feel now, trying to remember things other people told him were true.

They told her that once she came home from a Baptist church announcing to her family she'd gotten in line with the sinners and was now saved, even though they were Presbyterian. They assumed that she must have remembered singing Bessie Smith at her mother's funeral, "Baby, Won't You Please Come Home." Even now people recalled that funeral and little Paige with her voice so big out of that little body; even now people would start crying when they talked of that day. But Paige was not sure if she remembered any of those things.

What she did remember were the tea parties. Her mother dressed up, wearing gloves and a hat, Paige in her poofy white dress with the red sash. The hat and gloves ceremoniously removed, the white gloves trimmed in lace dropped in her pocketbook. Her mother was the guest and Paige was the host. Her bear, Barry, was the other guest, crowded around the cramped table with weak tea warming in the antebellum tea set, buttery boxed cookies sparkling with rock sugar, Joy dabbed on their wrists. She remembered her mother talking to her then, so seriously, as if there was an unburdening of all she kept inside. She talked of the tea set and how it had come from the family plantation in Georgia, how they'd moved to Chattanooga after the war because an uncle had done well with the railroad, how all they'd had was their name to start over. They'd prospered, with servants and society and an understanding that people knew what was what. "But that's all gone now," her mother had said. "And why is it gone?" Paige had asked, trying to sound like an adult. Her mother must have forgotten, too, that she was talking to her five-year-old daughter instead of a neighbor. "Because," she said, "I became with child, and they banished me, even after I married him." "Whose child were you with, Mommy?" Her mother didn't answer at first. Then she patted Barry's head, tugged his ear. "All of you. I'm with all of you." For years Paige had kept those words, *with child* and *banished*, a secret in her mouth. She'd whisper them, unsure of their meaning, when she played with her dolls. *You're banished.* She'd finally asked Claire, whom Paige believed back then knew everything. "Well, with child just means you're pregnant. And banished means sent away," Claire said. "Why do you ask?" "No reason," Paige had said, as lightly as possible. And when Claire didn't stop staring at her, Paige added, "Just something from TV." Even now she kept her memory, her mother's words secret, for they were words her sisters—especially Claire—were never meant to hear.

One night a week before their father's death, Claire came over so that Paige, who had not left the house all week, could go out. She went to JJs, bought a PBR, and went to the back deck, where music throbbed distantly away. Even though she didn't talk to anyone, she usually felt at home here, as if she could pick up her guitar and sing on stage and people would like her well enough. But this night with her father dying, she no longer wanted to sing in front of people. She only wanted to sit on the deck with him nearby and listen to songs from an earlier time. When the barman came around for that night's cover, Paige finished her beer, saying she wasn't staying for the show.

The lights were off, but Claire's car was in the driveway. Paige barely noted the other car on the side of the road, dark in the night so that she couldn't see how old it was. She let herself in quietly, more to not wake Claire, who seemed to travel in a cloud of

exhaustion, who stayed over it seemed more for the allure of unin-
terrupted sleep than seeing their father, who was already more in the
other world than this one.

When Paige entered the hall, she heard something upstairs
in Claire's room. A squeak of the bed or floorboard. She paused at
the stairs. It was probably Claire, getting ready for sleep. Then she
remembered the car parked on the side of the road. She listened to
the noises upstairs, a creaking and then a slamming sound. She heard
a moan—Claire's?—and then a deep masculine voice. She looked
around for something blunt and heavy. Shannon had played softball
as a child, but where would that bat be now? Probably long gone to
Goodwill or hidden in the attic. She heard shuffling again, a man's
voice, for certain. There was a large umbrella by the door, so she
picked it up and ascended the staircase. As she got closer to Claire's
room she heard the voices again, her sister's, more of a mumble, and
a man's, also mumbling, and then a kind of quiet. Paige threw open
the door and the umbrella exploded open, shielding her momentarily. She tried closing the umbrella, but it wouldn't, so she lowered
it instead to the floor. A shirtless black man hovered over Claire,
whose wrists were tied to the bed.

"Go away," Claire said, evenly. "I'm okay."

Paige stared at the man. The room was almost dark, but she
could see his boxers with hearts stamped on them and the thinnest
film of sweat on his skin. He did not move, perhaps in the hope he'd
become invisible, a statue, no longer real, and she would not see him.
She tried again to close the umbrella but the clasp felt stuck, and the
open umbrella was too large to get through the narrow bedroom
door. Claire remained in the bed, her hands pitched up behind her,
almost as still as the man. She lay there with abandon, something
Paige had never seen in Claire before.

She left the umbrella on the floor, closing the door behind
her. Downstairs she checked on her father, who was sleeping on
the cot in the living room. She wondered if this is what Claire did

the nights she came when Paige was out, left their dying father on a hospital cot unattended while she had sex with someone who was not her husband in her old bedroom.

On the porch she smoked a cigarette and watched the city lights glisten beyond the fist of a forest that sloped below the yard. She had slept with a married woman with children, but that did not stop her from being angry with Claire, who had now thrown away all that Paige had never had. Paige wondered if any of them were doing anything right when it came to love, if any of them were capable of it.

Paige was awakened by Claire the next morning. She'd fallen asleep only a few hours earlier on a lounge chair on the porch, a half-finished bottle of wine and an ashtray of cigarettes beside her.

Her eyes hurt. Claire was dressed in her trademark dark tailored suit and tiny diamond stud earrings. Her eyes were dark and despairing half-moons, red rimmed. Her makeup could not hide her hollowness.

"Listen," Claire said. And then she said nothing.

"The kids." Paige had thought they'd not have to grow up with pain or sorrow.

"I love him."

"You don't seem very happy."

"Happy?" Claire laughed. "Happy is a star. This is the sky that holds the stars and everything between them." Her voice was raspy, the thinnest thread about to break.

So this is what happens, Paige thought, when you don't sleep around before marriage. You confuse sex with the world. She never thought she'd feel older, wiser than Claire, but here she was.

"I won't tell," Paige said. She wanted to feel more for Claire, more compassion, more love. But at the moment she felt cold and distant. Later, she'd know it wasn't Claire she was angry at so much as it was herself for hurting people without care or thought so many times for the sake of feeling alive. Claire covered her face, sobbing. "And you can't either. You can never tell anyone." Claire wrapped her arms around Paige and then stood. Paige wondered how long Claire had been exhausted, years, maybe decades, maybe since their mother had died. Paige knew that Claire would not end things with the man she claimed to love, not yet at least. She knew she would bring the man here again, because there was nowhere else to go. That this man would tie Claire up and they would have sex in her old childhood bedroom while their father died below, while Aimee read about wizards to her father and Dez, and the children were without their mother just as she and Claire and Shannon had been, absence repeated again and again.

The night after Paige discovered Claire with the man, as her father sank farther into a world that was more real than the one he was escaping from, Paige took one of the fentanyl patches she'd saved and stuck it on the small of her back. His face was a large swollen mass, as if he were growing a horn. Soon he'd be on a morphine drip. "Where are the penguins? Where is Maria?" he'd asked her earlier that day. Yesterday morning, he had asked Paige again to end things for him. She had raised the teacup to his lips so the water could wet them.

Not yet, Daddy. Not yet.

Those evenings in high school when it was still warm, she and her father would sit on the deck and listen to the whippoorwills and watch the fireflies after the sun set. Her father would try to get her to listen to his music. Tinny, whiny country songs that Paige thought were about nothing but the so-called good old days. One day she put on a Wilco CD, to share what she was listening to, and after a few songs, her father said, "That sounds right much like country to me." Paige laughed because to her the two sounded nothing alike, and she put on her Janis Joplin CD instead.

"This is the kind of singer I want to be," she said.

"Drinking and drugging wrecked her life," he said.

"So much pain," Paige said. "All the women singers who follow her are just cheap imitations of her."

"I got some music for you," he said, standing. He went to the living room and turned on his old stereo from before the girls had been born, his one big investment, he said, before he met Lila and had other things that demanded his money and attention. He leafed through the stacked albums, the jacket covers kicking up bits of dust with each flip. Paige sat on the couch. It was the first fall after Shannon had left for college, and Paige and her father were still establishing their routine. "Close your eyes," he said. "I don't want you peeking at the cover." She heard the slight scratch of the needle as it settled on the album.

The woman's voice was far away, almost as if she were singing under a scarf someone had wrapped around her, but even so, the voice was powerful, confident, an instrument that delivered unmitigated sorrow, not just of a person but of the world.

"One of Janis Joplin's favorite singers," he said.

Paige hadn't considered that Joplin too would have influences, inspiration. "Who is she?"

"You sang her at your momma's funeral."

Bessie Smith—how could Paige have forgotten her? One of the songs she'd memorized and sung for her mother bubbled up, a tune, a few words, a chorus. For years she'd lived with the music in her head instead of pursuing where it came from or why. Her mind had seemed like the right place for the music to live.

"Why didn't you play her before now?"

"After Lila died, I guess Bessie was too much for me. I didn't think I could take it."

She remembered her mother's comments at their pretend tea parties, her nostalgia for the old South and the lost plantation. But maybe she'd remembered that wrong, too, maybe there was some nuance to her mother's nostalgia, or other reasons for it that Paige had missed or not noticed. Her mother had loved Bessie Smith from Chattanooga, said she was one of the best blues singers of all time. Bessie sang about love and pain and hurt the way Paige wanted to someday. After that night, she and her father gave up their battle of country versus alternative music, and instead, they listened to Bessie's voice access pleasure and pain. And for Paige after that, whenever she got on stage and had to sing about those things, she tried to summon Bessie, tried to do her right.

Now, her father didn't seem to care about any of the music she played. Paige stood, loose-limbed, and put on Bessie. Her father was asleep, so this time the music was for her. As her own pain drained from her body, she listened to Bessie singing about too much love and not enough love, and her voice was nothing but a sweet, sorrowful release.

SHANNON

For their father's funeral, she arrived with Jeremy and David in the convertible at the Episcopal church. She was one month pregnant, inseminated with Jeremy's doctor-approved sperm.

Paige had saved a space for Shannon at the end of the front pew, in case she needed to pee or throw up. David and Jeremy sat behind her, occasionally patting her shoulder. Every minute or so, Shannon would turn to see who was coming in. Most were people she recognized, except for one woman sitting in the back pew alone, dark skin and hair and eyes, in a Chanel-type suit with round brocade buttons. Her hair was done up in a tight bun looped and braided in such a way that suggested long, glossy hair. She looked like she belonged in a foreign film instead of at a funeral in Chattanooga, like a femme fatale who smoked cigarettes and stubbed the butts out with the tiny heel of her stiletto shoe. Maria, Shannon thought. It must be her. And then the service began and Shannon faced the minister.

The sisters did as their father had asked, recalling stories from when they were young. Claire described her father helping her choose her first outfit for a job interview, offering his opinion like a *Vogue* editor. Shannon told them about going to the Aquarium with him, how he quacked at the penguins and then translated their conversation. Paige talked about him taking her to the Opry and then sang George Jones. Then they sat down and the service resumed its more traditional trajectory.

Shannon felt herself float above the congregation until she was hovering over all of them. She saw the woman walk to the coffin, the gentle sway of her hips, her generous bust hidden and bound under the buttons of her suit as she walked toward the door. She did not wear stilettos and seamed stockings as Shannon had expected, but sturdy black leather pumps, worn and shined. Then Shannon was no longer floating, and she felt she would throw up on the cold church floor.

Shannon stood and pushed herself through the church doors. The squeaky sound of her shoes on the wood floor. Everywhere, wood floors. A muffled sound of the congregation singing. Outside the woman was getting into an old BMW in the parking lot. Her hands were on the steering wheel, but the car was not running. The window was rolled three-quarters down and as Shannon reached the car, she asked, "Are you Maria? Are you my father's wife?" The woman looked up, reflexively.

"I'm sorry for your loss," the woman said, closing the window and starting the car. Shannon rapped on the door; the woman shook her head slightly and backed out. As she drove away, Shannon saw the license plate was from Dalton, Georgia, about thirty minutes away. And then she was gone.

Bile rose in her throat. She hurried back into the church to the bathroom, rushed to the first stall, and threw up. The world felt silent. She flushed the commode and listened to the water echo down the pipes. She turned the sink on and waited for the water to warm, pretended the water was a stream and she was floating on it. She floated by her father, then her mother. She wondered whom she would float by next.

When the water was warm, she soaped and rinsed her hands. Was that the love of her dead father's life? Could she be, in some way, his wife? The restroom door opened. A woman took the sink next to Shannon. She wore a nondescript black dress slightly stained in the armpits. Her hair was cut at an unflattering length that emphasized her slight double chin. She didn't turn on the water, only stared at the empty bin. She whispered something that Shannon couldn't quite make out, and then the woman said it louder, and Shannon realized the words were meant for her.

"I'm sorry?" Shannon said.

"I said I forgive you." The woman wrapped her arms around Shannon and held her more in a grip than an embrace. She smelled slightly stale, as if her clothes had been washed but then not dried properly. Like mildew.

"I'm sorry?" Shannon said again.

The woman released Shannon. "You were right. I did marry twice and have two kids and bad haircuts and work a dead-end job. And much worse than even you thought."

Shannon reached out to touch the woman in front of her, make sure she wasn't a hallucination. "Julie? From senior prom?" And from *Jail Break*, Shannon almost said.

"You were so hateful to me."

"I'm sorry about that," Shannon said.

"I'm sorry about your Daddy. He was my husband's supervisor for a while. Always said he was a fair man." Julie looked down at Shannon's belly, even though she wasn't showing yet.

"I'm pregnant. Isn't that funny? You're the first person I've told."

Julie touched Shannon's stomach where the baby, invisible, was growing. Shannon knew she would hate it when people touched her belly as if it was a lamp or a wish generator.

"Who's the Daddy?"

"Jeremy. And David."

She drew her hand away from Shannon's stomach and quickly wiped it on her dress. "You always did have a weird sense of humor. I remember you told me that that night would be the best of my life. You were wrong about that." Julie seemed comfortably sober. Her eyes and skin were clear. "I bet it wasn't your last night of life sucking either, like you said it was."

"We were so young back then. I was wrong about a lot of things."

"God bless your baby." And then she left.

Shannon washed her hands again. Her forgiveness of Julie (but what was there to forgive?) slid toward a hateful feeling, even after everything, after all these years. She still felt that Julie looked down on her, judged her as a loser. She should have mentioned Julie's appearance in *Jail Break*, but then Shannon would have to admit that she worked there now. Besides, her father would not have wanted her to do something so spiteful at his funeral. She pushed open the door from the bathroom to the hallway. The service would be ending soon. She leaned against the cool tile of the wall, listening to the muffled sounds of her father's funeral as if she were wrapped in cotton.

And then at the end of the hall appeared a young Asian girl in a dress with a wide bow, patent leather shoes, and turned-down anklet socks. She could have been from any time. She was thin and solemn, about Dez's age, she guessed. She was standing in the hallway by herself, and the light from the large church window shone on her as if she were an actress on stage, as if the world existed to watch her. Shannon placed her palm against the cool tiles of the wall, for her legs were suddenly twitching. And then she saw him, a man in a dark somber suit, slight as the girl's hand he reached out to grab. He stepped into the light with her and they stood, father and daughter, she guessed, in that block of light, looking at her, and she wondered if she were hallucinating again, and she shielded her hands over her belly, for she would not lose this baby, and no one would take it from her, she would never let it go.

She leaned back against the wall and waited for them to come. They stopped a few feet in front of her. She reached out her hand and fingered the rough fabric of his suit. He looked the same except a little older, a bit thinner, almost gaunt. Was this the man she'd been dreaming about for the past ten years? Was this the repository for all she'd thought had been missing in her life?

"I'm so sorry," Ben said.

"It's you."

"Yes."

"You came all the way from Korea for his funeral?"

Ben shook his head. "We're setting up here. Lots of new business here with the new Volkswagen plant." Such everyday words. Ben cleared his throat. "I'm here for a while, to oversee startup operations. I was going to call you as soon as we got settled." He took the girl's hand. "This is my daughter, Hye Jin." The girl half-nodded, bowed, and then looked at the ground where the tips of her patent Mary Janes met.

"Hi, Hye Jin. Nice to meet you."

The girl would not look up.

"She's still adjusting," Ben said. "She's shy, like her father. Right, Hye Jin?" Then he said something in Korean and the girl nodded again. "Anyway, before I could get in touch with you, I read your dad's obituary in the paper."

"I wrote it."

"I thought so. It was a nice obituary."

"Why didn't you email me? Something?" Hye Jin was still staring at the floor. She hoped the girl didn't understand English. She lowered her voice. "Were you just going to call me up one day for coffee or something? Like we were nothing?"

"That was a long time ago."

"Yes. It was." She hated herself for hating a man whose wife had recently committed suicide. She opened the door to the church service, which continued on without her. "I'll see you around."

A week after the funeral, the sisters were on the Walnut Street Bridge facing the city. The Market Street Bridge, the Aquarium, and the Hunter Art Museum crested the skyline. It was late fall, the leaves were brown, and the city looked bare. They each held plastic baggies of their father's ashes. They'd just come from the lawyer's office, where they'd learned their father had secretly married Maria a few months before he'd been diagnosed. In his new will he instructed Maria to put the house on the market one year after his death, and to divide the proceeds equally in thirds among his daughters.

"Daddy would say her name sometimes," Paige said. "But he never told me who she was." She scooped some of the ashes out of the bag and threw them over the bridge. The ashes settled like snow into the river below them. "At least I have a year before I'm kicked out of our own house."

"Maybe it will take a while to sell. The market's still not that great." Why Shannon didn't tell them she'd suspected the woman from the funeral was Maria, that she'd even talked to Maria at the funeral, she couldn't say. She wanted to keep it to herself, to talk to Maria again before she told them.

"How could he do this to us? Ask a stranger to sell our childhood home." Claire threw her baggy over the bridge and then buried her face in her hands.

"We all have our secrets, I guess," Shannon said. She tossed ashes from her bag into the air, watched them scatter like seeds.

Ben emailed her his phone number and she waited a few weeks before she called him back. They agreed to meet at a coffee shop downtown. She arrived early. While she waited for him she sucked her grapefruit juice loudly through a straw, still trying to decide how angry she was for him showing up and destroying her fantasy of him. She'd made an attempt to look reasonably attractive, blow-drying her hair, taking a bit more time with her makeup, wearing an empire-waist dress that hid any sign of a pregnancy. He arrived wearing a polo shirt and chinos, and she had to remind herself that he was some big executive whose TV star wife had killed herself, not the young man she'd thought she'd been in love with more than ten years ago.

"You know these coffee shops are nice, but I kind of miss those IHOP days," he said.

"Why?" Shannon said.

Ben looked down at his coffee. "Lots of reasons."

"You used to be so talkative."

He shook his head, pinched the bridge of his nose.

He'd worn glasses in college and he seemed to be reaching for an invisible pair. LASIK, she guessed. "Tell me about you," he said.

"I sent you an email a few years ago. Did you get it?"

"Yes."

She waited for him to continue.

"I'm sorry about your divorce, about things not working out. But I couldn't write you back. You understand, don't you?"

His hand shook as he raised the mug to his lips.

She told him about Maria and her father's secret marriage, how he'd put her in charge of selling their house. She told him about Claire and Paige, about how, when she realized her father was dying, she'd decided to have Jeremy and David's baby to have some family of her own.

"Oh. Congratulations. I mean it."

"I don't regret it," she said. "Even with all the first-trimester baggage."

"You shouldn't."

"How is Hye Jin adjusting?"

"I don't know," Ben said. "She's always been a quiet child. Even before Ji Young's death."

"Do you want to talk about it?"

Ben shrugged, as if it didn't matter either way to him. Except that his hand, resting on the table, was still shaking. "Ji Young had been battling depression for a long time."

Shannon stilled his trembling hand. "I'm sorry, I really am. There's no rush. You can tell me when you're ready."

He squeezed her hand. "So," he said.

"So," she said. "Friends?"

"I'd like that." And then he palmed a tear on the side of his face.

BEN/HA BIN
(as told by Shannon)

While Ben had been taking photographs for the *College Cri-er*, trying to resist his crush on Shannon, and half-heartedly studying his business major, Ji Young had started a modest acting career, taking small roles in Korean TV dramas. When he returned to Korea, Ji Young's career began to take off, and she had recurring TV roles first as the young ingenue from the wrong side of the tracks and then later as a young mother with a career. Ben's family, initially against Ji Young's acting career, embraced it after they saw how the company benefitted from her growing celebrity status. In the months leading up to Ben and Ji Young's wedding, a year after he'd arrived back, tire sales jumped twenty percent. A previously untapped demographic, working women who wanted to be the people Ji Young played, was responsible. That Ben and Ji Young had known each other for years when they'd been students made their story even more romantic, a sign of true love.

When Ben returned, Ji Young had just started her first major TV role as a conflicted college student, unsure whether to follow her mind or her heart. On the screen and in front of her fans, she was outgoing and expansive. But when it was just the two of them, she was quiet and reserved, as if the world were too much for her and she did not want to disturb it. She was like a glass of cool clear water that could not be touched.

Ben should have taken her behavior as a warning, but he had not. He'd considered himself perceptive about these things, but he did not see her darkness below the surface, or rather he did see it, but he took that to mean there was depth underneath her still, symmetrical beauty. Despite her coolness, their marriage started off well, quickly becoming one of comfort and ease. They lived in a fashionable apartment in Gangnam and owned a SsangYong Chairman sedan, equipped with an always-new set of his family's brand of tires. In return for their material comfort, the marriage of Ha Bin Lee and Ji Young Kim gave the tire company some glamour, and helped Ji Young's career by representing the Korean woman's fantasy of an ideal couple.

And then, a few years after they'd been married, Ji Young would not get up one morning. Reluctantly, Ben called her agent, who sent a doctor over. After he met with Ji Young, the doctor told Ben he'd readjusted Ji Young's medication, that this happened sometimes with people like her, and that she would return to her normal self; she always did. Ben thanked the doctor and then sat on the floor of their living room and stared at the prescriptions. She'd never told him about this. Drugs, depression. How long had she been this way? And was the "normal" self he knew the medicated one?

The next morning, he asked her. She said she'd started feeling depressed when he was in the States, and that was when she'd started taking the antidepressants. They'd enabled her to go on auditions, to get an agent, to land a few roles. Before then, she said, she just stayed in her one room, not eating, looking out the window onto the ugly world below. She felt so much better for so long, and she didn't tell him because she was afraid he wouldn't marry her if he knew. What she meant was that his parents probably would not have allowed their only son to marry a woman who had gone to a psychiatrist and was on antidepressants.

For the first few weeks after the doctor's visit, Ji Young did not get better. She refused to eat. She was already tiny and delicate, not a big eater, and Ben worried that her health would deteriorate even more. He was not a good cook; maids or his mother or cafeterias had provided his meals for most of his life. In the States he'd supplemented his school cafeteria food with ramen and tuna and scrambled eggs. So he hired an *ajumma* to come in and cook soothing meals like rice porridge and seaweed soup, which he'd dip into her mouth on tiny spoons. Meanwhile, he had his grueling schedule at the company. As the son of the president and heir, he was expected to lead by example, working long hours, taking his employees and clients out for dinner and drinks most nights. His *soju* tolerance increased and he also learned how to appear to have drunk more bottles than he had, to act drunker than he was, to never do anything that would embarrass him or the family, to never promise or extract anything beyond goodwill while clients were drunk.

He stole moments from the office on this or that pretext and taxied to their apartment to check on her during the day. He nursed her as best he could, when he could, combed her hair, promised her that she would get better. And she did, after a few weeks, as the doctor had said, returning to the person he'd known for so many years, except maybe a bit brighter, a bit more serious, her skin always cool to the touch. She reassured him that now that she had him and her pills and her work there was no reason for her ever to be depressed again.

And so their lives continued. Ji Young was busy with her steady work in serial dramas and occasional films, while Ben struggled to fulfill his filial duty as the president's son. He was being groomed to eventually take over the company. Ben, however, was not naturally good at business and had to work hard at general competence, unlike his sister Min Ju who, with her MBA degree from Wharton, was more suited to run the business. If only his sister had been the first-born male. For even in the new millennium, the company was not ready for a woman to take the lead in such a male-dominated field, especially when a first-born son, not entirely incompetent, was at the ready. Min Ju, ever pragmatic, understood that if she officially took over, the company's brand would be ruined. She said that Koreans were modern enough for the next tire president to be married to a beautiful actress who played a powerful career woman, but not for a single woman to actually run the show. Not yet.

His sister remained stubbornly single, resisting pairings and matches, and as her thirtieth birthday loomed, she approached "old maid" status, and the possibility of her remaining forever single was higher than not. But it was difficult for her or her family to find a man who would not begrudge her her power, intelligence, and status, for the company depended on her too much to relinquish her to the role of housewife and mother. Min Ju agreed, saying that she was married to the company and that was enough for her. Ben wondered if the truth was rather it was enough because the type of marriage that would enable her to work as she did wasn't possible.

After Ji Young got better, they both almost forgot about her depression, and a year later she got pregnant and they were both happy, even, or especially, when they found out the baby was a girl. Ben took out his camera, relegated to the back of his wardrobe since he'd returned, and began taking photographs of his pregnant wife with black-and-white film. She wore the rough white linen of Korean mourners in a *hanbok* style, sheer in the light, hair draping her shoulders like a shawl, her mouth a wistful smile. He only had to find the right light to render her as a study of light and dark, shadow and sun.

One night when Ji Young was eight months along she'd awakened and shuffled into the hall, her pale nightgown a diaphanous and shifting image. He followed her with his camera. She looked out the window for him, the sleeve of her gown slipping, exposing her shoulder, her darkening and rounded nipples growing visible, spilling over the fabric. She looked at the city beyond them, the cramped apartment buildings that seemed to go on forever. He'd asked her what she was thinking. Nothing, she'd answer. *There's nothing there.*

He knew Ji Young kept secrets, but this time she wasn't lying; she probably was thinking of nothing, and it vaguely frightened him. For he did know that hers was not a Buddhist nothing, reflecting an absence of suffering, the edge of detached enlightenment. This was a nihilistic nothing, an annihilation. Oblivion. He hoped their daughter would be the something she needed to bring her back.

Hye Jin was born during the monsoon season, when mold flourished in humid rooms and floods brought tragedy. One year when his family was living back in Korea, Ben remembered the family returning to their house in Seoul after two weeks in Jeju Island during the monsoons. When they opened the door to the apartment, Ben thought there'd been a snowstorm or volcanic ash. A white musty mold coated their clothes, chairs, everything. His own leather jacket his father had bought for him in Italy was creased with the stuff. He wiped the sleeves attentively with a damp sponge, hoping he could bring the leather back to its original supple sheen. The dehumidifier containers put out to absorb the moisture were brimming with water. Before they'd moved back to Korea, they'd endured a shimmering, sometimes painful heat in South Africa, but there'd not been the humidity, and the nights in Johannesburg had been pleasantly cool. Even though his mother had begged his father to buy some AC units for their Korean apartment, his father had been against it for health reasons. It was not good for someone to go from hot to cold in such extremes, to breathe artificial air, Ben's father had said. Also, Ben said, in Korea in the early 1990s AC was still a luxury, and his father, ever mindful of his image as a hardworking man from humble beginnings, didn't want such luxuries associated with him or his children. His mother had wept when they found the silk duvets hand-stitched by her grandmother, duvets that had survived the Japanese occupation and wars and repression, a reminder of poverty and survival, a reminder that even in difficult times beauty could abide. Now those blankets were white and green with mold, forever ruined. It was, Ben told Shannon, the beginning of the rift in his parents' marriage, for his mother never forgave his father, even when the following day his father had the AC units, tall lumbering machines that stole a corner in each room, delivered and installed, so that afterward in the summer there always whirred a cool chill no one ever quite got used to.

After Hye Jin's birth, Ben's mother helped out (usually it would have been Ji Young's mother, but she'd died when Ji Young was a teenager), and the *ajumma* stayed on as well. Even with the dark skies and the rain, because of the air conditioner, there was no mold in their pricey modern apartment. Yet, a few weeks after Hye Jin was born, Ji Young became convinced mold was all around them, in the air, and if it started to grow it could never be stopped. She'd wake up in the night, scratching her arms to clean them of the mold that had grown on her in her dreams.

In those early months, baby Hye Jin slept with them, with Ji Young nursing her through the night, half asleep. Ben was afraid he'd roll over and crush the baby, so he took to sleeping on a *yo* beside them on the floor. He'd wake up sometimes to crying, not the baby's but Ji Young's, and he'd crawl up and ask her why she was crying and she'd tell him she'd dreamt the baby was covered in mold and when she'd tried to wash it off, she'd accidentally drowned her. She was terrified she'd kill her own baby, even though she was an attentive and careful mother, not letting the baby out of her sight. Yet at nights she cried from her own dreams, and some days when he came home from work, she'd call to him from the bathroom, asking him to examine the bathtub for mold before she washed the baby. He'd tell her it was clean, gleaming, couldn't she see? And she'd shake her head no, biting her lip. No, she couldn't. One day, in September, after the monsoon season had ended, he came home from work and found her scrubbing the tub with her plastic gloves, the baby sleeping beside her on the spotless white tile. His nose burned from the bleach. He was afraid she'd rubbed her own skin raw. "She can't touch any mold," Ji Young told him. "It will kill her." Ben lifted the sleeping baby, pulled the kneeling Ji Young off the floor.

"Let me take a photo of you two on the balcony," he said. "Here, we'll crack open the window, just for a bit of fresh air." And she followed him and posed, her fingers curled as if they were still holding imaginary sponges. Each day it went until she was better again, sometimes for years. When she was better she'd get a job on a TV drama series for the year or two the series lasted.

Being rich was just another fantasy that life wouldn't be as hard, Ji Young told him. She used to believe the fantasy because her mother had. Ji Young did not often speak of her mother or her father, an abusive alcoholic, neither uncommon nor surprising. How her mother died was unclear except that it was because of her father in some way. He wore her down, was all Ji Young would tell Ben.

In 2008, when Hye Jin was seven, the spate of celebrity suicides began. By the end of 2008, nine celebrities had committed suicide, resulting in many copycats, which then resulted in a spike to almost 15,000 suicides, high even for suicide-prone Korea. First was a man who was part of a celebrity couple, who committed suicide because he was massively in debt. Other celebrities, actors, sports stars, and models, followed, with a celebrity suicide almost every month. In March 2009, a famous soap opera actress left a seven-page letter condemning sexual exploitation in the Korean entertainment industry. She was the seventh in six months. Ji Young had known several of the actresses who hung themselves, and she was deeply affected by their deaths. That spring of 2009, she lingered in bed a little longer in the mornings before rising for work, and Ben worried she was falling back into depression. He made her promise she would not hang herself, reminded her she had a daughter to live for. One night when Ji Young was sleeping, Ben scoured the apartment for ropes, belts, and cords and took them to his office, where he put them in a file cabinet that had a key. Still, Ben saw their apartment provided all kinds of options for suicide. Knives, razors, the open balcony, the array of Ji Young's prescription pills. He wanted her to see a therapist, but she refused, saying that it would tarnish his company and her career if word got out. She seemed to rely more on her pills, which she took to sleep at night, to wake up in the morning, to alleviate depression and anxiety during the day. He was terrified to leave her in the mornings and terrified to come home. He paid for the *ajumma* housekeeper to stay during the day so that Ji Young was never alone.

One morning that spring, Ben emerged from the shower to find the words "I'm sorry" in Korean steamed into the mirror. When they'd first moved into the apartment they'd often left messages for each other on the steamed mirror—"Have a great day," "I love you," "Miss you"—generic but heartfelt missives that newlyweds all over Korea would leave each other in text messages and Post-it notes. Sorry for what, he wondered. Ji Young was still alive, sleeping in their bed. Hye Jin was up and ready for school, eating toast and jam the housekeeper had prepared. Ben had his rice and fermented bean soup and tried to coax Hye Jin, eight now, to sample some, but she refused, already preferring Western food, much to Ben's chagrin. He was relieved Hye Jin would not be as beautiful as her mother. There was a coarseness to her features that did not make her ugly but also not exceptionally pretty. He kissed Ji Young, still in bed, goodbye, dropped Hye Jin off at school, and then went to his office.

A few hours later when Ben was coming out of a meeting, his sister grabbed his arm and pulled him into her office. She was usually quite blunt, and in fact tact was one of the few skills Ben was better at. But this time she looked at him with penetrating stark eyes, and he could tell she was deciding how to tell him whatever it was. Finally, she exhaled a noisy puff of air and silently brought him around to her computer screen. She quickly typed something in the search engine and when she hit return, the screen filled with images of Ji Young, naked, straddling her manager Mr. Choi, lying underneath Mr. Choi, and resting on all fours while he penetrated her. Whenever her face was visible her eyes were closed. He could tell from her hairstyle, no bangs, almost elbow length, that the photos were from before he'd moved back to Korea. He could guess what happened; it was not a new story. Managers traded roles for sex and kept evidence of the encounters as a way to bribe the women as they became more famous. He retrieved his cell phone in his suit pocket and called Ji Young's cell, which was turned off, and then the housekeeper's, who also didn't answer. His own phone was lighting up with texts and unanswered calls from no one he recognized, but none were from Ji Young. He ran down the stairs of the building, to avoid any kind of notice in the elevator, and caught the first cab that stopped for him.

He felt as if he were in a movie, with the cab moving so slowly through thick traffic that he finally thrust a bunch of bills at the driver, jumped out, and started running down the street. It was April and yellow dust from China and Mongolia filled the air. The sun hadn't appeared in weeks, it seemed. He ran through the haze that clouded his vision toward their apartment building, weaving through crowds wearing white masks. When he got to the apartment, his suit was powdered with gold, as if he were wearing armor. He called Ji Young's name. He called the housekeeper. Then he saw the sliding door to the balcony cracked open and the dusty floor. He padded to the balcony door and opened it to a sunless sky. And then, as he stepped onto the balcony, Ji Young fell past him to the street below, like an angel kicked out of heaven, like a large doll dropped from inattentive hands, like someone trying to fly. She'd jumped from the roof of their building, since the balconies were built to prevent accidental and planned deaths. She'd at least spared him the memory and bad energy of jumping from their house. It was if she'd waited for him to arrive, to watch her fall, to witness her final act. It was some strange surreal moment, him witnessing his wife's suicide. He looked down from their fourteenth-story window and saw her body splayed on the top of a parked car.

She'd left a note for Ben. She'd started having sex with her manager, Mr. Choi, when Ben was in the States. Like many of the women actors and singers, she'd felt she had to. Since then Choi had been blackmailing her, but after her friends' suicides, she'd grown so tired of his manipulation she'd stopped paying him. She wasn't sure if he'd really release the photos of their affair from more than ten years ago, but he did, and now they were all ruined. She could not face her daughter, his parents, him. She apologized for the shame she'd brought on his family.

To escape some of the media frenzy, he and his family agreed that he and Hye Jin would spend the rest of the summer at the family's condominium on Jeju Island. They hadn't used it much since his grandmother, who'd lived there after selling her farm, died a few years earlier. He decided that they would take a ferry from Incheon to Jeju instead of flying, which was what they usually did. He wanted to do something that was different, an adventure, something out of their routine, something that might distract them.

The ferry was enormous and lumbering, packed with more people than Ben thought should be allowed, but no one seemed to be bothered. The rooms below were wide open and people rushed to claim their space for resting or sleeping, their blankets or *yos* spread out next to strangers until the rooms were filled with bodies claiming every extra space. Hye Jin asked him if the ferry was safe, if it could hold so many people and the cargo underneath, and Ben reassured her that, yes, the ferry was safe, that there had never been an accident, and anyway, there were lifeboats and preservers, but they wouldn't need them because the ferry was large and sturdy and reliable. He felt hypocritical telling her that because her mother had just killed herself, which meant that nothing was reliable or guaranteed in this life. They ate tuna and ramen on the deck, watched old men play *paduk*, smoke, drink *soju*, and eat dried squid. Korean *agashis* were as foreign to Ben as traditional men from any other culture. If the ferry drifted into the middle of the sea, if it lost its way, had nowhere to dock, Ben would have not been surprised. More than ever, he felt adrift and burdened at the same time.

For the first few weeks in Jeju, Ben and Hye Jin existed anonymously, ignored and unknown. The islanders were not that friendly to the mainlanders, for reasons Ben could understand. Korea had not treated them well—it had promised them many things it had not delivered, it had stamped out rebellions, allowed massacres to happen under the pretext of quashing communism. The islanders were poor and isolated. Tourism had mostly benefitted the hotel chains and wealthy investors from the mainland. But now the islanders' standoffishness was good, for they left Ben and Hye Jin alone to wander the island, to eat sushi and grilled pork in restaurants, to visit cheesy tourist sites around the island in the car Ben had rented for the summer. But after a few weeks, Ben saw the isolation was getting to Hye Jin. She cried for her mother; she missed their apartment in Seoul, her friends, her grandparents. She wanted to know why her mother had died, why she had left her. Ben tried to explain that Ji Young had not left Hye Jin, but that she'd been very sad about things that had nothing to do with Hye Jin. He didn't tell her they couldn't return to those things she missed because they would never be the same. That her friends would abandon her; Hye Jin would be an outcast—a *wangda*—mercilessly teased. That at this very moment their apartment was being sold and when they returned they would live somewhere else, a place that held no trace of her mother. That her loneliness on the island would not disappear, not ever. He despaired because he could not tell her those things, but he knew she would find out soon enough.

When they returned to Seoul in September, Ben was cautiously optimistic. They lived in a different apartment complex and the Ji Young sex-suicide scandal was no longer of major interest. He hoped Hye Jin could attend her new school and her new friends would not punish her or say too much. But then another actress hung herself and then a model did, both due to depression, and celebrity suicides was the top trending topic on the Internet by the fall of 2009. It was his mother who told him she did not think it would be good for Hye Jin to stay in Korea, and she suggested they live abroad for a few years until things cooled off. There were offices he could go to in Rio, Shanghai, or Mexico City, but the family agreed that it would be best for him, Hye Jin, and the company if he oversaw the new office being developed to capitalize on the new German car plant in Chattanooga. They'd liked the area when they'd visited Ben for his college graduation. His parents believed Chattanooga was in the middle of nowhere, which was a good place for Hye Jin to be, they decided. They pulled Hye Jin out of school and he and Hye Jin returned to Jeju until the family could prepare for their departure.

They'd arrived just a few weeks ago. Of course he'd thought of Shannon and had planned to contact her once they'd settled in, but then he saw the obituary and decided to go to the funeral. And that was where he saw her, rushed and puffy-faced emerging from the bathroom. He was surprised how comforted he was by the sight of her in her loose black dress and scraped-back hair, of her sharp brown eyes that recognized him immediately. But it was when she reached out so easily and fingered the fabric of his suit that he knew.

Here they were again, but this time united by grief.

2010

It's as if I am seeing for the first time in my life these fir trees, these maples and birch trees, and everything looks at me with curiosity and waits. What beautiful trees, and, in reality, what a beautiful life they must have.

Three Sisters, Act IV

When we are born, we cry that we are come
To this great stage of fools.

King Lear, Act IV, Scene 6

SHANNON

Soon after the funeral, Shannon knew she should try to track down Maria. But first there was the business of her first trimester, the fatigue, and the nausea. Then there was the much more enjoyable second trimester, learning she was carrying a girl, whom they'd agreed to name Jodie. Figuring out how to be a mother. There were Jeremy and David, of course, the endless discussions of how they were going to make this threesome parenting work. There was her job at *Jail Break*, of rising in the dark and driving around to distribution centers in Chattanooga. There was her blossoming friendship with Ben, the real one, not the fantasy from college, and that was enough for now. There was her sadness and the tediousness of dissembling her father's life, of packing his clothes off and sending them to the various charities that would take them. Stacks of shirts unworn, presents from all of them through the years, the pins still in them. Why had they given him so many shirts? Checked, and flannel, crisp no-iron Oxfords. Had they not known how many shirts he owned? Jeans and sweatpants and chinos folded in dresser drawers, now to be stacked in boxes. The underwear, plain cotton boxers, to be thrown away. His bathroom had for so long held only the essentials a single older man would need: an electric toothbrush, floss, toothpaste, deodorant, aftershave, Pepto-Bismol. When he got sick his sink and shelves became cluttered with the needs of the dying: rows of prescription pills, salves, Depends, acid reflux medicine, stool softeners, foot cream for his peeled and reddened feet, eye drops. They threw it all out.

In the cluttered drawers of her father's large desk, Shannon stumbled upon the notebook their father had shown them at his fifty-fifth birthday party, which included a detailed accounting of his expenses over the years. Tucked in the back of the notebook was a smaller book, which Shannon didn't remember seeing before. It was a ledger of descriptions and payments, beginning with the last year their mother was alive. In the first column was the date, in the second was a description such as "Woman, freckles," or "Woman, large lobes," and in the third was a sum. There was one name, written in block letters, appearing with increasing frequency until after a few years it was the only entry in the second column: Maria. So it went until Paige was starting college, and Maria's name also disappeared and the ledger stopped.

Had her father married a prostitute? Worse, was he seeing prostitutes when their mother was dying? And why would he ask this mystery woman Maria, his secret wife, to sell their family home?

One day, seven months pregnant, Shannon ate a lamb sandwich and decided it was time to talk to Maria. She wanted Jodie to be born without secrets. Even though it wasn't much to go on, she searched "Maria" and "Dalton" on the Internet. Eventually she found a slick website based in Dalton offering cleaning services to houses and companies. Maria's photo was on the "about" page; it was the same woman Shannon had seen at the funeral. She wrote Maria through the website's contact email, and surprisingly, Maria agreed to meet her for lunch the next week. When she wasn't working or thinking about Ben or her sisters or Jeremy and David and what she was going to do with her life, Shannon thought of this meeting. She was ready for answers.

But before lunch was her regular dentist appointment, which she'd been unable to reschedule, and she was determined to have it before Jodie was born. As she'd adjusted herself in the dental chair, the hygienist walked in, introducing herself as Cheryl.

"I'm replacing Ellen. I'm just letting you know that we do things a bit differently from her. Not that one way is better than another."

Cheryl fastened the bib around Shannon's neck and then asked her to open her mouth.

"I reckon you're about seven months along, am I right?" She probed Shannon's mouth with her metal instrument.

Shannon nodded.

"Margie up front thought you were eight, but I said no, that you were just carrying big was all."

Despite her father's death, Shannon was the happiest she'd been since college. Maybe happiness wasn't the right word, she thought. Well-being, at-oneness, groundedness. Doors were starting to close, loss would only continue, but she had a grand solace and comfort in friends and family that might have been denied her otherwise. She knew that no matter what happened to her, there would be people in the world who would guide Jodie and protect her from the harshest of storms. When she had wanted to be a world-famous journalist, she'd not wanted to have children because she felt she could not have done both well or fairly. She did not want to be the person who was always saying goodbye. She did not want to give up time with her imaginary children or, worse, somehow put them in danger, or leave them motherless because of her job. But now that door had closed, and the reasons for not having a child were no longer there. Watching her father die had reminded her how much she loved her sisters, Dez and Aimee, and Jeremy. How she was coming to love David. Over those months they'd all gotten closer, and Jeremy had refused to leave her side for a week after her father had died. And there was the gift of Ben and Hye Jin in her life here in Chattanooga, at least for a while.

She'd had to give up her fantasy of him being the one. She knew that if they'd tried to stay together back then it wouldn't have worked out. And now, well, Ben was grieving and had a daughter, and she was pregnant with another man's child, and neither seemed to have any space to feel anything close to what they'd felt a decade ago. But she could still talk to him in a way she could with few people, and she hoped she'd become that way to him. Friends, the way they'd started.

Now in the dentist's chair she could feel the baby pressing into her bladder, but she'd take that pregnancy inconvenience for the absence of blood, headaches, and cramping. She did not mind her ballooning stomach or swelling feet or sleeping on her back. She felt full and content and once Jodie started kicking, not so alone. Her sisters were happy for her, sort of, and now that Paige had stopped drinking, no AA or anything like that, just, she said, she wanted to take a break from all that for a while, Shannon would go over to their childhood home where Paige was staying a few evenings a week and they would spend quiet evenings together in front of the fire, sometimes talking about the past, sometimes not. Shannon could smell the smoke on Paige's clothes sometimes when she came back in from smoking on the back porch, her butts buried in the sand of an old paint bucket. Even though she rarely watched TV on her own, Paige would watch documentaries with Shannon, who was particularly interested in the ones that showed how the government had screwed up and allowed the financial crisis to happen. Shannon worried about the world she was bringing Jodie into, but not Jodie, who she knew was going to be one of the strong ones, someone who might even thrive in a world gone awry. With her sisters and Jeremy and David on her side, she believed they could handle anything.

Except that the sister she thought would be helping her the most through her pregnancy with unwanted parenting advice and baby accessories, Claire, had disappeared from everyone's lives.

Cheryl was just as chatty as Ellen had been and, like Ellen, kept the radio tuned to a Christian talk station. Cheryl was a master of the Southern art of the underhanded backstab, so subtle that one usually didn't even realize it until well after the conversation had ended. "You're so brave to go out without makeup; me, I've got to have my face on before I'm in public," or "I could never carry that off, but it suits you," or "I wish I could be as relaxed as you are about housework." What was it about hygienists that made them so chatty, Shannon thought, when their patients, mouths full of cotton or water or grit or utensils, were not in the best position to talk? And that Christian talk show, fundamentalist stuff, was extra torture. Shannon just hoped nothing about gays and hell and reconverting them back to heterosexuality or abortions are murder or a hundred other things would come on while she was in the chair. The tiny outdated TV in the waiting room was tuned to a conservative Christian station, and issues of *Guideposts* were scattered among *People* and *Good Housekeeping*. Did people still read *People* magazine, Shannon wondered, as Cheryl scraped the pre-pregnancy coffee stains from her bottom teeth. Why would they read it when there were so many better gossip sites online, as Shannon, a closet online gossip reader, well knew. The stories of the faraway and unreachable pseudo-stars interested her the same way the figures in *Jail Break* did, the same way that people she'd interviewed had when she'd been a journalist. The difference was that the famous had money; money to look good, to hire lawyers to get them out of trouble, money to nip and tuck and suction off the signs of abuse, whether drug, alcohol, or physical. Aside from that, the stories of addiction, shoplifting, and prostitution in *Jail Break* and the gossip websites were remarkably the same. Especially the drugs. Only rich people pretend that money doesn't matter, Shannon thought, just as they pretend that race and gender and who you know don't either. She wondered if the dental practice was funneling some of its profits into causes she did not support, the anti-causes reframed as "pro"— pro-life, pro-family, pro-America, etc. She was not one to keep up with that stuff about what to boycott and when. Paige refused to shop at Walmart, for example, but Shannon believed all stores and places were corrupt, and some just hid their corruption better. Besides, Walmart was where the poor people shopped, and Shannon wondered if the real reason people boycotted Walmart was to have an excuse to avoid them. When you criticize the people who shop at Walmart, you criticize the poor, Shannon thought self-righteously.

The only place she couldn't bring herself to go in Chattanooga was the Yellow Deli, a religious "organization" that ran a popular restaurant near the UTC campus. The workers, all part of a religious sect called the Twelve Tribes, worked for free as part of their communal duties. The women wore ankle-length drab-colored skirts and kept their long mud-colored hair in braids while the men sported long beards and billowy shirts. The Twelve Tribes had been run out of Chattanooga in the 1980s on child abuse charges, but they'd returned a few years ago and built a soothing restaurant with fresh iced tea, coffee, baked bread, and sandwiches. The sliced lamb sandwich, with yogurt sauce and lettuce and tomato, had achieved its own cult status—Jeremy brought them home regularly. Shannon usually left the room when he started eating them, but now pregnant, she felt compelled to linger. A week ago he'd come home with one. David, who had gotten a job at Chattasys doing systems organizational something or other, had been working late. Jeremy sat at the kitchen table and folded down the waxed paper on the sandwich with a certain amount of relish. He waved the sandwich, releasing its aroma, before he took his first bite.

"They're against miscegenation," Shannon had said.

"Miscegenation? Really? Who even uses that word? Anyway, I don't care if they're devil worshippers."

"Homosexuality!"

Jeremy bit again into the sandwich, allowing the white dressing to seep through to the waxed wrapping. "If I boycotted every place or person against the gays and interracial marriage, I'd be homeless and hungry. Hell, even half the homeless shelters wouldn't take me on account of their beliefs." He chewed meaningfully, swallowed, and took another bite. Another shiny dollop of grease and dressing glopped onto the paper. "You're just upset that they're too upfront with their backassedness," he said. "It's not the proper Southern way."

Shannon sniffed, grabbed for a tissue. She didn't want Jeremy to know that the sandwich, its grease and lambiness, smelled really,

really good, even if it was made by a cult. "If people want to be homophobic and racist and sexist, I'd rather they keep it to themselves, instead of using their close-mindedness as recruiting tools."

"Just admit you want it," he said, smiling. "I got half for Jodie. We'll pretend she's the one who wants it. You're pregnant; all is already forgiven."

She'd not been a big lamb eater before, but being pregnant had made her want all kinds of things she'd never known she'd desired. The past few weeks she'd been drawn to brown food. Jeremy handed her the half sandwich, the wrapping peeled and sopping. She closed her eyes and breathed in the sweet muskiness of the lamb.

"I hate you." She bit into the sandwich. "Damn, this is good."

"Your secret's safe with me." Jeremy wiped his mouth.

"I'm quitting these as soon as I'm out of my brown phase. And once she's born we will never talk of this again." And it was after she finished that sandwich, for reasons she still wasn't sure of, that she'd decided to find Maria.

Cheryl was reminding Shannon not to brush so hard, that her teeth were showing toothbrush stress. Shannon had never heard of such a thing. She told Shannon her own daughter was a junior in high school. "I'm just trying to keep her on track. So far she's got A's and B's and headed to college. Praise be to God."

Shannon grunted.

"She's just doing too much, I say, cheerleading, and student government, and youth group, Facebook and Pin-ter-est, and all that other stuff. She's going steady too."

Going steady, what is this, the 1950s? she heard Jeremy snidely whisper in her head. "It's not easy," she said through a clenched jaw as Cheryl scraped a back tooth.

"Don't I know it." Cheryl hummed something sappy Shannon couldn't quite identify. A woman happy with her daughter. "Your husband must be excited."

"There's no husband," Shannon said before she could think about it.

"Well, bless your heart," Cheryl said. "You've got a tough road to hoe."

Her mouth was gritty and the scraping continued, worrying a spot in the back of her mouth. And still she could not stop herself. "Her father's gay."

"Dead?" Cheryl brought the suction cup to Shannon's mouth. "I'm so sorry, honey."

Shannon's teeth felt polished and gritty at the same time. When Cheryl pulled out the suction cup, Shannon said, "I said he was gay. Not dead. Homosexual."

Cheryl pulled a string of floss and wrapped it around her index fingers. "Well, God bless you. They say the Lord only gives us as much as we can bear."

So, was this all she could bear, a mother who died when she was young, a father dead before his time, a divorce, distribution manager of *Jail Break*, pregnant with her gay cousin's child? It apparently was not all she could bear, because there was also Maria, former prostitute and her father's long-term secret lover and wife. This very Maria she was supposed to meet right after this dentist appointment at some tapas place on the North Shore, where she was going to interrogate her about her relationship with her father. What else was there to bear?

And yet, her life was not as bad as it sounded. Jodie was going to be born into love. She'd have two wonderful fathers. Aunts and cousins. Shannon had been promoted to distribution manager of a wider area, which gave her more money and more flexibility. And Ben. Ben was back.

Her mouth still gritty and sore from the dentist, Shannon walked into the restaurant with its desert-colored tiles and thought of turning around and going home. Of pretending she knew nothing, that this Maria did not exist. But then she thought of Jeremy's mother and how she did that with Jeremy, pretending her gay son could not be gay, and she remembered her resolve that Jodie would not be born into a world of secrets and lies, and she was strengthened.

Maria was just as regal and foreign looking as when Shannon had seen her at the funeral. Shannon realized she'd assumed Maria was Hispanic, but now that she sat next to her, she saw that Maria could have been from many places. Her Southern accent was jarring, and it bothered Shannon that this jarred her. There was something racist about her unexamined assumptions about what kind of people could have a Southern accent.

Maria was probably a few years younger than her father, Shannon guessed, in her early sixties. Her face did not have the unlined waxy sheen of women who used Botox and fillers. She seemed to be comfortable with her wrinkles, which crinkled around her eyes and mouth, along with a few deeper grooves across her forehead. She'd been a smoker, Shannon guessed, for her upper lip had the vertical creases of one who had spent a lot of time pursing her lips around a cigarette, so that her red lipstick now bled slightly into those fine lines. Maria smelled like roses, lemon, and every now and then, when she raised her arm or touched her neck, like bleach. She wore sparkly earrings and rings with gems patterned in simple designs. Shannon couldn't tell if the gems were real or not; she'd not been educated in such things. Maria wore a deep purple low-cut dress with a green chiffon scarf that billowed with the occasional gusts of air conditioning in the restaurant.

"Honey, why didn't you tell me you were pregnant?" She drew the word *pregnant* out into three syllables. Maria held a large glass of white wine in front of her. There was already a slight lipstick imprint on the glass. Shannon ordered sweet tea, her nonalcoholic drink of choice, even though the doctor had told her to cut down on sugary drinks.

"I'm so sorry your Daddy's not alive to see his grandchild."

Shannon swallowed. Closed her eyes. How could she explain how complicated it was, that the reason she'd decided to have Jodie was because she knew her father was going to die?

"Me, too," she finally said. "I'm glad you met with me. I wasn't sure if you would."

Maria studied her. "It was so sad and overwhelming, the funeral. Seeing Ed's daughters the first time. Y'all looked so sad. I just figured it wasn't the time." Maria's canary-colored purse, the Coach label embossed on the side, was slightly open, revealing a soft pack of Virginia Slims. Not a former smoker. Shannon had never been a smoker or touched a drink since she'd gotten pregnant, but suddenly she wanted both desperately. She wanted to smoke and drink with Maria and listen to her tell her everything about her relationship with her father. Shannon was feeling expansive and full of love. She felt she understood Jesus and his admonition to turn the other cheek, to not cast the first stone, that first commandment to love, love, love, that was the most important one of all. And Lily Tomlin as well, who had said, "Forgiveness means giving up all hope for a better past." That shit was so deep it ached. But this place, all part of the progressive North Shore where, now that Shannon was looking around, Maria was the only non-Caucasian in the place, here was not the place for that kind of talk. She needed to be not-pregnant and to be smoking cigarettes and drinking vodka. Or tequila. That could work. But what if she did get Maria into a more intimate setting, and Maria told her everything? Could she bear it? Would she still be able to forgive her father? Perhaps it was best not to know, after all. Bury her father's secrets with him. But they were here now, and Maria was waiting for Shannon to ask a question.

"Why didn't you come see him? You were married, after all."

"That—getting married—was Ed's idea. He wanted to do it before he turned sixty-five, so if anything happened I could get his social security benefits. I never thought he'd really get sick."

"But you're getting his social security?"

Maria shrugged. "Seemed silly to let it go."

"And why did he put you in charge of selling our house?"

"That was a shock. He never discussed it with me, directly. But I've been ruminating on it and I have a theory."

"What's that?"

"Well, right before we got married he was reading a lot of Shakespeare. He was enjoying it, especially the comedies. Then he read *King Lear.* Said it spooked him. Said he didn't want his daughters fighting about his inheritance like that."

"But it was a play," Shannon said.

"That's what I told him. And then he started reading Chekhov. That was okay until he read *Three Sisters.* Seems they lost their fortune after their father died, too."

"That doesn't make sense. They were plays."

"I know that," she said. "Maybe his brain was already a bit off, who knows. I remember what he said once, although I didn't make much of it at the time, he said, 'I want to rewrite my daughters' endings.' Anyway, my guess is he wanted to sell the house so y'all wouldn't fight about what to do with it."

"Because of Shakespeare and Chekhov?"

"It's just a theory."

Shannon decided to be direct. "Did you love him?"

"At first, when he was just a client, no. I mean, none of us got crushes on those men, even the regulars. I was flattered when he quit seeing the other girls, and only requested me. My ego was happy, but my bank account was happier. And then later, when I got out of it and started my house-cleaning business, he still wanted to see me because he said there was no one else he wanted. He wanted to pay me still, just to keep things simple, but I said no. Just a dinner and a movie once a week was enough, and that's how it was until he got sick. He said he'd loved me for a long time, and sure, I came to love him, too. He was a gentle man, in all of its meanings. I mean, it's been, what, almost twenty-five years? You have to love someone to keep them in your life that long."

Shannon fingered her notepad sprouting out of her tote. She wanted to take it out and start writing everything down, but she didn't want to scare Maria either, as if she were a skittish horse, who might run away at the sign of any sudden movement.

"We were going to move to Puerto Rico, you know," Maria said.

Shannon shook her head. "I don't know why he never told us."

"Would you have been okay with your father dating and then marrying a former prostitute?"

Shannon shrugged. "We'll never know, will we?" She looked Maria in the eye. "He started this before Mom was even dead."

"He was depressed, overwhelmed. We were his coping mechanism."

"I just feel like I didn't really know him."

"Did he really know you?" Maria asked. "We all have different selves."

She did not ask Maria much more, and they chatted sociably about their current lives. Her cleaning business was successful. She'd started dating a younger man she'd met on an online dating service. She asked about Claire and Paige, as if she'd known the girls most of their lives, which Shannon guessed, she had.

"I guess you're Jodie's grandma, in a way," Shannon said.

"Honey, that's sweet of you. But I think it's best if we just go our ways. I'll arrange to put the house on the market next fall, just like he wanted, and then after it sells, I'll be out of your lives."

When they got up to leave, Maria reached out and patted Shannon's hand.

"Don't be angry with your father for not telling you about me. Or about the house."

"There's no point in being angry at a dead person."

"He needed something that was only his," Maria said. "We've all got something like that."

What was hers? For a long time it had been Ben, the imaginary one in her mind. Was it Jodie? But Jodie was not only hers. What was it?

When they left the restaurant, Maria walked down the street to her car, her hips swinging in a way Shannon's never could. She saw the woman reach into her purse and take out the pack of cigarettes.

The story of Maria—that was what was hers.

When she got home, Jeremy was sitting on the wicker chair on their front porch, drinking from a large clear glass with a lime in it. His pack of American Spirits rested on the balcony, a V of smoke opened into the sky. While she'd been expansive and forgiving of Maria's smoking, she was angry at Jeremy, as the father of her child.

"I thought you quit." She reached for the door. "For the baby," she added, although it did not need adding.

"Ages ago." He patted the faded yellow cushion beside him. "Please come and sit with me." His words were long and loose. The last time she saw him drunk was before she was pregnant.

She sat next to him on the old wicker chair, the strands broken, shooting up like runaway grass. She picked up the glass and put the rim to her lips before she remembered. Even six months not drinking still felt like forgetting. Some nights she'd dream she'd drunk two glasses of red wine but then suddenly remember she was pregnant. She'd awaken cupping the soft rise of her belly, scared, then grateful she had not yet betrayed her daughter.

"Missing David?" He'd left a few days ago to visit some friends who'd returned from Iraq and were now in DC.

"I just feel there's that part of his life I'll never understand." He took a long drag on his cigarette. "It's not that he doesn't try to tell me. It's just that I wasn't there."

"I feel the same way about Ben." And her father. She closed her eyes, rubbed the sides of her temple. A fire truck's siren wailed in the distance. They hardly noticed them anymore. "His life in Korea sounds like a dream. Not good or bad. Just a dream." She slipped off her shoes, comfortable and sturdy Clarks with their sad attempt at fashion, but she didn't care. She'd never be a Maria.

"Exactly," Jeremy said. "I just worry this baby, this—" he swept his hand expansively to the street around them, the semi-tidy gardens, the vegetables David had started trying to grow—"is just a consolation prize."

Shannon cupped her hands over her belly, as if to shield Jodie from Jeremy's words. "Don't say that."

Jeremy put his hand over her stomach, laced his fingers in between hers. "I'll take the consolation prize."

He reached for his drink. She ran her hand over his hair, thick with a slight wave, the type of hair people had loved to run their hands through since he'd been a boy.

"He'll be back soon enough," she said.

"God willing and the creek don't rise," Jeremy said. She couldn't tell if he was being sarcastic or not.

For the next week David was gone, Jeremy spent much of his time in his room on his computer. Shannon watched TV shows she'd recorded from earlier—there was so much good TV on now, she wondered how anyone got anything done anymore. *Friday Night Lights*. She wanted to be just like Tami Taylor, the coach's wife. *The Wire*, especially the fifth season, which was about the Baltimore newspaper world. *The Sopranos*. *Mad Men*. In the evenings she didn't see Ben, she watched her pre-recorded shows while eating tiny spoonfuls of ice cream until the pint was gone. Her fingers left sticky prints on the remote; her mouth was ringed with a white glaze. When she fast-forwarded through the commercials, the Smiths, Joy Division, and the Cure thumped through Jeremy's muffled door. Occasionally when the music stopped, she heard him typing frantically on the computer. An online conversation with someone, probably David. When she came home from work before him, she'd stare at his closed door, wanting to open it and see the world he was living in. But she saw one of his old tricks from high school he'd used to check if his mother had been in his room. He'd stuck a piece of tape on the top of door and the wall, and if the tape had come off the wall he knew someone had been in his room. She didn't open his door; instead in the afternoons she made lists of things she thought the baby needed.

They were moving into a larger place with three bedrooms after the baby was born. They were going to try and stay in Chattanooga for the first year or two, so that Shannon's sisters could help. But after that, they talked of moving somewhere else, where David and Jeremy could legally marry, where they would all be accepted as a family, and where Shannon could get a different kind of job and maybe meet a man who could accept them. Ben would be returning to Korea in another year or two. Even though she was increasingly having romantic feelings for him, she kept reminding herself there was no point going down that road again. Right now boxes of baby items, hand-me-downs, and still-tagged clothes purchased by David and Jeremy were stacked in a corner in her room. Plus, there was the baby shower, another event Shannon knew little about. She'd been to a few, mostly for friends from high school who still lived here. Each one was different: some expectant mothers had long complicated registries at multiple stores, others wanted nothing except books. At some showers she wore a pin affixed to her shirt, a new one collected each time another person said "baby." She often won the most pins, because baby just wasn't in her vocabulary, and her journalistic ear was attuned so that she'd hear the word "baby" before anyone else. And then, when she was close to winning, she'd purposely say the word—*baby*—and let someone else collect all her pins and the prize, a gift certificate to someplace she didn't want to go. Claire and Paige were supposedly planning the shower. She told them she didn't want any pins, no registry, but instead wanted things the baby would eventually need to remember a time before she was born—photos, songs, stories. When Paige asked for a list of people to invite, Shannon only gave them her two sisters, Jeremy, David, Ben, and a few girlfriends she still felt close enough to.

After their father died, Shannon would get together with her sisters for brunch. Paige was doing surprisingly well. She'd gotten a job at the downtown local bakery, rising as early as Shannon did, and then a few days a week she'd go to the Folk School, where she took banjo lessons. On Friday nights she'd go to the Mountain Opry. She made enough to pay the bills related to the upkeep of the house until it had to go on the market. She brought loaves of bread for Shannon and Claire when she met them on Sundays: kalamata olive, sourdough, dense multigrain, sweet raisin and cinnamon. She seemed to be in a good space, even if this space were temporary. In another year, Paige said, she'd be ready. She'd have a plan.

Claire was the one who seemed to be falling apart. She was all nerves and frizzed hair and wild eyes, a bit too large and open, her naturally pear-shaped body whittled away so that she was, for the first time ever, skinny. Shannon was reminded of when her own marriage had fallen apart and she'd cried for hours in her cabin in the small town until she could no longer bear being alone and moved back to Chattanooga. She was reminded of their mother during one of her spells, as they were called then, when she was wired and frantic, cleaning the house at two in the morning, singing at double speed, her laugh high-pitched, carrying throughout the house. At brunch Claire was unsettled, fingers moving in her lap, tracing the edges of her cell phone, feet tapping some unknown tune, looking as if she were about to collapse into a brittle bone heap, and yet she didn't. Her cheeks were hollowed out, her skin pale and clammy, but that thrumming beneath her skin, as if she were a conduit through which currents of electricity passed, made her sexy and slightly dangerous, in the way her hair fell from bangs growing out, like unruly grass or weeds uncut, something alive and deadly in those pieces of hair, nails, bones that poked out, begging to be noticed.

At these brunches, they talked about the kids, Shannon's pregnancy, something they remembered about their dad, or what Shannon should do about Ben, which they all agreed was nothing. But mostly they talked about Maria, their father's mystery wife. Shannon didn't tell them that she'd met Maria at the funeral and that later she'd discovered Maria had been a prostitute their father had started seeing even before their mother died. She liked that Maria was the one thing that was hers, something that brought her closer to Dad than them. Maybe she was protecting her sisters (or was it her father?) from the man he was.

After she finally met Maria for lunch, she had to tell someone. One night, the week David was in DC, she went to Ben's house on the excuse that she'd run out of ice cream.

"She's not really interested in being a grandmother," Shannon said. They were in the living room drinking barley tea. Hye Jin was in her room doing homework.

"Do you want her to be?"

"I don't know. I don't know her. Not really, I guess." Shannon stretched her legs out on Ben's lap. Had they become so comfortable they were more like brother and sister now, or was it mild flirtation? She wasn't sure, except she felt so pregnant she couldn't think about maneuvering her body into actual sex much at all, even though she had to admit that against all her good judgment, she wanted to. "It's just so strange that my father was in love with a prostitute."

"She was other things, too," Ben said.

"I'm sorry; you're right." Shannon was horrified. She'd not been thinking of Ji Young.

"Well, maybe she'll change her mind. Or you will," Ben said. He absently rubbed her swollen ankles. "You'll have to tell your sisters, you know."

"I know," Shannon said. But she didn't plan on doing it anytime soon.

By the end of the week, David returned as promised with presents for all of them, fussing over Shannon, apologizing for leaving her just when the pregnancy had gotten rough. David presented her with a tiny coffee maker with a morning timer that brewed decaf just for her. In the evenings, when she was coming home from seeing one of her sisters or Ben or having dinner with a friend, she'd find them laughing on the porch, arms around each other. They joined her in the evenings for TV or sometimes went out for dinner with friends or to some benefit or another that she had no interest in.

"How are Salim and his son?"

"He's worried, now that the troops are pulling out. Just the other night there were people on his roof with machine guns."

"Al Qaeda?"

"He called the police. Eventually they arrived and chased the men away. But that is his life now until his application for refugee status gets approved."

David talked of his friend Salim and his son Ali even moving to Chattanooga. Salim practiced English with Ali, who was now composing short emails to David. Vague, generic expressions one writes when learning a foreign language. *How are you? I am fine. I had a good breakfast this morning. I am studying hard at school. I miss you.*

And then a few weeks after David returned, Shannon came home from work one afternoon and saw a half-finished bottle of Jack Daniels. Jeremy was moaning in his bedroom, a bucket next to the bed.

"He's gone again," he said.

"Who?" But she knew.

He moaned again and closed his eyes.

She opened the closet door. The carry-on Samsonite David had used when he last went to DC was not there. "Where'd he go?" But Jeremy was already passed out.

She called David's cell, which was turned off, then Paige, and then Ben, but there was nothing to do until morning. She wasn't worried yet, just angry at David and Jeremy for falling apart on her just when she was about to have their baby. She'd been an idiot.

She had to get to work before Jeremy was up, but she left a message on his phone, and he agreed to wait for her at home after work. He had a less-than-demanding job at one of the large charities, a family thing, and he was able to use his time as he wanted. This time he was on the porch, drinking more of the Jack but not drunk, smoking, his face cracked with dried tears.

David's friend in Iraq, Salim, and his son, Ali, were dead. An IED. They were in a car and there it was. Targets or just in the wrong place, they didn't know. David had flown to DC to be with his friends who'd known Salim and were going to have a private memorial service. Jeremy had wanted to go with him, but David had refused.

"We'll never be his life," Jeremy said.

"He'll be back." Shannon was sitting next to Jeremy, holding his hand.

Jeremy sighed the way you do when you are tired of crying but aren't finished yet.

When David was there, the pills prescribed for Jeremy's anxiety stayed in the medicine cabinet, untouched. In that week after David left, Jeremy was okay even though David had not contacted them and Jeremy's calls went to voicemail. But when David had not returned after a week, the pills began to disappear, and then the bottle was removed from the cabinet and appeared at his bedside, so that Shannon could no longer keep track of his use. She tried talking to him, but he often wasn't home when she was, and then once or twice she awakened to Jeremy and another man's voice so clear she couldn't tell if it came from the computer or if someone was in his room.

On the predawn morning of her father's birthday, the first one he'd not been alive for, Shannon awakened to Jeremy clattering in the kitchen and then slamming the door to his bedroom. It was four in the morning and she had to be at work to distribute papers at 5:30, so she got up, peed, and then opened Jeremy's door without knocking. His bedside lamp was on, and he was lying in bed in his Calvin Klein briefs, pale and shivering, holding a glass of clear something—vodka she supposed, since a bottle of it was on his dresser. His shirt and jeans were crumpled on the floor, stained and smelling like cigarette smoke and spilled beer.

She sat on the bed. He did not acknowledge her. His eyes were half-closed. He was slurring a song. "I would go out tonight but I haven't got a stitch to wear."

"Jeremy," she said. He looked up at her then, astonished. "We are having a baby. This was y'all's idea, remember? So what the fuck is this?" She swept her hands across his bedside table so that the orange vial fell to the ground, the pills scattering around them. He reached out with a spidery hand but only grabbed air. He covered his face with his hands and began wailing. She'd never heard him cry like this, more guttural keening than tears. "Oh God, oh God, oh God."

"Why are you sabotaging all the good things in your life?" she said.

"David's missing." Jeremy sobbed even louder, bringing in full rasping breaths, as if he couldn't catch air.

"He's just not in contact. He'll probably be back today."

"He's disappeared. I've talked to his friends in DC. After the first night they never saw him again."

"Dead?" Shannon hated to say the words.

"Just gone." Jeremy shook his head, palmed the streaks on his pale face.

He took a film canister out of his pocket. "I found this in his dresser drawer."

She enclosed the canister in her fist. "Who takes real pictures anymore? And doesn't develop them?"

"He showed his old camera to me, when we got back together. He told me he was only a few pictures into the roll when he got a digital camera. And then he got the idea to only take a photo when he wanted to show something really important, to take his time to finish the film. Then when you got pregnant, he told me he wanted the last photo on the film to be of Jodie after she was born."

"But the roll's finished."

"Exactly. He's not coming back." He took the canister from her and put it on the dresser. Then he laid his head on her lap, hiccupping. She stroked his hair, smoothed the damp clumps from his forehead.

"Have you talked to his parents?"

"Nobody's heard from him."

"People are easy to find these days. We'll file a missing person's report, check his bank account." She stopped stroking him and gripped his shoulders.

"It doesn't matter. What matters is he doesn't want us to find him."

She felt her face warm and her eyes water. She took Jeremy's hand and placed it on her belly. "Do you feel her?" She rubbed Jeremy's hand in slow relaxing circles. In a rare instance of perfect timing, Jodie kicked, a flutter through Shannon's abdomen, echoing through Jeremy's hand to hers. Jeremy looked up at her and smiled briefly, wide and open, as he had when he and David were first together over a year ago. And then it was gone, and he was staring at her intently with bloodshot eyes.

"David so loves her." Jeremy removed his hand from Shannon's stomach, and it fell, curled inside itself beside him. He sat up and put his arm around her. "It's your dad's birthday." He drew her to him, and kissed her forehead, something he'd never done but her father had, and then her forehead burned. She pressed her lips together and inhaled.

"You remember."

"It's okay to miss people," he said, smoothing her hair, but it was more like he was talking to himself. "All those people who love you." He took her hand, and they sat together, quietly, until it was time for her to get up and go to work.

When she came home from work the house smelled of lemons and incense. The windows were open and the bright April sun beamed into the rooms. She ran to the bathroom as she always did, having stopped once on the way home to pee, and sat with what felt like a basketball on her stomach, heavy on her thighs. After she finished she called Jeremy's name. He was in the kitchen, clean-shaven, his hair still damp from a shower. He met her in the living room and handed her a glass with soda water, a lemon, and a sprig of fresh mint. He held his own glass, which looked the same as hers, and they clinked glasses. He showed her his bedroom with its made bed. The pills were gone. An old-fashioned suitcase, beat-up leather, no wheels, rested by the door. He sat on the bed. It was as if he'd never lived there.

"Paige is coming in about fifteen minutes to help you move back into your house. I'm checking into Horizons, and I'll feel better if you're there instead of here until I get out and David's back."

"Will you be back for the birth?"

He opened his closet door and reached for the top shelf, where he took down a stuffed dog, worn and faded. "Remember?"

"Boxer." There was a small zipper pouch under the dog's tail where Jeremy used to hide candy, and later pot and magazine photos of shirtless men.

Jeremy kissed the dog and then handed it to her. "This is for the baby shower."

She sat next to him, took his hand. They sat quietly as she tried to figure out what to say. "I'll help you look for David."

"I told you. He doesn't want us to find him. I want to be in good shape for Jodie."

"I'll drive you, then."

He handed her keys. "Use the car while I'm gone." He still still owned the convertible he'd received for high school graduation. He swore he'd never sell it.

The doorbell rang. He let go of Shannon and opened the door. Paige held a lopsided cake. "For Daddy's birthday."

After they each ate a thick slice of cake, they loaded Shannon and Jodie's stuff into Paige's car. Paige and Jeremy hugged and she drove back to their house on Missionary Ridge.

Shannon didn't believe he was really checking in, but when they arrived at Horizons, a treatment facility outside Chattanooga, the staff welcomed him by name. Jeremy's mother was supposed to meet them there before he checked in, but she hadn't arrived. The staff told Shannon she could visit after a week. They hugged and he kissed her fast on the lips, as they sometimes did. He was thin and pale, but still beautiful.

"Jodie's lucky to have you for a father," Shannon said. "David, too."

He disappeared into the treatment center. Shannon cried all the way to Missionary Ridge. By that evening Shannon had moved into her father's old room.

On the back porch, Shannon listened to Paige pick out a song on her banjo. They drank sweet tea and watched the first fireflies of the season.

"I feel like I'm moving backward," Shannon said.

Paige didn't answer. She hummed along with the song, something old and familiar. "Just seems that way."

"I can't do this without Jeremy and David."

Paige stopped playing. "They'll be here. And even if for some reason they aren't, we are. We just have to hope it takes a while to sell the house."

"I guess I should call Ben." But she didn't move. The fireflies were little lighthouses, ephemeral beacons in the distance. She was surprised she'd not thought to call him earlier, but she hated to burden him with one more thing.

That night, she didn't sleep well. She didn't feel alone, exactly—she rarely did now that Jodie was with her—but she felt like she had right before her father's MRI, when she'd tried to pretend nothing was wrong. She tried to convince herself otherwise, but she feared David would never return. She wasn't sure how the rest of their little family—her, Jeremy, Jodie—could cope with his absence. She decided to stop by the house the next morning, a Saturday, to pick up the little coffee machine David had bought. And then she'd have lunch with Ben and tell him the latest.

The sun was out again, the day after her father's birthday. Aimee's birthday. Was there a party? She couldn't remember. Day one of Jeremy's rehab. She'd never believed he was an alcoholic or an addict, merely that he self-medicated when he was in pain. Many times in his life, as when things were good with David, he didn't seem to need anything at all.

Their house was quiet and half empty. Shannon picked up the coffee maker, unplugged, scrubbed clean. The birds were chirping outside the living room window, busy building nests, and then the garbage truck was drowning them out, idling in the street as the workers dumped the bags of trash into its loud spinning tumbler. Jodie pressed against her kidney. Shannon walked to the bathroom, thankful there was still toilet paper left on the roll. She sat on the commode for a while and stared at the tub, which was so bright and white she guessed it must have been cleaned with bleach. She couldn't imagine Jeremy cleaning all this yesterday, by himself. Maybe he'd called a cleaning service like Maria's. He was not normally a neat person, although he'd been better after David moved in.

It was like he was saying goodbye. She flushed the commode and rinsed her hands under the cold water, not patient enough to let the water warm up. She walked past Jeremy's room, where the door was closed. The garbage truck was gone, but she could no longer hear the birds, either, and the moment then was of only silence. She knocked on the door and called his name. There was no answer, of course; he was in rehab, she reminded herself. Was he suicidal? The tape on the door had been ripped. She opened the door.

His room was the way he'd left it yesterday, emptied of clothes and personal items. And yet, she felt someone had been there. Probably his mother, cleaning things out. On his desk was a slip of paper in Jeremy's writing. *God Bless You All. I Am An Innocent Man.*

1906. The words on Ed Johnson's tombstone Jeremy had shown her many times. The black man Jeremy's great-great-great-grandfather, wearing his forty-year-old Confederate uniform, had helped shoot and hang from the Walnut Street Bridge. It was, she thought, like a suicide note.

Shannon called his rehab facility from her cell phone, but the receptionist reminded her that patients were to have no contact with the outside world the first week. Shannon drove to the facility and demanded to speak with someone higher up. She was worried, she told the receptionist, that Jeremy was suicidal. After a few minutes, a counselor came out to the front holding a box.

"You're Shannon Nash?"

Shannon stood, staring at the box.

"Jeremy checked out this morning." The woman handed the box to Shannon.

"He's alive."

The counselor nodded. "Probably at a bar, if you're lucky. That's usually the first place they go."

In his box was his iPod and a few T-shirts, a pair of jeans, underwear. There was no message for her.

For the next few days, Shannon tried everything she could think of. She kept her phone beside her at all times. His cell phone had been turned off, but she still left messages. She sent private messages through his dormant Facebook account. She finally accepted Dennis's Facebook friendship request, and then without delay wrote him a frantic email asking if he could help her. He was a senior reporter, now, certainly he could find something. To her surprise he wrote her back almost right away. He started with a concise paragraph, apologizing for his part in the divorce, hoped she was doing well. Did she have Jeremy's social security number? She did not, but she'd tried to find it. He'd make some calls, check around. And that was how she and Dennis became casual friends on Facebook.

She called Jeremy's mother, who claimed to not know anything, and who said she'd have to look around for his social security number. It could take a while. She talked to Ben, Paige, left a voicemail for the permanently unreachable Claire. She Googled. She filed a missing persons report—now there were two. She went to Alan Gold's, but none of the bartenders had seen him. Jeremy's mother finally gave her the social security number, saying she'd too been in contact with the police, but, in the end, he was a grown man. What could they do? Shannon gave Dennis the number, and he wrote back saying Jeremy had not used his credit cards or left any trace of where he'd gone or what had happened.

It was as if they'd both conspired to disappear all along. Like the police told her, like Jeremy said, it's hard to find people who don't want to be found.

And then, after a week had passed, she awoke in darkness, dreaming of his note.

She hadn't been to Ed Johnson's grave since the senior prom, but as she drove Jeremy's car down McCallie she remembered the drive with the roof down, with David and the girl—Julie—in the back. She remembered how good the cool air had felt against her rashy face and arms, how she was so ready to leave this town. She parked the car and sat for a moment in the dark. Technically, it was not safe for a pregnant lady to enter an almost abandoned cemetery in the middle of the night. But she'd not be able to sleep or eat or take care of this baby in her body until she'd gone to Ed Johnson's grave and made sure Jeremy wasn't there.

She used the tiny light on her key chain to light her way to Ed Johnson's half-neglected tombstone.

"Jeremy," she called in a whisper at first and then a louder voice. "You there? Please come out."

There was nothing. She lay on the ground to rest. A few hours later the stars ceded to the sun, and the birds began to chatter. It was time to wake up.

She got into her car and drove to Ben's. It was early; he'd not yet left for work. He and Hye Jin were eating bowls of cereal at the kitchen table. She waited in her muddy dress stuck with leaves, refusing to wash up, until they'd finished eating and Hye Jin left with a neighbor for school. And then, without saying anything, almost eight months pregnant, she went over to Ben, who was in the kitchen putting Hye Jin's bowl in the dishwasher, took his shoulders so he faced her, and kissed him. He pulled away, studying her.

"Back in college, you were right about two things," she said.
"First?"
"That in photos, so much is left out of the frame."
"Second?"
"That I would be surprised what I could recover from." She fingered the buttons on his shirt. "The thing is, I don't want to recover from you again."
"Are you sure?"
She nodded. "You?"
His hands slid up her waist and belly, the pressure firm and warm, until they cupped her swollen breasts. "Where?"
"Your bedroom. My car. Korea. Wherever you want," she said. "It's time."

PAIGE

She was becoming obsessed with him, or more accurately, his music. After she got off work at the bakery she would sometimes go to the Folk School to continue her banjo lessons, which she wasn't very good at, but that didn't matter so much, at least for now. She was enjoying learning a new instrument, of being a beginner, of starting over. She allowed herself to play the instrument for the joy of playing rather than to go anywhere with it. She wrote a few unfinished songs, but spent most of her time listening to the songs of those she loved, the ones that took her breath away, old and new, on her father's old record player or iPod. But Fridays at the Mountain Opry were what she'd come to live for. It was there she discovered what had surrounded her for her whole life, the families and people making music, born to it, playing because that's what you did, you made music and shared it with others. You played an instrument or danced or sang. The crowd did not look anachronistic as much as she looked like someone from the future visiting the present. She with her cropped hair, her tattoos, her nose and tongue rings. She was the interloper, the outsider. She didn't care. Occasionally she'd see people from her demographic, twenty-somethings with beards and black-framed glasses, clad in flannel shirts, skinny jeans, and boots. "Hipster-redneck," she called them. She looked like one of them, the hipster types, but she didn't feel like them. For the people her age, the Mountain Opry was a diversion, a sideshow, a warm-up before the real music began at the clubs downtown. Paige, though, felt like she belonged more with the old white-haired people who made up most of the audience. She'd get her dollar bag of popcorn and sit at the edge of one of the middle rows. As she fed bits of salt and fake butter into her mouth, she warmed up as the audience did with the house band, which played the first hour. By the end of the first hour, Paige would turn her attention to the area behind the open stage, where kids and cloggers sat near the musicians' entrance.

He wasn't there every Friday. Billy Wilson. He was a wiry man with gray hair cut in a mullet that tipped his collar. He wore flannel shirts and his hands shook when he wasn't playing. His voice was scratchy and plaintive, still as deep as it had been when he'd played years ago, people said, only slightly thinner. He played the guitar mostly, the fiddle sometimes, as if they were extensions of his hands, and Paige thought that was the reason why his hands were twitching—because they weren't attached to an instrument. He played songs sung by Hank Williams and Jimmie Rodgers and Bob Wills, but he sometimes played his own music, so similar to the greats that it took Paige a long time to figure out they were his own songs and not hidden gems from a long-lost era. She tried to find his music to listen to at home, but he did not have a website or a Wikipedia page or any songs to download from iTunes. She haunted the local used record shop and CD stores and still she couldn't find him, although she'd heard he was big for a while in the late sixties. She was determined to find a way to take his music home so she could listen to it every night without rushing through, giving his songs the attention she believed they deserved. She decided she would introduce herself to him one night after he played at the Opry. She would ask him for his songs.

She was nervous meeting him, and she wasn't sure why. She usually wasn't that way, shy with musicians. She'd met so many famous musicians and singers that after a while it no longer mattered. Hell, her own old band was famous now. They'd just been interviewed in *Spin*, and her name had appeared in the article when the reporter asked about their band's earlier incarnation. Her former bandmates, her former best friends, had been nice, vague, not implicating her in the way she'd fucked them over, the way her own irresponsibility and dramas had overwhelmed whatever music they were trying to make. She'd believed back then that because she could write songs and sing, they were the ones holding her back. She'd had the hubris to believe she was Bessie Smith. Now she saw she'd gotten what she'd deserved, to be kicked out. And now her old band, reincarnated as the Caves, was headlining instead of opening. They were as big as one could be for a while if they played their cards right.

But her old band and its sudden fame did not concern her. What did concern her was Billy and his music. Once Billy started singing he didn't stop; he instead moved from song to song without pause or explanation. She needed to learn whatever this man would teach her. She'd heard many great musicians before with a technical virtuosity that far exceeded his. She'd heard great singers sing with great passion. She herself had sung with great passion once. But this was something else, as if he were only playing for himself and God. But everyone said that about musicians. What was it, then? That when he started playing she wanted to lean in and listen to whatever he had to say. And whatever that was would allow her to feel something she'd never felt before. Because she could not find his music anywhere, she could only listen to it in her head, hum the tunes, sing a few words, make up the others. She did it at the bakery, even when other music was playing, a hum so low only she could hear it. At night she tried to re-create the songs on her guitar, just to touch him a bit more, to understand how he'd moved so simply, so unexpectedly from one chord to the next and yet how in the end it felt inevitable.

One Friday night in April, Paige was determined to finally meet him. After his set, he ambled behind the open stage, placed his guitar in its case, and walked out the rear exit. She rose from her seat and sidled backstage, where she followed him outside. When she first stepped out she could not find him in the darkness, as if he'd simply disappeared. But then she saw him not far from the door, smoking a cigarette, his guitar set down beside him. She moved close to him and tapped out a cigarette of her own. He smelled like cigarettes, like her, but more than that there was a slightly comforting, slightly curdled odor of the unwashed that clung to him. In the light, so close to him, she noticed his hair was grayer than she'd thought, a bit matted, as if he never bothered to run a comb through it. It wasn't greasy exactly, but had a dry clumpishness to it of someone who might not be concerned about grooming.

How did people meet and talk without cigarettes, she wondered? She'd met so many people outside bars and clubs and parties smoking, had the best conversations then, late at night or early morning when the nondrinkers and then the nonsmokers, without the perfect mix of stimulant and relaxant, had long ago called it an evening. As she saw it, it was only when the smokers were left that people were finally able to admit that the world and their lives were short and serious. It was if smokers were put in touch with their mortality in a way that nonsmokers were not—nonsmokers still believed they would live forever, and therefore did not have to be serious about life for a long time.

She smoked silently for a moment, treating Billy as if he were some skittish animal, allowing him to get used to her, so he wouldn't run away.

"Your set was amazing," she finally said. They were not the right words. She'd said them to many people and people had said them to her many times. And yet she meant them. She had been amazed.

"'Preciate it," he said.

An old truck came rattling up the road and pulled over near him. Billy tossed his cigarette butt on the ground and rubbed it with his boot.

"That's my ride," he said.

"Will you be here next week?" She had to see him again.

"I reckon," he said. He leaned to pick up the guitar case and hobbled to the truck. He was not much taller than Paige. He could have been fifty or seventy. He walked unsteadily, as if he were drunk or about to collapse. The driver, a man about Paige's age wearing a baseball cap, opened the passenger door and hoisted Billy in. He nodded once at her, said a few words to Billy, and drove away.

She waited for the next Friday, and to her relief, he appeared in what seemed to be the same flannel shirt as the week before, the battered guitar case by his side. He sat in a chair behind the stage, still and quiet.

When it was his turn, he introduced himself and launched into the same breathless, continuous playing as he had the weeks before, pausing for neither applause nor explanation. And again, she followed him out, and again she lit her cigarette and smoked silently beside him.

"You're just about the best person I've seen live," she said, and again she felt the words weren't right. For all he knew, she'd never seen anyone live before, except the range of folks stopping by the Mountain Opry.

"'Preciate it," he said. They smoked in silence. She waited for him to speak again. "I saw Bob Dylan play in the Village in the sixties. I reckon that was the best I seen."

"My daddy said George Jones was the best he saw."

"Did he? Every time I played with him he was drunk or passed out."

"Daddy must have caught him during one of his sober times."

She watched a slight smile creep up. "I did hear he had those from time to time," Billy said.

The old truck pulled up. Billy tossed out his cigarette.

"There's my son."

"See you next week?"

"I reckon."

The son didn't nod at her this time. He talked to his father a bit more, as if he were berating him, but in a loving, concerned way, as if he were protecting him from the world, from the likes of Paige. She wondered what Billy had that his son was worried she would take.

During the next week, she hummed the songs a little better, but they were never as good as when he sang them. She just wasn't able to go where he did and pull herself out again. In the past, whenever she'd gotten too close to the songs she started doing drugs. After her father had died and she'd used one of his fentanyl patches, she asked around and found out where she could get OxyContin, and that had been her plan to get through her father's death. But then Claire asked if she could watch the kids in the afternoon and Shannon was officially pregnant, and she got the job at the bakery. And then she found out her father had married a woman named Maria and they had to sell the house in year. She flushed the pills away as soon as she bought them, and hadn't touched a drink or anything except her cigarettes for the past nine months.

She'd hated this type of music as a child, but now nothing aggrieved her more than the knowledge that the music she'd ignored for so long was disappearing. She saw it in the thinning crowds at the Opry, the demographic endpoints of very old and the very young, forced to come because their grandparents made them. After these old people left, there would be no one to keep this thing going. So each Friday when she went, she reminded herself that one night this too, like everything else, would end.

She could accept that for herself, for her mother, her father. But for Billy Wilson? People should hear his music. She wanted to one day sit Aimee and Dez down and play it to them, tell them about those nights at the Opry. She wanted to live in a world where his music still existed even after he was gone. She wanted his music to last for as long as the world did.

Which was why when she was getting nowhere with her backstage smoking sessions with Billy, she secretly recorded him on her iPhone one night at the Opry. She usually sat in the back, but this time she took a seat up close, and when he started to play, she started recording. She got about six of his songs. At night, with her headphones on she'd listen to him, his voice far away and echoing and she'd imprint the songs in her mind so that she could recall or play them herself at will.

She might not have taken her secret recording any further except that one day she saw the Caves were playing in Atlanta. They were big now, big enough to sleep in nice hotels and to have a real tour bus. What she'd wanted once upon a time. Now they were just what the country wanted, or at least a certain part of the country; they were what her demographic wanted, a sound familiar yet different enough, with electronic keyboards and synthesizers so you could dance with them if you wanted yet tortured enough that they were still deep. Becky/Becca had transformed. She was no longer the shapeless almost red-haired drummer, but now a chanteuse in clingy vintage dresses, hair dyed a deep intentional red, her eyes frightfully blue under the lights, sexier and more charming than Paige had ever been.

Paige bought a ticket for the show and drove to Atlanta and watched her former best friends and her former girlfriend play on a stage larger than she'd ever been on. While the band played and Becky/Becca seduced the audience (when did she learn that, Paige thought, and then she thought, from me, she learned that from me) in a way that looked effortless but Paige knew was so much work, she thought of Billy at the Opry, stripped down to nothing but a ragged voice and beaten-up guitar.

She hoped that after the show she could talk to them. Probably they'd assume her wanting to see them was about her wanting something from them, closure, forgiveness, money, a second chance. But that was not why she'd come. It wasn't about her or them, it was about this guy, better than all of them. It was like when they'd listened to Big Star together and wondered how they'd done it. So much had changed, but she remembered when they lived in Fort Wood, and these people, her old bandmates, would fall in love with his music as she had, and they'd want more people to listen to him, to have their worlds transformed.

After the concert she waited in the bathroom until it emptied out. She splashed her face with water. Her hair was growing out unevenly and her bangs were jagged from her impatient self-hair trim. Her bare face was pale, but her skin and eyes were clear. Outside, the venue was dark and almost empty before she made her way to their tour bus, not at all like their old minivan with its door swung open, the carpet worn to the rusted bottom. This bus was large and hummed in the night, like a tiny village that provided warmth and food and comfort to those who lived there. Security guarded the perimeters. Trespassing was not allowed. Paige waved helplessly at the lit windows, but the bus was too far away, and no one inside was looking out. The guard stopped her as she approached the bus.

"Tell Becky that Paige is here. I used to play with them. We started the band together in Chattanooga."

"Sure you did," the guard said.

"I have something to give her."

"I bet you do," the guard said. "If you're such good friends with them, why aren't you on that bus right now? Why don't you call her? Or send her a Facebook message."

Because when they'd first kicked her out and she'd been drunk and high, she'd left long angry messages on their phones and Facebook pages. She'd emailed rambling explanations and defenses. She'd accused them of many things. So they cut her off, blocked her email, phone number, Facebook. Then her father was dying and she left and they became famous.

And then she saw her walking across the parking lot, red hair and mini-dress. "Becky!"

The woman did not turn or acknowledge Paige. Maybe it wasn't even Becky. Maybe this person was someone's new girlfriend or part of the staff on the tour.

"It's Paige!"

The woman stopped and turned. They stared at each other, across that parking lot, and then Becky started walking toward her.

With each step closer, in her baby doll dress and lean limbs and combat boots and red lipstick, she looked less and less like the Becky playing drums in the basement so long ago and more like someone Paige might see in a music magazine. But when Becca got a few feet away, with the makeup sweated off, her crazy red hair about to spring, she looked more like Becky, her old love, again.

The security guard approached. Becky did not wave him away.

"What?" she said, already weary. Even though it was dark, Paige could feel Becky staring at her. God, she wanted to hug that girl.

Paige patted the satchel slung over her shoulder. "There's someone I want you to listen to."

"You sound okay." By *okay*, Paige knew Becky meant *sober*.

"I am."

"I heard about your dad. I'm sorry. He was a sweet man." Her accent had all but disappeared.

"Yeah, it sucks," Paige said. "But I have my family. I've been really getting into some of the older Americana stuff. This guy, he plays at the Opry."

"The Mountain Opry?" Becky laughed. "All those blue hairs and racists and God Bless America songs?"

"There's a lot of good music there, if you give it a chance," Paige said.

"Yeah, well, I've given people enough chances," Becky said.

There was more silence. Becky was waiting for her to apologize. "I'm happy you guys are doing so well and I'm sorry I fucked things up." It was hard for her to say, for her to string the words together, but there, she'd done it.

"All right."

"I appreciate it." Paige reached her hands out, stepped forward. Becky leaned in and allowed Paige to embrace her.

"So what's this you want to give me?"

Paige reached into her satchel. The CD was not there. "I must have left it in the bathroom."

Becky shook her head. "Still a fuckup I see." She turned. "Goodbye Paige."

"I am not a fuckup," Paige yelled at the disappearing figure.

She ran back into the arena and into the bathroom where the envelope rested next to the sink. She put the CD back in her satchel.

"I am not a fuckup," Paige said, walking back to her car in the emptying lot. *But I would have been if I'd given Becky the CD.* She was about to betray Billy just to impress Becky. Becky who would not have heard what she did. You really had to see him live, she thought. She was in love with his music, and therefore, in a way bigger than sex or any of that other stuff, with him. From that moment, she was his.

Billy did not come to the next two Opry's, and Paige wondered if she would ever see him again. She heard him singing in her head almost every day, and she hummed his songs while she set out pans of warm loaves at the bakery, strummed chords on the porch at night while Shannon, heavy with pregnancy, rested in the chair beside her before trundling off to sleep. That third Opry she finally saw him entering the back entrance, the same red-checked flannel shirt and battered guitar case. After his set she joined him outside to smoke.

"I thought you'd never come back," she said.

"Billy Junior is working nights, hard to get a ride," he said. He stroked the beaten guitar case leaning against the brick wall. "I got here, but I don't got no way to get back. Think you can give me a ride home?"

Home, she discovered later that evening, was in Sand Mountain, a rural area on the border of Georgia and Alabama, an area she'd grown up knowing as a place of extreme conservatism, ignorance, and the KKK. She couldn't see much in the night, although as she drove up the gravel driveway, she did hear Billy's dog barking from the darkened cabin. If she weren't with Billy, so old and frail and kindhearted, she would have been terrified to be in this area. She figured people around here might not like the way she looked with her short hair streaked purple, her nose and tongue rings, her not-so-hidden tattoo.

When they parked in front of his house, he surprised her by inviting her in. She realized then that he was a little bit lonely. As they walked toward the frantic barking, Billy told her he'd built the cabin himself with money he'd made when he was "almost famous" for five minutes. Even in the dark, she could feel the woods behind them. He told her Billy Junior lived with him off and on, as did his other children when they were between jobs or marriages. Billy opened the door, and a pit bull named "Dog" greeted Billy with a panting, unreserved happiness, and after Billy introduced him to Paige, Dog settled down.

"You want some coffee?" he asked her. "I got some I can reheat."

"Sure," she said. She would have said yes to whatever he offered, just so she could spend a bit more time with him.

He came back after a few minutes with two stained mugs. The coffee tasted more like dirty dishrags than brew, and she was sure it was one of the name brands her father used to drink before she took over the coffee buying in high school, Folgers or Maxwell House, coffee she hadn't had in years, since before she moved to Seattle. Even after she swallowed, her tongue burned with the bitter aftertaste of charred sludge sunk to the bottom of the pot.

Except for the large flat-screen TV dominating the living room, the house could have been from a time before Paige was born. Along with a stained coffeepot, the kitchen housed an old white refrigerator and splattered stove that must have been decades old. The rest of the house was spilling over with books stacked on shelves and chairs, its walls papered with yellow-taped posters of Dylan, the Stones, Hendrix, and Joplin. There was a stereo in the corner and surrounding it like a moat were towers of CDs whose spines Paige couldn't read. The mustard-colored couch and matching chair sprouted rusty springs unsuccessfully contained with old duct tape. After a few sips of her coffee, she excused herself to the bathroom, which Billy pointed to down a small, narrow hall. The bathroom reminded her of those in the bars she'd played when first starting out, filmed with mildew, stray hairs embedded in the soap like secret messages, the seat lid forever lifted, splattered with dribbles of urine and vomit. When she returned from the bathroom he was fiddling with the stereo, and then she heard Bob Dylan.

"You lived here long?" she asked.

"Only since my wife kicked me out. Seven, eight years ago."

"Where'd you learn to sing like you do?" she said.

"I reckon it's from all the Sacred Harp singing I did when I was growing up."

"What kind of singing was that?"

"You know, shape-note singing?" He looked disappointed.

"I guess not." She cast about the room, fixed her eyes on the piles of CDs, precarious, tottering. "Do you have any recordings of it?" She was imagining a singer with a harp, an angel on a cloud, strumming.

He shook his head. "It's not for recording." And that was all he said. He sat on the couch and lit a cigarette and she joined him. She hadn't been inside a house that allowed smoking since those parties back in Fort Wood. She tapped her ashes into a tuna can lined with a few mashed butts; Billy tapped his own ashes in his flannel shirt pocket.

She wanted to ask him more about the Sacred Harp singing but decided she would learn more about it before she embarrassed herself again. Instead they listened to Bob Dylan and talked about their favorite songs. He told her about when he'd lived in the Village in the sixties, when he thought he'd live there forever. That he chose his girlfriends by whether they liked Bob Dylan or not back then, since most didn't know who he was. "There was so much good music back then," he said. "You could walk into any place and hear good music."

"Dylan deserves the Nobel Prize," Billy said. "But I reckon it won't happen. People are too damn ignorant."

When she finally got up to drive home, Paige told him she could take him to the Opry next week if he needed a ride. He wrote his phone number on a scrap of paper and said she could call him and he'd let her know. He didn't have email or a cell phone, didn't see the need for those things, he said.

When she called him later that week, his other son, Vince, answered and said she could take him, but to come over early so he could meet her.

That next Friday when she arrived, Vince was there and Dog, too, barking from the entrance. Even in the daylight, the inside of the cabin was dark. Billy and Vince were watching basketball on the large flat-screen TV and smoking. Vince had a beer, and Billy was drinking from the same stained and chipped mug he'd used last week. Paige brought a six-pack of Yuengling and handed it to Vince.

"It's from Pennsylvania," Vince said, showing Billy a bottle.

"I don't reckon I ever had one of those," Billy said.

"Maybe when you come home you might want to try one."

"I might," Billy said.

Paige sat quietly while they watched the game. An hour before the Opry was to start, Paige said she thought they might get going. Billy stood. He picked up his guitar case, and they went to the door. He was wearing a different flannel shirt, blue-checked, that looked almost clean. He smelled like industrial soap and his hair was wiry from being washed. They got in the car and started the drive.

"I don't think Vince likes me," Paige said.

"It's nothing personal. He thinks you're after something," Billy said.

"If wanting to listen to you play your songs means I'm after something, then I guess he's right," Paige said.

"I'm not recording anything, if that's what you're after," he said.

"Why not?"

"Don't see the need," he said. He felt his front pocket for his cigarettes. "Mind if I smoke here?"

"Not at all."

And so it went through April and May with Paige picking up Billy and taking him home. Some nights he'd invite her in and they'd drink burned coffee or she'd maybe have one beer, Miller was what he usually had, and they'd listen to music and talk about it some, the way a line or two or a hook was perfect for that song. Other nights he'd leave her in her car, the engine idling, barely saying goodbye.

At home now, Shannon was exhausted and grieving, and Ben, her old boyfriend for a minute in college, was coming around more often. And Claire had moved out of her big home and into her old bedroom. Claire, distracted and fidgety, had sabotaged her own life for something elusive and illusory. Paige, the one who'd been the fuckup, was the only one who seemed to be getting her life together. She worked at the bakery and wrote music and played with her niece and nephew when she saw them. She cleaned the house and did the shopping. She tried to soothe Shannon's grief and help her prepare for Jodie's arrival as the due date was only weeks away. She left food for Claire in the fridge because otherwise she wouldn't eat. She did all of this while waiting for Friday night.

One Friday she drove Billy home and he invited her in, but this time, instead of putting in a CD, he took his guitar out and started playing. He told her to fetch her guitar from the car, and she played with him, but she wouldn't sing because she was afraid she'd ruin it. There were so many things she was afraid of with him; he was so skittish she was afraid he'd one day never want to see her again. After that on some Fridays they played music together in his house, sometimes his own songs but usually the old stuff, not just the guys but songs sung by Patsy Cline and Loretta Lynn and Kitty Wells and Dolly Parton and June Carter. She tried not to ask of him anything except what he would offer. Each Friday she'd arrive at his home and take him to the Opry and back home. That was what she could offer him.

One night, after they'd been playing in his living room, Billy stopped at the end of Johnny Cash's "Chattanooga City Limit Sign" and set his guitar in his lap. "You ready to see the source?"

"Nickajack," she said.

Billy drained his coffee, lukewarm and oily in an orange UT plastic cup. "Just need a refill for the road. You're driving."

Paige knew the legendary story of Johnny Cash's resurrection. Nickajack Cave, the site of Civil War battles and Native American bones and artifacts, a cave running all the way from Tennessee to Alabama. A cave people never emerged from again. How in 1967, Johnny Cash, humming with drugs and booze, entered the cave intending to walk until he got so lost he'd never be able to get out. He walked until his flashlight battery died out, and then he sat down in the dark, ready to die. Except instead of dying, he saw God, who told Cash it was not up to him to decide those things. Realizing he should not die there and then, he began crawling in the dark until he could stand, and then, when he smelled the gentle breeze before him, he knew he was close to the mouth. Outside June Carter and his mother were waiting for him, for they'd known he'd gone there even though he'd told no one of his plans. A year later the cave was half flooded and then closed off to everyone except the clouds of gray bats swirling like dervishes.

She drove in the darkness, the radio tuned to a classic country station, while Billy smoked and sipped from his plastic cup. Her truck was humid from the air gusting through the half-cranked window Billy blew smoke out of. They listened to the music with the attention and joy of musicians returning to old favorites, songs that continued to surprise and enlighten. They didn't want to talk over the music, but after a song, Billy would say, "that was a good one," or Paige would say, "that one still holds up," and that was all. After one song by a singer Paige didn't know well, she said, "I've never heard that one before, but it's so good, I don't know why." Billy laughed and then coughed, turning to the fogged window. "That's cause it's one of mine," he said. She knew Billy had probably worked with half the musicians they heard on the radio, but he never said anything about it, and she knew better than to ask. Instead she hummed the refrain to the song, *you can't never get nothing until you want something, and nothing's all you'll get,* so she could search for the song online when she got home.

When they arrived at the lake, Paige saw the cave in the distance, shrouded by bats, like gray ashes floating in the moonlit sky. Paige was about to park the truck on the side of the road when Billy instructed her to park in an old church lot off the main road. She followed him to a dilapidated shed on the edge of the church property. Inside, among the rusted gardening tools, was a small fishing boat.

"You gonna help me with this?" Billy tugged at the boat. Paige took the other end and they dragged it to the edge of the lake. She didn't ask him how he knew about the boat or if they were supposed to use it. None of that mattered really.

The night was humid but the water was dark, still, and cool. They hoisted their guitars into the boat and paddled toward the cave. She'd driven by before, of course, and had seen fishermen on boats skirting the wired-up mouth, but she'd never been so close. What would it have been like, to enter that cave expecting never to come out? Would she be as lucky as Johnny Cash, or would she remain in the dark, wrestling her demons, forever lost? Paige, who had run out of cigarettes at Billy's, took the one he offered her from his crumpled pack.

"Johnny always said I should make a record," Billy said. "George, too, a few years later. I told them no."

"Why?"

"I figured if I made a record it would sound nothing like the way I think it sounds when I'm playing. I figured it wouldn't be no matter in the scheme of things."

"That's depressing."

"It's reality." Billy took out his guitar. "The printing press. The automobile. The light bulb. Those are things that changed the world. My songs won't do that." He looked up at her. "Ready?" Paige snapped open her case and pulled her guitar out, rested it on her knee.

"I like to think music can change the world," she said.

"I reckon it can. Just not mine." He strummed a G-chord. "After I figured that out, I felt free. I can play whatever I want and it don't much matter except to the people hearing it."

"If it don't much matter either way, then why can't I record you?"

"A song is alive when we're playing it. After it's done, it's done. Besides, I want to die in obscurity."

Her hands shook as she strummed the chord. Was that what she was afraid of, dying in obscurity? He was right: sooner or later, everyone did. One day even earth would end. One day everything and everyone would be forgotten. Why did it matter one way or the other what her—or even her band's—brief spot on the world amounted to? Only moments like this mattered, and they would be secret and unknowable to everyone except her and Billy.

"Let's just play some music," he said.

"As long as we can play some of your songs," she said.

"All right. For every song of mine you've got to play one of yours."

Her songs were rough and unfinished, some of them fragments, thoughts, and rhythms and patterns that hadn't found their ending. But she knew enough not to say no.

At first they played some Johnny Cash, but after a half dozen of those they moved into their own songs: one of his, then one of hers. She was embarrassed playing after him; her songs felt trite, casual, burdened with effort compared to his, but she said nothing. She might as well have stripped off her clothes and stood before him under a harsh unflattering light, like a bug under a microscope. But he did not laugh or offer praise or criticism. He listened, and that was enough. They played under stars fading as the sun threatened to rise, the bats disappearing into the dark mouth of the cave. They played to the crickets and cicadas, to the earth's noises from places they could not see. They smoked his cigarettes and sipped from warm tall cans of beer she'd found in the back of her truck, and as the sun rose they wrote a song together, something she could never have written alone, a song that took her own longing and then pushed it back further to meet his, which stretched back even further to the people alive when he was little and the stories they told about those before them. She did not dare write anything down for fear that it would spook him, and he'd realize what he was doing and snap his guitar back in its case before they reached the final chord. Instead she committed the song to memory, as well as the way his tar-stained nails strummed the guitar. She watched the way the early sun bathed him in the faintest of pink. She had to remember as much as she could because she knew this moment would be what she would measure her happiness against for the rest of her life.

And then it was over and they paddled back to shore and dragged the boat back to the rundown shed and drove back to Billy's, the sun bright on the road ahead of them. They did not listen to music. Instead she silently hummed their song over and over, for she was afraid to sing it out loud. He'd not asked her, but she knew that she was not to record it or even play it for anyone else. She hoped she would remember what he wanted and not be tempted to betray him, that her desire to share, to tell the world that she'd done this with him, with Billy Wilson, would not overtake her commitment to keep their song to herself as he wanted.

"What's that tattoo on your shoulder?" Billy reached over and lightly touched the Miro painting, broken only by the spaghetti strap of her top. It was the only time she remembered him touching her.

"It's a painting by a guy named Miro."

"I've heard of him." He paused, then flicked his cigarette ash out the crack of the window. "Some girl talked you into it, I bet."

"You'd be betting right." And that was all they ever said about her sexuality.

When she pulled into his gravel driveway, he invited her in for coffee before she drove home. The sun was up, casting their world in a pale pink. They drank coffee and smoked cigarettes. He ashed his cigarette in his pocket while she tapped hers into the empty tuna can. She took her guitar out of her case, and they sang their song one last time.

They were on the last verse when the screen door slammed.

Vince placed his long hand on her guitar, so that her hand was trapped under his mid-strum. He was more of a shadow, a presence than anything she saw. "What the hell are you doing?"

She looked up at him. Her head ached from coffee and cigarettes and lack of sleep. "Singing a song we wrote."

"And then what? You'll record it and tell the world how you got Billy Wilson to write a song with you." Vince put his hand on Billy's shoulder.

Paige stood. She looked at Billy. "He can trust me." But was it true? Could she be trusted with this, his gift to her, for her and no one else?

"I'll walk you out," Vince said.

Outside she shielded her eyes with her hands. The insides of her eyelids felt scraped and scratchy. "I get it," she said as she unlocked the truck door. "Your daddy's music is like Sacred Harp singing. Don't worry, I won't mess with it."

Her hands shook as she started the truck. As she drove home she tried to remember his voice, how it sounded like that cave, like the bats beating their wings. As long as she could carry that song with her, could sing it to herself, she could believe that the world could change.

Thursday after she got home from the bakery, she discovered Billy had called and left a message on her cell phone, something he'd never done before.

"This is Billy Wilson," he said, as if his deep Southern voice, slow and syrupy, needed identification. "Don't be too mad about Vince. He's just looking out for me. Trying to do what's right. I told him you didn't mean no harm." There was a pause in the recording and Paige thought he'd hung up. Then she heard an exhale, and she guessed he was just taking a drag off his cigarette. "Some of your songs are all right. Recording's not for me, but that don't mean it ain't right for you." And then he hung up.

All right. The faintest praise she'd ever heard and yet it meant more than any other. For Billy to say some of her songs were all right meant that she wasn't wasting her time.

She called him to thank him and to see if he needed a ride to the Opry, but his phone rang with no response. She supposed he or Vince had unplugged it, as she knew they sometimes did.

Even though he'd not asked her to take him to the Opry, she decided to surprise him Friday late morning with a visit. If Vince were there she'd have to explain to him that she didn't mean Billy harm. She'd promise not to record their song or play it for anyone.

She'd write something out, sign it, and make it legal. He was right, she knew. Recording their song would only lead to all kinds of temptations she wouldn't be able to resist. Like Charlie in *Willie Wonka and the Chocolate Factory*, when he returned the Gobstopper because he knew if he kept it he'd betray Willie Wonka. By giving up her desire for him to be recognized and, by extension, for her to be recognized, she could be right with him.

She'd driven over after her shift at the bakery ended, with the idea she'd make coffee, fry some eggs and bacon if he had any in the fridge. He loved IHOP, told her breakfast was his favorite meal, that he could eat it any time of the day. In the passenger seat cheese biscuits from the bakery steamed through the folds of the white paper bag. She was relieved that Vince's truck was not in the driveway. She knew he usually slept at his girlfriend's house, checked on his dad closer to lunch time. He might show up while she was still here, but at least then she could give Billy breakfast.

Dog started barking as she neared the door. She yelled Billy's name and waited. Dog kept barking. She rattled the knob of the door, letting him know she was about to enter since he never locked it. She was afraid Dog might run to her and attack her without Billy around, but instead he stood in the hallway to the bedroom as if his legs were pinned to the floor and kept barking. She called Billy's name. In the kitchen, the coffee was cold and oily, last night's pot. The bathroom door was ajar, but he was not inside. Dog was still in the hallway, and when she neared him he turned, still barking toward the bedroom door, cracked open. Dog nuzzled into the room. She felt it then, the terribleness of what would come next. She didn't want to follow him, didn't want this moment to ever happen, because she'd never be able to take it back.

His face was shockingly still, his mouth slightly open, his skin already sinking toward the floor. She palmed her hand over his mouth, in the blasphemous hope that air might escape. He was wearing a stained T-shirt and boxers. His left hand was flung out; his right lay on his chest, as if he'd died playing guitar.

Next to his bed on the nightstand was an issue of *Rolling Stone* from the 1970s, folded back to an article on Bob Dylan. The clock radio buzzed the classic country radio station, barely discernible above the static. There was a window above the nightstand that looked out into the woods in the back of the house. She watched the trees, listened to birds chirping as if it were any other day. She opened the top drawer, not sure what she was seeking, but she was only half surprised that it was cluttered with vials of prescription opiates. How he, and Vince probably, made some money. She was still holding the white paper bag of biscuits. She opened the fold, and stuck her hand in, allowing her fingers, chilled for no real reason, to warm against the bread. She removed two of the biscuits and fed them to Dog, who ate them in one gulp.

The night Paige's father died, he could no longer ask her to end it for him. He'd eased in and out of consciousness. When she tried to get him to sit up and drink some water from the teacup, he told her, "I don't think I can anymore." She told him it was okay. She called her sisters and told them it would be soon, that she thought he would make it through the night, but that they should come in the morning. She could have waited. But instead she played George Jones and wheeled him out on the deck so that even though he couldn't see the stars he could hear the birds in the trees, the rabbits and squirrels in the woods below them. She dotted their temples and throat and wrists with Joy perfume. Hearing is the last to go. *I love you.* As she squeezed his scabbed and flaking hand, he opened his eyes one last time, and he seemed to be telling her, *now, now, now.* Then he shut them. He faded out again, his breathing shallow and difficult. She covered his face with a pillow and released him. She forgot so much, but this night she would remember. She would remember the way he looked before he closed his eyes for the last time, as if he'd been underwater and had struggled to get to the surface and didn't see much that he liked. She would remember the stars half-hidden by clouds. She would remember the scratching sound on the record player as the needle met the end of the track.

She remembered that now, as she looked at Billy. She also remembered finding her mother that morning when she was six, the way the color was already gone. She was sure she'd seen her mother's ghost rising, but now she supposed it was just the play of early morning light. He was the third person she'd loved that she'd been the first to see dead. As if she were some terrible angel whose purpose was to bear witness to the loss of the most important things in the world.

At least her father had not died alone.

She got on her knees so that she could breathe puffs of air on his sunken cheeks.

"Billy. I'm sorry I recorded your songs. I'm sorry I wanted to give them to Becky. It was wrong of me. I hope you'll forgive me."

If she could have, she would not have left his side until they'd taken the body away. But now was not the time for grieving. That would come soon enough, and when it did, it would never leave her. Now was the time for decisions. Better for Vince to find him, she thought, better for him to hide what he wants to hide, to save what he wants to save. Better for the child to find the dead parent, better for him to grieve directly, better for him to hold his father's frozen hands.

She took a bottle of Oxy and dropped it in the paper bag on top of the remaining biscuits. She walked out of the house without looking back.

She stopped and bought a six-pack of Miller tallboys at a service station, drove to Nickajack, and parked her truck in the church parking lot. Even though it was midday, the lot was still empty. It was harder, but not impossible, to drag the boat out and into the water by herself. Even when she got the boat in the water and her guitar in the boat, she waited for someone else to show up. No one did. She was alone.

Not quite a week ago, the two of them had been here playing their songs. Now she sat in the rusted boat with its slow, almost imperceptible leaks and played the song they'd written. She could play it a thousand times and never tire of it. She opened a beer, the first one she'd had since last week. It had been a long time since she'd craved a drink, and sipping a beer occasionally with Billy had not led her to want anything more than to share a moment with him. But now she craved the beer and the pills, which she fed into her mouth, calibrating the dosage she would need for the pain to disappear into a dark hole. She threw what remained in the bottle into the lake. She closed her eyes and waited.

As if she were already dead and watching the world from some quiet comfort of the sky, she saw herself swimming to the cave, ripping off the mesh wall, tearing down fences with her hands. There she submerged herself in the water, half wading, half swimming deeper and deeper, waiting to get lost, encountering all the forgotten ghosts, slaves, soldiers, Native Americans looking for people to tell their stories to. When she found them she would announce herself to them. Here I am: haunt me.

CLAIRE

When she was called into HR Monday morning, Claire was thinking that her period was three days late, but she couldn't be sure because her cell phone, which had her calendar on it, was missing. She was pretty sure she'd left it at Joseph's house Friday, but she wouldn't know until he stopped by her office, which he hadn't done yet. She was feeling the familiar warning signs that her period was about to begin, a bit of cramping, a craving for sweets, the bloat around her middle. And yet, for every day her period was late, she had to allow the possibility that she might be pregnant. So she willed her period to arrive (she imagined her finger being pricked, the drops of blood staining a creamy muslin cloth). She knew what pregnant felt like, nauseated and maternal, and this wasn't it. When she'd been pregnant with Aimee and Dez, she'd puked her morning sickness into the toilet bowl while she gently gathered her hair back so it wouldn't stick to her neck, and then she'd wiped her face with a warm thick cloth, as she'd done when her mother was sick from chemo. A mother to herself. Now she didn't feel like a mother to herself or to anyone. She felt full of love and life and also scraped and raw, but who and what was feeding her mind was not a child waiting to be born. Her body belonged to Joseph, and when she was not with him, her body became a useless deflated thing, crushed by desire and exhausted from hiding what it was to the world. It had been three days since she'd last seen him, and she felt bloated and husk-like at the same time.

She attributed the ache in her bones, the heaviness in her stomach, to withdrawal symptoms from not seeing Joseph. Her throat was scratchy and her legs tingled where he'd gripped her legs in his, his own legs phantom limbs cut from her. Usually they arranged these things through text messages, but since her phone was missing, she had no idea what he'd texted. She must have left it in his room, forgot to put it back in her purse in the dark. For a while, she'd had the cabin, and Joseph had met her in her old bedroom, and that had worked until Paige had discovered them. Then her father died and she found out about Maria, and that was when she told Jim she'd fallen in love with someone else and needed to move out to think about things and that was all she could do at this point. It was everything, and yet it wasn't enough. What was enough? She'd had enough, that had been her life, and she'd given it away for one small, deep thing. And the house she'd grown up in, the one she'd thought would always be hers, was to be sold by a woman named Maria her father had secretly married. That she'd hidden Joseph and her love for him the way their father had hidden Maria was what had finally made her decide to tell Jim the truth. She'd followed the rules for as long as she could remember because she thought she owed it to her parents, when she saw now she owed them nothing.

Still, standing in the elevator as it rode up to HR, willing her period to arrive, dreaming of Joseph, telling the truth to Jim, she believed the worst was over. That had been the hardest, watching him slump over on the table, hearing the low keening of someone who would never see the world or trust it in the same way again. (And what of it, Claire thought, he's come to that notion so much later than I have. He's been lucky to have believed in the world for so long.) When she told him of the affair, he'd squeezed his eyes shut, but only after she said, "I don't know if I love you anymore," did he break down. The one thing he'd always believed in, he no longer could, he had said. They'd agreed she'd move back in with Paige and still pay for the mortgage and bills until the housing market revived and Jim could get work. In that separation she'd tarnished her roles as mother, wife, dutiful daughter, pillar of the community, Lila's daughter. Since then, Jim had lost even more weight than she had, going on a hunger strike of sorts (but what was he denying himself, she wondered, was it the same thing she was?), his self-confidence in his own roles as breadwinner, father, husband, shattered.

Now Shannon had moved back into the house, and even though no one said anything, she knew she could no longer meet Joseph there. She was still trying to figure out what to do.

Friday she'd surprised Joseph at his aunt Alma's house in the Martin Luther King neighborhood where he lived. Alma had told everyone in the office she was taking a long weekend to visit some relatives in Knoxville. Claire had brought this up with Joseph. Perhaps they could go away, spend more than a few stolen hours together. He told her he couldn't, that he'd promised Aunt Alma he would stay and watch the house. They'd have to wait.

But Claire couldn't wait. She didn't see the point of waiting. She'd moved out of her house and into her childhood bedroom, leaving her husband and children, so she wouldn't have to wait. So the Saturday evening Joseph's aunt Alma was in Knoxville, Claire drove up and down the road in front of his house and looked for him. A single bright light shone from the second floor. The first floor was darkly curtained, and Claire could not tell what was behind it. She parked the car a block down and texted: *I'm here.* She turned on the radio to a station that played music from the sixties and seventies, music that was the soundtrack to a stranger's life. She sat on her hands so she would not text or call him again. She waited for a light to turn on or off, a Morse code to her call in distress. The house was in the family, like theirs, his Great-Aunt Alma, the youngest sister, the only surviving of the three who had grown up there and lived until their deaths. Claire knew that Joseph mowed the lawn and had painted the outside trim and fixed broken screens and commodes, but she saw that the house needed much more work. In a few months Joseph would move to Atlanta to start graduate school, and Alma would live alone in a house she could not care for, a house that might fall apart before she did.

He texted her: *Meet me at the front door in 5.*

She smiled at the phone but did not reply; there was no need to. Marvin Gaye was singing from the seventies about the sadness of wars and the future of the world's children. She wanted to worry about those things, but she could not, not now, for in four minutes and thirty seconds she would see Joseph. She stepped out of the car and walked across the street to an empty playground a few houses away from his. In the darkness, under a half moon and blinkering lamps, she sat on the plastic swing and clenched the chains holding it. She pumped toward the sky and counted to ten. Tomorrow there would be work and the pain she'd caused her family and her deep sadness she was just beginning to understand, but for now she was flying.

He answered the door before she even knocked, silently pulling her in, as if he were admitting her to a speakeasy or underground political meeting. He did not show her the house, even though she was curious—anything she could learn about him, the way he lived, had lived, she wanted to know. The first floor smelled like a strange perfume: the crisp top note of lemon furniture polish with a lingering scent of urine and dust. Dark, heavy curtains hid the windows on the first floor so that the rooms glowed an eerie orange from old-fashioned, dimly lit bulbs. She could see the living room, crowded with heavy wood furniture, draped in doilies and tablecloths, yellowed from age and dust. The sofa and matching chair shone under clear plastic wrap as if saving themselves for an event or time that would never come. Most of the wood floors, stained and darkened, were covered in big rugs, faded and worn.

She followed him up the creaking stairs to a room so austere it was hard to believe anyone lived there at all. Like a cell or a monastery, she couldn't help but think. A twin bed, corners tightly tucked, a dresser, and on the floor books, mostly library books, none new, stacked neatly against the wall. There was an aged photo of a man with slicked-back hair. Claire traced the silver frame.

"A relative?"

"Distant. He invented the straightening comb. He was a millionaire. He slashed his throat and killed himself when he thought the government was going to take his money."

"I didn't know that."

"My family's lived in Chattanooga longer than most of those—including yours—who live on a mountain."

"Why didn't you tell me?"

"You never asked."

"A black woman named Tammy grew up with my mother. When she was dying my mother said Tammy was her sister. I don't know if it's the truth."

He sat on the bed. "This whole thing has been about you, not me."

"Then why have you been with me?"

"I didn't have much choice."

She didn't dare ask him what he meant by that. She wanted him to say then that he loved her, but he did not. They sat on the bed and did not touch. The lights were off, shades drawn. It was the darkest room she'd been in with him.

"I want to go to Atlanta with you," she said.

"This is dangerous," he said.

"I'm ready." Did she mean it? Would she really move two hours away from her children to be with him? Jim would not allow her to take them with her. She swallowed. Her skin was hot, burning from the inside out. She wanted to fall on him, cover him with her own heaviness, and then submit to whatever he wanted to do, whatever knots and tricks he could come up with. Once, early on, she'd asked him to give her pain, and he'd responded by asking her: how much pain can you take? It was, she realized when he asked her, the one question in her life she wanted to find the answer to. Despite the handcuffs and blindfolds and ropes and candle wax and clothespins, the pain never went deep enough, past her father to her mother. "Do you hate me yet?" he'd asked, and she said quickly, easily: "No." How could she hate the one person who made her feel alive?

That night in his room at Alma's house, he surprised her. For the first time, they had regular straight-ahead sex, missionary position. In some ways it was the strangest thing they'd done, something that required nothing but the movement of their hips, his strong muscular arms next to her shoulders, her legs swung over his. Even though he wore a condom, he pulled out before he came, and then with his hand brought her to orgasm. She then did the same to him. They lay twisted together like a candy wrapper, the smell of them quickly filling the stuffy box-like room. Usually his skin disappeared when they were in the dark, but that night Claire pulled the shade up a crack so that the faint streetlights crept through and she could see his leg twisted around hers. Different shades of the same color, and she thought of that first day when he'd shook her hand and she'd seen her own skin as not white for the first time. She thought she could stay there forever, in that room, the sweat off their skin and their smells their only nourishment. If she did not leave this room, she would never need anything else.

She didn't notice her cell phone was missing until the next day when she wanted to text him. She didn't let that stop her: she typed messages to him in the air with her flying fingers, like a madwoman knitting with invisible needles.

Now going up in the elevator to HR, she tried to think of where they might meet next. Chattanooga was so small it was hard to find a place where they would never be seen. His aunt's house had been a one-time thing. She and Joseph had resorted a few times to renting a room by the hour at Lamar's, an old-school bar and hotel on Martin Luther King near Joseph's aunt's house. Late at night the bar, which was owned by a black family and still had its original velvet wallpaper, vinyl couches, and jukebox that only played blues and jazz, would fill with white people who wanted to feel like they were in what they thought was a black bar. But early in the evening, the bar was usually empty, and she and Joseph would meet there, and over one stiff drink, listen to Nina Simone and Charlie Parker and Bessie Smith, before retiring next door to the chlorine scented rooms. Even though the sheets smelled of bleach and they showered before and after, and now that she no longer was living with Jim and the kids and in that sense she was no longer lying to the important people, Claire felt for the first time that she was engaged in something cheap and tawdry.

She did not want to think of what would happen in a few months when Joseph moved to Atlanta. He had been giving her Chekhov to read. No more worldview-bending novels with big ideas. After she'd read some of the stories, he asked her for her thoughts as he always did, and she said, "It's so different from Baldwin," and he said, "Why? They both ask questions." She wondered if their fate would be the same as the couple in "The Lady with the Dog." She wondered how long could they go on like this. Their challenge was how to make it work indefinitely. She didn't think they could last that long hiding; this wasn't nineteenth-century Russia. She could get a divorce and they could marry and live in Atlanta where their relationship would not matter to anyone, with their pasts unknown and of little concern. Maybe she would have his child. What if she were pregnant with Joseph's child? A sudden irrational part of her wanted to be. The child would be a tangible thing. The child would be the end of secrets, hers and her mother's and her father's, her grandfather's, and the grandfather's before that. The child would be the beginning of truth.

They would be just another couple with no need to hide or feel shame.

But then what? Joseph still had his future, his own career, his own family, his own home. He'd first get his MBA and then he'd have to start at the bottom, working those long hours indefinitely, and who was she to bring more children into the world when she was neglecting her own? How could she have told him she'd go with him to Atlanta, live two hours away from her children? Certainly Jim would get custody. Her head ached. She was merely on a vacation away from her kids, that's what she told herself, and they'd live together again soon.

The truth was, though, she did not see them any less than she had before she'd moved out. She would still spend evenings with them after work four or five days a week. Aimee would answer the door. Jim would stay upstairs; she never saw him. Dez, as far as she could tell and from what Jim told her in his brief email updates to her, was adjusting well enough, being a nine-year-old boy who loved it when his mother was around, but occupied himself with the rest of the world when she wasn't. But it was Aimee, already reeling from the death of their grandfather, and now David's and Jeremy's disappearances, who made Claire wonder if what she'd gained had been at the expense of her own daughter. Joseph was the one who made Claire want more than she had, she who had never known what it meant to feel weight and lightness at the same time, that deep irrational longing for a meaningful life beyond her children and the world she'd grown up with. Because before Joseph, hadn't Jim and her children and her career been enough? Hadn't they and the love she had for them not only been enough, but everything? She'd thought so for so long. But now, after Joseph, even if she never saw him again, those things would never mean the same thing, the only thing, because now she knew there was something unnamable, unseen. It was not the accretion of days, the small moments people claimed that mattered, it was not the daily patterns that varied so little from human to human. It was not life. It was not death. It was a force of energy that made those things feel small and sad and ordinary. It wasn't Joseph even, it was what Joseph had brought her, what she was seeking, what, she supposed now, in the elevator, she might have found in anyone who had come upon her when her father was dying. For to find the depths of her pain allowed her to feel joy.

She could trace her pain back to her father's cancer and, before that, her mother's death. But shouldn't she trace it farther than that to her family's larger pain, back to slavery and plantations and immigrants coming in boats, unleashed from their own oppression so they could oppress others? Wasn't that how it always worked? Or maybe it was none of that. Maybe she was just selfish. Narcissistic.

A bad mother. Maybe it didn't matter what she felt, really. Maybe, as Joseph had said, it was about her. What did she know about him, really? Had she tried at all to move beyond those moments with him hidden away? Was she ready to share toothpaste and bills and car payments? Those were things she had to consider. And the letters, of course. It was after she'd found those that she knew for sure she would leave Jim and the kids.

Soon after her father had died, Claire was cleaning out his sock drawer and found a thin stack of letters rubber-banded together. They were dated from the time when her parents were in college and were addressed to Claire's father. The stationary was a light cream and personalized, and her mother's cursive was elegantly even, each loop almost a perfect oval, the result of a generation of women who spent a lot of time on their handwriting and its presentation. A way of being seen and perceived. Her mother had attended Hollins College in Roanoke, Virginia, a respectable women's college, small and Southern. She'd met Claire's father, Ed, a junior in engineering an hour away at Virginia Tech, at a mutual friend's house one weekend in Roanoke. Claire supposed she was looking for some kind of spark from her mother in those letters, some flight of imagination, some revelation of dreams or a vision of the world or possibilities beyond her own. But the letters, hardly romantic or intimate, revealed nothing. Her mother wrote Ed about the new dress she'd bought for a night in Roanoke with some of the sorority girls, she wrote about one of her friends from school who was now in college up north, and it appeared, was getting "a reputation." She wrote about her classes, which she diligently studied for, although none seemed to inspire her. She wrote about the girls ironing their hair to keep it straight and long, but she was afraid to do that because she'd heard it would fall out. Her roommate brought some key lime pie from home one weekend, which she and her friends devoured in one sitting because there was nowhere to refrigerate it. Lila politely asked Ed how classes were at Virginia Tech, and then confirmed that, yes, she could go to the movies with him in Roanoke a few weeks from now and reminded him of her dorm curfew.

Was that all that occupied her mother's mind, Claire wondered. Certainly there had to be more. But on it went, the short,
remote detailing of the quotidian. And then, toward the end of the
stack of letters, in the second paragraph, after the usual description
of the usual food and clothes and school, she read: *About the other
thing. It is yours and I'm having it and I'm not moving to California. My family
will grow to like you, I'm sure. They'll help to set us up in Chattanooga after you
graduate. You'll like it, you'll see.*

Was the "it" that he'd come to like the baby or Chattanooga,
Claire wondered bitterly. The letter confirmed what she'd felt but
never named, had suspected but never had the courage to ask. It was
here, oblique and cruelly casual. Her parents had gotten pregnant—
with her—and then married under duress. More important: she'd
not been wanted. She'd always thought they'd loved each other, and
maybe they had, but the marriage had not been their first choice.
Claire was not their choice. And her mother—the "is" underlined
three times. As if there had been an accusation. Or a question? Had
that been her mother's rebellion—to have sex with a man (or men?)
before marriage? Perhaps she had simultaneous lovers. It thrilled
Claire to think her mother might have been up to it, that there was
that slim possibility her father was not her biological father. But she
did not believe it. That was not where her mind went. Neither did
her mind go to the place that might make her father into the villain
here, that he knew he was the father and didn't want to own up. The
man she'd known was not that person. But had she'd known him,
really? Suddenly, her dead father, the one she'd loved the best, was
capable of anything. And if he was, then she was too.

The last letter was not addressed to her father but to Tammy
and had never been sent. There was no address or date on it.

She did not tell her sisters about the letters. The only real
information, that their parents had married because her mother
was pregnant, seemed more for Claire than them. Protecting them
still. But it was after she'd read the letters and learned about Maria
that she began to think she might leave Jim and, yes, the kids, too,

temporarily, just a month or two, a vacation, until she could begin another life. A real life instead of this shadow play she was acting out.

She'd not questioned doing it, any of it, taking care of her mother, her sisters, Jim, the children, taking care, taking over. Why hadn't any of the adults stopped her? Why hadn't they said, you're too young to be doing this? Why had she continued for so long, not stopping until she'd moved out and back into her childhood bedroom? She did not want to go to all of Aimee and Dez's concerts and shows and games. Did they really need her to witness everything they did? Couldn't they just get on and do things because they wanted to and not because a parent was watching, approving of their every move? She knew her thoughts were selfish and self-serving, but she also wondered, genuinely, if giving her kids some space so that they were not always being watched might not be that bad in the long term. She was exhausted thinking about the parade of recitals, games, and performances she'd be attending for the next decade, pretending her children were more special than anyone else's, that if she were a good mother she'd make sure they knew how special they were, that every day she'd tell them they were loved. But no one was too special to avoid life, to avoid death. Her life, everything she'd imagined—no, that wasn't the right word—everything she'd assumed it would be, was so terrifyingly not special.

So as she took the elevator up to HR, she did not worry about the meeting, what it might be about; instead she was imagining those tiny drops of blood, scarlet stains on her underwear, and waiting for them to release her. She was thinking about her mother's letters and her children, and most of all, she was thinking of when she'd next see Joseph. She was also thinking of his words to her that last time she'd seen him, that this, her love for him, was all about her. She would change that, she thought. The next time she saw him, before they talked about books or kissed or did anything, she would sit quietly and ask him: *what are you thinking.* And she would listen, again and again and again. And because she was thinking all those things when she entered the office she did not worry at first that Shirley, the HR manager, had asked her to shut the door.

She'd assumed she'd been called in because of some kind of personnel issue, which was usually why she was summoned to Shirley's office. Every few months a new hire or an intern landed in HR complaining or crying that he was not being recognized or rewarded for his efforts, or that she was being unfairly criticized or reprimanded for spending too much time on her cell phone or for arriving "just a few" minutes late. Claire and Shirley would commiserate and then strategize as to the best way to deal with them. Shirley was sympathetic, said that people in their twenties had always been that way, but Claire could not remember herself being so insecure, confused, needy. Perhaps that had been her problem, that she'd not allowed herself to be those things back then.

She'd arrived in Shirley's office and taken a chair. She was thinking of the latest Chekhov story she'd read, about a man who died on a ship and whose body was tossed overboard. The story ended with the ocean scowling. Scowling! She wanted to ask Joseph about that scowl, after they'd had sex (but when? where?). She wanted to ask him about the deceptively simple opening sentence: "It was getting dark; it would soon be night." But first this meeting in which, under the fluorescents and beige walls, they would discuss how to manage this or that issue. After the meeting she would try to find Joseph and see if he had her phone. Then they'd plan their next place to meet.

"We're just waiting on Mr. King and Mr. Grimsley," Shirley said in her purring, soothing voice. Claire wondered if maybe this meeting was good news, perhaps an early promotion, which was not due until next year. It would explain why King and Grimsley were coming. She was still performing as well at Chattasys as she'd always done, the one area that seemed to be boxed off from the free fall that was her life.

King and Grimsley, two of the vice presidents of Chattasys, entered the room laughing about one of the many politically incorrect inside jokes they shared. They'd both gone to Baylor and then on to Sewanee (King) and Vanderbilt (Grimsley). Good old

Chattanooga boys who had known Claire's mother, ten years older than them, from parties on the Mountain and dinners at the Club—Lila before she married the man from up north.

Claire greeted them and they grunted, arranging their seats on Shirley's side. They'd never sat across from her like that before, all three of them. The joking stopped so suddenly, as if they'd not been joking, as if the joking had been a ruse, a cover for something more nefarious, a diversion, a practiced empty gesture used to fill space and time. Shirley was known for being calm in the worst situations, such as when they'd had to lay off a bunch of mid-level managers after the crash two years ago.

Shirley cleared her throat. She spoke as if she were reading from her computer screen.

"There's been a charge of sexual harassment and racial discrimination."

It was only a matter of time, Claire thought. These guys, all of the older ones at least, not all, but many, had been screwing around with the secretaries and interns since the beginning of time. It was an open secret that the secretaries came and went at about the same time their affairs with them began and ended. Grimsley and King had not harassed Claire, though; rather they'd been condescending and patronizing. After all, she was Lila's girl, and that had worked against her as much as for her. The men did not take her as seriously as she believed they should, as she witnessed men her age or even younger move up Chattasys's ladder more quickly than she did, the implication being that she didn't work as hard—or shouldn't—being a mom and all. But she knew what she produced, what accounts she'd brought in, managed, and maintained, saving the company more money than they even knew. She knew her gender and her ties with her mother worked against her, except when they didn't. But she was good at what she did and she believed it was only a matter of time before she was recognized. Once she became a VP, slowly, carefully, she'd change everything. She was playing the long game.

She would outwait and outlive them. But now two of those she hoped to outlive and outwork were looking at her as if they were awaiting the revelation of some secret knowledge that only she possessed.

"Is it serious?"

"Yes." Shirley opened her drawer and took out Claire's cell phone.

"Where'd you find that?"

"Alma gave it to us."

And then Claire saw that she was the one about to lose everything, and those men never would.

Before they could stop her, Claire rushed out and down the hall to Alma's office.

"I figured you'd come here," Alma said.

Claire fell to her knees and pressed her head against Alma's desk. "I love him." Claire thought that if Alma understood that, then she would understand everything.

"Then you should have quit your job," Alma said.

"He loves me."

"Did he have any choice?"

Claire raised her head. Alma impassively handed her a tissue.

"I never said nothing about all that goes on here," Alma said. "But when you start messing with my family? You crossed a line."

Claire saw that Alma had threatened the company not with just a lawsuit against Claire, but much more. She had the goods on all of them.

"What do you want?"

"For you to leave Joseph alone."

She raised her head and pushed herself up. "And if I don't?"

"You will be on the five o'clock news." She didn't have to say anymore.

"Okay." It surprised Claire how easy it had been for her to give in, when it came down to it.

"And you have to resign."

"I can't quit," Claire said. "It's the only thing I—my family— has."

"Well, I suppose, then, you don't mind me going ahead with my lawsuit and dragging all that dirty laundry in the paper and the news stations," Alma said. "Up to you."

"If it was up to me, I'd be with Joseph."

"What do you know about him? Do you know his favorite color? The way he likes his burgers? What his favorite song is? You know what kind of trouble he was in when he came to live with me? Do you know anything about his momma?"

"Blue. His favorite color is blue. And he likes his burgers plain. His favorite song is 'What's Going On.'" Claire dabbed her eyes with the crumpled tissue. "He wouldn't tell me about his mother."

"Then you at least know you aren't his first white woman, either. And, although I warned him, you probably won't be the last." Alma picked up her phone. "Yes, she's here. I'll send her back your way." She hung up her phone and looked at Claire. "Go on. They're waiting."

As Claire walked back down the hall, she did not think then of the collapse of her life, of how Jim and the kids would manage if she were not working, of how they would lose the house she'd once dreamed of. She did not think that she might never be able to work in business in Chattanooga again because she'd be blackballed. She only thought of the last time she saw Joseph, in his room, her hand resting on his chest on his tiny bed. He'd kissed her gently and he'd taken her hand off his beating heart and told her, "It's time to go." She silently dressed, his sweat, the smell of their lovemaking still heavy in the air, and then he'd walked with her down the stairs and kissed her in that same soft way. "Goodnight," he'd whispered. "Until next time," she said, her throat tight. Then he'd closed the door and she'd walked to her car in the dark. She watched his form appear upstairs where the light was on. She didn't want to believe what he'd said, that it was all about her, that she knew so little about him. But if it were true, she wanted to make up for it, she wanted to love him better, starting at that moment. She would learn about him, and his life, and his sufferings, not just the ones in the books they read. She would do what it would take, even if it meant giving up her childhood dreams. She willed him to come to the window so she could see him again, but he turned off the light. If he'd done even that one small thing, come to the window and pulled up the shade, she would have turned around then and run back into the house and begged him to leave with her, right at that moment, and elsewhere she would do better, damn the regrets. She was that far gone. But he'd kept the shade down and turned off the light, so that he was invisible to her, and she to him, both disappearing into the night.

She'd needed only one box to take what she'd wanted from her office: a mug painted with Dez's five-year-old fingerprints, Aimee's Mother's Day card from last year that read, "You're the best mommy ever," *The Invisible Man*, a framed photo of Jim and the kids hugging her so hard she could barely breathe, a photo she'd tucked in a drawer in her desk six months ago because she could no longer bear looking at them, the Montblanc pen her father had bought her when she'd earned her MBA. Her father, her father, her father. Even that one box had been heavy. Driving away from Chattasys was driving away from the last thing she'd had that tied her to the life she'd so carefully built and thought she'd loved.

She'd never been a big drinker, especially of hard liquor. When was there the time? She could go months without drinking anything alcoholic. Instead she'd taken the other route—prescription drugs, legal and sanctioned: Adderall, Ambien, Xanax. All of those pills sat in their plastic containers at the bottom of her purse. She could take one or a few or many and something would happen—she'd fall asleep or relax or focus on one small thing. She hardly thought of those pills, though, as she drove away from Chattasys for the last time, a place she'd spent as much time at—no, more—as with her children or Jim or her father.

What she did next she did without thinking. It was almost automatic, as if she'd been born for this moment, and she was being tested in ways she might never fathom. She pulled into Jax Liquors downtown and reached for her cell phone that wasn't there to text Joseph. She banged her head against the steering wheel until she finally felt something, the soft beginning of a bruise above her eye. Leaving the car running (if someone drove away with the car, she thought, then, finally, there really will be nothing left for me), she went into the store and bought a bottle of Jack Daniels, a drink she'd sipped only once or twice with Coke in college, although she had gone on the Jack Daniels tour at the distillery forty-five minutes from Chattanooga with Jim once, but since the distillery was in a dry town they hadn't been allowed to drink any. Now with the bottle she returned to her running car, which for better or worse, was where she'd left it, and she drove up Fifth Street to the UTC campus, where she'd once been an honors student, and even though she lived on campus she was near her father and sisters just in case they needed her. But had Shannon ever worried about those things, about money and leaving and all that? She had not. Had Paige, who had left without even finishing college, who had moved to the other side of the country, worried about how their father might be doing with her so far away? Paige had not. Claire parked her car in the gravel student lot. The spring semester was over and there was space for her, even though she didn't have a parking pass. Let them give me a ticket, she thought. She rested her head on the steering wheel and closed her eyes. She breathed deeply. Then she got out of the car with her purse and the bottle conspicuously silhouetted in a brown paper bag. She walked the block down the sidewalk to the entrance to the Confederate Cemetery, the place she'd lost her virginity freshman year, to the guy before Jim, a virgin named Bobby she'd dated her first semester freshman year. They'd come to the cemetery in the middle of the night, sober, because there was nowhere to make out privately in the dorms. She showed him her great-great-great-grandfather's grave, and then in the grass nearby, they made out under the trees and the grave markers and the moonlight. She was the one who'd brought condoms. It was time, she'd thought then. Time to be done with this and to move on.

Now she found her great-great-great-grandfather's grave-stone, faded, barely legible, and leaned against it. It would still be light out for hours. Because they were only thirty minutes away from the Central Time Zone, Chattanooga nights were light for so long it seemed darkness would never fall. It was funny how if you don't want to be seen you don't have to be, she thought, even if you're right in front of people. They don't expect you to be there. Invisible. She unscrewed the cap and took a swig from the bottle. It did not taste as bad as she thought it would. She took another swig, thumped the gravestone. He'd been a Confederate soldier just like almost every white man from the area had been. He'd died before the turn of the century, before Jeremy's great-great-great-grandfather had led the hanging on Walnut Street Bridge. She cursed her great-great-great-grandfather and all those before and after him, for refusing to admit—still!—they'd been wrong.

And yet, even here, in a cemetery drinking Jack Daniels from a bottle, living in her childhood bedroom away from her kids, estranged from her husband, jobless, which meant they would have to put the house on the market, which might or might not sell, even here, where it was as if all that taking care of people she'd done her whole life was for nothing, even here, now, she wasn't sure if she'd been wrong. For she couldn't imagine not choosing Joseph, even now in the dirt with all these horrible ghosts, even if she never saw him again. This moment in the Confederate Cemetery was in some way right and inevitable. She took another drink.

She opened her purse, unzipped the side pocket, and removed her mother's letter to Tammy.

For the next year, whenever she missed Joseph, whenever she missed her father, her mother, she would read the letter out loud, as if it were a prayer. She never knew who the letter was about, but she liked to pretend it was about her father. That evening in the cemetery she recited the letter over her relative's grave, like a spell or an incantation, until she was drunk and dreaming.

There is a God. I tasted purple and it was caught between my teeth, like royalty, like blood. There was skin and something that smelled like the river near our house, near the green hideout, which I showed you once and you made a crown of leaves for me to wear. There was something about his legs, the way the hairs curled like snail shells, how his toes pointed like a ballerina's. For all of my days I will not forget how the sun parted through the strands of his hair growing like flowers reaching toward the sky. Leaves fell but never landed. I rested my palm on his stomach and I watched him glow. He carried me until I flew and from the clouds I saw how the world is all connected. We're all baptized, so it doesn't matter. We're all going to heaven. We're all holy. There is a God. The universe is ordered. We live on a pin's head. Never fear the letting. When I touch him he touches the ground and things grow and reach past this tiny, tragic world. Tomorrow I will get in our river and I will swim until it becomes the ocean until it becomes Kenya until it becomes you so I can give you this letter. Tammy, you're the only one besides me who knows this kind of love. L

The next thing she knew someone was jabbing her in her ribs. She opened her eyes, and it was dark. A darker shadow, some large imposing figure loomed over her. She opened her mouth to speak, but it was scraped out and coated with a dry cakey film of vomit.

"Ma'am. Where do you live?" The policeman said something into his walkie-talkie, something about her.

"Here," she mumbled, then pawed the stone.

"I'm not from around here." He shined a flashlight in her eyes and then waved it over to the half-drunk bottle of Jack Daniels. "You'll have to come with me."

As he tried to lift her, she felt the wet stickiness between her legs, smelled the dark smell of her own blood.

"Can't you hear them all weeping?" Claire pushed him away and pressed her ear to the ground.

"Who?"

"All the dead people. Soldiers, Indians, slaves. They're all here beneath us."

She heard the policeman speak to someone else she'd not seen before, and then another police officer, a woman, emerged from the darkness. The blood, as if it had been dammed up, trickled down her legs.

She heard many voices, not just the police officers, but other men and women and their babies crying. She heard Aimee crying alone in her bed; she heard Dez crying, too, in his dreams because he never cried when he was awake. Her hearing was so acute she heard Jim's tears as they crunched up the corner of his eyes. She heard Shannon and Jeremy and her father and her mother. She heard her great-great-great-grandfather cry when the slave who took care of him died because now he was alone. She heard her mother's maybe-sister Tammy sobbing softly before they sent her away.

"Can't you hear them?" Claire said again through ragged sobs.

"No, ma'am, we can't. The only person crying right now is you."

JEREMY'S CAR III

Shannon runs the engine, her stomach ballooning against the steering wheel. She feels a kick and a rumble. "Not now, Jodie," she says. "No more surprises." As if the baby has heard her, the kicks suddenly stop. On the floor beside her is a stack of *Jail Break*, late for delivery. Paige emerges from the courthouse, leading a slumped and shrunken Claire. Shannon toots the horn and waves. Claire chooses the back seat and buries her head in her hands.

It's too hot to drive with the roof down, but she's got it down anyway. Shannon's skin is all sheen and sweat, the light so strong that even with sunglasses on she has to shield her eyes to see the road in front of her.

"How about some music," Shannon says, tiring of Claire's sobbing. She turns on the car stereo and pushes Play on the CD changer. "Hey Paige, it's your old band. Shows how often I change the CDs in here."

"Change it," Paige says.

"I still love your voice on this," Shannon says.

"Please," Paige says. "Anything. You must have something better than this."

"What about your friend from the Opry? Do you have some of his stuff?"

"No," she says, her voice low. She pushes the player to the next CD. "Lucinda," she says. Paige sings along about losing something still not found.

They pull into the recycling center on Third Street and drive up to the newspaper bin. Shannon turns off the car. "Claire," she says. Shannon takes one of the papers and hands it back to her. She turns around. "Look at this. You're on the front page of *Jail Break*. Paige and I have had to post your bond. And why?"

"For love," she sobs.

"Listen to me. I've got a baby coming out any day now, and both fathers are MIA. Now my niece and nephew are about to endure the humiliation of their mother being arrested for public drunkenness and resisting arrest. What's worse, whenever they walk into a convenience store, they'll see the mug shot of their own mother. So, you know what I'm doing? Instead of delivering all these papers, which is my job, but which I'm now about to lose because of what I'm doing, we're dumping them here. This is the last batch." Paige picks up the stack of papers and drops them on Claire's lap. "Do it."

Paige gets out of the car and opens Claire's door. She pulls Claire from the car and pushes her over to the recycling dumpster. Claire tosses the papers in, and they disappear into the dark empty space. She returns to the car, still sobbing.

"We're going to live together in our old house until it sells, and I'm going to have a baby and we're going to take care of her and we're going to take care of you, Claire. We will take care of you until you get through this."

"As long as it takes," Paige says.

"Paige and I are going to throw something away, too," Shannon says.

Paige waves a CD in front of them. "This," she says, "is my Gobstopper." She gets out of the car and throws it in the trashcan next to the recycle bin.

Shannon pops the trunk and eases out of the convertible. She pulls a stuffed dog out of the trunk.

"You can't," Paige says. "That's for Jodie. You can't throw Boxer away."

"I can," Shannon says, walking to the trashcan. She drops the animal in and walks to Paige's side of the car. "You're driving."

Claire stops crying. Her hair is stringy and greasy, her hands thin and fluttery. She opens the door and runs to the trashcan. She returns with the dog. She gets in the back seat and hugs the stuffed animal close. "We are not letting Jeremy go."

Before Shannon shifts the car into gear, Claire says, "Hey, there's something here."

"Jeremy used to hide stuff there when we were kids," Shannon says. "Pass Boxer up."

Shannon unzips the bottom of the dog, and pulls out something she keeps in her hand. She drops the object in her purse. "Just some undeveloped film he forgot about. It's probably nothing."

"Just like Dad's secret wife is nothing?" Claire says. "Why could he have her when I can't have him?"

Shannon pulls the car away from the dumpster and pulls into a space in the nearby lot, turns off the car. "You don't want to know."

"What do you know, Miss Reporter?" Paige asks.

"A little. That she'd been with Dad for a long time."

"How long?"

"Long."

"Why didn't he tell us?"

"Well, it seems when they first met, for the first few years or so, let's just say their relationship was transactional."

"A prostitute?"

"He was seeing her when Mom was sick, wasn't he," Claire says.

"It appears that way," Shannon says.

"Wow," Paige says.

Claire gets out of the car and throws herself on the ground, sobbing again, muttering indecipherable things.

"Goddammit, Claire," Paige says. "This has got to stop."

"No!" Claire brings her hand up to silence them. She crawls to the curb of the parking lot. "I promise after this I'll do the right thing. I'll beg Jim to take me back. I'll be a good wife and mother. I'll find a job. But for now, be here with me and let me have this."

They sit on the sidewalk beside her and hold her hands. A car with two children singing in the back seat passes them. Snatches of a joyful song, muted from the closed windows, speed by. Claire picks up the tune, hums it softly, so that her sisters can barely hear it.

DAVID'S PHOTOS, DEVELOPED

In reverse chronological order. Some dates approximate.

1. April 2010. The last photo on the roll. David's hair is neatly combed and he is freshly shaven. His white cotton shirt is buttoned almost to the collar. His smile is formal, one practiced for photos. He projects responsibility. In the photo's world of black and white, he looks like a father from an earlier era.

2. March 2010. Jeremy and David hastily huddled, their kiss for the camera blurred. They smell like soap and Calvin Klein. Jeremy's hand crosses the frame, so that his fingers are looped around David's jeans. David's hand is on Jeremy's chest, directly over his heart.

3. 2009. David's Army buddies together in DC. A long line of togetherness, pretending to smile for the camera.

4. 2008. An Iraqi man and a small boy. Standing together, not touching or smiling. Behind them are trees, not the desert one might expect.

5. 2008. David squatting, his arm around the boy from the previous photo.

6. Film overexposed.

7. 2005. David in front of a school he's helping to build, surrounded by Iraqi children, wild-haired and tattered.

8. 2002. Germany. David in uniform, kissing another uniformed man, arms flung around each other's necks.

9. 1999. Jeremy, shirtless, jeans unbuttoned, on Jeremy's childhood twin bed.

10. 1995. Julie, her eyes half closed, hair damp and long, wrapped in a towel in the hotel room.

11. 1995. Jeremy, on the bridge, his body an energetic X, stretching from the beams, grinning madly.

12. 1995. Shannon and Jeremy dancing. She is a blur of violet, spinning out from his arm past the edge of the photo, laughing, not miserable at all.

SHANNON

Shannon was sitting at Ben's kitchen table. Still pregnant. Forever pregnant, it felt in those last long weeks. Ben had developed the roll of film in the canister hidden in Boxer. She guessed that Jeremy had put the roll there for her to find after Jodie was born, that he too had planned to disappear, perhaps with David. Or maybe he had left Boxer and the roll for safekeeping until he—or both of them—returned. She couldn't give up hope.

They passed the photos back and forth, as if they were trading baseball cards. After Shannon flipped through the photos several times, she stopped on the one of Jeremy from 1999.

"This was the night of Paige's party. Remember Jeremy said he'd hooked up with David, and he'd run out when his mother arrived?"

"Kind of."

"He was in the cottage on her property." That cottage. The one place she hadn't checked. She stacked the photos and put them in a manila envelope. "I've got to go somewhere." She kissed Ben lightly. He tasted of salt and lemons. "I'll call you later tonight."

She got in Jeremy's car and drove the windy road up to Lookout Mountain, to the guest cottage where he'd been with David that night of Paige's party. There were a few lights on in the main house where Jeremy's mother lived, but the cottage was dark and shut tight. Shannon banged on the door anyway.

"Jeremy? David?" She banged again, stuck her nose to the curtained window. She listened for something, a scuttle, a sneeze. Nothing. She turned toward the main house. Jeremy's mother. Even when Shannon had last talked to his mother, she'd not seemed to care too much about Jeremy's disappearance or that she was going to have a granddaughter. Still, Shannon thought she should try and talk with her, Jodie's only grandparent. So she waddled to the house, her breaths deep and grasping. She rang the doorbell, banged the door.

A porch light turned on. She felt eyes on her through the peephole.

"Hello, Mrs. Hamilton. It's Shannon!"

She heard the unlatching of the chain, the creak of the door.

Jeremy, full of color and weight, stood in front of her, grinning. "I was wondering how long it would take you to find me."

She stepped toward him, her belly forcing distance, and slapped him. He grabbed her wrist and pulled her to him in an embrace.

"Jeremy, do we have company?"

Susan Hamilton, dressed in a cream silk blouse, gray pencil skirt, and low heels, appeared in the hallway.

He released Shannon, but still held her hand. "Yes, Mother. It's Shannon."

"Lila's daughter? The homely one, right?"

Jeremy smiled at Shannon and shook his head slightly, to warn her. Not that she would say anything. Typical Susan Hamilton. Shannon slapped Jeremy again. "How could you do this, you selfish prick?"

"Why are you slapping my beautiful son?" Susan looked as if she might cry, something Shannon had never seen her do.

"Mother, it's okay. Why don't you go into the living room? I'll make you a drink."

"Okay, son." She disappeared.

"Beautiful son? What's her deal?"

"Dementia. All the edges are gone." He smiled at her. She hated him for looking happy. He pulled her inside. "Look, I'm sorry. You were right. I had to get my shit together before Jodie was born.

But I couldn't do it with you around living in that house. I was too depressed about David, and every time I'd see you pregnant, all I'd do was think about him being away. I'm sorry. But I had to be alone for a while."

"That's what rehab is for."

"I was going to call you, like tomorrow. I promise."

"Jeremy?" Susan had reappeared. "Shall we invite our guest in for cocktails?"

"We'll meet you in the living room, Mother."

As soon as she was down the hall, Jeremy leaned in. "We'll get a few drinks in her, and you are not going to believe what she's got to say."

"I bet." Shannon punched him in the arm. "I'm still angry."

"I know, I know." He smiled. He looked good, a healthy flush in his cheeks. Sober. He'd let his hair grow out so that bangs as dark as eyelashes winged his eyes. "I'll make it up to you, I promise."

"There's no making it up, Jeremy," she said. She would not let him off for this one.

She sat on the sofa patterned with pale blue birds. Susan took the matching chair opposite. Jeremy brought one gin and tonic speared with cucumbers on a tray and two tonic waters for him and Shannon. They sat for a few minutes, quietly sipping their drinks. Shannon was fighting back tears, she was so furious and relieved, but she wouldn't let Susan see her cry. Finally, Susan set her drink down.

"I wish y'all had told me about your scheme before you were inseminated."

"We didn't think you'd approve," Shannon said.

Shannon listened to Susan's pantyhose rasp as she crossed her legs. "You're right about that. If I'd known, I'd have tried to stop you."

"Because homosexuality is genetic?" Shannon couldn't help herself.

Susan looked at Jeremy, her head bent slightly, as if there were a crick in it.

"It's all right, Mother, you can tell her."

She nodded. "You know why we didn't like your father Ed so much after Lila died?"

"Because he wasn't from around here."

"That's what he wanted you to think. It's because he was cavorting with prostitutes while poor Lila was dying of cancer."

"I know," Shannon said.

"We told him to stop with the call girls and we'd support you girls' education. But there was one woman he just wouldn't stop seeing, a Mexican or something. Just to spite us."

"Maria."

"That's her. Besides, he wanted to prove a point, about public school education and all that, I suppose. But if he'd just stopped with the Mexican prostitute and married a nice woman, we didn't care where she was from, just a good woman, you girls could have had a new momma. And you would have gone to your mother's old school."

"It doesn't matter now," Shannon said.

"I suppose not. You turned out how you turned out. And Jeremy, here. We'd tried to shield him from the worst, you know, by adopting him." Susan picked up her drink, took a long draw.

"It's okay, Mother, you can tell her," Jeremy said again.

"You see, Thad and Lila grew up with the housekeeper's daughter, just a few years older than them. Her name was Tammy."

"Mom talked about her."

"Well, she was the result of an unfortunate liaison between her mother, Eva, the family housekeeper, and your grandfather. He must have loved her because he risked just about everything to keep the both of them in the cottage house on their property."

"Tammy is my mom's sister?"

"Half-sister. I guess it was an open secret who she was. She and Lila were close, but when she got older Tammy started getting wild, going downtown on her nights off, meeting men. She was light-skinned, you know, and this was the 1970s; all kinds of things were changing. She became with child. She told Lila, who was about to go off to college, about it, wouldn't name the father, only said he was white, asked her to help her get rid of it. But Lila, that good Christian woman that she was, convinced Tammy to keep the baby, give it up for adoption. Then she talked her father into giving Tammy enough money to move away and start a new life. Tammy said she was going to Africa, Kenya, I believe, but we knew that was just a story."

"Where'd she go?"

"We didn't try to find out."

"There's more," Jeremy said. "Go on, Mother."

Susan Hamilton sighed, like someone bored with life. "So, Thad and I had just been married a few years when we found out we were unable to conceive. We came to the conclusion that, if the baby were light enough to pass, we'd adopt Tammy's child."

"Luckily I didn't look too black or anything," Jeremy said.

"As soon as you were born, we knew you were ours, no matter what you looked like. We were prepared to accept the consequences." Susan sighed again. She lifted her glass and jiggled it at Jeremy. He put the glass on the tray and went into the kitchen. "Let's hope your baby doesn't have any deficiencies."

"What do you mean?"

"Of course you're barely related, like half cousins twice removed or something."

"Did you make Tammy give up her baby just so you could have one?" Shannon said in a low voice. "Because I wouldn't put it past you."

Susan shook her head, but Shannon didn't know if Susan was communicating denial or a refusal to accept the truth.

Jeremy returned with a fresh gin and tonic for Susan.

"Our baby will be without deficiency," Shannon said. "Right Jeremy?"

"She'll be perfect," he said.

But Susan didn't seem to be listening. Her eyes were fixed on a point far away. "Look at the light," Susan said, pointing to a window at the end of the hall. She stood and started walking toward it.

Jeremy scooted to Shannon. "She came to me that first day in rehab and told me the story. I freaked out and went home with her."

"I thought you might be dead."

"I'm sorry. I knew your sisters would take care of you."

"Not good enough."

"I know," Jeremy said. "But I missed David so much. And then, I found out about Tammy. I just needed to get my shit together. I was afraid if I contacted you, you'd come see me, and I couldn't handle it."

"I'm so pissed off at you, I can't even think." Shannon leaned back, closed her eyes, sipped her tonic water. But she was thinking. She was thinking that yes, Jeremy had been a little darker skinned and haired than the rest of the family, but she'd never thought anything of it, especially after he told her he was adopted. She was thinking that Jeremy had flaked out on her when she really needed him and she could never be certain that he wouldn't do it again. She was thinking she kind of understood why he'd disappeared these past few weeks, but that didn't excuse what he'd done to her, to their daughter. She was thinking that the doctor had told her that everything about the baby seemed healthy, normal, but now she wouldn't know for sure until after she was born. She was thinking that her own mother had a sister, and that she might still be alive. She was thinking that her daughter should know her grandmother and her story. She was thinking reparations. She was thinking that her journalism dreams had been misguided. She was thinking that everything she'd been working for had been leading up to this.

"I'll do whatever you want to make it right," Jeremy said.

"Anything?"

"Name it. Hell, I'll even go to Korea if you move back there with Ben."

She looked him in the eye. She hadn't gotten together with Ben until after Jeremy had disappeared. How much did he know?

Susan was at the window now, with her fingers spidering up the pane.

"Did you find David's photos?" Jeremy asked.

"We developed them. Some good ones of you."

He smiled slightly, and it looked painful.

"Jeremy, come here, son, and look at the light."

"In a minute, Mother."

Shannon stood. It was time for her to go. He grabbed her to him before she left.

"We have to find out what happened to her," she whispered in his ear.

And then, if she wants me to, I'll help her tell her story. Our story. If she's okay with that. No more secrets. This is the thing I was meant to do.

2011

Oh, dear sisters, our life is not ended yet. We shall live! The music is so happy, so joyful, and it seems as though in a little while we shall know what we are living for, why we are suffering ... If we only knew—if we only knew!

Three Sisters, Act IV

When thou dost ask me blessing, I'll kneel down,
And ask of thee forgiveness.

King Lear, Act V, Scene 3

AIMEE

Papa Nash's house had been on the market for five months, but it finally sold. Mom and me and Dez and Dad and Aunt Shannon and Jodie and Aunt Paige had all been living there. After we'd all moved out of the house, Aunt Shannon, Ben, Jeremy, and Jodie were taking a road trip to meet Jeremy's mother, who lived in Santa Fe, New Mexico. And then Aunt Shannon and Jodie were going to move to Korea with Ben and Hye Jin. Jeremy was going with them, too, at least for a while. Aunt Paige was taking a bus to New York. She'd met a girl there and they were planning to join some protests against Wall Street. We were going to rent a three-bedroom house in Highland Park because that was what we could afford. Fine with me. I was ready for my own room instead of sharing one with Dez, who woke me up in the middle of the night yelling at monsters from bad dreams.

Sometimes in the evenings or early mornings, I'd find Mom and Aunt Paige and Aunt Shannon talking in lowered voices; they stopped when I came into the room. I hated their secrets. I heard them say they couldn't understand why Papa Nash had lied to them. I heard them say they wanted to buy the house, but there wasn't any money. They said things about Maria, too, Papa Nash's secret wife, but I couldn't hear what exactly.

It pissed me off, their hypocrisy. It wasn't Maria's or Papa Nash's fault that we were poor and about to be homeless. It wasn't their fault that Mom and Dad were both working now at crappy jobs, at least compared to what they used to have. It wasn't their fault that Daddy was sleeping on the foldout couch in the living room most nights because he didn't want to sleep in the bedroom. It was Mom's.

Mom, who decided I needed to go to the girl's charter school that was a mirror of the private girl's school I was supposed to go to. Now I went to school in the hood, and I was one of ten white girls out of the two hundred girls who went there. She said she didn't want me to grow up like her. The thing was, I liked my new school better than the boring private girls school, but I didn't tell her that. I also didn't mind when she took me with her to the neighborhoods I didn't even know about until last year, when she volunteered, helping people with their taxes or advising them about starting a business. It was important that I lived in the world, she'd tell me. And I'd tell her that the world I lived in was the one where she had ruined our family. And she'd bite her lip and nod and say, she knew. But she'd never say she was sorry.

The storm hit on Papa Nash's birthday, a week before we were supposed to be out of the house. I was the only one who remembered it was Papa Nash's birthday because it was the day before mine. But it was okay; I was turning twelve, and it wasn't so important for me anymore. Not after last year when I was still trying to figure out how to put my life back together, but now that I was pretty much twelve, I'd decided things were never going to be the way they were, for better or worse.

On the day of the storm all the news stations were warning us—this was it, and we should be ready. The house was already half boxed up with dishes and books and items that had no future home. We didn't go down to the basement until late morning, when things got serious. First we taped the windows with duct tape, threw blankets and sheets over the furniture. Ben gathered us all together in the living room and with the self-timer took some pictures of us—Mom and Dad and me and Dez and Aunt Paige, and Aunt Shannon,

Jeremy, and Jodie, Ben and Hye Jin. It was as if we knew that after this we'd be different again. I'd made sure my phone was charged so I could text my best friend Laila. I was hoping to get some photos of damage with my phone. We were competing to see who had it worst.

We descended to the basement and waited. We sat on Aunt Paige's bed and on the floor facing the TV, which wasn't a flat-screen but one of those old big sets people used to have. We watched the tracker on the news as the storms moved toward Chattanooga. Me and Dez and Hye Jin watched the news and ate cereal with milk from Paige's mini-fridge while the adults drank coffee from a French press. They'd gathered lots of food—water and granola bars and bread and cheese and dried fruit and bars of chocolate—a French-style picnic, Aunt Paige said. Dez was hyper and excited and Hye Jin seemed to get quieter every minute. I got them to play Go Fish and Uno for a while, and then I found the old crochet dollhouse that my grandmother had made for my mom and then my mom had given to me. But then Dez decided the house had been hit by a tornado and he swept the furniture and everything with it so that house was a mess. Before I would have complained to Mom and Dad about Dez ruining everything, but now that I was about to be twelve, I decided he wasn't worth getting upset about.

On some days, everything seemed back to normal with Mom and Dad; on other days, Dad couldn't be in the same room with her. Today, because of the tornado I guess, his arm was around her and her head rested on his shoulder. Aunt Shannon and Ben were talking together in low voices, something secret that they didn't want us to know about. I'd decided they were going to get married before they went to Korea. (Two months later, I found out I was right.) I wanted them to stay here, mostly because of Hye Jin and Jodie. As if he were reading my mind, Jeremy, who was holding Jodie, let her go and she crawled to me. Hye Jin sat beside me and dangled Boxer in front of Jodie's laughing face. They were my sisters.

And then Aunt Paige said it's happening and we all crowded around the TV and watched the trees blow and bend and topple

over onto cars and houses and buildings. After a flash, the lights
went out.

I texted Laila: *No power.*

For the first few minutes it was strangely quiet. Dez turned
on his flashlight and beamed it onto face after face, as if to reassure
himself there was nothing to be afraid of. When Dez's light landed
on Ben and Shannon, they were making out like teenagers. "Stop it,"
Dez said. "That's gross." And then everyone laughed.

Then we all turned on our flashlights and pointed the beams
at the ceiling so that we cast long shadows.

Paige said it was time for tea and then we'd sing some songs.
She set up a china tea set and poured juice in the cups and passed
around cookies. She said she used to have tea parties with her mother when she was little and that tea set was used on her mother's
family's plantation in Georgia from before the Civil War. Then Mom
said that wasn't true, that grandmother's side of the family didn't
even live on a plantation, it was more like a little farm they lived off
of, and her grandmother had bought the tea set in the forties from
a traveling salesman. And Aunt Paige said how did Mom know and
Mom said that her mom had told her, didn't Aunt Shannon remember, and Aunt Shannon said she didn't remember either way. Aunt
Paige just laughed and said that was probably true, but she loved the
tea set anyway, and then she asked if me and Hye Jin would like a
few dabs of Joy perfume, and we said yes, and she shone her flashlight on her dresser until she found the bottle. She put some on our
wrists because she said that was the best place for perfume and Dez
complained that it was getting too smelly in the basement, but Aunt
Shannon and Mom said we smelled nice.

Text from Laila: *Window smashed. Chair in the road. Roof ripping apart.
You ok?*

Yes. Al made us get in the bathtub.

Al, Laila's big brother. I had a secret crush on him. At least I
hoped it was secret. He was twenty years old and in college studying
engineering. He had black hair that was cut super neat, like there

was always this straight line on the back of his neck and he had one of those V bodies that were never sloppy. Plus he was nice to me. Sometimes he took my hand and shook it when he saw me, as if we were at a business meeting. It wasn't gross or anything, more like a joke between us. I always made sure I put hand lotion on before I went to Laila's in case he was there.

U r in a bathtub?

Just me and mom. Al & dad are fighting, as usual.

Laila's Dad never said hi to me or anything. I think he hit their mom sometimes, although Laila never talked about it. He was a jerk.

Text me when it's over. I paused. What the hell, it could be the end of my life. *Please give a handshake to Al for me.*

Lol. Will do.

Then Aunt Paige took out her guitar and played some songs by a guy named Billy Wilson, who had been a friend of hers, but he'd died last year, too. She said he should have been famous but wasn't, but it was okay because he didn't care about that anyway. She played three of his songs and taught us the lyrics, so that after a while we could sing along with her. Then Dez said he was hungry, and Aunt Paige said we'd have our Paris picnic and then she'd teach us Sacred Harp singing. So after our bread and chocolate and cheese, Aunt Paige took out some old hymnals and taught us how to read shape-note music and after a while she had the whole family singing in different harmonies—Ben and Dad on bass, Mom and me on treble, Aunt Shannon and Hye Jin on tenor, Dez and Aunt Paige on alto. We practiced for a long time, and then we finally sang a song called "My Home."

On Jordan's stormy banks I stand,
And cast a wishful eye
To Canaan's fair and happy land,
Where my possessions lie.

Don't you feel like going home,
My home it is in the promised land,
And I feel like going home.

It sounded kind of eerie without any instruments. But we also sounded really good and loud and in harmony. Dez asked what the promised land was, and Mom said in this song it meant heaven. Dez said was that where Papa Nash was, and Mom said yes, even though I knew she didn't believe in heaven (neither did I). Nobody mentioned the others: Hye Jin's mom; Jeremy's mother, Mrs. Hamilton, who'd died a month ago; Papa and Momma Patrick; Momma Nash. Nobody asked if David was there. It was as if we didn't want to know.

Then there was a loud crash right above us. Hye Jin screamed, and since she was sitting next to me I put my arms around her before Ben crawled over and held her. Until then we'd all kind of been having fun singing songs and picnicking under flashlights, but then we all got kind of scared. We waited for something else, but there was nothing.

I texted *House falling in*. And then, because I didn't know when I'd have power again, I turned off the phone.

"I'll go check," Dad said.

"No," Mom said. "It's too dangerous. We'll wait until we know the storm is over."

"What if we can't get out?" Dez said.

"We'll get out," Mom said.

"Hey, everybody," I said. "Today is Papa Nash's birthday."

"Oh my God," Aunt Shannon said. "I can't believe we forgot."

"Hey, Dez, you want to do our birthday dance? We can teach Hye Jin."

"That's dumb. We don't even have a cake. Besides, Papa Nash's in the promised land."

"Come on, Dez," Hye Jin said. "Show me." They were her first words all day.

"I've got something," Paige said. Using her flashlight, she walked over to her bed and pulled a box out from under it. She took out something that looked like a book, wiped the dust off it with her sleeve. "Here. Papa Nash's birthday."

We huddled over photos Ben had taken the day before I was born. Mom looked miserably pregnant with me, her smile strained as she posed with Papa Nash and Paige and Shannon. Jeremy, dark

haired and disheveled, handsome and hungover, was there too. So
was Dad.

"You should have this, Aimee," Shannon said. "Daddy would
have wanted you to have it. A birthday present a day early."

I took the photo album before Dez could grab it, and put it
in my backpack. (For the next few years I would take that album
out every few months or so and examine the world the day before
I entered it.)

By the early evening the storm had passed. Dad went upstairs
to check things out and said it was okay to come up.

(Even now I remember quietly walking up those dark stairs behind Mom, my flashlight guiding me, and then entering a house, un-
recognizable with its crashed-in ceiling from the tree collapsed in the
middle of the living room, its sodden furniture covered in damp leaves
and twigs, all silent except for the crunch of glass under my shoes.)

For a long time no one spoke. The kitchen was blocked by
the fallen tree, and the rest of the rooms on the floor were damp
and windblown. I picked up one of Hye Jin's dolls, gathered colored
pieces from one of Dez's games, found an ink-stained sheet of my
unfinished homework. But I didn't know what to do with them,
so I dropped them back on the floor. That was the place where I
watched *American Idol* with Dad, I thought, and there was where I
played video games with Dez, and there was where Hye Jin and I
drew imaginary cities, and there is where I fed Jodie her bottle until
she fell asleep.

"It's all gone," Dez said.

"Nothing's gone. We're all here," Mom said. Then she sat on
the edge of the wet armchair and cried. Aunt Shannon and Aunt
Paige sat on either side of her and held each other and drew each
other in so tight that it seemed for a moment the rest of us weren't
even there.

And then Dad was holding Dez and Jeremy was holding Jodie
and Ben was hugging Hye Jin. It was just me, alone, and I wanted to
be away from all of them. Especially my mom.

We'd been told not to go upstairs because the roof might collapse. But I had to be alone, and I figured I'd be okay as long as I didn't go near the parts the tree had fallen on.

The bathroom was at the top of the stairs, intact. I wasn't even sure if the toilets were working, I mean, there was no electricity, nothing. It was kind of thrilling, not having a house anymore. Real dystopian.

I sat on the commode lid and wondered if I should turn on my phone and text Laila. Then I decided I should use the commode before anyone else did, before things got really gross since it probably didn't flush. So I pulled my underwear down, and there they were, those tiny dark spots of blood. My first period. Unbelievable. Getting my period the day before my birthday without electricity or water or tampons or anything. And to top it off, I thought I felt a cramp. Even my own body was betraying me.

"Fuck," I said. "Fuck." I'd never said the word *fuck* so many times before, even in my head. It felt good.

I turned on my phone.

Got my p. Can u believe it?

No response. Her phone was probably turned off, too.

"Aimee? You're not supposed to be up here. It's too dangerous."

"Go away, Mom." I watched a drop of blood fall into the commode. "That's what you want to do, anyway."

I heard her gasp, which is what I wanted. I was getting good at hurting her.

"Please, Aimee, I hope one day you'll forgive me."

I didn't answer.

"You know, when I turned twelve my mother died. I wanted to be different than her for you. I didn't want to burden you with all of my secrets. Maybe I didn't tell you enough. But more than anything now I want to be here with you. I want to be here for your soccer games and your plays. I want to help you pick out your prom dress and the bedspread for your freshman dorm. I want to hear about your first boyfriend, your first kiss. Your first everything, all those firsts my own mom missed."

"Like your first period?"

"Yes. Your grandfather went to the store and bought a bunch of stuff for me because he didn't know what I needed."

"Well, I need a tampon."

"Now?"

I didn't answer.

"Oh, my baby. I think pads are better to start with. Don't mess with tampons until you have to. I have some downstairs. Just wait here and I'll be right back."

I heard her go back downstairs. I checked my phone.

Hi Aimee, this is Al. Laila asked me to tell you she's OK. Busy with Mom. RU OK?

Yes. And then I turned off my phone again. If Al saw my text about getting my period, if he figured out what "p" meant, I would die right now.

I didn't even try to flush the commode. I wadded up a bunch of tissue and stuck it in my underwear and pulled up my jeans. I scrambled downstairs and hurtled outside before she returned.

The ground was crisscrossed with fallen trees and branches. In the valley below, Chattanooga looked dark but whole. I knew better. Everything was broken. The world smelled like the bottom of a mud puddle. Sirens everywhere, although I couldn't see any trucks.

I made my way down the street, climbing over logs and side-stepping trash cans and chairs that had blown into the road. No one was outside except me. I pretended I was the last survivor. I pretended I would have to live off whatever I could find in the empty, crushed houses. I pretended I was trailing blood.

One of the memorial sites for the Missionary Ridge Civil War battle was ahead of me on the side of the road. Cannons and artillery and boring explanations—another dumb reminder of a very dumb war. I was glad the South lost. I mean, it would have been even more embarrassing if we'd won. Racists should never win.

The site didn't seem much affected by the storm. Statues and the plaques and artillery slick and unmoving watched over the valley. I climbed on one of the cannons that pointed to the city below. How hard would it be to blow the city up? To start over? I stretched across the cannon and hugged it like it was a person.

Eventually they'd notice I was gone, and they'd start to panic. Maybe they were running around the house right now, calling my name.

(It's impossible to imagine them not calling my name.)

I turned on my phone.

Stay safe—Al.

Better than a handshake. *Ok.*

I look back.

Even though she can't see me yet, I spot her zigzagging down the hill. Mom looking wild and crazy.

She calls my name. I don't answer.

(It's impossible not to forgive them. It's impossible not to ask them to forgive me. But not then. Not there. Not yet.)

I straddle the cannon, hug the cool, wet metal. I imagine staining the cannon with my blood.

I steady my cell phone camera, turn on the flash.

I text Laila a photo of our house, collapsed.

I hear them calling me now. Mom, Aunt Shannon, Aunt Paige. Dad. Dez. Ben. Hye Jin. Jeremy. Jodie. Papa Nash.

Clouds stretch the sky. The earth opens. The tang of blood, the bite of metal. The smell of fallen trees.

Listen to the wind howl through the trees beyond your window.

Listen to the wind whisper your name.

JEREMY'S CAR IV

Even though it's early morning and almost cool, the top is down. Shannon idles the convertible near the Walnut Street Bridge where Ben shoots one last sunrise photo. The tangerine sun spreads like an open hand.

Jeremy, in the back seat behind Shannon, fusses with Jodie's car seat while the baby sleeps. Hye Jin, buckled in, watches her father from her rolled-down window. He scoots to the left and right, stands, then squats, and then waits for the light to come to him.

"I'll miss this place," Hye Jin says.

"We'll be back soon enough."

While they wait for Ben, Shannon turns to the back and lightly squeezes Jodie's chubby ankle. "You ready to meet your grandma Tammy?"

"Don't wake her," Jeremy says.

"Don't worry, she's out," Shannon says. "But when she wakes up screaming you have to deal with her." She sighs and turns to the front. "It's going to be a long trip."

"I can't wait to meet her," Jeremy says.

"Me, too."

"Let's hear Paige's song again," Hye Jin says.

Shannon plays the song Paige wrote just before she left for New York. The sound of oars in the water. Laughing in a truck with the windows down. A tobacco-stained finger tracing a red and black tattoo peaking from under a shoulder strap.

Ben approaches. He gets in the passenger seat in the front. "I think I got it," he says. He and Shannon bend toward each other and kiss.

"Jo-ah," Shannon says.

Time to go.

Jodie opens her eyes, punches her legs, and laughs. Bah, bah, bah, she tells them. Here we are. The faint perfume of morning dew. Whisper of the engine. Sun on skin.

Amazed to be alive.

ACKNOWLEDGMENTS

This work was supported in part by a MakeWork Grant and the University of Tennessee at Chattanooga English Department.

I want to thank those who read some or parts of drafts of this novel and gave me invaluable feedback: Rowan Johnson, Caleb Ludwick, Brian Beise, Catherine Meeks, Kris Whorton, Ravi Shankar, Lorraine Johnson, Earl Braggs, and Stacy Chapman.

A special thanks to Bob Boyer, who was infinitely patient helping me take photos for the research for this project.

Thanks to Beth Partin, copy editor and proofreader extraordinaire.

Thanks to John Gosslee, Andrew Sullivan, and Katie McGunagle of C&R Press for their energy, vision, and support. Thanks to Jessica York, for helping me with the final version of the manuscript.

And as always, I am grateful to Rowan Johnson for his encouragement, inspiration, and love.

OTHER C&R PRESS TITLES

NONFICTION

Women in the Literary Landscape by Doris Weatherford et al

FICTION

Made by Mary by Laura Catherine Brown
Ivy vs. Dogg by Brian Leung
While You Were Gone by Sybil Baker
Cloud Diary by Steve Mitchell
Spectrum by Martin Ott
That Man in Our Lives by Xu Xi

SHORT FICTION

Notes From the Mother Tongue by An Tran
The Protester Has Been Released by Janet Sarbanes

ESSAY AND CREATIVE NONFICTION

Immigration Essays by Sybil Baker
Je suis l'autre: Essays and Interrogations
by Kristina Marie Darling
Death of Art by Chris Campanioni

POETRY

Dark Horse by Kristina Marie Darling
Lessons in Camouflage by Martin Ott
All My Heroes are Broke by Ariel Francisco
Holdfast by Christian Anton Gerard
Ex Domestica by E.G. Cunningham
Like Lesser Gods by Bruce McEver
Notes from the Negro Side of the Moon by Earl Braggs
Imagine Not Drowning by Kelli Allen
Notes to the Beloved by Michelle Bitting
Free Boat: Collected Lies and Love Poems by John Reed
Les Fauves by Barbara Crooker
Tall as You are Tall Between Them by Annie Christain
The Couple Who Fell to Earth by Michelle Bitting

CHAPBOOKS

Atypical Cells of Undetermined Significance by Brenna Womer
On Innacuracy by Joe Manning
Heredity and Other Inventions by Sharona Muir
Love Undefind by Jonathan Katz
Cunstruck by Kate Northrop
Ugly Love (Notes from the Negro Side Moon) by Earl Braggs
A Hunger Called Music: A Verse History in Black Music
by Meredith Nnoka

CPSIA information can be obtained
at www.ICGtesting.com
Printed in the USA
LVHW04s2305240618
581768LV00002B/173/P